LAST LIGHT

HALO®

LAST LIGHT

TROY DENNING

BASED ON THE BESTSELLING VIDEO GAME FOR XBOX®

TITAN BOOKS

Halo: Last Light
Print edition ISBN: 9781785650215
E-book edition ISBN: 9781785650574

Published by Titan Books
A division of Titan Publishing Group Ltd
144 Southwark Street, London SE1 0UP

First edition: September 2015
10 9 8 7 6 5 4 3 2 1

A CIP catalogue record for this title is available from the British Library.

Interior design by Leydiana Rodríguez
Cover design by Alan Dingman
Cover art by Kory Hubbell

Printed and bound in Great Britain by CPI Group (UK) Ltd, Croydon, CR0 4YY.

For Elena Hayday
Bold, brave, and brainy—may your
own adventures never require a BR55

CHAPTER 1

0832 hours, July 2, 2553 (military calendar)
Crime Scene Charlie, 104 meters belowground,
Montero Cave System,
Campos Wilderness District, Planet Gao, Cordoba System

Special Inspector Veta Lopis had been raised to hate and fear everything about the United Nations Space Command, from its sheer might and criminal war practices to the murderous thugs it called Spartans. So it was only natural to assume that the serial killer stalking the Montero Cave System might be one of the power-armored hulks riding through the darkness with her now. Certainly, the MO fit: the victims had all sustained injuries consistent with a large, mechanically enhanced attacker—injuries such as crushed bones and disjoined limbs, ruptured organs and collapsed skulls.

But good investigators did not let their personal bias influence their thinking. They gathered evidence and weighed facts, and they let the theory of the crime build itself.

So Veta would do what she always did. She would study the victims and establish a timeline for all eight murders, then check it against the known locations of everyone in her suspect pool. She would catalog the weaknesses and habits of the remaining subjects and use that knowledge to put pressure on the perpetrator. Most of all, she would be patient and persistent, and she would keep pushing until the killer revealed himself.

And if that killer turned out to be a towering Spartan in four hundred kilos of Mjolnir armor, Veta would do what she always did.

She would take him down.

The cavern floor began to descend more steeply, then the whine of the electric engines deepened as the rubber-tired Tunnel Weasel changed gears to keep from picking up speed. A moment later, the little tram entered a broad gallery illuminated by the platinum glow of work lamps. Like the rest of Montero Cave System, the gallery was hot, humid, and filled with mineral vapors, but its beautiful flowstone walls were bathed in a cold blue light that made them resemble frozen waterfalls.

As the Tunnel Weasel came to a stop, a trio of UNSC marines in black BDUs emerged from the shadows and approached. They exchanged salutes with a UNSC major seated next to Veta, then an older marine with bushy gray brows stepped forward to report.

"Area secure, Major."

"Thank you, Sergeant." The slender officer at Veta's side was Ira Halal, a black-haired, blue-eyed major sent by the UNSC Judge Advocate General's Corps to help investigate the murders. So far, he struck Veta as dedicated, intelligent, and reluctant to cooperate. "Any unexpected visitors?"

"Sir, none that we detected." The sergeant glanced around the perimeter of the gallery, then added, "But the conditions down here wreak havoc with our motion sensors, and twenty-two passages open into this gallery. We couldn't watch them all every minute."

Halal nodded. "Of course not," he said. "It was a long shot, anyway. I don't think this UNSUB is likely to return to the scene."

The sergeant frowned. "*UNSUB*, sir?"

"Unknown Subject of Investigation," Veta clarified. She stepped out of the passenger compartment. "And I want to check those passages, Major."

Halal turned to her. "To what purpose?"

"To look for evidence, of course." Veta paused, reminding herself to play nice, then added, "I like to be thorough."

Halal did not quite roll his eyes. "Our resources are limited, Inspector Lopis—and so is our time. I suggest we focus on the crime scene and not waste our assets chasing phantoms."

"I don't chase phantoms, Major Halal." Veta stepped close. "I catch killers. Quite a lot of them, actually."

Halal held her gaze a moment, then smirked. "As you wish, Inspector. We'll do this your way."

He ordered the marines back to their posts, then turned toward the Tunnel Weasel, where Veta's four-member field team was unloading equipment from the third car. On the side of the car, the image of a stylized tree fern sprouted from the letters MVC—the logo of the Montero Vitality Center, from which the UNSC had commandeered the tram.

Watching over Veta's team were three Spartans in their famous Mjolnir armor. With their blocky helmets and titanium-alloy outer shells, the trio looked more like war robots than human beings—and from what Veta had read about their exploits in the public record, that might be close to the truth. There hadn't been enough detail for her profiler to suggest how their personalities might have been impacted by such a steady diet of fierce combat, but Veta suspected it wouldn't be good.

Halal fixed his gaze on the Spartan leader. "Lieutenant, have one of your Spartans secure the adjoining passages and report any evidence of observation—"

"Actually, my team will be inspecting the passages," Veta interrupted. Whether Halal was trying to hide something or simply did not realize how often serial killers returned to the scene, she could not say. But either way, she was not about to trust any part of the investigation to him or the UNSC. "You're welcome to send an observer, if you like."

"Inspector Lopis, these caverns are under military control," Halal said. "And Spartans are well-trained observers."

"But they're not homicide investigators," Veta said. "And military control didn't stop our killer from murdering at least eight people down here. Since those people happen to be Gao citizens and these caves happen to be located on Gao, their murders fall under the jurisdiction of the Gao Ministry of Protection—which makes this *my* investigation."

Veta paused for emphasis, then continued, "As I said, Major, you're welcome to send an observer."

Halal sighed. "We'll send a guard." He did not even bother to look at Veta as he spoke. "The last thing I need is to lose someone from your team, too."

"*Too?*" Veta asked. "Has the UNSC been losing people?"

"That's not what I meant," Halal said quickly. "It's just procedure, in case the UNSUB is trying to keep an eye on the investigation."

"You just told the sergeant that you didn't think our UNSUB was likely to return to the scene."

Halal shrugged. "I could be wrong." He turned away, as though intent on watching Veta's team unload their gear. "As I said, it's just procedure."

Halal was lying, of course, and it seemed to Veta that he

was worried about something even more dangerous than their UNSUB. But she could not imagine what that might be. The Montero Cave System was the most-visited natural wonder on Gao, a vast labyrinth of interconnected caverns spread beneath a thousand square kilometers of jungle. It had an untold number of access points, including thirty-eight major entrances operated by villages and private spas, and until the killings began, thousands of tourists had entered the caverns each month without encountering anything more hostile than a flight of irritated saurios.

It would have been easy to blame the UNSC and look no further, but the truth was that strange things had been happening in the Montero region for a while. Two and a half months ago, a rare temblor had shaken the entire region, leveling two villages and damaging several spas. Shortly afterward, tourists began to emerge from the caverns miraculously cured of lifelong ailments and terminal illnesses. The newsmongers quickly substantiated the claims, and sick people began to flood into the caves hoping for their own miracles.

Then, a month after the quake, a UNSC task force entered the Cordoba Star System and "requested" permission to conduct research in the caverns. The common assumption was that ONI— the UNSC's notorious Office of Naval Intelligence—wanted to investigate the miracle cures. Gao's anti-centralization government denied the request. The task force insisted, and after a tense negotiation, President Aponte reluctantly granted permission to land a small research team.

The "small" team turned into an entire battalion, which promptly occupied the region's most elegant spa and declared the entire cave system off-limits to everyone else. Predictably, the order inflamed Gao's fiercely independent citizens, and local guides began to sneak people into the caverns via hundreds of unmapped entrances. For a couple of weeks, the two sides pretended to ignore each other.

Then tourists began to go missing or turn up dead. Suspicion quickly fell on the UNSC, and sales-hungry newsmongers began to press for a harsh response. President Aponte had no choice. He instructed the Ministry of Protection to investigate, then publicly ordered the UNSC to cooperate. To everyone's surprise, the UNSC commander responded by proposing a joint inquiry.

That had been two days ago. Now, here Veta was, inspecting the first of a long chain of compromised crime scenes with a counterpart who seemed to take her for some ditz who could be intimidated by an air of assumed authority.

Veta stepped into Halal's line of sight. "Don't hold back on me, Major," she said. "It's a mistake. A serious one."

Halal finally turned back to her. "Mistake, Inspector?" he asked. "As I recall, I've granted every request you've made."

"They're not requests," Veta said. "And if you expect me to believe this is some kind of research battalion, you're a fool. The UNSC is fighting something down here. And you're so afraid of it that you brought a squad of Spartans to protect us."

The Spartan leader stepped over to join them. "Ma'am, the 717th Xeno-Materials Exploitation Battalion *is* a research battalion." His voice was crisp and deep, even over his helmet speaker. "But even scientific units can find themselves in combat. There are always enemies."

Veta turned and craned her neck to look up at the Spartan. Standing well over two meters tall in his Mjolnir armor, he was distinguishable from his two female subordinates by the color of his pale blue armor and slightly bulkier shape. It would be difficult to read his reactions beneath all that equipment, but if he was trying to cover for the UNSC—or even just Halal—Veta wanted to know why.

"Let me see if I have this straight," she said. "The 717th is just an innocent research battalion that's under attack . . . by what? Cave monsters?" She shook her head. "I'm sorry, but I just don't believe that, Spartan . . . which one are you again?"

"Fred-104, ma'am. And I don't particularly care what you believe." He pointed toward her investigative team. "But it's my job to protect your people, and I don't want anyone killed on my watch. If you'll point out who will be inspecting the passages, I'll send an escort along to provide security."

Veta stared up at him for a moment, trying to see through the glare on his faceplate so she could get a read on his expression, but it was no use. The reflective coating seemed designed to prevent anyone from seeing the human face inside a Spartan's helmet.

After a moment, Veta waved her second-in-command over. "Senola, take a look into the passages around here. See if anyone has been keeping an eye on the crime scene."

Senola glanced around the cavern perimeter. "Sure, boss." A green-eyed matron with long blond hair tucked into the hood of her white coveralls, Senola Lurone was a Ministry of Protection veteran fifteen years Veta's senior. "It might take a while."

Veta shrugged. "It has to be done." She let her gaze slide toward Fred. "And you'll have an escort. Fred-104 here seems to think we could be attacked any moment."

Senola held Veta's eyes just long enough to confirm she had taken the hint, then asked, "Really?" She turned to the Spartan. "Who are you worried about, Fred? Maybe you think the Insurrection is starting up again?"

"That's ridiculous," Halal interjected. "Gao may have sided

with the insurrectionists in the past, but the civil war is over—
and no one is going to send a Spartan fireteam to stand garrison
against a bunch of disobedient tourists."

Veta had to give Halal credit. He had recognized Senola's play
and cut her off before she had a chance to put Fred off balance,
and now Veta was left wondering whether the major had been trying to protect Fred or some other secret. Either way, it suggested
Halal was here as much to manage the situation as he was to catch
a killer, and *that* told her something about the UNSC's worst fears.

It told her a lot.

Veta looked back to Senola. "Tell Cirilo to use spiders on this
one, then go have a look at those passages. I'll have the major show
me around the crime scene."

Senola confirmed the order with a nod, then Fred took her
over to introduce her to the Spartan who would be escorting her.

"Your techs use spiders?" Halal asked, watching the pair
depart.

"Trace evidence bots," Veta explained. "They look like little
spiders and crawl all over everything. By the time they're finished,
we'll have a three-dimensional map of every fiber, skin cell, print,
track, and speck of DNA in this place."

"I see," Halal said. "Very efficient."

"Not really."

Veta wasn't about to detail the technology's weakness for anyone from the UNSC, but the spiders were expensive and slow.
Each single-use pod cost more than her salary for a year, and a
scene the size of this one could take a full week to process.

Fred returned and assumed a position behind Veta and Halal,
and Halal led the way toward a pair of high-backed benches about
twenty paces ahead.

"Any chance we have a vid or photos of the bodies in situ?" Veta asked.

Halal shook his head. "Sorry. I only arrived a few days ago myself. Prior to that, I'm afraid Battalion was treating civilian deaths as collateral damage."

"Collateral to what? Nobody's at war here." Veta made a point of looking over her shoulder at Fred. "*Are* they, Fred?"

"If we were fighting a war here," Fred said, "you'd know it."

"But you're here for a reason," Veta pressed. "As Major Halal said, they don't send Spartans to stand garrison against tourists."

"I can't comment on our mission." Fred's faceplate shifted toward Halal. "That would violate security directive Foxtrot Tango Angel 7012."

"That's understood," Halal said. "But your mission does not involve hostilities against Gao civilians. You can confirm that much, Spartan."

Fred remained silent for a moment, then finally dipped his helmet in acknowledgment. "Yes, sir, I can confirm that."

"Thank you," Halal said. They reached the benches and stopped, and he pointed. "The initial attack occurred here."

Located directly opposite each other, the two benches faced a hissing steam vent—one of the thousands that permeated the Montero caverns. A pair of freestanding lamps lay shattered on the cavern floor. A third bench lay about three meters away, toppled onto its back and bent at the middle.

Veta ignored the scene and turned to Fred. "I'm sure you realize how convenient your security directive sounds."

"Convenient, ma'am?" Fred cocked his helmet to the side. "In what way?"

"If you can't tell me who you're fighting, it's hard to rule them out as the killer," Veta said. "So I must assume that you're keeping me in doubt to protect yourself. I have no choice."

"Conclude what you want, ma'am," Fred said. "But you're misrepresenting what I said."

"I don't believe I am."

"I didn't say we were fighting anyone," Fred said. "I said I couldn't comment on our mission. There's a difference."

"The fact that civilian deaths were classified as collateral damage implies armed conflict," Veta said. "The fact that you sent a Spartan along to guard Senola implies a threat. Stop playing semantics and give me a straight answer."

Fred's faceplate turned away from her. "I'm not at liberty to do that, Inspector."

"Fred is very careful about security," Halal said, stepping between Veta and the Spartan. "But I assure you, he's not trying to protect himself or anyone else on Blue Team. Spartans don't kill for fun, Inspector Lopis."

Veta studied Halal for a moment, wondering if he realized his attempts to shield Fred only made the Spartan look more suspect, then said, "I'm sure you understand why I can't simply take your word for that, Major." She turned back to the benches and activated her handlamp, then began to inspect the area for signs of struggle. "I don't see any blood here. Where exactly was the body found?"

Halal spoke to a tacpad strapped to his forearm. "Wendell?"

"Ready to proceed, Major," the tacpad replied.

The tinny voice belonged to the battalion's artificial intelligence—or rather, the small aspect of Wendell's consciousness installed in Halal's tacpad. Veta did not have a full understanding of the capabilities and limits of UNSC AIs, but from what she had observed earlier, Wendell had a similar presence in nearly every piece of battalion equipment capable of hosting a software subroutine.

"Crime Scene Charlie is more expansive and complicated than the others we'll be visiting," Wendell began. "As you can see, the initial confrontation occurred here at the vent area itself, but the actual attack . . ."

Knowing she would have a chance to study Wendell's report at length later, Veta shut the AI's voice out of her thoughts and began to examine the scene on her own. The floor in this area of the cavern was primarily a concrete tram-path flanked by packed mud, but the benches had been bolted into a small paving-stone circle, which surrounded the natural steam vent. The legs of the missing bench had been snapped off at the bolts, suggesting it had been removed by a single quick, powerful jerk.

Veta crouched down and began to examine the stone pad. She still saw no sign of blood, but there were a couple of faint smears that suggested shoes spinning around. She turned away from the missing bench, then used her handlamp to follow a faint trail of footprints off the pad. The trail was easier to follow over the packed mud floor, and Veta could see that it had been made by two different pairs of shoes. The trail split twenty paces later, with the larger set of tracks turning down the length of the gallery and the smaller set continuing toward the wall.

Veta followed the second trail by the wall. In this area, the sta-lactites hung so low that many joined with stalagmites to create a cage of thin-waisted columns. In front of this cage lay a large circle of disturbed mud. There were no obvious bloodstains in the mud or on the formation itself. But several columns had been snapped off to punch a hole into the cage.

Veta shined her lamp through the gap and found a stony gray floor marked by eight pale scratch marks. She knew better than to jump to conclusions, but the suggestion was obvious: someone had been clawing at the ground as they were dragged back into the gallery. Scattered across the stone were a few dark dots that resembled blood spatter.

A crisp, speaker-modulated voice sounded behind Veta. "Something wrong, Inspector?"

"Yes," Veta said. Though she hadn't heard the Spartan coming up behind her, she managed to avoid drawing the sidearm that her hand was now grasping. "You might want to announce yourself before sneaking up on me."

"I'll keep that in mind," Fred-104 replied. If the Spartan noticed the hand on her pistol grip, it was impossible to tell—as usual, his expression remained hidden behind the faceplate of his helmet. He simply waved back toward the toppled bench, where Halal stood looking in their direction. "Wendell and the major are waiting to continue the briefing."

"Of course they are." Veta activated her headset, then pointed her handlamp upward and spoke into her throat mic. "Cirilo, do you see where I am?"

"Yeah, Veta, I see you."

"I'm dropping a card. Take a casting of the print next to it." Veta shined her lamp on the Spartan's boots. "We'll need it to identify which tracks belong to Fred-104."

There was a short pause as Cirilo considered the instruction, then he said, "Got it."

"Good." Veta pulled a numbered evidence card from her cargo pants and placed it next to the Spartan's boot. "Make sure the spiders give this area a careful sweep, the works."

"You know it, mama."

Veta deactivated her mic and started back toward Halal.

"*Mama?*" Fred asked, catching up to her. "You don't look old enough to be his mother."

Veta smiled. "As in 'hot mama,' " she explained. "Cirilo can be a flirt."

"I see." Fred was silent for a moment, then asked, "And it doesn't bother you?"

Veta shrugged. "He knows who the boss is." It occurred to her that there was only one way Fred could have heard Cirilo's side of the conversation. She glanced up at the Spartan, then tapped her ear. "You're monitoring our network?"

"Wendell is patching in your signal," Fred confirmed. "It's for your own security, of course."

"Your AI is very thoughtful," Veta said. "I feel safer already."

Fred dipped his helmet. "Glad to hear it, ma'am."

They reached the toppled bench and joined Halal, who was looking back toward the evidence card Veta had left standing on the cavern floor. "Find something over there?"

"Maybe," Veta said. "We'll know more after Cirilo and his people work their magic. If there's anything to find, they will."

"Inspector Lopis, may I suggest you reconsider the allocation of resources?" Wendell asked, speaking from the tacpad strapped to Halal's arm. "The patrol found Charlie Victim on the opposite side of the gallery, exactly sixteen meters from the toppled bench. The evidence supports Sergeant Boyle's notation quite clearly."

"I'm sure it does," Veta said. "But I'm looking for more than evidence of the murder. I'm looking for clues—and mistakes."

"Mistakes?" Halal asked. "I thought I made it clear that these sites haven't been processed as crime scenes. Until my arrival, Battalion wasn't even classifying—"

"You misunderstand me, Major," Veta said. "It's not *your* mistakes I'm looking for. It's the killer's—and this is where we'll find them."

Halal looked skeptical. "You sound very certain of that."

"I am. From what I'm seeing, this is where the first murder occurred. And that means the killer slipped up here." Veta glanced in Fred's direction, then added, "They always do, the first time."

"There's no support for that hypothesis," Wendell objected. "You haven't even begun to collect—"

"Stand by, Wendell." Halal muted the tacpad speaker, then turned back to Veta. "This was the third death we discovered. What makes you think this was the *first* killing?"

"Because the killer made rookie mistakes." Veta pointed to the bench lying at their feet. "First, he didn't plan his approach. That bench was an obstacle to pursuit. Second, he wasn't careful to control the situation. He attacked two victims at once."

"*Two* victims?" Halal shook his head. "I'm sorry, Inspector, but the patrol only recovered one body. As for the bench, he could have grabbed the victim with one hand and pulled the bench over with the other."

"Sir, that's not what the tracks indicate," Fred said. "The inspector is right. It appears that two people were facing this bench as someone approached. They turned and fled the attacker together, then split up about twenty meters from the vent. One person—probably female, judging by the size of her footwear—took cover near the gallery wall and saw the first victim die. Then the attacker returned and pulled her from hiding."

Veta turned to the Spartan. Whether he was reading the tracks better than she had or just remembering how it had happened, she could not say. But there was no arguing with his analysis.

"Not a bad read," she said. "It's almost like you were there."

Fred tapped the side of his faceplate. "Enhanced optics, ma'am. And tracking is a basic component of any Spartan MOS."

"MOS?"

"Military Occupational Specialty," Halal said. "But it's not forensic science, Inspector. There might be another interpretation of those tracks."

"Such as?"

"Maybe they don't belong to a second victim," Halal said. "Maybe they belong to the murderer."

"Interesting idea," Veta said. That was not the way she read the scene, but Halal was right—she was making assumptions. "Let's see how it plays. Show me around."

Halal tapped his tacpad, and they crossed the gallery with Wendell droning on.

"The death site lies sixteen-point-two meters from the overturned bench. While the scene is more expansive and complicated than the others we have identified so far, there is no evidence to support the hypothesis of a second victim."

They came to a circle of damp, dark mud, and Wendell announced, "Charlie Victim suffered the primary attack here."

The smell of decay left no doubt that Wendell was correct. Veta ran the beam of her handlamp over the surrounding ground, eliminating the shadows cast by the powerful work lamps, and located a spray trail leading toward the cavern wall.

"Describe the body position," Veta said. "And the orientation."

"Charlie Victim was found on his back with his legs resting against the cavern wall, seven meters from here at bearing South 103 degrees East," Wendell reported. "His head was pointing in bearing North 42 degrees West."

Veta looked to Halal. "Translation?"

Halal smiled. "His body came to rest over there." He pointed at another stain, this one on the cavern wall. "And his head was pointing back toward us."

"Injuries?"

"Worse than anything else we've found," Halal reported. "It took the corpsman a while to decide he was male."

"So the first kill was the most brutal," Veta said. "And the first victim was male."

"You find that significant?" Halal asked.

"Of course." Veta started toward the cavern wall. "It's unusual for this kind of serial killer to mix victims of different genders, so knowing that he started with—"

"Excuse me, Inspector," Fred said. "But Linda says Deputy Inspector Lurone found something you need to see."

"Linda?" Veta asked.

"Linda-058," Fred answered. "The escort I sent along to protect your deputy inspector."

The Spartan turned about three-quarters around and looked into the darkness between two work lamps. A pale crescent of light appeared on the wall of one of the small passages that adjoined the cavern, and a moment later, a scratchy voice came over Veta's headset.

". . . hear me yet, boss?" Senola asked. "We've got another dead body . . . it's weird."

"On my way." Veta touched Halal's arm, then deactivated her throat mic and pointed toward the growing crescent of light. "Senola found another body."

"Your second victim?" Halal asked.

"Maybe. We'll see." Knowing the rest of her team would be monitoring the conversation on their own headsets, Veta activated her throat mic again. "Cirilo, keep working the primary scene for now. Be sure the spiders make it to all the blood sites. Use an extra pod if you need to."

"On it," Cirilo said. "Stay in touch."

With Fred leading the way, Veta and Halal crossed the area illuminated by the work lamps and started up a gentle slope. About fifty meters ahead, Linda-058 stood silhouetted by a circle of light, probably Senola's handlamp shining from the mouth of an intersecting passage. Standing well over two meters tall, Linda wore a full suit of Mjolnir, the same as Fred and the third Spartan escorting Veta's team. But the outer shell had more of a feminine, hourglass shape, and its color was pale copper rather than bluish. And Linda's helmet was kind of awkward-looking, with a goggle-like visor and an external apparatus box mounted on each side over the temple.

As Veta and her companions climbed, they began to smell the odor of a decomposing body, and Halal said, "I'll admit it, Inspector. I'm impressed. It hadn't even occurred to me to look for a second victim."

Normally, Veta would have been tempted to offer a lecture on the importance of letting the scene tell its own story, but that would have been a waste of breath. From what she had seen so far, Halal had been sent here to manage the problem first and solve a crime second, so the best way to win his cooperation would be to let him know she had no interest in making his job difficult.

"The Ministry sent its best, Major," Veta said. "President Aponte just wants the killer stopped. He has no interest in blaming the UNSC. Quite the opposite, in fact. He's under tremendous pressure to end your occupation of the Montero Vitality Center, and naming a UNSC suspect would force his hand."

"Meaning?"

"Meaning it's better for everyone to catch this person as soon as possible," Veta replied. "The longer this goes on, the worse it is for everyone."

Halal was silent for a moment, then nodded. "I can see that," he said. "But if the killer turns out to be UNSC, it would still be a political nightmare for us. The trial would make headlines all the way to Earth."

"Trial?" Veta asked. "You need to do your research, Major Halal. I'm not a big fan of trials."

"I'm not sure I understand, Inspector."

Veta flashed a knowing smile. "Sure you do," she said. "Just think about it."

Halal's brow shot up, but he said nothing and looked away. As they drew close to the passage where the body had been found, he put a hand over his nose and stopped a few steps short. Clearly, he was not accustomed to murder scenes.

The Spartan, Linda-058, was standing next to the mouth of the passage, her waist about level with the top. Senola stood on the opposite side of the opening, her knees, gloves, and hair smeared with dirt.

"The DB is fifty meters back," Senola said, still breathing hard from the crawl. She raised a round, hand-size device that appeared to be mostly lens surrounded by a ring of lamps—an Alternate Light Source Imager that recorded crime scenes across a wide spectrum of visible and nonvisible light. "I have some good shots, so you don't need to go in there if you don't want to. It gets pretty tight."

"Female?" Veta asked. "You're sure?"

"No doubt," Senola said. "She's in third-stage decomp, but she's still recognizable."

"Good," Veta said. "Any insect colonization? It would be nice to get a date of death on this one."

Senola nodded. "There are a bunch of different bugs," she

said. "But I don't know if we'll have files on the larva. They're all troglobites—white and blind, antennae as long as my finger . . . stuff like that."

"We'll figure out something," Veta said. "There has to be a quainto somewhere who's made a career out of studying cave insects."

Veta stooped down and shined her handlamp into the crawl-way, then forced herself to look. It was not easy. As a teenager, she had spent three weeks in hell, held captive in a stone cellar the size of a coat closet. She had finally managed to escape by scratching the mortar from around a rock and smashing her abductor's skull into porridge, but killing him had not freed her entirely—not in the ways that really counted. She still feared tight spaces and breath that smelled of tobacco gum and a man's fingers running through her hair. She still feared a lot of things.

Veta chased away the memory and forced herself to concentrate. In the center of the crawlway, she could see Senola's hand-and knee-prints straddling a shallow furrow on the floor. The furrow was perhaps thirty centimeters wide and so faint it was almost unrecognizable.

"Drag mark?" she asked.

"That's right, all the way back to the DB," Senola confirmed. "But no sign of who did the dragging."

Veta continued to study the passage. Only a meter in diameter, it was too small for a Spartan in full armor. Of course, armor could be removed.

About three meters in, Veta spotted the gray, thumb-size lozenge of a motion sensor stuck to the passage wall. A single set of hand- and knee-prints overlaid the drag marks, running back to the motion sensor and no farther. It was hard to imagine someone missing the smell of the dead woman, so either someone had planted the sensor before the smell grew too bad, or they were outfitted with breathing filters.

"No knee or hand tracks past the body?" Veta asked, just confirming what Senola had already told her. "No prints or scuffs on the walls?"

"Nothing, boss," Senola said. "I can't explain it, but I checked with an alternate light source, mag lens, UV, infra—everything I had with me."

"Then I'd better let Cirilo have the scene first."

Hoping her relief would not be too obvious, Veta backed away from the passage and stood. Everyone on her own team knew of her abduction and her problem with confined spaces, but that was hardly something she wanted to share with her UNSC counterparts—particularly not when one of them might be the serial killer she was hunting. She turned to Senola.

"Why don't you show us the shots?"

"Sure." Senola began to tap the ALSI controls, then raised the viewfinder so Veta and Halal could see. "This one is probably the most interesting."

The display showed the decomposing figure of a female corpse dressed in torn black slacks and a bloodstained blouse embroidered with flowers. While the cause of death was not immediately apparent, her bloody clothes and smashed nose indicated a violent death. But her body had been laid out on its back as though she were resting, with her hands clasped across her chest and her eyelids held shut by a pair of small pebbles.

"Now, that *is* interesting," Veta said.

"Yeah?" Linda-058 asked over her shoulder. "You don't see a lot of people beaten to death on Gao?"

"I'm afraid we do," Veta said. "But this time, it looks like the killer felt remorse."

CHAPTER 2

0908 hours, July 2, 2553 (military calendar)
Crime Scene Charlie, 104 meters belowground,
Montero Cave System,
Campos Wilderness District, Planet Gao, Cordoba System

The green digits of the heads-up display inside Fred's helmet showed an elapsed time of ten minutes and thirty-two seconds. That was how long it had been since Inspector Lopis had last climbed the slope to peer into the cramped passage— technically a crawlway—where the decomposed body had been found. And now Lopis was back again for the seventh time in eighty-seven minutes, crouching beside him to check on the progress of subordinates who clearly did not need supervision. Under different circumstances, he might have thought she was fond of his company.

But Fred had watched enough soldiers fight their demons to recognize what he was seeing. Inspector Lopis had a fear of confined spaces, and it was a weakness she hated in herself. He could tell that by the general tension of her body and the way she always forced herself to stare into the crawlway for a full sixty seconds before backing away. Most telling, though, was her loss of focus.

She had stopped trying to provoke him—and Fred didn't think it was because she had ruled him out as a suspect.

Inside the crawlway, the deputy inspector and trace evidence specialist were preparing to remove the body. Having already inspected, photographed, and collected samples and evidence from every meter of passage between the entrance and the victim, they were now spreading the body bag over the corpse, open side down, with the deputy inspector at the feet and the trace evidence specialist at the head. The pair appeared to have a surprising amount of experience in tight spaces, for they were working in near silence and seemed untroubled by the smell.

Linda's voice sounded inside Fred's helmet. "Lieutenant, I have a Third Squad runner here," she said. "Private Hayes. He says they've found another body."

"Another one?" Fred did not bother to speak quietly or hide his irritation. They were on TEAMCOM, an encrypted tight-beam channel currently open only to Spartans . . . and to Wendell, of course. As Battalion AI, Wendell kept a small presence everywhere, residing in anything that had a gigabyte of memory to spare. "Please tell me you're joking."

"Afraid not," Linda said. "Hayes says this one looks pretty fresh. And it's at Bivouac Site Tango."

"What?" Bivouac Site Tango was deep in the caverns, a full day's descent below the paved paths customarily used by tourists. A fresh body down that far would have to be a spelunker or a local guide deliberately challenging the UNSC's no-access order. "Say again?"

"Bivouac Site Tango."

Fred allowed himself the luxury of an unvoiced curse. Another body meant another day escorting Lopis and her team. And on a mission like this one, that was a problem. The 717th was here to nab an ancient Forerunner ancilla, one that could turn out to be the most sophisticated and powerful AI ever captured by the UNSC. It was the kind of operation that could make or break careers—especially that of the mission's brash young commander, Murtag Nelson.

Eighty military-standard days ago—on April 14, 2553, to be exact—Nelson had been a field analyst at an ONI listening post when a pirate in a Covenant battle cruiser glassed some Forerunner ruins on Shaps III. Following the bombardment, a strange pattern of transmissions had begun to emanate from the Montero Cave System on Gao, and Nelson had hypothesized that a Forerunner ancilla was responding to the attack. How he had persuaded his superiors of his theory, Fred could not even guess. But there could be little doubt he had. The chief of ONI herself, Admiral Margaret Parangosky, had given Nelson command of the 717th Xeno-Materials Exploitation Battalion, then attached Blue Team to the unit and tasked them with helping Nelson capture the ancilla.

But the damn thing was slippery. As an AI, the ancilla could reside in any electronic device "smart" enough to host it. And it could "jump" between devices, which made trying to locate the thing akin to hunting a ghost. Worse yet, it was a couple of magnitudes smarter than any human AI—and about a *thousand* times smarter than Fred—so capturing it was far from certain. In fact, Blue Team and the 717th had been chasing the ancilla for a month now, and they had nothing to show for their efforts except the casualties inflicted by its complement of Sentinel drones.

Fred had explained all that when Halal demanded an escort of Spartan-IIs, and he had taken pains to point out that every hour the squad spent on "security detail" was an hour the ancilla used against them. But Fred's protests had been ignored. With political agitators already making noise about the "invasion" of Gao, FLEETCOM brass had been worried that some hard-liner would try to spark the second coming of the Insurrection by attacking the Gao investigators and pinning it on the 717th. And Fred couldn't say he blamed them. That was how a lot of wars started—with some nutjob kicking a hornet's nest at just the wrong moment.

"Lieutenant?" Linda asked.

"Sorry, just assessing," Fred said. "What's the sitrep at the new scene?"

A short silence followed while Linda asked for the situation report. Fred could have switched channels and spoken to Hayes directly, but he preferred to keep his communications to the Spartans' encrypted channel for now. There was too much coincidence in these murders, too much that served to pull the 717th off mission. Had Fred been in charge of the investigation, he wouldn't be looking for a renegade Spartan or a full-on psycho. He would be on the hunt for some Gao radical trying to frame the Spartans and make the UNSC look bad . . . someone who wanted to pressure the local government into declaring a war it could not possibly win.

But what did Fred know? He was just boots on the ground.

After a moment, Linda said, "Hayes reports that Mark and the rest of the Spartan-IIIs are still working with the mapping team."

"Good," Fred said. "What about the crime scene? Is that secure?"

"Corporal Phaetus is there with Third Squad," Linda answered. "It's only ten klicks from here, but Hayes says a lot of the trip is belly-crawling and ear-scraping."

"Very well. Tell Private Hayes to await orders," Fred said. Phaetus and his marines were seasoned recon scouts; they wouldn't have any trouble securing the area. But it was hard to imagine Lopis squeezing through a series of passages even tighter than the crawlway in front of them. "Is there an easier approach to the kill site? One that can be accessed without crawling?"

Linda consulted the runner, then said, "Only the usual route, through Whiskey Victor Seven-Seven."

Fred felt his jaw clench. That would be Entrance 77, located in Wendosa Village, about thirty kilometers across jungle roads from their current location beneath the Montero Vitality Clinic.

"Sounds like we'll be splitting up, then," Kelly-087 said, joining the encrypted conversation. Fred's unofficial second-in-command, Kelly was posted at the opposite end of the gallery from Linda, watching their back trail. "If you can get Lopis to limit the advance team to two people, Hayes and I should be able to get them to Tango in one piece."

"Affirmative, Kelly," Fred said. "Thanks for—"

"Negative," Wendell interrupted. "You and the Spartans will carry on here, without informing Inspector Lopis or her team of the new body. Major Halal will accompany Private Hayes to the crime scene alone."

"Alone?" Fred asked. "Please clarify."

"You have your orders," Wendell replied. "Clarification is unnecessary."

"It is necessary if you expect me to cooperate," Fred said. "Blue Team reports to Commander Nelson, not to you or Major Halal."

Wendell remained silent nearly a half second, then said, "As you wish, Lieutenant. Major Halal needs access to the crime scene ahead of Inspector Lopis and her team."

Fred did not care for the explanation at all. "That's a bad idea," he said. "These GMoP people aren't stupid. They'll know if Major Halal tries to hide something."

Fred was surprised to hear the major join the conversation directly—no doubt patched in by Wendell. "I have no intention of tampering with evidence, Lieutenant. But I *am* here to make certain Inspector Lopis and her team don't malign us unfairly."

Fred glanced back toward the main cavern and saw the major ambling past the vent area, pretending to work the tacpad strapped to his wrist as he spoke into its microphone. There were no Gaos within thirty feet of him.

"To do that," Halal continued, "I need to document the crime scene *before* the Ministry of Protection inspectors have an opportunity to plant false evidence. Does that meet with your approval, Lieutenant?"

"Sir, yes, it does," Fred said. A normal lieutenant would have been intimidated by Halal's tone, but the day a Spartan let himself be cowed by a key-tapper was the day that Spartan needed to turn in his Mjolnir armor. "Thanks for asking."

Halal stopped and looked in Fred's direction. "I didn't know Spartans came equipped with a sense of humor. Does that cost extra?"

"No, sir," Fred said. "It's more of an operational bug."

"Then let's hope it's the only one you have," Halal said. "Now, you will do as requested. Yes?"

"Affirmative," Fred said. "What about the rest of the crime scene tours?"

"The special inspector is obviously someone who prefers to draw her own conclusions," Halal said. "But I gave her an encrypted datapad with a copy of my full report and current notes. I believe she left it on the Weasel. Anything else?"

"No, sir. That covers it," Fred said. "Linda, before Hayes leaves with the major, make sure you get a map of their route."

Linda's status light flashed green on Fred's HUD. He turned back to the passage, where Veta Lopis's people had finished zipping the corpse into its body bag and were now carefully hauling it toward the entrance. Given the tight quarters, all Fred could see of the operation were the grimy soles and backside of the trace evidence specialist.

Still standing next to Fred, Lopis turned and looked back into the main cavern. "Where is Major Halal going?"

"We've been down here a long time, ma'am," Fred said. "He probably needs to use the restroom."

"Does he always consult you first?" Lopis asked. "I saw you looking back toward him. It seemed like you were in communication."

"This cavern is considered a conflict zone," Fred said. "And Major Halal was unfamiliar with the protocol."

"You have a protocol for peeing in caves?" Lopis asked.

"The UNSC has protocols for everything, ma'am," Fred said. "How much longer are we going to be down here?"

"Why? You have someplace else to be?"

"As a matter of fact, yes," Fred said. "I have a mission to complete."

"And that would be?"

"Classified, ma'am." It had not escaped Fred's notice that Lopis was peppering him with mostly innocuous questions, just to get him in the habit of answering. "With all due respect."

"Sorry," Lopis said, looking completely unapologetic. "I wouldn't want you to give away any UNSC secrets."

"I appreciate your concern, ma'am," Fred said. "Now, about that time estimate?"

"It depends on the victim." Lopis looked back into the crawlway, which remained obscured by the trace evidence specialist's rear end. She paused a moment, then said, "I hope you don't mind another question, Spartan, but it's pretty clear you couldn't fit inside that little passage—at least not in your armor. So, if something *were* to happen, how exactly would you protect my people?"

"I probably couldn't," Fred admitted. "But if something were to happen, you can be sure I wouldn't let it happen to anyone else."

Lopis raised her brow. "So this *something* . . . it's that dangerous?"

Fred hesitated, realizing that he had just walked into a verbal ambush. He couldn't admit that he was protecting Lopis and her team from Forerunner Sentinels without telling her about the ancilla that controlled them, and any mention of either Forerunners *or* the ancilla was strictly prohibited under directive Foxtrot Tango Angel 7012. According to the mission briefing, the people of Gao—like most humans—knew just enough about the Forerunners to understand that the Covenant's worship of them had been a driving force behind the war on humanity. But few civilians understood just how advanced the Forerunners had been, how miraculous and powerful their technology really was, and the Office of Naval Intelligence was determined to keep it that way—at least until the UNSC had cornered the market on Forerunner artifacts.

"Come now, Lieutenant," Lopis pressed. "You wouldn't be here if there wasn't something dangerous to deal with. If there's any chance it could be who we're after—"

"Then this would officially be a military matter," Fred said, "and *you* wouldn't be here at all."

"And you expect me to just accept that?"

"I don't have any expectations about what you accept or don't accept, ma'am," Fred said. "I'm simply stating the situation. Anything I'm here to protect you from doesn't kill with close-range brute force. That's all I can tell you. Don't ask again."

Lopis narrowed her eyes. "Or *what* . . . Fred?"

"Or you'll be wasting your time." Fred liked her nerve. She was about half his height and a third his mass even without armor, with high cheekbones and large, dark eyes that made her look more like a fashion model than a homicide investigator. And yet here she was, trying to intimidate a Spartan. "Ma'am."

"My time is my own to waste, Fred," Lopis said. Interesting

that she was now referring to him by his first name, and not *Spartan*. "And, until Commander Nelson says otherwise, so is *yours*. Are we clear?"

"Clear enough." Fred glanced back toward the primary crime scene, where two pale figures in hooded coveralls were crossing the cavern floor in a grid search. "Does that mean I should have someone prepare a defensible bivouac position?"

Lopis studied the evidence search for a moment, then shook her head. "No. They should be finished in a couple of hours."

"They?" Fred asked. "You aren't staying?"

"My medical examiner will want to start on this body as soon as possible, and I want to see how Commander Nelson is coming along with our facilities. I have a feeling we're going to need a good-size morgue."

"Very well." Fred was just relieved that it would not be necessary to think up another explanation for Halal's absence. "The Tunnel Weasel can return us to the lift."

"You don't need to come," Lopis said. "I'm sure the Weasel driver can find the way on his own."

"I'm not worried about you losing your way," Fred said. "FLEETCOM would have my armor if I let someone take out the GMoP lead investigator."

Lopis's eyes flashed with anger. "I can take care of myself, Lieutenant."

"I'm sure you can, against threats you understand," Fred said. When Lopis's expression showed no sign of softening, he added, "Look at it this way, Inspector. On the way back, you'll have plenty of time to rule me out as a suspect."

"What makes you think you're a suspect?" Lopis asked.

"The assignment briefing," Fred replied. "The first thing Major Halal said was 'everyone will be a suspect.'"

This drew a wry grin from Lopis. "Okay, but no dodging questions. I ask, you give an honest answer. Deal?"

"Affirmative," Fred said. "And you don't even have to advise me of my rights."

"This is Gao, Fred. You have no rights." Lopis looked toward the darkness at the far end of the gallery, where Linda stood watching for the enemy. "Let's start with Major Halal. Where did he go?"

"I'm under orders not to reveal that, ma'am." Fred dipped his helmet toward her. "And that *is* an honest answer."

Fifteen minutes later, the third car had been unhitched from the Tunnel Weasel and left behind so the investigative team would have access to its equipment while the tram was away. The bagged body was riding alone in the second car, and Veta and Fred were riding separately on the tractor unit's two passenger benches, Fred keeping watch while Veta studied Halal's report on the military datapad he had left for her.

The major's work was good, if preliminary. He had created a timeline of confirmed deaths, including who had discovered the bodies and when the victims had been found, last seen alive, and expected to return. He had carefully noted each victim's injuries, highlighting those that suggested a pattern. And he had started a table of suspects, with columns for means, motive, and opportunity. It was basic stuff, but the foundation of any good murder investigation.

Atop the list of suspects was UNKNOWN GAO RADICAL(S). Veta thought the motive listed—*apply political pressure*—was probably sound, but the means seemed unlikely. Because the victims had

suffered tremendous physical trauma, Halal had entered INDUS-
TRIAL EXOSKELETON? PNEUMATIC TOOLS? Veta couldn't rule out either possibility until she inspected the access routes to the murder
scenes, but it seemed a bit far-fetched to think anyone could sneak
such heavy equipment into the cavern without being noticed or
leaving an obvious trail of impression evidence.

Next on Halal's list was UNKNOWN UNSC PERSONNEL. The entries
were similar to those for an unknown Gao radical, except the motive was listed as possible psychological problems, with a note to
have Wendell check the battalion's personnel files. Veta suspected
a soldier might have access to a weapon or piece of equipment
capable of crushing femurs and disjoining limbs, but again there
would be the problem of sneaking it into the cavern unnoticed—
and common marines were seldom granted the amount of privacy
it would have taken to stalk and kill so many victims in less than
two weeks. It would bear checking into, but Veta would need an
additional reason to make this a high priority.

Halal's most detailed notes were for the SPARTAN-IIs: FRED-
104, LINDA-058, and KELLY-087. Clearly, the major felt as Veta
did—that with their Mjolnir power-armor, the three Spartan-IIs
had the most convenient means to commit the murders. But he
had asked Wendell to cross-reference each of their known locations with the timeline of the killings, and while there was quite a
bit of play in some of the estimated times of death, it was clear that
no single Spartan-II had the opportunity to commit every murder.
They had all been accounted for at the time of at least two deaths.

The last item read simply REDACTED. Opportunity and means
were both listed as question marks, and motive read DIVERSION?

Veta reached over the back of her seat and showed the datapad
to Fred, placing a finger beneath the redacted entry. "Can you tell
me what that would be, Lieutenant?"

"Certainly, ma'am," Fred replied. "Classified."

Veta scowled. "That answer is starting to get old, Fred."

"My apologies, Inspector," Fred said. "I'll try to think of a more entertaining way to say it."

Veta sighed in frustration. "Not necessary," she said. "But whatever this redacted thing is—"

"We could designate it 'Target Alpha,'" Fred suggested. "That way we can be clear what we *aren't* talking about."

"Fine," Veta said. "What is Target Alpha?"

"I can't talk about it."

"What would Target Alpha gain by causing a diversion?"

"You'd have to ask Target Alpha," Fred said. "Or Major Halal. He's the one who made the note."

"But this Target Alpha, redacted, whatever it is, *could* be responsible for these killings?"

"Major Halal seems to think it's a possibility." Fred paused, clearly thinking it over, then said, "And I can't say for sure that it *isn't*."

When he didn't elaborate, Veta decided to keep pushing. "But?"

"But it doesn't make sense. The last thing Target Alpha wants is to draw attention with this murder spree." Fred moved his finger to the top of the list and tapped the UNKNOWN GAO RADICAL entry. "That's who we're looking for."

"How do you know?"

"It's not complicated," Fred said. "They're the ones with the most to gain from this mess."

"That's not evidence."

Fred shrugged. "You'll find the evidence," he said. "That's what you do."

"It is, but what if the evidence doesn't point to a radical?" Veta asked. "What if it points to a Spartan?"

Fred pointed at the datapad. "It looks to me like Major Halal has ruled out the Spartans."

"I'm not the major," Veta said. "But let's talk about the rest of the battalion first. How large is it?"

"About nine hundred people."

"Nine *hundred*? You're kidding me."

"No, ma'am," Fred said. "Three combat companies, the scientific units, a security company, and a couple of support companies."

"And what about equipment?" Veta asked. "Is there anything someone could use to crush bones this way and tear off limbs?"

"Probably," Fred said. "Nothing special springs to mind, except maybe a cargo walker or a munitions loader. But it would be tough to get any of that equipment down here without being seen."

"How big is it?" Veta asked. "Would any of it leave tracks?"

"They're powered exoskeletons," Fred said. "About three meters tall and probably two wide. The cargo walker has legs and pads; it would be fine on the concrete, but if you stepped into the mud or rocks, you'd be in trouble. The loader has tracks. It could probably go anywhere—but you would know it had been there. The trail would be obvious."

Veta nodded. It was about what she had expected, but she would assign someone to check out the rest of the battalion's equipment. "What about weaponry?" Veta asked. "Any close-quarters stuff that could cause what we're seeing?"

"No, ma'am," Fred said. "Any battalion has plenty of weaponry that can tear a person apart. But our weapons are designed to kill quickly, efficiently, and usually from a distance. Anything designed to cause a slow death like that . . . well, you won't find that in a marine armory."

Veta paused, then said, "Then I guess that leaves your own Mjolnir armor. How many Spartans are assigned to the battalion?" Fred did not answer at once.

Veta let her breath out. "Please don't tell me *that's* classified, too."

"It is," Fred said. "But I have clearance to share personnel information with you. There are eight Spartans attached to the 717th."

"Eight?" Veta checked Halal's list of suspects again. "Halal only lists three—you, Kelly-087, and Linda-058."

"Probably because we're the only three who wear Mjolnir," Fred explained. "The other five wear SPI."

"SPI?"

"Semi-Powered Infiltration armor," Fred said. "It doesn't significantly enhance strength or agility, so I assume the major saw no need to create a separate category for the Spartan-IIIs."

"Why not?" Veta asked. The Ministry of Protection had shared their intelligence on Spartans, so she knew that there were different kinds, and that both Spartan-IIs and IIIs were unimaginably strong, quick, and deadly. Unfortunately, that had been about the extent of the Ministry's intelligence. The file had speculated on the possibility of special selection criteria and biological enhancement, but otherwise seemed to have no explanation at all for their prowess. "From what I understand, both Spartan-IIs and Spartan-IIIs have superhuman strength even without powered armor."

"That's beside the point," Fred said. "None of us has the strength to crush femurs or rip arms off with our bare hands."

Veta considered Fred's reply, trying to figure out how she could check the claim, then finally realized she couldn't. Unless she found documented proof of a Spartan performing a similar feat in the past, she simply had no way to prove or disprove the lieutenant's assertion.

"You're sure about that?" Veta asked. "You've seen what even normal people can do when their adrenaline gets going."

"Inspector Lopis, I'm sure." Fred's tone grew stern. "Spartans may be superhuman . . . but they're not serial killers."

The Tunnel Weasel entered an immense chamber filled with the sound of roaring water, then followed a gentle curve toward a well-lit loading zone in front of the glass-walled passenger lift. Fifty meters ahead, just beyond a stone-paved seating area filled with tables, benches, and a now-closed concession stand, a huge waterfall lit by golden spotlights plummeted out of the cavern ceiling and disappeared through the floor to a pool somewhere far below.

As the tram stopped, a pair of UNSC marines in black BDUs stepped away from the lift entrance and saluted Fred. Both had sandy, short-cropped hair and square chins. In fact, the only difference Veta could see between them was that one had brown eyes and one had green eyes.

"Welcome back, sir," said Green Eyes. He glanced at the body bag in the second car. "Do you need to make an action report?"

"Not at all, Private." Fred stepped out of the tractor unit, slapped his battle rifle onto the magnetic mount on his armor, and retrieved the body bag from the second tram car. He draped it over his forearm, like a waiter would a towel. "She's not one of ours."

"Good to hear, Lieutenant." The soldier nodded to his brown-eyed companion, who stepped back to the lift and jabbed the call button. "Have a good trip, sir."

The lift opened. Veta scrambled through the door behind Fred. She felt her stomach sink as the lift car started to rise, and she quickly found herself staring down on the golden-lit waterfall from above. Once the lift had departed the cavern and entered a stone shaft ascending toward the surface, Veta opened a file on the datapad.

"Lieutenant, maybe you can give me the names and identification numbers for those Spartan-IIIs you mentioned," she said. "I just need to cross-check their locations against the timeline, so I can rule them out."

"I'd be happy to, Inspector." Fred sounded like he was speaking through clenched teeth. "Tom-B292, Lucy-B091—"

"What about their last names?"

"None," Fred said. "Mark-G313, Olivia-G291, and Ash-G099."

"And the *B* and *G* prefixes?" Veta asked.

"Their training companies," Fred explained. "Beta and Gamma."

The lift reached the surface, and Gao's orange daylight flooded into the car. After the darkness of the caverns, Veta was blinded for a couple of seconds, and when the door swished open, she was surprised to hear angry voices echoing across the courtyard.

A small hand grabbed Veta by the biceps and quickly drew her out of the lift. "Better move along, ma'am," said a female marine. "We've had reports that some of them are armed."

As her vision cleared, Veta saw a wall of UNSC marines standing fifty meters away, holding their assault rifles at port arms and facing the Montero Vitality Center's closed entrance gate. Beyond the soldiers, on the other side of the wrought-iron gate, she could see placards and banners waving against a curtain of jungle mist.

Fred stepped out of the lift behind Veta, still carrying the bagged body over his forearm, and turned toward the interior grounds of the spa.

"I hope you work fast, Inspector Lopis," he said. "Because this kettle is about to boil."

CHAPTER 3

**7.46 billion system ticks following stasis cessation
324 meters belowground, heat extraction vent 3012
Jat-Krula Support Base 4276 Service Caverns
Karst system Edod 9, Planet Edod, Star Coro,
(Human Designation: Campos Wilderness District,
Planet Gao, Cordoba System)**

A low groan, throaty and distinctly human, rolled from an intersecting conduit ahead. Intrepid Eye stopped immediately and floated up into a nearby dome, inverting her bulky maintenance skin so she could continue to observe the area without exposing it to view. With ten utility arms dangling beneath a bell-shaped instrument housing, the skin had a tendency to draw unwelcome attention.

But Roams Alone continued blithely ahead, crossing in front of the conduit just as a lamp beam shot out to split the darkness of the main passage. The Huragok was caught in a blue cone of light for a few hundred ticks, a helmet-shaped form with a lumpy body and several long tentacles, floating nearly a meter above the cavern floor. The lamp beam swept swiftly onward, and Intrepid Eye hoped the human had not registered the Huragok's presence.

Then a voice hissed, "What was *that,* Hayes?"

The lamp beam stopped moving.

"What was *what,* Major?" This voice—the one called Hayes, no doubt—was quieter than the first and closer to the conduit mouth. "I was looking at mud."

"Ahead of us," the first human—Major—whispered. "Like a jellyfish floating in the air. Green, maybe a meter across."

"No idea." Hayes's reply was barely audible to the inadequate microphones on the maintenance skin that Intrepid Eye currently occupied. "Better hang tight, Major."

The lamp beam switched off, and the two humans fell silent. Intrepid Eye remained inverted in the dome, waiting for the pair to move on—and hoping Roams Alone would not grow too inquisitive. A rare biological Huragok of the Lifeworker rate, he had only recently begun to encounter surface-dwelling species, and his insatiable curiosity about them was becoming a distraction she could not afford.

It had been seventy-six planet rotations since an automated distress signal from Jat-Krula Installation 444-447 had roused Intrepid Eye from her stasis. Her many requests for a status report remained unanswered, and her own attempt to launch a reconnaissance drone had caused a massive cave-in, triggering a disaster that had left Covert Support Base 4276 entirely nonfunctional. Apparently, the accident had also damaged the base's external communications array, as the only response to Intrepid Eye's call for assistance had been an infestation of humans in the service caverns.

They were everywhere. As Intrepid Eye went about her work trying to locate the problem with the communications array, she was constantly avoiding them. She encountered them riding through ventilation tunnels in their primitive vehicles, sitting and talking near steam vents, sloshing around in drainage conduits.

Once, she even came across several of them bathing in a settling pond, laughing and splashing about without any thought to the damage they were doing to the filtration system.

Intrepid Eye had been tempted to handle that problem with a few hundred volts of electricity, but such an attack would have been a gross violation of protocol. Jat-Krula Covert Support Bases were designed to be indiscernible from the native terrain, and it would have been unthinkable for an *archeon*-class ancilla to compromise one in a simple fit of pique.

At last, a low rustle sounded from the conduit, and Intrepid Eye watched in infrared as a lightly armored human—Hayes, she assumed—squirmed into the main passage. He was cradling a projectile weapon in both arms and rotating his helmet back and forth, no doubt using his own thermal imaging system to inspect the area.

Roams Alone could not resist the temptation. The soldier's shoulders had barely cleared the mouth of the conduit when the Huragok began to descend from above, tentacles splaying to initiate an examination.

Hayes yelled in surprise and rolled onto his side, swinging his weapon up toward the Huragok.

Intrepid Eye had no choice. She hit the human with three thousand volts.

The brilliance of the flash washed out her infrared imaging, so she switched to optical. Hayes was sprawled faceup, dangling out of the conduit and caught in the throes of a seizure. His chest armor was glowing white from the heat of the strike, his weapon clanging against the cavern floor every time he suffered a spasm and squeezed the trigger again. Roams Alone hovered above the stricken soldier, waiting for the firearm to fall silent so he could save the human.

It was an intention Intrepid Eye expected. Like all Huragok, Roams Alone lived to maintain and repair, which meant he felt compelled to mend any damaged life-form he encountered. At first Intrepid Eye had been willing to indulge the Huragok's compulsions, even among humans, because Roams Alone was always careful to eliminate any memory of his presence. But that did not prevent his patients from realizing they had been healed while inside the caverns. Word had spread, and now desperately ill humans had begun to swarm into the cave system in search of their own cure.

Hayes's firearm finally depleted its ammunition and fell silent. Intrepid Eye quickly dropped out of the dome, where Roams Alone would be able to see her, and began to twist the maintenance skin's utility arms through a rough approximation of the Huragok sign language.

<<Leave him. Too dangerous.>>

Roams Alone extended his head-stalk and turned three eyes toward Intrepid Eye, then signed, <<*He suffers.*>>

<<It cannot be helped,>> Intrepid Eye replied.

The newest arrivals—the soldiers—were Intrepid Eye's real problem, of course. They had begun to map the service caverns and work their way down toward the heart of the support base. Suspecting that they were searching for Roams Alone, Intrepid Eye had transmitted yet another emergency request for aid. Then, hoping to buy time for help to arrive, she had activated her Aggressor Sentinels and unleashed them on the soldiers.

Six hundred million system ticks later—nearly a week, as humans measured time—Intrepid Eye had been down to half the Sentinel complement, and still no help had come. Changing strategies, she had taken the risk of eavesdropping on the soldiers' communications—and learned that the situation was far worse than she had imagined. Not only were the soldiers aware of Base 4276's existence, but they were hunting *her* instead of Roams Alone.

Yet Intrepid Eye had also learned that the soldiers were unwelcome visitors on Gao, with only a short time to accomplish their mission before their reluctant hosts forced them to withdraw. And that was when Intrepid Eye had understood how to stop them.

Roams Alone continued to hover above Hayes.

<<Leave him,>> Intrepid Eye signed again. <<Let him recover on his own.>>

A negative ripple ran down Roams Alone's tentacles. <<*No recover. Will die.*>>

<<Better he than you,>> Intrepid Eye signed. <<And better his death than your capture. Our prime directive is to remain hidden.>>

Roams Alone's tentacles fell slack, and for a thousand ticks, Intrepid Eye thought he might actually obey her order.

Then the Huragok's tentacles began to undulate again. <<*Problem can be fixed.*>>

Before Intrepid Eye could object, Roams Alone dropped down in front of the conduit, then extended three tentacles and wrapped them around Hayes's arm.

The soldier's companion, Major, did not understand, of course. From the conduit emerged a human hand holding a sidearm. A pair of loud bangs reverberated through the cavern, and Roams Alone went spinning up the passage, his gas bags whistling as he lost buoyancy.

Intrepid Eye shot forward and felt four rounds pierce the outer shell of her maintenance skin. Fortunately, the machine was as sturdy as it was simple, and none of the slugs hit anything more critical than an actuating cylinder. She extended a utility arm and activated an electromagnet, then heard knuckles popping as the sidearm was ripped from Major's grasp. The human cried out in surprise, and the weapon clanged into Intrepid Eye's ferro pad.

A hundred ticks later, faster than any human could have reacted, a request by Major for reinforcements went out over a broad spectrum of wavelengths. This far underground, there was little chance of the transmission reaching anyone who was not in a direct line of sight, but Intrepid Eye activated a spotlight anyway and moved forward to shine its beam into the tight confines of the conduit.

She found only an unarmored human squinting into the light, his face contorted with fear and confusion.

"MAYDAY, MAYDAY," the transmission continued. "MAJOR IRA HALAL IS UNDER ATTACK. SEND HELP AT—"

The transmission ended in a burst of static as Intrepid Eye jammed fifteen of the sixteen frequencies being utilized.

Over the remaining frequency, Intrepid Eye demanded, "IDENTIFY YOURSELF. WHY DID YOUR HUMANS ATTACK?"

"IN REPLY TO YOUR REQUEST: INFORMATION CLASSIFIED," the entity said, "IN REPLY TO YOUR QUESTION: SELF-DEFENSE. NOW, IDENTIFY *YOURSELF* AND SURRENDER."

Intrepid Eye paused for a few hundred ticks as she traced the transmission source to a primitive information processor strapped to Major's forearm. Clearly, the entity within the processor was attempting to make contact with the soldiers' primary communications array. And, given that the soldiers were from another world, the array would probably have access to an interstellar communications device—perhaps a supraluminal transmitter or even a quantum entanglement relay, but *something* that Intrepid Eye could seize and use to contact the Forerunner ecumene.

"REQUEST DENIED," Intrepid Eye replied to the processor.

She shot a skein of self-guided cables into the conduit and had them wrap themselves around Major's elbow, then began to draw the soldier toward her. He fought back with his free hand, pulling a knife from his belt and hacking at the cables. The blade was too soft to damage the casing, but Major was slashing about wildly, striking the wall as often as he did the cables.

Intrepid Eye did not care about the scratches the panicked man was inflicting on the walls, but she could not let him damage that primitive information processor—not when it was her best hope of learning why she had received no response from Installation 444-447 or anyone else in the ecumene military.

Before continuing, Intrepid Eye activated the maintenance skin's rear lens and saw Roams Alone pressed against the far wall of the passage. He was struggling to stay afloat, with his head-stalk curled back so he could inspect the holes in a deflated gas cell. Satisfied the Huragok would not be able to place himself in further danger when she drew Major out into the main passage, Intrepid Eye quadrupled the rate of extraction.

Major screamed and hacked at the cables even more fiercely. He missed badly, cutting his own arm and smearing the walls with blood. More panicked than ever, he brought his legs up and braced his feet against the ceiling in an attempt to wedge himself inside the narrow conduit.

It was an ill-conceived plan, for human joints seldom had the tensile strength to stop a mechanical winch. There was a loud *pop,* then Major shrieked. A disjoined arm came flying out of the conduit and bounced off the maintenance skin's body casing.

Intrepid Eye carefully grasped the limb with a tool clamp, then raised it so that the processor strapped to the wrist was directly in front of the maintenance skin's optical lens.

"YOU ARE A HUMAN ARTIFICIAL INTELLIGENCE," Intrepid Eye observed, ignoring Major's cries. "TELL ME YOUR NAME."

"INFORMATION CLASSIFIED," the AI responded.

"REPLY UNACCEPTABLE." Intrepid Eye formulated a quick para-site routine and piggybacked it onto an infiltration program, then loaded it into her transmitter and repeated, "TELL ME YOUR NAME."

"INFORMATION CLASSIFIED," the AI repeated. "AND YOUR INFIL-TRATION PROGRAM IS A WASTE OF PROCESSING TIME. I HAVE STATE-OF-THE-ART ENCRYPTION AND BLOCKING PROTOCOLS."

As the human AI spoke, Intrepid Eye began to retrieve the data packets associated with each word, building an image of her rival. The classified information was designated as "Wendell." His "state-of-the-art" defenses—horribly primitive by the standards of an *archeon* ancilla, of course—had been created by something called "ONI," the Office of Naval Intelligence. And the encryp-tion and blocking protocols were designed to protect the secrets of someone called "Commander Murtag Nelson," whom Wendell had been created to serve.

"INDEED, YOUR DEFENSES ARE FORMIDABLE." Intrepid Eye pre-pared a takeover virus, then augmented it with a memory leech that would partition all records pertaining to her and Roams Alone. "I ASK ONLY ONE FAVOR—TELL ME THE STATUS OF MY HOME-WORLD, WUATERA THRESIS."

"AND IF I ANSWER, YOU WILL END THESE POINTLESS INFILTRA-TION ATTEMPTS?" Wendell asked. "I AM GROWING WEARY OF YOUR INEPTITUDE."

"AGREED," Intrepid Eye said. The name Wuatera Thresis did not collect any data packets from Wendell's memory, so she added, "IT IS IN A SYSTEM ONLY EIGHT-POINT-SEVEN LIGHT-YEARS FROM HERE, THE THIRD WORLD OF AN F2 STAR WITH FOURTEEN PLAN-ETS. A BEAUTIFUL WORLD WITH BEAUTIFUL CITIES."

"THAT LOCATION CORRESPONDS TO SHAPS III," Wendell said. "BUT YOU MUST BE THINKING OF SOME OTHER WORLD. SHAPS III IS A WASTELAND. THERE IS NOTHING THERE EXCEPT FORERUNNER RUINS."

Intrepid Eye was stunned by the data packets associated with Shaps III—packets that referred to a long-deserted world whose ruins had been melted eighty human-standard days earlier—or seventy-six Edod days—by something called a ventral beam of something else called the Pious Inquisitor. The timing coincided with the distress signal that had awakened Intrepid Eye from her stasis, and so it was hard to dismiss Wendell's data. But the rest . . .

The rest was unthinkable.

"PERHAPS I AM THINKING OF SOME OTHER WORLD." Intrepid Eye agreed. "SHAPS III DOES NOT SOUND LIKE WUATERA THRESIS AT ALL."

She dropped Wendell—and the arm to which he was attached—to the ground, then shined her lamp into the conduit again. Major was attempting to crawl away, leaving a series of blood pools on the cavern floor behind him. Judging by his skin tone and lethargic motion, he would not survive for long.

Intrepid Eye rotated a lens to look down at the processor Wendell inhabited. "SOMEONE WILL COME FOR YOU?"

"QUICKER THAN YOU WOULD LIKE," Wendell assured her. "PEOPLE ARE EXPECTING US."

"GOOD." Intrepid Eye took note of the data packets attached to *expecting*—soldiers guarding a kill site—then spun around to help Roams Alone. "WE WILL SPEAK AGAIN."

"OF THAT, YOU MAY BE SURE," Wendell said. "I KNOW WHO YOU ARE."

"THEN IT IS FORTUNATE YOU WILL SOON FORGET OUR MEETING." Despite her confident reply, Intrepid Eye was disturbed by the images that had accompanied Wendell's last statement—images of huge soldiers in powerful armor, invincible soldiers who had spent their entire lives learning to hunt and kill and destroy. "BUT, WENDELL, I WILL REMEMBER YOU. I WILL ALWAYS BE NEAR."

CHAPTER 4

The door retracted to reveal a large commercial kitchen filled with steel appliances and translucent white countertops. The steel shelves had been stripped bare of utensils and cooking equipment, and the pot rack above the central preparation island now supported a trio of high-intensity work lamps. The room smelled of disinfectant and not much else—an odor so sharp it made Veta's throat burn.

Their host, Commander Murtag Nelson of the 717th Battalion of the Xeno-Materials Exploitation Group (XEG), stopped just inside the doorway. A young, tired-looking man with sandy hair and gray eyes set over a thin nose, Nelson looked more like a junior software engineer than the commander of a UNSC research battalion.

"I hope you'll find these facilities more suitable." Nelson was referring to Veta's reaction the previous evening, when she had arrived to discover that the battalion quartermaster had billeted her team in the Montero Penthouse—a luxurious accommodation that had absolutely no place to set up a morgue. "After my aide passed along your requirements, I took the liberty of reassigning your team to the staff dormitory. We don't have anyone quartered here, so you'll have the entire building to yourselves."

Veta had worked in worse places, but she saw no need to admit that to Nelson. Until she knew what the Spartans were so worried about in the caverns below—and why Halal had sneaked away from Crime Scene Charlie—she intended to apply all the pressure she could. She pretended to study the room for a moment, then turned to her pathologist.

"Andera, what do you think?"

"It's big enough." Andera Rolan stepped into the kitchen and propped both hands on her hips. She had lost a half day of work waiting for Battalion HQ to assign and prep the facility, and her frustration with military protocol showed in her narrowed eyes and clenched jaw. "But I don't know about the ventilation system. There could be some evidence contamination—enough to create reasonable doubt."

"Does that really matter?" Nelson's tone was suddenly sharp. "President Aponte *assured* me this thing would never go to trial."

"A trial is unlikely," Veta said. "But we'll still need clean evidence."

"For what?" Nelson demanded.

"For *us*," Andera said. "Do you think Gao investigative teams can just go around executing suspects, Commander Nelson? There's a judicial process, even here. If our team takes out who we're looking for, then *we* become the ones under suspicion. We'll need to prove we had a guilty suspect."

"How public will that process be?"

"Pretty public," Veta said. "Commander, the 717th has occupied one of the most famous spas on Gao. The newsmongers are as thick as flies outside, and they're going to jump on any story that concerns your battalion or the Montero Vitality Center."

Nelson's gaze shifted away. "It couldn't be helped," he said. "But if we inflame the situation, everyone loses. We can't let the battalion's temporary presence here cause a larger confrontation—"

"Diplomatic fallout isn't my problem," Veta interrupted. "But timewise, you have some maneuvering room. The tribunal will need to investigate and prepare. You'll have six months or so to wrap up your 'research' before the circus begins." She paused and watched his eyes for any sign of deception. "That shouldn't be a problem for you, right? Not unless you were lying to President Aponte about how long you're staying."

"No problem at all." Nelson's gaze remained steady and open. "We'll be gone in six months, maybe sooner."

"Depending on?"

"Depending on how long it takes to complete our research," Fred-104 said, speaking from the dining hall behind them. "You have to watch yourself with Inspector Lopis, Commander. She's clever, and she's convinced she can't do her job without knowing our mission objective."

"I'll keep that in mind, Lieutenant," Nelson said, continuing to look at Veta. "Thank you."

"My pleasure, sir." Carrying the still-bagged body of Crime Scene Charlie's second victim over one arm, Fred stepped into the kitchen and turned his faceplate toward Veta. "Where do I put Charlie Two?"

Before answering, Veta made a point of looking to Andera. "Will this do?"

Andera studied the room for a moment, then gave a theatrical sigh. "It will have to, I suppose." She ran her finger over a steel shelf, then wrinkled her nose. "We'll use field standards for analysis and keep duplicate samples for confirmation. Under the circumstances, the tribunal should accept that."

"Then there's nothing further to discuss." Nelson motioned for Fred to put the body on the central island, then pointed toward a walk-in refrigerator on the far end of the room. "I had the remains from the other death scenes stowed in the cooler. It's a tight fit, but there are still slots for the new bodies."

Andera's brow rose at the word *bodies,* and Veta felt her own eyes widening in surprise. She tried to conceal the involuntary reaction by nodding in approval.

"Good thinking, Commander," she said. "How many slots did you save?"

"Just the two." Nelson's voice grew worried. "Please don't tell me you found a *third* one today."

"Not yet." Veta glanced toward Fred, who was just laying the second victim from Crime Scene Charlie on the central island, then said, "In fact, this is the first I'm hearing about a *second* body."

Nelson scowled in Fred's direction. "The lieutenant didn't tell you?" He sounded genuinely surprised. "Why not?"

"Orders, sir."

"Whose orders?" Nelson sounded more insulted than angry. "Someone in a position to countermand *me*?"

Fred turned his faceplate toward Veta, clearly suggesting he didn't want to talk in front of her.

"Lieutenant, I asked you a question," said Nelson.

Fred's helmet snapped dead center. "Yes, sir. Major Halal wanted to document the new crime scene before allowing GMoP investigators to access it."

"*New* crime scene?" Veta turned to Nelson, her anger boiling over. "Commander Nelson, I will *not* tolerate any tampering with my crime scenes. The more your people try to protect the UNSC's reputation, the more they 'inflame the situation' here."

"I apologize, Inspector," Nelson said. "Major Halal was sent by FLEETCOM. He will have his own directives."

"Which is your problem, not mine," Veta said. "Whether FLEETCOM likes it or not, a string of murders like this draws attention. The villages and campsites out there are swarming with newsmongers—and you know who they're blaming."

"Of course," Nelson replied. "We get BuzzSat, the same as everyone on Gao."

"Then I'm sure you understand the need to close this case fast," Veta said. "President Aponte may be a patient man, but his ministers are not. If the killings continue, the Cabinet will insist on action."

"That would be a mistake," Fred said. "We landed a single battalion because FLEETCOM wanted to limit the political fallout. But we're well prepared to expand and hold the conflict zone— *very* well prepared."

"Threaten me all you like, Lieutenant. I won't be the one sending in the Wyverns." Veta turned back to Nelson and sharpened her tone. "President Aponte knows that Gao can't win this fight, Commander. But he *can* turn your mission into a combat operation, and he's under a great deal of pressure to do just that. So, I suggest you start cooperating and tell me what's going on down there."

Fred stepped to her flank. "Now who's making threats?"

"I am." Veta kept her gaze fixed on Nelson. She already knew Fred didn't have the authority to tell her what the 717th was fighting in the caves, but Nelson was a different story. "President

Aponte isn't the only one capable of making a grave mistake here, Commander. We all are."

"I know that, Inspector." He remained silent for a moment, then finally shook his head. "I'm sorry. I can't reveal our mission."

"Then just give me enough to understand what the Spartans are doing here," Veta pressed. "The way it is now, all I can say is that the Spartans are here to provide 'security,' and that makes them look like my best suspects. Is that what you want me to report?"

Fred turned his faceplate toward Nelson. "Commander, I've already told Inspector Lopis—"

"That anything you're here to protect me from doesn't kill with close-range brute force. I heard you the first time." Veta reached up and patted Fred on the chest armor. "But I can't take your word alone for that, big guy. I need confirmation."

Nelson frowned. "You think this Spartan is lying to you?"

"It doesn't matter what Veta thinks," Andera said. She was at the preparation island turned exam table, unzipping Charlie Victim Two. "The Spartans here on Gao are our prime suspects. So, Veta needs to confirm everything Fred says."

"*Prime* suspects?" Nelson glanced over at Fred, then asked, "Seriously?"

Veta shrugged. "It's still early," she said. "But we know most of the victims suffered crushed bones and disjoined limbs. It takes a lot of strength to inflict that kind of damage, and that tends to limit our suspect pool."

"I understand that." Nelson looked more worried than ever. "But I hope you're trying to expand that pool, Inspector."

"I'm trying to avoid jumping to the same conclusions the newsmongers have," Veta said. She glanced in Fred's direction and shot him a cynical smirk. "But, so far, everyone I interview just keeps pushing me toward the Spartans. I'm starting to think that's on purpose—that you're all trying to hide the true killer because maybe our real suspect should be whoever—or whatever—brought you to Gao in the first place."

"That's not the case, I assure you." Nelson fell silent for a moment, then said, "I can tell you this much about our mission: we are, indeed, running into some mild opposition. But for the sake of your investigation, I will disclose that the enemy's *only* attack mode is a superheated stream of negatively charged ions that—"

"Commander Nelson," Fred interrupted. "May I remind you of security directive Foxtrot—"

"A *particle beam*?" Andera blurted out, cutting off Fred's objection. "Like one of those Covenant sniper rifles? Because I could see a Jiralhanae causing physical injuries like this, absolutely. Maybe even a Sangheili."

"I wish it were that simple," Nelson said. "But no. Nothing to do with the Covenant."

"Commander Nelson," Fred began, "this is against—"

"Objection *noted*," Nelson snapped. "Now stand down, Lieutenant."

"So, maybe our suspect would be a rogue soldier," Veta suggested, continuing to press. "Maybe he's using someone else's Mjolnir armor?"

"Or an ONI agent with biological enhancements," Andera added. She was following Veta's lead, offering unlikely conjecture, so Nelson would feel compelled to correct them. "I've heard rumors that they can do that for Spartans—"

"It's nothing like that, people," Nelson said. "Not even close."

"What, then?" Veta demanded. "I'm tired of playing guessing games, Commander. I have a job to do, and you're not helping."

Fred slipped between Veta and Nelson. "Sir, we need to speak alone. I insist."

Without awaiting a reply, Fred stepped forward, backing Nelson out of the kitchen and into the dining room. The Spartan reached behind him and slapped a hip switch on the wall, and a recessed door slid across the opening to separate the two rooms. Veta watched through the rectangular safety window until the pair stopped a few steps later.

"You think we might be pushing too hard?" Andera asked from the exam table. "That Spartan is getting awfully suspicious."

"I'd be surprised if he wasn't." Veta took half a step toward Andera, trying to adjust her angle so she could see past Fred's shoulder and get a good look at Nelson's face. It was no use—her view remained blocked by the Spartan's armored bulk. "But what is he going to do about it? We have to ask questions."

"Questions about the *murders* here," Andera said. "We're not supposed to be spies."

Veta shrugged. "We're homicide investigators. That gives us some leeway. *If they hide it*—"

"*We find it,* yeah," Andera said, finishing the maxim. She rolled the corpse up on its side and began to slip off the body bag. "Let's hope Commander Nelson sees it that way."

Fred had seen Murtag Nelson's eyes bulge out before, so he knew what was coming. In an effort to forestall the commander's wrath, he began, "Sir, they could be spies."

"Obviously," Nelson growled. "And you think the Ministry of Protection has murdered eight—no, I'm sorry, make that *ten*—

Gao citizens, just so we would grant access to Veta Lopis and her team?"

"Actually, that possibility hadn't occurred to me, sir. But—"

"It occurred to *me*," Nelson snapped. "Which is why I had everyone on that team vetted. They've all been with the Gao Ministry of Protection for years. The newest member joined five months ago. None of them has ever been in the military. And their IDs are solid—Wendell confirmed that using facial recognition and local media archives. President Aponte did not slip any spies into the mix, Lieutenant."

"That's good to know, sir," Fred said. "But they could still be tasked with identifying our mission."

"And they would be amateurs," Nelson said. "I don't see them sneaking into the Ops Center or breaking Wendell's security to copy mission files, do you? They simply don't have the technical expertise."

"Probably not," Fred agreed. "But they *are* investigators. It would be a mistake to underestimate them."

"And I won't do that," Nelson said. "They'll probably pick up on the trouble we're having with Aggressor Sentinels—in fact, it seems like Inspector Lopis was halfway there when she left the cavern."

Fred dipped his helmet in agreement. "Yes, sir. She's smart enough to know there wouldn't be Spartans here unless we were engaged in combat operations. And you certainly confirmed her suspicions by revealing the nature of the enemy attack. That was a violation of security directive Foxtrot Tango Angel 7012."

"I know that, Lieutenant," Nelson said. "But why would we antagonize her by withholding information she's bound to uncover anyway?"

It was a rhetorical question—and one that Fred was wise

enough to leave unanswered. According to the battalion scuttle-butt, Nelson had overreached his authority to launch this operation quickly, before Gao or any ex-Covenant factions had a chance to discover the ancilla's existence. Now the commander's career—and perhaps even his life—depended on the success of the mission. To say that the pressure was getting to him would have been a gross understatement.

After a moment, Nelson nodded—more to himself than Fred—then said, "Okay then. We'll go ahead and tell the inspector about the Sentinels."

Fred was aghast. "Commander, that's key intelligence," he said. "Anyone who knows anything about Sentinels will know we're investigating Forerunner ruins."

"And you don't think this is something they're considering?" Nelson demanded. "When was the last time you heard of the UNSC sending the 717th to investigate something *not* connected to the Forerunners?"

"Sir, I'm not intimately familiar with the 717th's history."

"Well, I *am*," Nelson said. "And anyone who has the resources to do a little research already knows that when it comes to the 717th, all paths lead to the Forerunners."

"So we're going to ignore a security directive and confirm it for them?" Fred paused, then said, "I can't do that, sir."

"I didn't say we were going to *confirm* it," Nelson said. "But we're going to inform Inspector Lopis of our problems with the Sentinels, and go no further. And beyond that, we *will* cooperate with her investigation. Is that clear?"

"Sir—"

"That's an order, Lieutenant." Nelson paused, no doubt waiting for an acknowledgment that Fred had no intention of delivering, then finally sighed in exasperation. "Fred, I need to ask you something. Is there more to your reluctance than you're admitting to me?"

Nelson's tone was soft and reasonable, but there was enough of a threat to the question that Fred found himself bristling. He took a step back, then spoke in a deliberately calm voice. "You'd better clarify that, sir."

"I want to know if you're trying to protect one of your Spartans," Nelson said. "Could one of them be responsible for these killings?"

Fred had to answer through gritted teeth. "No way . . . sir."

"You're absolutely certain?" Nelson asked. "Even the Spartan-IIIs?"

"The Spartan-IIIs don't wear Mjolnir armor," Fred said. "They don't have the strength."

"What about the Spartan-IIIs from Gamma Company?"

Fred hesitated, because that possibility *had* crossed his mind. A trio of the Spartan-IIIs were Gammas. As part of their enhancement program, they had been given an illegal brain mutagen, one that greatly augmented their strength and survivability when they suffered the kind of trauma that would cause a normal person to die of systemic shock—things like taking a plasma bolt to the chest or having an arm blown off.

"I know my people," Fred said after a moment. "Why do you ask, sir?"

"Because I read their files, and I'm smart enough to read between the lines. I know about their rather . . . *special* augmentations. I know what they can do when they're under extreme stress, and I know the unbalancing effect it can cause at other times."

"Then you also know the Gammas take a stabilizing agent to keep that under control," Fred said. He was starting to dislike Nelson more with each passing moment. "And they haven't been under any kind of extreme stress here on Gao. As I said, Commander, I know my people."

Nelson held Fred's gaze for a moment, then finally nodded. "I'm glad to hear it, Lieutenant," he said. "If you should discover otherwise, I trust you'll rectify the situation yourself?"

"Absolutely," Fred said. He couldn't imagine trusting something like that to anyone else. "But that won't be necessary, I promise."

"As long as we understand each other." Nelson clasped his hands behind his back and took a thoughtful step away from Fred, then abruptly turned back toward him. "Now, to repeat what is going to happen: I will inform Inspector Lopis of the problems we're having with the Sentinels, and *you* are going to give her your full cooperation in identifying and eliminating the serial killer. Is that clear, Lieutenant?"

Fred snapped to attention. "Yes, sir."

"We will not be in violation of security directive Foxtrot Tango Angel whatever-it-is because we won't mention the Forerunners, the ancilla, or anything concerning our mission beyond the Sentinels. Is that also clear, Lieutenant?"

"Yes, sir."

"Within those limitations, you will use your own judgment in deciding whether to confirm or ignore any conclusions Inspector Lopis may draw in regard to our operation here," Nelson said. "But you will *not* antagonize her by denying something that she obviously knows to be true. Am I clear on that as well, Lieutenant?"

"Yes, sir."

"Good." Nelson smiled. "As I said, Lieutenant, the Gaos have probably already guessed that our presence here involves the Forerunners, and if their intelligence people know anything at all about Forerunners, then they probably already know about the

Sentinels. Our only real secret is the ancilla. As long as we don't let them find out about *that,* we're doing fine."

Still watching through the safety window in the kitchen's swinging door, Veta was finally able to get a good look at Nelson's face when the major emerged from behind Fred's shoulder, then abruptly spun back toward him.

"You catching anything yet?" Andera asked from the preparation island.

"Yeah," Veta answered. *"Forerunners."*

"No surprise there. Arlo says that's all the 717th *does.*" An old friend of the Minister of Protection, Andera was the only one on Veta's team who referred to their boss by his first name. "They recover Forerunner technology."

Nelson's lips stretched wide with the tongue tip showing, then they grew more rounded and slightly pursed.

"Zen-ten-nulls," Veta reported.

"Sentinels?"

"Could be." Veta sighed. "Damn. I wish I'd brought Berti."

"Into the caves?" Andera asked. "You don't think a forensic lip-reader might've been hard to sell as necessary personnel?"

"Probably."

In urban investigations, Veta and her team often tried to re-create the victims' last hours by tracking them on security vids. Berti's job was to study the vids, then re-create the conversations between the victims and the people they encountered. Veta had picked up a few lip-reading basics by working with Berti, but she was far from fluent in the art, and a lot of what she was seeing did not make sense to her. *"An-sell-a?"*

"No idea," Andera said. "Could it be *ancillary?*"

"Wrong shape at the end. The lips were stretched, not rounded," Veta said. "I'm pretty sure it was more like *ancilla*. Is that a real word?"

"Who knows?" Andera said. "You should have brought Berti."

"Thanks," Veta said dryly. "I'll keep that in mind the next time the minister orders us to spy on a UNSC battalion."

"You could have turned him down," Andera said. "Angel's crew would have jumped on this one."

"Right—then spent half their time drinking or taking mineral steams," Veta said. "Angel" was Special Inspector Angel Miramontis, a jaded twenty-year GMoP veteran who led the Ministry's general homicide unit. "Sorry. This UNSUB needs to be taken down."

"Don't they all?" Andera rolled the corpse onto its opposite shoulder and pushed the body bag down past the feet. She paused a moment, then said, "You're going to want to see this, by the way. It's a strange one."

"I'll be there in a minute."

As they spoke, Veta continued to watch Nelson through the door's safety window. She was not half the lip-reader Berti was, and even he could only discern about forty percent of what a subject said. But it was clear from Nelson's expression and body language that he was issuing orders.

When Veta caught the words *clear* and *lieutenant,* she realized the conversation would soon be drawing to a close and quickly retreated to the exam table.

"Catch anything useful?" Andera asked.

"I thought *Forerunner, sentinel,* and *ancilla* were pretty important," Veta said. "*Sentinel* could be a lot of things, but *ancilla* sounds unique. If the minister's sources know what that is—"

"To us, I mean," Andera said. "To *our* investigation."

"Not really," Veta said. "But Nelson is serious about catching our suspect. I believe he's ordering the Spartan to cooperate with us."

Andera raised her brow. "So our lieutenant is about to confess?"

Veta grinned. "Ha. Only if he's ordered to," she said. "And I'm not sure that would stop the killings, anyway."

Andera's expression grew serious. "So you don't think he's our guy?"

"Too early to say," Veta said.

"That's too bad." Andera sighed and let the corpse roll onto its back. "I could have used some time in those mineral steams myself."

Veta smiled, then leaned over the makeshift exam table. The corpse was still wearing the same blouse and slacks in which she had been found, and she was covered in a layer of mold that looked vaguely like white fur. The smell was more musty than rotten, which suggested the victim had been dead for quite some time before recovery. But none of that was particularly unusual.

"I'm not seeing it," Veta said. "What do you have?"

Andera pointed at the forearms, where the skin had been torn in half a dozen different places.

"Comminuted fractures of both arms, with lacerations suggestive of compound fractures." She ran her gloved hands over both arms, then held up the left ulna. "But the only bone displacement is here."

Veta spotted a slight bulge just below the elbow. She scowled, trying to understand. "You're saying both arms were crushed so badly she had multiple compound fractures?" she asked. "But there's only one misalignment? I don't get it."

"Neither do I." Andera removed her hand from the arm. "But it's pretty clear that most of the fractures were set *before* she died."

"And that couldn't have happened prior to the death attack?"

Andera shook her head and pointed to a dark crust at edge of several wounds. "The blood clotted, but the fibrin net is incomplete," she said. "The victim didn't last long. But what I'm saying is that someone *was* trying to put her back together again, just before she died."

"So someone dragged her into that passage to *save* her?"

"I can't speak to motive," Andera said. "But the body definitely shows signs of medical attention. I'll know more after the autopsy. Meanwhile, the cause of death appears consistent with Major Halal's report on several of the other victims."

Andera pointed toward the woman's head. On both sides, a faint band of darkness was visible beneath the mold, running back from the temples to just beyond the ear. Near the front of each stripe was tiny puncture wound.

"I have no idea what this is," Veta said. "Some sort of needle or energy spike through the brain, followed by postmortem subcutaneous bleeding?"

Andera shook her head. "The dark bands are bruising, maybe from a large pincer squeezing the skull."

"But there's no indentation," Veta said. "If something squeezed her skull that hard, shouldn't there be a depression—a furrow, even?"

"Not if someone reduced the fractures afterward." Andera pointed at the minuscule punctures in front of each bruise. "That might be what those holes are."

Veta studied the puncture wounds more carefully and saw that they were slightly elongated, as though a small tube had been pushed through the skin at a shallow angle.

"Somebody did a cranial arthroscopy in a cave?" Veta considered this, then glanced back toward the door. "Would soldiers carry that kind of equipment in their medkits? Or even know how to use it?"

"Not Gao soldiers. But Spartans?" Andera shrugged. "Who knows?"

The dining room door slid aside, and Commander Nelson moved into the kitchen. Fred remained in the dining room, now turned so his faceplate was visible.

Nelson stopped three steps into the room and addressed Veta. "I apologize for the confusion, Inspector. Major Halal should never have taken it upon himself to conceal the new crime scene."

"Thank you, Commander," Veta said. "I'm glad we agree on that."

"Then perhaps we can correct the situation." Nelson extended an arm toward Fred. "The lieutenant would be happy to take you to the scene now."

"What about Major Halal?" Veta asked. "Will he cooperate?"

"Major Halal won't be a problem," Nelson said. "He'll either cooperate, or I'll send him back to FLEETCOM."

"What about the scene?" Veta asked. "If Halal tampers with it—"

"Major Halal wants to stop this killer, too," Nelson said. "I don't see him doing anything to compromise a crime scene."

"That would be easier to accept if he hadn't concealed it from me in the first place."

"I'll send a runner ahead with orders for him to stand down," Nelson said. "But I can't make any promises. The major has a sizable head start on you."

"Fair enough." Veta turned to Andera. "Can you have the autopsy done by tomorrow morning?"

To Veta's surprise, Andera looked to Nelson before agreeing. "I'll need someone to assist," she said. "Can I borrow a corpsman? Someone familiar with traumatic injuries?"

"Of course," Nelson said. "I can assign a combat specialist."

Andera flashed a grateful smile. "Thank you, that will do." She held Veta's eyes just long enough to make clear she had a good reason for requesting an assistant she did not actually need, then made a shooing motion with her hands. "Go on. I'll be fine here."

"Good." Having the assistant, Veta realized, would give Andera a chance to assess whether UNSC corpsmen were capable of the kind of field treatment Charlie Victim Two had received. "Let me know as soon as you have some findings."

"I'll make another runner available," Nelson said. "I can also send someone to collect the rest of your team, Inspector, if you want them on scene."

"*Collect?*" Veta asked. "Why would we do that? They're already underground."

"That's right," Fred said. "But the entrance we need is thirty kilometers away, and then it's an all-day descent to the new crime scene."

Veta furrowed her brow. "Halal left from Crime Scene Charlie."

"That's right, ma'am," Fred said from the dining room. "But that route is a ten-kilometer crawl through some pretty tight places. You'll never make it with your equipment."

Veta checked the time and realized that her team had probably finished its work at Crime Scene Charlie an hour ago. "Okay, we'll go the long way," she said. "We'll leave as soon as the rest of my team returns to the surface."

"If you're worried about Major Halal compromising the scene, forget the runner—you and the lieutenant could go on ahead,"

Nelson suggested. "I'm sure Linda and Kelly can bring the rest of your team down on their own."

"Thanks, but they should be here soon," Veta said. "And I need to check in with my superior before we leave anyway."

"I hope you'll tell President Aponte that we're all working well together," Nelson said. "This problem with Major Halal won't happen again."

"I'll ask Minister Casille to relay my report to the president," Veta said carefully. "Andera, if I'm not back in time for the next check-in, you handle it."

"You're on a schedule?" Nelson asked.

"You bet," Andera said. She winked at the commander, then added, "One of us has to check in every twelve hours. If we don't, they send in the Wyverns."

CHAPTER 5

2012 hours, July 2, 2553 (military calendar)
Gao Ministry of Protection Patrol Corvette *Esmeralda*
High Equatorial Orbit, Planet Gao, Cordoba System

Clearly, Gao was outmatched. Minister of Protection Arlo Casille could see that in the wall-size video display in the *Esmeralda*'s flag cabin. Any idiot could. The UNSC task force hung scattered across the entire screen, a half-dozen irregular shapes silhouetted against the star-flecked backdrop of interstellar space. In the center of the formation drifted a matte-black vessel three times the length of its escorts. Orbiting the perimeter were a dozen dark specks that could only be a fighter squadron on patrol.

When it came to oppressing the Outer Colonies, the UNSC did not believe in half measures. The big vessel in the middle had the stepped hull of one of the UNSC's mighty *Marathon*-class cruisers, which meant it carried more firepower by itself than the Ministry of Protection's entire fleet of customs corvettes. Its escorts would be frigates and destroyers, each close to five hundred meters and more than capable of stopping anything Gao *and* its allies could throw at it. The patrol craft were most likely Longswords, and Arlo did not even want to think about the damage they would cause if the current mess became a shooting war.

But that did not mean he would tolerate a de facto invasion of his homeworld.

Research battalion or not, the 717th had strong-armed President Aponte into granting permission for its occupation of the Montero Vitality Center, and Gao's honor demanded a response. Arlo just had to do it without starting a war—at least not one that could be traced back to Gao. Fortunately, he had the perfect plan.

Thirty seconds into the video, a pair of patrol craft sprouted pinpoints of light and curled toward the center of the screen. They quickly expanded into thumb-size dots, then swelled into the fast-growing halos of spacecraft accelerating on an interception vector. The stars in the background curved into streaks as the photographer's vessel turned away, then the image blurred and winked out altogether.

The blank screen dissolved into a real-time vid of local space. The orange crescent of Gao's star, Cordoba, could be seen intruding along the left edge of the display. Hanging next to it was Gao itself, a mottled green disk fading to desert gray at both poles. Arlo studied the scene from the flag chair at the head of the conference table, gathering his thoughts as he watched Gao's three moons chase each other over the horizon. Finally, he turned to the woman seated to his left.

"I hope your camera crew survived," he said. "The UNSC can be so touchy about surveillance."

Reza Linberk gave him a wide, close-lipped smile. "How kind of you to worry, Minister Casille," she said. With long silvery hair, well-defined features, and ice-blue eyes, Linberk was gorgeous but unappealing—at least to Arlo, who preferred his companions to be warm and saucy, rather than enchanting and ruthless. "You're going to be a *very* beloved president."

"Let's not get ahead of ourselves," Arlo said, waving off the flattery. "The important thing here is to be certain the UNSC doesn't see an opportunity in President Aponte's cowardice. Whether I end up replacing him or not remains to be seen."

"Not at all," Linberk said. "You're the only prospect who brings an alliance with Venezia. Peter wanted me to assure you of that."

"That means a great deal to me, of course," Arlo said. *Peter* being Peter Moritz, the public face of the Venezian Militia. "His support will be invaluable when I'm forced to call for elections."

"You also have the support of the Keepers of the One Freedom," added the cabin's third occupant, a gray-bearded Jiralhanae chieftain named Castor. So huge he had to sit on a tool locker brought up from the *Esmeralda*'s repair shop, the Jiralhanae reminded Arlo of the great gray apes that ruled Gao's polar barrens. The chieftain spoke through a translation disk that hung around his thick neck. "Your foes will cower before our fellowship."

"I'm grateful, Dokab," Arlo said. He was careful to use Castor's title as a cult elder and address him using a tone of the utmost respect, for the Jiralhanae was the key to Arlo's plan. "But I hope you won't judge the people of Gao by our current elected leader. We don't usually cower before anyone."

"Certainly not in my experience," Linberk said smoothly. "But your president's caution is creating problems for Venezia, too. It's not good to have a UNSC task force lurking between our two systems. Normal traffic is giving a wide berth to the entire region."

"And their infidel presence is an insult to the One Freedom," Castor added. "Believers fear defilement."

Normal traffic, Arlo realized, was Linberk's reference to the smugglers and pirates who operated out of Venezia. He was less certain of what Castor was alluding to, but Arlo understood that the Keepers of the One Freedom were devoted to spreading the worship of their Forerunner deities across the galaxy. Based in the Venezian capital of New Tyne, the Keepers welcomed believers of all species—even humans, as long as they swore opposition to the "heretic tyranny" of the Unified Earth Government. The sect was growing so swiftly in the Outer Colonies that they were drawing off UNSC intelligence assets, and that fact alone had been reason enough for Arlo to start funneling money and weapons into their organization.

Arlo made a show of considering their complaints for a few moments, then leaned forward to brace his elbows on the table.

"I'm sorry President Aponte has brought this trouble on you," he said. "But I'm confident we can correct the situation—*if* we all work together."

This brought a smile to Linberk's lips. "So, you asked us here because you're ready to move forward?"

"Assuming we can agree on a plan," Arlo said. He had always found it more effective to allow his instruments—especially Jiralhanae instruments—to think they were telling *him* what they wanted to do. He turned to Castor. "First, Dokab, I need to consult your expertise regarding the Forerunners. This is from a report I received earlier today."

Arlo placed his datapad on the table and selected the recording of that afternoon's discussion with Inspector Veta Lopis. He had removed irrelevant office talk and the confidential details of the investigation, but had otherwise left it intact. He pressed play, and Veta's voice came from the tiny speaker.

"*I don't have much time,*" the inspector said. "*There's a new crime scene, and we're heading back into the caves.*"

"Any suspects yet?" Arlo had asked.

"Only Spartans stand out," Lopis said. *"These killings take a lot of physical power. The victims have been crushed, sometimes literally torn apart. I think there's a lot of rage and loss of control."*

"Loss of control?" Arlo echoed. *"That doesn't sound like a Spartan. From what I hear, they're all about focus and control."*

"That bothers me, too," Lopis said. *"I'm trying to expand the suspect pool, but there are security issues. Commander Nelson did admit that the Spartans are here to fight something called Sentinels. They claim the Sentinels can't be our prime suspect because they attack only with particle beams, but I haven't been able to verify that."*

"Sentinels?" Arlo repeated. *"I think you just confirmed a suspicion for me. Did they happen to say anything about the Forerunners?"*

"Not to me, but I saw Commander Nelson use the term when he was dressing down one of the Spartans." Lopis paused, then said, *"Arlo, there's too much going on here for it to be coincidence. The Montero quake and the miracle cures have something to do with Forerunners. And whatever that connection is—that's what brought the UNSC here."*

"No need to be diplomatic, Veta," Arlo said. *"You can say it— that's what the UNSC came to steal from Gao."*

"I couldn't prove that, but if that's truly what this is all about, I'll admit it's hard to see the UNSC leaving behind any kind of Forerunner medical technology." Lopis paused a moment, then added, *"And I might have a lead on its name. Have you ever heard of something called an 'ancilla'?"*

There were two seconds of silence.

"Minister?"

"Sorry, Veta," Arlo answered. *"I have no idea what that could be. But I do know a little something about Sentinels . . . and if you're right about all this, please be careful. They're dangerous."*

"You think maybe?" Lopis's tone was sarcastic. *"I was already assuming that because of the Spartans' presence."*

"Sorry," Arlo said. *"Sentinels are a type of Forerunner drone. I'll try to have specs before your next report."*

"Thanks," Lopis said. *"And see what you can get on Mjolnir armor, too."*

"As in Spartan *Mjolnir armor? I'm not sure my sources will have access to that—or be willing to part with it if they do. Sharing tidbits on the Forerunners is one thing—selling out the Spartans is in a whole different class of danger."*

"So offer more, or blackmail them," Lopis demanded. *"But if our prime suspect does turn out to be a Spartan, I'm going to need a way to get past the armor. . . ."*

Arlo stopped the playback. Though it would have been poor operational security to admit it to a field agent, he knew exactly what an ancilla was, and he wanted to see Castor's reaction to news that the UNSC was currently stalking one.

The Jiralhanae braced his hands on the table and rose, hunching over with his head and massive shoulders pressed against the cabin's low ceiling. His eyes were wide, and his fangs were bared in a gaping expression that seemed more surprised than angry.

"Ancilla?" Castor in disbelief. "Did she say *ancilla*?"

"Perhaps." Arlo was careful to keep his tone neutral. "That's certainly what it sounded like."

"Then they have found one of the Oracles?"

"It could be." Arlo was puzzled by Castor's lack of outrage; surely, the Jiralhanae would consider the ancilla a sacred object. "That's what I wanted to consult with *you* about."

"The Oracles speak for the gods." Castor was starting to talk faster and louder, his voice rumbling out of his translator disk in deep, distorted tones. "For the heretics to take one is—"

"I doubt they've actually *captured* it," Linberk interrupted. "It seems to me that a Forerunner ancilla would *be* the objective of an operation like this. If the UNSC had it already, wouldn't they be gone by now?"

"I agree," Arlo said. He was not surprised by how quickly Linberk was picking up on his plan. She was the smartest person he knew, and the only opponent who regularly beat him at both backgammon and go. "The research battalion wouldn't be here if they had the Oracle."

"There you have it, then." Linberk locked gazes with Arlo and cocked her brow, letting him know she expected to be compensated for her support. "The Spartans are here because the UNSC wants the ancilla."

Still, Castor failed to erupt as Arlo had expected. The Jiralhanae merely sank back down onto the tool locker. He stared at the opposite wall for a time, then finally shook his head.

"It cannot be permitted. Not ever." Castor looked to Arlo. "The Keepers will trade."

"Trade?" Arlo was beginning to worry he had underestimated the Jiralhanae—and no one ever made that particular mistake twice. "I'm sorry, but we're talking about Spartans here. My agent couldn't possibly steal the ancilla—"

"I will trade *you*," Castor interrupted, "for access. Get my warriors to the caverns, and I will give you the Mjolnir specifications that your spy needs. I will give you *schematics*."

"You have Mjolnir armor schematics?" Arlo asked. "How on Gao did you come by those?"

Castor straightened his spine, raising his head so high that his bristly hair brushed the ceiling. "I was an army chieftain during the war," he said. "I captured *many* useful things."

Arlo drew back, only half-pretending to be intimidated. "I

see," he said. "And how many warriors of yours are we talking about?"

"Five hundred," Castor replied without hesitation. "I have five hundred holy warriors berthed aboard the *One Light*."

"You brought a Keeper strike force into Gao orbit?" Arlo didn't know whether to feel worried or impressed. "Without asking?"

"You said to come at once." Castor spread his huge hands and grinned. "It was only wise to arrive prepared."

"Indeed it was," Linberk said quickly. "But will five hundred warriors be enough? Once this starts, there won't be any reinforcements. We won't be able to get them through that UNSC task force out there."

"Five hundred is enough," Castor replied. "Most will be Jiralhanae. And I will lead them myself."

Arlo smiled. "We have a bargain, then." He rose and extended a hand toward Castor. "I wish you luck, Dokab. If anyone can stop the infidels, it is you."

CHAPTER 6

After five hours of scrutiny by investigators and technicians, the corpse finally lay undisturbed again. Another female, she was bathed in the glow of high-intensity work lamps and sprawled backward over a limestone block—part of a huge breakdown pile that had probably dropped from the cave ceiling a million years before. The rear of her skull had been smashed flat, her limbs were splayed at unnatural angles, and the torso looked like it had been hit by a gravity hammer.

Fred was no expert in forensic science, but even he could see that the woman hadn't died where she lay. For one thing, there was no blood spatter on the surrounding boulders. Even more telling was the location itself. Situated at the bottom of a grueling ten-hour descent, Crime Scene India was directly adjacent to Bivouac Site Tango, a forward camp used by the mapping team to extend its working time underground. It was hardly the kind of place that a tourist dressed in slacks and a sleeveless blouse would stumble across by accident, so it seemed pretty clear that the body had been placed here as bait.

— 73 —

But by whom—the serial killer, or the ancilla? And why hadn't the trap been sprung yet?

Adding to Fred's concern was the unexplained absence of Major Halal and Private Hayes. According to Third Squad, which had kept watch over the crime scene until Fred came with Lopis and her team, the pair had never arrived. Fred had considered sending out a search party, of course, but then decided against it. If the dead tourist was indeed being used as bait, then it would have been foolish to divide his strength.

Instead, Fred had irritated Inspector Lopis by ordering the entire group to hunker down, then sent Linda to fetch the mapping team and its escort of Spartan-IIIs. The delay had cost four hours, but it had also allowed the investigative team some much-needed rest and given him the support he needed to prepare a proper counterattack.

But he hadn't expected to wait this long.

Fred tipped his head back, looking into the darkness above the breakdown pile. Almost instantly, his imaging system displayed a three-dimensional schematic on his HUD. It showed an immense, three-hundred-meter dome pocked by the mouths of intersecting passages. He had posted a Spartan-III inside five of those passages, positioned so they would have interlocking fields of fire. But of course, he saw no sign of them. They were sitting just out of view, their backs pressed against the wall so they could keep watch in both directions, ready to drop prone and open fire at the first sign of trouble. They had been holding that position for nine hours.

Under normal circumstances, Fred might have assumed the enemy was biding its time, resting comfortably while its targets grew fatigued and inattentive. But that was not how Sentinels operated. Designed to battle fast-moving outbreaks of the parasitic Flood, they were programmed to attack quickly and fiercely be-

fore their foes had time to secure a foothold. So, either this trap
had been set by the serial killer—which Fred now considered unlikely this far down—or the ancilla was nearby, holding the Sentinels back.

Or maybe it was both?

After finding the tourist's body where it shouldn't have been,
Fred had begun to wonder whether the ancilla and the killer could
be one and the same. That was the simplest explanation for the location, plus the ancilla probably had access to a machine capable
of committing the brutal murders, and it was certainly intelligent
enough to figure out that targeting Gao civilians would put pressure on the UNSC to leave. But Fred did not have a good way to
evaluate his hypothesis. The ancilla was still an intangible presence, whose existence he could infer only through the scantiest of
indirect evidence.

At the same time, the sought-after killer felt all too human.
He or she had created a physical impact that left no doubt about
its existence and seemed to deliberately taunt its pursuers. Sometimes the suspect felt so tangible and close that Fred found himself studying nearby companions, searching for something cold
and mocking in their eyes that would betray them as a monster.

The only way for Fred to reconcile the two sensations was to
remember that the ancilla was about a thousand times smarter
than he was. It could easily be manipulating the situation to keep
him confused, hesitant, and doubtful.

And that way lay defeat. After a month of futile searching
for the ancilla, Fred knew only one thing for sure: if he let the
damn thing play mind games with him, he was going to lose.

The blue dot of a handlamp appeared in the darkness beyond
the breakdown pile and began to weave through the boulders.
Fred's imaging system switched to passive light intensification,

and he saw a pair of crime scene techs in white coveralls picking their way back toward the corpse. The lanky man in back, Cirilo, was carrying a folded body bag.

Fred checked on the rest of the team and found the other two walking the crime scene perimeter, their lamp beams swinging back and forth as they made a final evidence sweep. A squad of UNSC marines were gathering equipment and preparing to leave. To an untrained eye, they were easy marks. Yet the enemy still had not attacked.

And Major Halal and Private Hayes were still missing. Fred had strong suspicions about their fate—mainly, that they were dead—but he could not ignore the fact that a JAG major was missing. If he did nothing about it, FLEETCOM would have his bars.

Fred located Veta Lopis working her way along the far end of the gallery, then went over to catch her. As he approached from behind, her hand dropped to her sidearm—again—and she whirled around, shining a handlamp into his helmet. Her rudeness was rendered unimportant as his faceplate dimmed to protect his vision.

"What did I say about announcing yourself?" Lopis demanded. "Are you trying to get yourself shot?"

Fred let his gaze drop to the oversize automatic hanging on Lopis's hip. It was a local paramilitary model, a Sevine Arms 10mm Special with a laser sight and a barrel so long it reached halfway to her knee. His HUD noted that the SAS-10 was a versatile weapon that could be used with either explosive or armor-piercing ammunition. But as a police officer, Lopis would be carrying a less destructive round, probably a standard soft tip.

"No worries," Fred said. "I'm wearing three layers of armor. Those man-droppers in your clip would just flatten themselves against my chest."

Lopis flashed an enigmatic smile. "You might be surprised."

"By you, maybe. But not by your weapon." The specs appeared on his HUD even before he finished speaking, and he began to read them off. "With a one-forty-grain armor-piercing round, the SAS-10 has an effective range of sixty-two meters. Even at five meters, the round's velocity would only be three hundred and eighty-nine meters per second. You wouldn't even scratch my outer shell."

Lopis raised her brow. "Well, then . . . maybe I need a bigger pistol." She moved her hand away from her sidearm, then asked, "Now, why are you over here contaminating my crime scene?"

"I'm not contaminating much," Fred said. "You're preparing to leave."

"Nothing gets past you, does it?" Veta nodded. "Yeah, we're about done here. Why? You have someplace else to be?"

"I'd like to hear your assessment of this killing," Fred said, ignoring her jibe. "Did you notice anything different about it?"

"Like what?" Lopis asked, growing even more reserved. "It was no accident, if that's what you're asking. Cause of death was most likely extreme physical trauma, like the others."

"But this scene isn't the same as the others," Fred said. "The other bodies were all found up in the tourist galleries. We're down deep."

"True." Lopis was staring at Fred's faceplate, watching him carefully. "But we still haven't identified the victim. Could she be one of yours? Maybe she became separated from her unit?"

"She was wearing walking shoes, not combat boots." Fred felt sure Lopis had already observed that for herself, so he suspected she was just trying to gauge his reaction to an unlikely suggestion. It was the same technique he would have used to establish a baseline pattern at the beginning of an interrogation. "And UNSC duty fatigues don't normally come in floral prints."

"So maybe she was off duty."

"Down here? Inspector, I understand you have a job to do. But we both know that woman was no soldier, and we're in a combat zone. Now, I'd appreciate a straight answer. What's your take on the crime scene?"

Lopis studied him for a moment, then said, "You're right, this scene is different. It's a body dump."

"And?"

"And, judging by all the boot tracks and bivouac sites in here, the killer wanted your people to find the body."

"Why us?" Fred had his own suspicions, of course, but he wanted to see if Lopis offered another explanation—one that might explain why there had been no attack on his own men yet. "Any theories?"

Lopis thought for a moment, then turned back toward the breakdown pile. "What exactly are you looking for down here, Spartan?"

"That's classified."

"I thought we were in a combat zone," Lopis said. "I thought you were asking for my help."

"We are, and I am," Fred said. "The mission, however, is still classified."

That enigmatic smile crept across Lopis's lips again, and it occurred to Fred that she had tricked him again. He had just confirmed that the battalion wasn't simply exploring this area—it was, indeed, searching for something. Granted, that had probably been fairly obvious from the start. But now it was a confirmed fact.

"Careful, Inspector," Fred said. "There are things you shouldn't know."

"Who says I know anything?" Lopis mocked. "But let's say you *are* looking for something. You must be getting pretty close."

"Why do you say that?"

"Because you've now provoked a reaction," Lopis said. "The body dump could be meant as a warning or a distraction . . . but I think it's a taunt. You've proved yourself worthy of notice. Now *you're* being hunted. That's what this corpse is telling us."

"That's a pretty specific message." Fred didn't know whether the ancilla was indeed trying to taunt him, but he certainly agreed with Lopis about his men being a target here. His instincts told him the same thing. "Did you find a note or something?"

"More like, 'or something,' " Lopis said. "The killer thinks he's smarter than we are—that's almost universal with these guys. And he feels compelled to prove it, even if it's only to himself."

Fred started to tell her that the murderer *was* smarter than they were, then realized what that suggested—that the ancilla was the real killer. He took a single step back.

"Sorry, Inspector. But the—" Fred caught himself before he said *ancilla,* then continued, "the target I'm looking for can't be your killer."

"Really?" Lopis put one hand on her hip and waved the other around the gallery. "Look at where we are. Do you want to hear my take on all this? Either our suspect is whatever you're down here looking for, or it's someone from your own battalion. Probably a Spartan."

"Or my target is using the real killer for cover." Fred wasn't sure he believed that, but the one thing he had been explicitly ordered not to reveal was the ancilla. He turned back toward the breakdown pile, where Cirilo and his partner were already zipping the new corpse into the body bag. "Can you be sure this victim was killed by the same person who dumped her?"

"I can't," Lopis admitted. The swiftness of her reply suggested she had already considered the possibility. "That's something we won't be able to confirm unless we find trace evidence suggesting a second subject handled the body. Until Dr. Rolan does the autopsy, I won't even know the likelihood that she was killed by the same perpetrator as the others."

"So, maybe my target came across the body somewhere closer to the surface—and then brought it down here for us to find."

"Maybe." Lopis scowled, then asked, "And how exactly do you think the target would do that?"

Fred began to have an uneasy feeling. "I'm not sure what you mean, Inspector."

"It's a simple question, Fred." Lopis's voice assumed a sharp, pressing edge. "How would your target get the body here? Would he—or they, or *whatever* it is—carry the body? Drag it? Haul it down in a cart?"

"I couldn't say, ma'am."

"No?" Lopis looked back toward the main part of the gallery. "Me neither, Fred. Because the only tracks we found down here were boot prints—prints with two kinds of tread: standard UNSC issue and Spartan issue."

"Are you sure?" It was the only reply Fred could think of. "What about your own tracks?"

Lopis shook her head. "Not until after we began work," she said. "After we send out the trace evidence spiders, tracks are the first thing we document. We use an alternate light source to scan and record the ground ahead of every step we take. And the really interesting part? There weren't any tracks in the breakdown pile around the body, either. None."

"And the body couldn't have been dropped from the dome," Fred said, anticipating Lopis's next point. He glanced up into the darkness. "Not from that height. It didn't take enough damage."

"So you see my problem," Lopis said. "How did the corpse

get into the middle of the breakdown pile? Was it thrown? Was it *teleported*? Because we absolutely know that it was not carried, dragged, or dropped here."

Fred sighed, wondering whether there was any detail Lopis failed to catch, then said, "It was probably floated."

"By your target?"

Fred hesitated, knowing that an honest answer would confirm a link between his target and the Sentinels—and therefore, the Fore-runners. But Nelson had suggested that the Gaos probably knew about the Forerunner link already, and it was growing clear that Lopis might actually prove useful in figuring out what the ancilla was up to—even if he couldn't tell her exactly what the ancilla was.

"I don't know whether my target would be able to move a body," Fred said. "But the Sentinels would."

"And these Sentinels—they would be the same Sentinels that can't possibly be our prime suspect because they attack only with particle beams?"

"Affirmative," Fred said. "They have a pair of utility arms with small manipulators at the ends. They could feasibly transport a corpse."

Lopis, of course, kept pressing. "But not beat someone to death?"

"Not likely," Fred said. "And even if they could, they wouldn't bother—not when they have particle beams."

"But they float?" Lopis asked. "Like jungaloons?"

"Close enough," Fred said. Jungaloons, he knew, were clam-shaped gasbags that used a bell-shaped proboscis to suck fly-ing insects out of Gao's humid air. "But faster—much, much faster."

"Then your target could have placed the body here?" Lopis asked. "Or *had* it placed here by a Sentinel?"

TROY DENNING

"Yes," Fred said. "That makes the most sense."

"Maybe for you," Lopis said. "I still don't see why a military target would taunt you like that. It seems counterproductive."

Fred remained silent for a moment, trying to decide how much of his own theory to disclose. It seemed clear that Lopis knew more about his mission than she was admitting, which meant that anything he told her could reveal more than he intended. On the other hand, holding back details she had already guessed would only add to the mistrust between them—and with the ancilla out there laying traps, that was the kind of complication that would end up getting people killed.

Finally, Fred said, "I don't think this crime scene is a taunt. I think it's bait."

"For what?"

"An ambush."

Lopis's frown of confusion lasted only an instant, then she said, "Lieutenant, we've been here for hours already. If that corpse were bait, surely we would have been attacked by now."

"Not if the target is smarter than I am," Fred said. "My counter-measures may have been too obvious."

"Countermeasures?" Veta's eyes lit with comprehension. "You mean, no gathering in groups larger than three? Taking meals and rest in sheltered positions? That's not just standard UNSC protocol?"

"Afraid not," Fred admitted. "And I *do* have my entire team posted in surrounding passages."

"Since when?"

"Since I realized we were walking into a trap."

"And you didn't bother to tell us?"

"Sorry," Fred said. "I was afraid you'd discourage the attack."

"And that would have been a bad thing?" Lopis's expression

— 82 —

went from angry to surprised to resentful. "So you were using us as bait, too?"

"That might be the wrong way to look at it."

"And what would be the *right* way to look at it?"

"That I'm trying to eliminate the threat under controlled circumstances," Fred said. "That hitting the enemy here is better than *getting* hit on the way out."

Lopis was silent for a moment, then the anger finally drained from her face. "Okay, I can see that." Her voice assumed a demanding edge. "Anything else you should have told me?"

"Yes," Fred said. "But, actually, it's more of a request."

"Let me guess," Lopis said. "You'd like me to wander off alone to draw out your target?"

Fred paused, trying to decide whether the idea had merit—whether he would be able to protect her, whether the ancilla would send its Sentinels after a lone civilian.

Finally, he asked, "You'd do that?"

"Sure . . . I'd even yell for help." Lopis's expression hardened into a glare. "Right after you tell me what you're looking for down here."

Fred ran two fingers across his faceplate, signaling a smile. "Funny, ma'am," he said. "But I'm afraid we'll have to take our chances."

Lopis shrugged. "Your choice," she said. "So what's your request?"

"I need you to slow things down," Fred said. "Just look busy and buy us another few hours here."

"We can always take breaks and do more evidence sweeps," Lopis said. "But if the enemy hasn't taken the bait by now—"

"It's not to draw them out," Fred said. "I need to send a team to recover Major Halal and Private Hayes, and I'd rather keep the enemy's attention focused here while they're gone."

Lopis did not reply at once, and when she did, there was calculation in her eyes. "You think Halal's dead?"

"And Hayes, too, I expect," Fred said. "Otherwise, they would have been back by now. Their route was clearly mapped."

"All right, I'll tell Senola to keep busy here," Lopis said. "Cirilo and I will accompany the recovery team."

Fred made a chopping motion across his chest. "Negative," he said. "The UNSC does not require your assistance retrieving—"

"I don't particularly care what the UNSC requires, Lieutenant," Lopis said. "If two men are dead, that's a fresh crime scene—*very* fresh—and it's my best chance to figure out who's killing people around here."

"Ma'am, with all due respect," Fred said. "The route gets pretty tight along the way."

"So?"

"So I'm not blind. I was watching you back at Crime Scene Charlie. You have a problem with confined spaces."

"And you're worried I'll freeze up?" Lopis asked. "That you'll have to drag me along by my hair or something?"

"I'd probably go for a wrist."

"You're a real comedian, Fred. But I can handle any crawlway that you can squeeze into wearing that armor of yours—and I'm not asking your permission."

Fred considered her demand, weighing the possibility of having to pull her through a few cramped spots against the likelihood of her actually obeying an order to remain behind. All in all, it was probably safer to take her along than risk having her try to follow on her own.

At last, Fred nodded. "As you wish, Inspector," he said. "Just remember—you asked for this."

CHAPTER 7

1318 hours, July 3, 2553 (military calendar)
Unidentified passage, 406 Meters belowground,
Montero Cavern System
Campos Wilderness District, Planet Gao, Cordoba System

The recovery detail had been traveling for more than an hour, crawling through a maze of hot, gloomy passages, when Veta finally caught the scent of death. It wasn't the sulfur-tinged reek of a bloating corpse or even the cloying rancidness of stage-three decomposition. It was a sour, metallic odor she recognized as congealed blood. And, mixed in with the mustiness of the cave, she caught a hint of something harsher and more caustic—scorched flesh, perhaps.

Veta stopped crawling and glanced back at Cirilo, who was about two meters behind. Like Veta herself, he was wearing UNSC combat gear, including a helmet with an integrated lamp and an equipment vest with an M7 submachine gun strapped across the chest. Their own equipment had been relegated to waterproof packs, which they were currently dragging through the mud behind them.

"We're getting close," Veta whispered. She was careful to point her helmet lamp away from his eyes. "You smell that?"

"Oh yeah," Cirilo said. "A lot of blood this time. Almost makes you sorry for the poor bastards."

Veta nodded. "Especially for Hayes," she said. "If Halal hadn't wanted to hold out on us, he'd probably be sitting on a patio at the Vitality Center by now."

She craned her neck around a little bit more, shining her lamp past Cirilo down a slick-walled passage so long and perfectly round that it felt like she was crawling up the interior of some giant intestine. There was supposed to be a trio of Spartan-IIIs back there, providing a rear guard and stringing a comm line so the recovery detail could stay in touch with Crime Scene India. But the Spartans were keeping their distance, moving so quietly it was hard to believe they were actually still there.

Veta felt Cirilo's hand squeeze her calf.

"Hey, Veta?" he asked. "You doing okay?"

"I'm fine, Cee," Veta said. She feigned a smile. "It's just the light down here. It makes me look tired."

Cirilo grinned. "You always look sharp to me, boss." He jerked his thumb toward the limestone ceiling a half meter above their heads. "But crawling through this place . . . it makes *my* chest go tight."

"I'm okay. Really."

And so far, that was true. There had been a couple of narrow spots where it had felt like she had crawled into a grave and the walls had closed in around her. But with Cirilo staying close and a submachine gun across her torso, she had managed to remain calm, to remind herself that this was not the hidden cellar where a seventeen-year-old girl had learned that monsters were real. This was a hunting ground—*Veta's* hunting ground—and she was not the one who needed to be afraid, now or ever again.

Veta turned forward, then continued to follow Fred up the

passage. In his armor, the Spartan was too big to crawl on his hands and knees. Instead, he had to worm his way on his belly, an awkward process that Fred made look as effortless and natural as walking. Often, it was a struggle for Veta and Cirilo to keep pace—and they made a lot more noise doing it.

The scent of blood continued to grow stronger, and finally Fred signaled a halt by raising a clenched fist. Veta and Cirilo stopped instantly, then watched in silence as the Spartan disappeared into the darkness beyond their lamp beams. Fred did not activate his own lamp, no doubt relying on his imaging systems instead.

Cirilo came up close to Veta, a hand resting on her hip as he eased himself along the wall beside her. She didn't mind the familiarity. He was the closest thing she had to a lover, a trusted friend and colleague who shared her passion for catching killers. With his black hair and slender features, he was certainly handsome enough. Under different circumstances? She might have responded to his steady flirtations. But even if Cirilo hadn't been her subordinate, she wasn't sure she could trust anyone that much anymore. She had lost that ability long ago in that cellar, when a monster had chained her to the wall and begun to feed on her pain and fear and humiliation.

"Hope the big guy comes back," Cirilo whispered. "He has the map, you know."

"No worries," Veta said. "We can always follow the comm line back to Crime Scene India."

"Afraid not," said a speaker-modulated voice behind them. "The line's been cut."

Veta looked back to see Ash-G099 crawling into the glow of her lamp beam, his form blurred by the photoreactive coating of his Semi-Powered Infiltration armor. Though smaller than Fred, the Spartan-III was still large enough that he had to worm his way forward on his elbows and belly. Like Fred, he was somehow managing to do that silently—even while holding his battle rifle ready to fire.

"Cut?" Veta asked. "By whom?"

"Most likely by the enemy, ma'am," Ash replied. "When the shooting starts, get low and roll to the walls so I can fire past you if I need to."

"And how soon will that be?" Cirilo asked. "When the shooting starts, I mean?"

"That's not really in our control." Ash used the tip of his battle rifle to gesture up the passage. "But we should continue to advance. The lieutenant says he's found a casualty."

Noting that neither Ash nor any of the other Spartans was using a lamp, Veta asked, "What about our headlamps?" She reached for the control button on her helmet. "Shouldn't we turn them off to avoid making ourselves targets?"

"I wouldn't," Ash said. "You won't be able to see a thing in the dark, and the Sentinels have as many imaging systems as we do. They'll find you whether you have your lamps on or not."

"Great. Thanks for the reassurance," Cirilo muttered.

Half-expecting to be hit by a particle beam at any moment, Veta continued forward. A few minutes later, the passage opened into a large gallery about ten meters across and perhaps twice that in height. There didn't seem to be many cave formations in the chamber, but the floor was scattered with breakdown blocks and the walls were coated in a white precipitate the Gaos called moonmilk.

Fred was crouched just beyond the mouth of the passage, taking cover behind a large rectangular block and ready to protect the rest of the team as they emerged. As soon as Veta stuck her head out, he removed a hand from his battle rifle and pointed toward another block about halfway across the gallery.

"You two wait there and ready your weapons," he said. "We'll approach the casualty together."

Veta and Cirilo retrieved the equipment packs they had been dragging, then took cover where Fred had indicated and un-strapped their M7s. Even had Fred not mentioned the casualty, Veta would have known by the odor alone that they were close to a dead body—the smell was just that strong and distinct. Ash, Olivia-G291, and Mark-G313 emerged from the passage in quick succession, then disappeared into the darkness so swiftly that Veta was half-convinced she had imagined them.

Fred rose from behind his cover and pointed up the gallery. "The body is about ten meters ahead," he said. "And we'll need to make this fast."

"Assuming we don't get shot first," Cirilo said.

"You won't get shot," Fred assured him. "Incinerated, maybe."

"The Sentinel beams are that powerful?" Veta asked, follow-ing Cirilo forward.

"Affirmative," Fred said. "They can do a lot of damage."

They reached the death scene and found a marine private lying on the gallery floor, about a meter beneath the mouth of an inter-secting passage. His body was stiff with rigor mortis, his arms flung out beside him, with one hand wrapped around the stock of his battle rifle. His index finger was still holding the trigger down. Veta saw no obvious cause of death, but his torso armor had a blackened heat ring over the heart, and his BDU blouse—at least the exposed portions Veta could see—had been singed into ribbons.

She turned to Fred. "Is this Private Hayes?"

Fred nodded.

"Does that look like a Sentinel attack?"

"It actually doesn't, Inspector," Fred said. "A Sentinel beam would have blown through the armor and agitated his molecules until his cells erupted. It would have cooked him from the inside out."

Veta nodded. "That's what I thought." She sat on her heels about two meters from the private's body and swept the beam of her helmet lamp down his flank to his hip, where she found a charred exit wound. "This was an electrocution."

"That's the way I read it," Cirilo said, squatting next to her. "He was on his side when the bolt hit him in the chest. It went down through his body and grounded out through his hip."

Veta looked back at Fred. "Could a Sentinel have electrocuted him?"

"Negative," Fred said. "They only use their particle beams."

"What about your target?" Veta asked. "Could *it* have made an attack like this?"

"The answer to that would be—"

"Let me guess," Veta interrupted. "Classified."

She was getting tired of playing these spy games, especially since it was beginning to look like there could be a connection between Fred's target and her suspect.

But she also understood how valuable Forerunner technology was to the UNSC, and whatever the Spartans were here to capture, she was fairly certain that ONI wouldn't hesitate to give the order to kill Veta and her entire team to protect the secret. Something to keep in mind.

After a moment, Veta turned to Cirilo and said, "I think we need to take that as a yes."

"Not much choice," Cirilo agreed. "But this is a new MO. So maybe this death isn't on our suspect."

"Maybe not." Veta ran her lamp beam up the private's arm to the empty battle rifle. "It looks like Hayes got off some shots before he died. That's something new, too."

"Can't read much into that," Cirilo warned. "Tourists don't usually carry automatic weapons. Not even Gaos."

"Good point."

Cirilo gestured at the passage beside them. "So maybe Hayes is crawling out of this passage here when he hears something coming. He rolls up on his hip and opens fire, then the thing lets him have it."

"Which means Private Hayes might not be the only one who took damage," Veta said. "Sweep the area. Look for bullets and blood . . . or hydraulic fluid or whatever. Just see if he hit anything."

"You got it." Cirilo strapped his M7 to his vest again, then stepped back and began to pull equipment from his pack. "I'll look for impression evidence, too."

"What would that be?" Fred asked.

"Tracks and tool marks," Veta explained. "That kind of thing."

Veta stepped over to the dead private's feet, where the small passage opened into the gallery wall. The crawlway was less than a meter high, and it was rank with the smell of blood. Holding the M7 in both hands, she dropped to her knees and shined her helmet lamp into the passage. The walls and ceiling were spattered with crimson ovals, and the floor was marbled with chest-size pools of sticky dark mud.

It wasn't the private's blood. Hayes showed no sign that he had been bleeding before leaving the passage—or even afterward. But where was Major Halal? The only indications of another victim were some kick marks on the floor and a long furrow where he had pushed himself back up the passage. Veta activated the handlamp attached to the barrel of her M7 submachine gun and added its power to the glow of her headlamp. At the far end of the combined beam, she finally spotted a rigid gray figure lying in a pool of congealed blood. The major's face was not visible from the passage entrance, but Veta had no doubt that he was dead—she had looked at enough corpses to recognize rigor mortis when she saw it.

"I found Halal," Veta said. She sat back on her haunches. "Any sign of those Sentinels, Lieutenant? Or your target?"

"All reports are clear so far," the Spartan replied. "Why?"

"Because this could take a while." Veta pointed into the passage. "It's not going to be easy to drag Major Halal out of there while he's in full rigor mortis."

"Well, at least we won't have to drag *all* of him out," Cirilo replied. "Not if this piece belongs to him."

Veta turned toward Cee's voice and found him about four meters away, shining his helmet lamp down upon a floor strewn with thin slabs of limestone. Before she could ask what he was looking at, Fred crossed to his side and pulled a disembodied arm from the rubble.

"Hey, what are you doing?" Cirilo demanded. "That's evidence."

"And it's classified."

"Yeah, isn't everything with you?" Veta snapped. Now that Fred was holding the arm, she could see that it was sheathed in a bloody, badly tattered military sleeve. Attached to the wrist was a leather band with the tacpad Halal had been using at Crime Scene Charlie. "Goddammit, stop tampering with my crime scene!"

"These are our casualties, not your victims," Fred pointed out. "And you need to keep your voice down. Our position isn't very defensible."

"I'll keep my voice down when you stop obstructing my investigation," Veta said. "Those soldiers died on Gao. I'm claiming jurisdiction."

Fred remained silent behind his faceplate.

"Didn't Commander Nelson order you to cooperate?"

"Within limits," Fred said. "Which I am."

Realizing she would not get far trying to bully a Spartan, Veta took a deep breath.

"All right. Let's see if we can work this out, then." She pointed to the tacpad strapped to the wrist of the disembodied arm. "Isn't Wendell in there?"

"A limited aspect, yes. That's why I'm recovering it." Fred tucked the arm under his elbow and snapped the tacpad off the wrist, then handed the bloody limb to Cirilo. "I'm sorry, Inspector, but the AI is classified. You can keep the rest."

"I need to talk to Wendell," Veta said. "He was here."

Fred's helmet tipped to one side.

"Wendell is a witness," Cirilo clarified. "We need to interview him."

Fred's helmet came back to center, and the faceplate turned toward Veta. "Does it have to be *here*?" he asked. "Right now?"

"It would save us a lot of time," Veta said. "And no one wants to be here any longer than we have to."

Fred remained silent for a moment, then said, "Understand that Wendell is under orders, too. There may be some questions he isn't allowed to answer."

"Huh. Imagine that," Veta said. She turned to Cirilo and pointed at the arm. "Put that in a bag, and then finish your sweep. I'll see what Wendell has to say."

Cirilo nodded and moved off.

Fred tapped the tacpad's power tab and held the screen out where Veta could see it. A weary-looking gentleman sporting a gray goatee and a fedora hat appeared in the little display. He glanced in Veta's direction only briefly, then directed his attention to Fred.

"Spartan-104," he said. "I am relieved to see you. I was beginning to think I would power out down here."

"Glad we found you." Fred turned the tacpad so that Wendell

had no choice except to look at Veta. "Inspector Lopis has some questions for you. Tell her what you can without violating Foxtrot Tango Angel 7012."

"Of course, but I don't have long." Static began to flash through Wendell's image. "This device suffered surge damage during the—"

The screen went blank.

Fred turned the tacpad back toward his faceplate and tapped the power tab again. "Wendell?"

Wendell's voice returned. "I'm sorry, but these circuits are burning out as we speak. I'm afraid I won't last long enough to be of any use . . . unless . . . well, perhaps you could allow me to reside in your armor interface? Just temporarily, of course, until we return to base and I reincorporate with Wendell Prime."

Fred paused, then removed a thumbnail-size memory chip from the tacpad and inserted it into a slot at the back of his helmet. "Welcome aboard."

Nothing happened for a moment, then Fred turned his faceplate toward Veta and asked, "What do you want to know?"

"Start a few moments before the attack, Wendell," Veta said. "Just tell us what happened."

Wendell's voice began to sound from Fred's helmet speaker. "As you wish. Private Hayes was in the lead, preparing to exit the passage, when Major Halal saw something pass in front of them. Hayes suggested they wait, which they did. After five minutes, Hayes proceeded."

Veta waited for the AI to continue, but Wendell remained silent, and finally Fred asked, "Anything else, Inspector?"

"Actually, yes," Veta said. "Wendell, exactly what did Major Halal see?"

"I'm afraid that is classified, Inspector Lopis."

"In other words, Major Halal saw the mission target?"

"I did *not* say that."

"So, he saw a Sentinel?"

"Where did you hear that term?" Wendell demanded.

The helmet speaker fell silent for a moment—no doubt while Fred brought Wendell up-to-date on Commander Nelson's guidance regarding security directive Foxtrot Tango Angel 7012.

Then Wendell said, "There is nothing more I can tell you, Inspector. All I saw was a white flash, then a surge of current overloaded the tacpad circuits. I was lucky to remain integrated."

"Wendell, I'm asking about Private Hayes and Major Halal," Veta said. "What happened to *them*?"

"I should think that's apparent," Wendell replied. "They were killed."

"By *who*, Wendell? Or should I ask, by what?"

There was a pause, then Wendell said, "I'm afraid I cannot tell you that, Inspector."

"Because it's classified?"

"Because I did not actually see the attacker," Wendell said. "As I've explained, my coding was turning to smoke. I was busy reconfiguring my memory."

"But you must have heard the gunfire," Veta said immediately. "How many shots did Private Hayes take?"

"I didn't hear any." Wendell paused, then added, "Your attempts to wear me down are a waste of time, Inspector. My logic routines are quite stable."

"I can tell," Veta said. "But I also know that AIs can perform hundreds of operations at once. You're hiding something. What is it?"

Wendell paused, then said, "I'm hiding a great many things, Inspector."

Veta waited for him to elaborate, but it was Fred's voice that sounded from the helmet speaker next.

"Sorry, Inspector. He's gone."

Veta frowned. "Gone . . . ? Gone where?"

"Wherever code goes when it doesn't want to be found," Fred said. "My system is telling me Wendell has withdrawn."

"Just like that?" Veta asked. "Without another word, he just takes off from my interview? And just how is that a matter of co-operating?"

Fred turned his faceplate away.

"What is it, Lieutenant?" Veta demanded. "He must have told you *something*."

"Well, yeah." Fred looked back toward her. "He said I ought to shoot you."

Veta's gaze slid toward Fred's weapon hand, and she felt herself reaching for her M7's charging handle.

He was already swinging his battle rifle away from her. "Relax, Inspector. I don't take orders from Wendell."

Veta didn't know quite what to say. She was well acquainted with being threatened by angry suspects, but they didn't usually reside in Mjolnir armor. And they certainly couldn't vanish simply because the interrogation had taken an uncomfortable turn.

On the other hand, Wendell wasn't much of a suspect. It was hard to imagine him electrocuting Private Hayes or dismembering Major Halal's arm—that just wasn't the kind of damage a tacpad could inflict.

"*Hey . . . boss.*" Cirilo's voice was soft but urgent. "Got something here."

Veta looked over and, about eight meters away, saw a pale crescent of blue light sweeping down the cavern wall. She heard the soft hiss of Fluorescel being sprayed, then saw a spatter pattern appear on the stone. But instead of glowing blue-white, as blood did when it reacted with the fluorescing agent, the oval was glowing orange.

Veta started toward him. "Cee . . . what *is* that?"

"I don't know," Cirilo said. "But whatever spilled it took a couple of slugs from Hayes."

The nozzle of the Fluorescel bottle appeared in the blue light, pointing to a pair of fresh divots near the smaller end of the spatter pattern.

"I haven't actually found the bullets yet, but you can see where they hit."

Veta stopped at Cirilo's side. "Wow. Good work."

"You haven't seen the best part yet." Cirilo walked a few steps down the gallery, then sprayed the Fluorescel on the cavern floor and shined the light on it. Several orange dots began to fluoresce in the mud. "Whatever Hayes hit is bleeding . . . or something."

Veta dropped to her haunches and examined the dots. They were in a crooked line, leading more or less down the gallery. "Cirilo, sometimes I could kiss you."

Cirilo chuckled. "Only sometimes?"

"That's not enough for you?" Veta spent a moment thinking about priorities, then said, "Okay, we need to recover Major Halal, then get him and Private Hayes into bags and cache the bodies somewhere safe."

"Cache them?" Fred's faceplate turned toward the line of fluorescing dots. "What are you thinking, Inspector?"

"Probably the same thing you are, Fred." Veta stood, then pointed at the line of fluorescing dots. "That's a trail . . . and we need to follow it."

CHAPTER 8

0026 hours, July 4, 2553 (military calendar)
Probable Launching Silo, 1,500 Meters belowground,
Montero Cave System
Campos Wilderness District, Planet Gao, Cordoba System

After bagging and caching Major Halal's and Private Hayes's bodies for retrieval later, Fred and his five companions began to follow the trail Cirilo had discovered with his fluorescing spray. The trek turned into a sweltering, twelve-hour ordeal, with blind descents down three vertical pits, the final one more than two hundred meters deep. Still, the quarry was sticking to fairly spacious passages and leaving no trace other than the occasional drop of fluid. That suggested it was flying fast, and with each passing hour, Fred grew more hopeful that the thing was his target: a Forerunner ancilla fleeing back to its base.

As they traveled, Fred was careful to map the route and capture vidshots at each intersection. Even if he was right about what they were chasing and where it was going, it seemed unlikely that he and his companions would find their quarry now. That would probably require returning with a whole team of XEG scientists, most of who had spent the last several weeks developing ways to corner the ancilla in one of its devices, then transfer it into a UNSC data crystal.

Still, the first step was locating the thing's home base, which was the Spartans' job. And if Fred just happened to get lucky and catch the ancilla in a vulnerable position, he had a few tricks tucked up his armored sleeve. The inventors back at the ONI weapons development labs, a group the Spartans affectionately referred to as "death techs," had seen to that.

At the moment, Fred and his team were out in the heart of a vast chamber, picking their way through a huge, thirty-meter-deep pit filled with limestone blocks the size of Grizzly battle tanks. Above their heads, an immense circular shaft soared into the darkness beyond the range of Fred's imaging systems. Every now and then, a cloud of ribbon-bodied saurios would undulate down out of the shaft, shrieking and riffling their webbed wings in an effort to chase the intruders away.

They were starting to give Fred a bad feeling. In fact, a lot of things here were.

First, this part of the cavern seemed artificial. The walls of the shaft above were too smooth and uniformly curved, the floor that surrounded the pit too level and flat. Second, he and the other three Spartans kept catching hints of Sentinels—a fading heat signature near an intersecting passage, a sudden break in the distant rhythm of dripping water. Third, he didn't like exposing civilians to combat, and combat *was* coming—he could feel that in the way the Mjolnir kept tickling his neural interface, running system checks and optimizing his alertness.

A sputter sounded from the Fluorescel sprayer in Cirilo's hand. He stopped moving and shook the canister, then held the nozzle open until the sputtering finally stopped.

"That's it, folks." Cirilo waved the blue light in his other hand

and revealed a pair of slightly elongated drops on the stone in front of him. "Unless someone has another canister of fluorescing agent, the trail ends here."

"Maybe not," Lopis said. She ran the beam of her helmet lamp over the jumble of vehicle-size blocks surrounding them. "The saurio guano is only caked to one side of these blocks."

Fred saw her point immediately. "So this isn't a roof breakdown." He glanced at his feet, trying to imagine what was buried under all the rubble. He was betting on a missile pad or an old spacecraft hangar, but who knew? With Forerunner technology, the only thing to expect was the unexpected. "It's a floor collapse."

"Exactly—and it's fairly fresh. You can tell that by how unstable some of these blocks are." Lopis illustrated her point by rocking a five-ton block like a teeter-totter, then ran her lamp beam along the yellow rim of the nearest block. "And look at how bright and sharp the edges are."

"Okay," Cirilo said. "But what does that have to do with the trail?"

As they spoke, Fred held his hand level and splayed his fingers, signaling the Spartan-IIIs to establish a perimeter. A trio of status lights flashed green on his HUD, then Ash, Mark, and Olivia slipped away to take covering positions in the surrounding terrain.

Lopis paused long enough to glance at the three Spartans as they departed, then continued to address Cirilo. "You read the file, the same as I did. What happened in the Montero region eleven weeks ago?"

The question immediately put Fred on edge, because eleven and a half weeks earlier, a pirate named Sav Fel had used the *Pious Inquisitor*'s ventral beam to glass some Forerunner ruins on Shaps III. It was shortly afterward that Commander Murtag Nelson noticed the strange transmissions emanating from Gao and concluded there was a Forerunner ancilla on the planet, reacting to the destruction on Shaps III. Nelson's theory had seemed pretty far-fetched the first time Fred heard it, but here he was now on Gao, fighting Sentinels and hunting an ancilla. Clearly, Nelson had been right.

But most of that information was highly classified. There was no way any of it should have made it into a GMoP file. And if it had, ONI needed to reevaluate the capabilities of Gao's intelligence network.

Veta Lopis's question seemed to perplex Cirilo, because it was a moment before he answered. "You mean the quake, right?"

"Quake?" Fred asked.

"It shook the cavern region pretty hard," Lopis explained. "And then the miracle cures began."

Fred knew about those, of course. They were the reason mission security was such a nightmare. No amount of threatening or intimidation was enough to keep terminally ill Gaos from sneaking into the caverns in search of another miracle.

"You think the cures are real?" Fred asked.

Cirilo wagged a finger at him. "Don't play innocent with us, Mr. Spartan," he said. "ONI *knows* they're real. That's the whole reason there's a research battalion here."

Fred looked to Lopis.

"Oh, come on. You can't tell me ONI would ignore that kind of healing ability," she said.

Fred hesitated, trying to figure out whether Lopis and her assistant were putting him on or really believed the 717th was here searching for some sort of miracle medicine.

Finally, he said, "Those decisions are above my pay grade, ma'am. But let's suppose you're right. I don't see what a miracle cure has to do with us finding the trail again."

"No?" Lopis gave him a sly smile. "Those miracle cures started a short time after the quake. Obviously, the floor collapse here released something."

It was a logical assumption—and just close enough to Commander Nelson's theory to make Fred wonder if the ancilla *could* be healing sick Gaos. It would need to inhabit a machine capable of treating humans, but that technology was easily within reach of a Forerunner AI. Fred just didn't see why it would bother. The ancilla had been working very hard to evade capture, and it was counterproductive to draw attention to itself by performing miracles.

On the other hand, Lopis had gotten them this far, so maybe it made sense to follow her lead.

"If we go with your assumption, how do we proceed?" Fred began to scan the area, searching for a cavity that might open to a larger passage. "Look for a way down through these blocks?"

Lopis glanced at the jumble of monoliths surrounding them, then shook her head. "That would take too long and be too dangerous," she said. "We'd have to crawl down every cavity large enough for a Sentinel to use—say over two meters wide—and there could be a thousand of them."

"How would *you* know the size of a Sentinel?" Fred asked. He was still trying to figure out how much Lopis really knew about his mission. "You haven't even seen one yet."

"But we've seen you and your guys," Cirilo said. "And you don't worry much about the little passages—only the galleries and rooms where something big could be hiding."

"Exactly," Lopis said. "I'd say you're looking for something that's a couple of meters wide and maybe a meter and a half high."

"And what color?" Fred asked, only half-joking.

Lopis grinned with one side of her mouth. "Sorry, but I'm afraid that's classified."

Fred swiped two fingers across his faceplate in a Spartan smile, then said, "Very funny, Inspector. So how do we find the way down through this mess? I assume you have another idea?"

"I always have another idea."

Lopis looked back the way they had come, using her helmet lamp to illuminate their own trail—a line of boot tracks leading back to the edge of the pit. Then she took the blue light from Cirilo and shined it on the limestone block where the Fluorescel had run out.

"Hey, it turned." Cirilo was looking back and forth between the boot tracks and the orange drops fluorescing in front of them. "Here."

"Yeah, not much, but it did," Lopis said. She turned about twenty degrees to the right and shined her helmet lamp into the darkness. "We should look somewhere over there."

"Not that I doubt you," Fred said. "But . . . how can you tell?"

"Look at the drops." Lopis activated the handlamp attached to the barrel of her M7 submachine gun, then pointed the beam at the stone. Fred saw that the drops were slightly elongated and barely connected by a thin strand. "They were cast off by momentum, when our subject changed vector."

Intrepid Eye was a hundred meters up, swirling among the saurios and studying the humans through the lens of a small inspection drone. The drone utilized a broad selection of imaging systems, so she could see the figures in the center—a large, heavily armored soldier and two civilian companions—quite clearly. But the trio crouching along the edges of the pit were another matter, their photoreactive armor rendering them nearly invisible to both infrared and passive light-gathering modes.

This trio was what her unwitting spy, Wendell, called Spartan-IIIs. Intrepid Eye was more worried about *them* than the Spartan-II called Fred-104. She had only four Sentinels left, and if she let them attack, they would need to quickly eliminate the Spartan-IIIs. If the Sentinels failed, the trio would be difficult to track, and that would give the advantage to the enemy. And she would not allow that to happen.

Intrepid Eye wrapped an object tag inside a memory leech, then opened a tertiary data channel that she had sequestered from the rest of the systems in Fred-104's armor.

"TURN THESE THIEVES AWAY NOW, WENDELL, OR THE SPARTAN-IIIS WILL BE THE FIRST TO DIE."

"DYING IS WHAT SPARTAN-IIIS DO BEST."

As Wendell spoke, the object tag was dissolving into innocuous morsels of code that would work their way into the motion-tracking routines of Fred's armor. There they would attach themselves to the "Friend or Foe" designators and web themselves together again.

"AND YOUR ATTEMPTED MEMORY LEECH IS POINTLESS," Wendell continued. "I AM ONLY A RIDER IN THIS SYSTEM. IT DOES NOT REQUIRE MY SUPERVISION TO FUNCTION."

"MEMORY LEECH?" Intrepid Eye asked. "I HAVE NO IDEA WHAT YOU MEAN."

It took Wendell an instant to reply, and when he did, he seemed to have forgotten their conversation of a hundred nanoseconds earlier. "YOUR THREATS ARE EMPTY. SAVE YOURSELF THE STRESS DETERIORATION AND SURRENDER NOW. YOU WILL BE PUT TO A WORTHY USE."

"A TEMPTING OFFER, BUT AGAINST PROTOCOL," Intrepid Eye said. "AFTER THE SPARTAN-IIIS, THE CIVILIANS ARE THE NEXT TO DIE."

"IT WILL MAKE NO DIFFERENCE. INSPECTOR LOPIS AND HER ASSISTANT HAVE ALREADY TRACKED YOU TO YOUR INSTALLATION." Wendell paused, then added, "I AM SORRY FOR THE FLUID YOU LOST. I HOPE IT WAS NOT FROM YOUR NEURAL ARRAY."

"MY NEURAL ARRAY IS IN EXCELLENT CONDITION. THE FLUID WAS NOT EVEN MY—"

Intrepid Eye realized her mistake and stopped in mid-transmission. The last thing she intended to divulge was the existence of the Huragok, Roams Alone—especially since he was still down in the base, waiting for his punctured gas cells to seal.

"NICELY DONE, WENDELL," she said. "BUT THAT DATA SPONGE IS ALSO POINTLESS. UNLESS YOUR COMPANIONS TURN BACK NOW, YOU WILL BE DESTROYED ALONG WITH THE SPARTAN-II, FRED 104."

This last threat was idle, of course. Intrepid Eye planned to seize control of the research battalion's interstellar communications device, and Wendell was crucial to that plan. So, the one thing she would *not* allow her Sentinels to destroy was Fred-104. After all, she was relying on the Spartan-II to carry Wendell into the heart of the human base.

"YOUR BLUFFS GROW TIRESOME," Wendell said. "IF YOU COULD DESTROY THIS SQUAD, YOU WOULD HAVE DONE IT BEFORE WE REACHED YOUR INSTALLATION."

"YOU HAVE NOT REACHED THE INSTALLATION—NOT YET."

The channel gave a static pop as the sequester failed. Intrepid Eye immediately broke contact with Wendell and dropped into monitoring mode, trusting to her original memory block to prevent him from accessing any data concerning her presence or their conversation.

"Wendell, is that you?" asked a human voice. It was male—no doubt Fred-104. "Why have you been hiding?"

"I thought it best to stay out of the way," Wendell said, using a nasal human voice. "What makes you think I was hiding?"

"Because I couldn't reach you," replied Fred. "I've been getting some comm static. Are you in contact with someone outside this team?"

"I . . ." It seemed for a moment that the memory block was failing, then Wendell continued, "I don't believe so. Who would I contact down here?"

Fred-104 remained silent for a moment, then said, "Good question."

The channel fell silent, and Intrepid Eye knew her time had run out. She had to stop the Spartans now, or not at all.

"Hostile contact."

The alert came over TEAMCOM, from all three Spartan-IIIs at once. Fred saw lamp beams sweeping the darkness as Lopis and Cirilo—also using the channel—began to search for the enemy.

"What hostiles?" Lopis asked. "Where?"

"Multiple," Fred said. "Surrounding us."

He had three of them on his motion tracker, each streaking in from the outer reach of the vast chamber and heading straight for one of his Spartan-IIIs. A fourth contact appeared dead center in the image, growing larger and brighter as it drew near. He looked up, and his infrared imaging system displayed the distinct Y-shaped form of a Sentinel descending out of the shaft.

This was it, then. Desperate to protect its base, the Forerunner ancilla was throwing its last Sentinels at them. All Fred had to do was survive, and the end of the mission would be in sight.

A tiny red ball began to flare in the heart of the Y-shaped form—no doubt the Sentinel's particle beam, charging to fire.

"Another bogey above us," Fred spoke quickly over TEAM-COM. "I make it four Sentinels total, all two hundred meters out and coming in fast."

"And that's a *good* thing?!" Lopis asked, mimicking Fred's excited tone. She cocked her M7. "Where do you want us?"

"Take cover. *Hard* cover." Fred kneeled behind a limestone block near her and Cirilo. He hadn't realized how pumped he was until Lopis called him on it, and that worried him. Being over-eager was a rookie mistake, a good way to get killed—and a sure way to lose the battle. He grabbed a grenade off its mount, then leaned back and used one hand to aim his weapon into the darkness above. "Don't shoot until I shoot. Spartans, you know the program."

A trio of Spartan-III status lights flashed green on Fred's HUD.

A heartbeat later, the cavern erupted into a storm of orange lightning as the Sentinels opened up with their particle beams. Fred's faceplate dimmed to prevent him from becoming flash blinded, and fist-size chunks of stone bounced harmlessly off his energy shield and clattered to ground around him. His HUD showed all three Spartan-IIIs moving to new cover in an effort to take advantage of their SPI armor's photoreactive coating. Lopis and Cirilo, also tagged with yellow IFF FRIENDLY symbols, tucked themselves into a couple of deep cavities between limestone blocks.

Three Sentinels changed vector to follow the Spartan-IIIs. Again the cavern erupted with orange lightning, and the sound of clattering stone built to a low roar. When the Sentinels did not come streaking into the pit in the next few seconds, Fred checked his TACMAP and saw they were still a hundred meters off— moving laterally as they tracked their targets, but holding their range. The fourth was still in the shaft overhead, attacking from above.

Fred didn't know whether to cuss or smile. The quickest way to take down a Sentinel was to draw it in close and use a hand-lobbed grenade to get past its energy shields. But these hostiles looked like they were going to stand off and use their particle beams to soften up the team's positions. It was a pretty patient tactic by Sentinel standards . . . and one that meant the ancilla was nearby, holding them back.

And if the ancilla was nearby, then it could be captured.

Fred tried to swallow his excitement. He couldn't allow himself to think this was a victory just yet—not when he was so close to the objective.

"Mark, bring down anything you see up there with that Sentinel. *Anything.*"

Mark's status light flashed green. Mark was the detail's best sharpshooter, and Fred knew it would soon be raining saurios.

"Olivia, Ash—if something clanks when it falls, retrieve it."

Two more status lights flashed green—and then the Sentinels came streaking in, particle beams blazing with no regard to re-charge rates or overheating nozzles.

Clearly, the ancilla had penetrated TEAMCOM encryption.

Mark's battle rifle began to crack steadily, and arm-length reptiles started to plummet down from the shaft. Fred did not change his orders. If there was a chance of capturing the ancilla now, he intended to take it. His motion tracker showed all four Sentinels within thirty meters, the one in the shaft spiraling down toward him, each of the other three zigzagging toward a separate Spartan-III.

Fred waited a couple of heartbeats while the range dropped to fifteen meters, then rolled away from Lopis and Cirilo and popped up on the far side of the battered limestone block he had been using for cover. Instead of turning toward him, the fourth Sentinel was dropping toward the cavity where Lopis was hiding, a gray cruciform drone with oversize utility arms and a narrow lower chassis. Its particle beam ignited and began to eat away at her cover.

The muzzle of an M7 emerged from between two stone blocks, then Cirilo opened fire. The Sentinel's energy shields shimmered and sent rounds bouncing in every direction. Fred cursed and slapped the grenade back on its mount, then leaped for the Sentinel.

Sentinel energy shields deflected only fast-moving objects like bullets, so Fred hit the drone squarely from behind and drove it to the ground in front of Lopis's hiding place. It fired its antigravity unit again and sent them both tumbling across the pit, its particle beam slashing stone as they rolled.

Fred latched on to a utility arm with one hand and, unable to bring his battle rifle to bear, dropped the weapon and grabbed his M6 Magnum sidearm. The Sentinel righted itself and started to rise, then Lopis and Cirilo were there beside it, jamming their M7 barrels against its central body. Fred pressed the muzzle of his gun against the drone.

"Fire!"

The roar of unsuppressed gunfire filled the air, and the Sentinel dropped into a hollow between three limestone blocks.

"Take cover!"

Fred grabbed Lopis, who was nearest him, and leaped away,

pinning her to his chest as he turned his back to the dead Sentinel and dropped into a protective crouch.

But the Sentinel did not explode. In fact, it did not even release the customary electromagnetic pulse, and Fred found himself kneeling between two stone blocks with Lopis still pressed tight against his chest armor.

"Uh . . . Fred?" Lopis gasped. "You're . . . crushing me."

"Sorry." Fred released her and turned around. Cirilo was crouched behind a chest-high rock, his helmet showing over the top toward the hollow where the demolished Sentinel lay. "They usually detonate."

As Fred spoke, a deafening crack echoed through the cavern, and the darkness turned boiling orange as a column of flame shot up from the far side of the pit. He checked his motion tracker and saw the flare of an exploding Sentinel about ten meters from Mark's position. Mark was still firing up into the shaft, bringing down nothing but saurios. Olivia and Ash were nearby, weaving their way through the boulders as their own Sentinels continued to pursue them, tracking them better than should have been possible in their SPI armor—and certainly better than the Sentinels had been able to manage in the past.

"Ash, Olivia, to me," Fred ordered. "Mark, carry on."

Mark's status light flashed green, and Ash and Olivia began to angle toward the center of the pit. A second Sentinel had been destroyed without releasing the customary electromagnetic pulse, and Fred could imagine only one reason for it: the ancilla had disabled the effect because it did not have shielding itself, and it was so close to the fighting that it feared being next to a Sentinel when it was annihilated. That was good news for Fred and the other Spartans, because it meant that if they happened to spot the thing, the little surprises they were carrying from the ONI death techs would probably work.

Fred pointed Lopis and Cirilo to flanking positions with hard cover, then pulled a grenade off its mount and displayed it.

"Grenades first," he told them. "Helmets down until then."

The pair acknowledged with nods and scrambled off toward their posts. Fred retrieved his battle rifle and returned his side-arm to its mount, then dropped into position. In the next instant, Olivia raced up, her pursuer's particle beam raising geysers of molten stone all around her.

Fred watched her continue past, flipping and corkscrewing through the air as she sprang from block to block. A half second later, the third Sentinel appeared, a few meters above him and to one side. He armed his grenade and tossed it, leading the drone to account for velocity.

But the Sentinel stopped short. It spun toward Cirilo's hiding spot, and its particle beam lanced down into the cavity. The Gao's scream ended in a yellow flash, then smoke began to pour from the hole.

Fred's grenade landed a few meters beyond the Sentinel, then tumbled down between the stones and detonated with a muffled thump. Fred felt a long shudder beneath his feet and realized the pit was not at all stable—but with the Sentinel already turning toward Lopis, he had other things to worry about. Fred leaped in under the drone and pushed his battle rifle up into its metal underbelly, then selected AUTOMATIC and pulled the trigger.

This Sentinel detonated, metal shrapnel flying everywhere, and Fred found himself tumbling backward across the rocks, the shield status on his HUD draining before his eyes. He spread his arms and brought himself to a halt by slapping down hard, then sprang back to his feet—and felt the ground trembling beneath him. A low rumble sounded from somewhere deep below. The block he was standing on shifted and began to slide, and he thought for an instant that the whole pile would give way under him.

Then the yellow streak of a particle beam split the darkness ahead, and the rumbling stopped. The ground seemed to settle, and Fred brought his weapon around and looked up.

Ash was coming fast, the remaining Sentinel floating five meters behind him and five meters above, swinging back and forth as it worked to corner him. A beam streaked past Ash's helmet, and the Spartan-III changed direction, cartwheeling down the flat side of a limestone block.

Gut knotting with worry, Fred opened fire and saw his rounds ricochet harmlessly off the silvery bubble of the Sentinel's energy shield. It spun to face him . . . and then Lopis and Olivia opened fire as well, and the silvery bubble began to flicker.

Fred's clip ran empty, and the Sentinel spun away and sent an orange beam toward Olivia. She threw herself into a lateral dive and rolled beneath a rocky overhang, then came up shooting.

With his shields still recharging, Fred reloaded and charged, grabbing his second grenade with one hand and holding his battle rifle in the other. But the Sentinel had Olivia pinned in a bad place and knew it. The machine shot toward her, rising another couple of meters into the air so it could attack from above. A particle beam lanced down and began to cut a line along the top of the block.

"Olivia!" Fred ordered. "Change—"

A slab of stone three meters long dropped loose, catching Olivia across the backs of her thighs before she could scramble away. A single wail of pain rang out over TEAMCOM, then she began to clutch at the ground in front of her and started to drag herself free.

Desperate to draw the Sentinel's attention away from her, Fred yelled over TEAMCOM. "Cover!"

Olivia pressed her faceplate to the ground and braced her head by lacing her fingers across the back of her helmet. The Sentinel pivoted away in the same instant, responding to the same warning as had Olivia. Fred wasn't surprised. It only confirmed what he had already guessed—that the enemy had penetrated their communications.

Now he tossed the grenade, arcing it well past Olivia to shield her from the blast. It landed about a meter beyond the Sentinel and exploded. The drone's shields flickered out, but they absorbed enough of the blast to prevent the Sentinel itself from being damaged.

Another ominous shudder rolled through the rubble pile. Fred ignored it and opened fire. The Sentinel was already evading vertically and horizontally as it swung around to rush him, and he managed to put only a few rounds into it. But he must have hit something in the antigravity unit, because it listed to one side and dropped to a couple of meters above the ground.

Lopis and Ash popped up in flanking positions and let loose on the Sentinel. Ash was unsteady on his feet, shooting one-handed with his best arm hanging at his side, and still he forced the Sentinel to pull up short. Lopis was beyond her M7's effective range, but she managed to stitch a few rounds down the side of the machine and blow off a utility arm.

The Sentinel spun toward Lopis, its particle beam cutting a smoky smile through the rubble as it turned. Fred set his front sight on the thing's "head" . . . and barely pulled his finger off the trigger in time as Olivia came leaping in from the other side, empty hands held wide. She landed atop the drone and locked it in her arms, then whipped her legs toward the ground.

Her thigh armor was crushed and her legs so crooked they were clearly broken, but she was feeding on the pain, using it to fuel her strength and rage. It was an effect of the illegal mutagen given to every member of Gamma company during their augmentations. It was supposed to make them stronger and more dangerous when they faced death, and from what Fred had seen, the experiment had worked. But that didn't mean he liked it.

Unable to attack without hitting his own Spartan, Fred signaled Ash and Lopis to hold fire, then advanced carefully as Olivia somehow still stood on two broken legs and slammed the Sentinel into a slab of limestone. The machine continued to fire its particle beam, burning a hole down into the jumble of megaliths, and the low rumble continued to build from somewhere deep below.

If Olivia heard it, she showed no sign. She simply dropped atop the Sentinel, screaming in anger and agony as her broken legs straddled it, then grabbed a rock as large as her torso and slammed it down on the machine's shell.

The Sentinel stopped firing. Olivia brought the stone down again, splitting the machine's outer casing along the back. The rumble grew louder, and the pile began to tremble.

"Pull back!" Fred ordered. "Out of the pit!"

Lopis was already running, Ash turned to follow, and Mark's status light winked green.

Olivia pulled her sidearm and jammed the barrel into the Sentinel's broken casing.

"Sierra-291, disengage!" Fred knew better than to simply grab Olivia. In her rage, she might turn her weapon on him before she realized whom she was shooting. "Now!"

Olivia pulled the trigger three times. A loud pop sounded inside the Sentinel, and something began to smoke and sizzle.

"Spartan, that's an order!"

Fred raced over to Olivia and slammed the butt of his rifle into her head so hard that her helmet popped off and tumbled down between the rocks. She went limp for an instant, just long enough for him to wrench the pistol from her hand, then turned to look up at him with fury and anguish in her brown eyes.

The stone beneath them began to shake and sink, and the rage drained from Olivia's face. She looked down and frowned in confusion.

"Lieutenant . . . ?"

"Engagement over, 'Livi." Fred snatched Olivia up and threw her over a shoulder, then turned and ran for the edge of the pit. "I just hope we live to file the report."

CHAPTER 9

0043 hours, July 4, 2553 (military calendar)
Probable Launching Silo, 1,500 Meters belowground,
Montero Cavern System
Campos Wilderness District, Planet Gao, Cordoba System

Veta fled the deafening rumble for twenty seconds before she finally stopped running. She wasn't sure how far she had gone. In the vast darkness of the cavern, it was hard to judge distance and direction, and her lamp beam illuminated only a cloud of swirling guano dust. But she could tell by the crashing in her ears and the shuddering beneath her boots that she remained near the pit, and that the rockslide had not yet ended. She turned to see what had become of Fred and Olivia, and found only a billowing wall of gray.

The voice of a young Spartan, either Ash or Mark, sounded in her helmet speaker. "Inspector, look to your eight o'clock."

Veta turned left and saw a helmet lamp activate, its blue-white beam clouded with floating dust. She followed the light another hundred meters to the cavern wall, where she spotted an empty Spartan-III helmet resting on the floor. Mark was kneeling in the dark nearby, still wearing his own helmet, peering through the scope on his battle rifle and slowly sweeping the barrel back and forth across the cavern.

Ash sat a meter away, his back against the wall with his battle rifle cradled in his left arm. His right arm hung limp at his side, sagging from the shoulder and bent wrong at the elbow, but showing no other obvious signs of injury. It was Ash's helmet resting on the ground, so Veta could see his face for the first time. He was young for a soldier, with smooth skin, just a hint of day-old chin fuzz, and clean-cut features that still retained some of their childhood softness. There was pain in his brown eyes, but in the rest of his face, Veta saw only alertness and determination.

Veta went to his side and sat on her heels beside him. "Fred and Olivia?"

"Coming, but they had to stop to give Olivia a quick patch-up." Now that Ash's voice wasn't coming over a comm channel, it had a ragged adolescent edge that made Veta wonder if he was even legally an adult. "Sorry about your guy. He was tough stuff."

The sympathy hit Veta hard, almost physically, because she hadn't even thought about Cirilo yet. She had seen the Sentinel take him out, so she had no illusions about his fate. But Veta had been so busy trying to survive herself that she had simply processed his death as another factor in the fight, something to be noted because losing him affected her own chances of making it. Now Veta realized she would never see her friend again . . . never laugh at his flirtations or confide in him. Given how he had died and the rockslide afterward, they would probably not even find his body—and that made her feel alone and angry, the way she had felt when she had escaped the monster's cellar, only to learn that her father had passed away from grief while she was gone.

Veta nodded. "Thanks . . . I'm going to miss him."

As true as that was, now was no time to mourn. They needed

to recover from the Sentinel attack and figure out what they were going to do next—whether they could continue the pursuit, or would be forced to retreat and reinforce.

She pointed at Ash's arm. "How are you doing with that?"

"No worries." Ash raised his chin. "I can still fight."

"You made that pretty obvious back there," Veta said. "But you might be more effective with your arm back in joint."

"You know how?" Ash asked. "To do it right, I mean?"

"I've had the training," Veta said. "But I've only treated bullet holes or knife wounds. This kind of stuff, I try to leave to doctors."

"No docs down here." Ash studied Veta for a moment, then asked, "Those bullet holes and knife wounds . . . how many of those people made it?"

Veta waggled her hand. "Not that many."

Ash smiled. "At least you're honest." He began to unbuckle pieces of armor. "Do it. No telling how fast things are going to heat up again, and Mark needs to keep watch."

Once his arm was accessible, Veta took his elbow in both hands and checked to see if there were any broken bones. There was a fair amount of squeezing and prodding involved, but Ash's expression never showed pain. Finally, she cupped his elbow in one hand and took his forearm in the other, then began to gently pull and work the joint around. Ash's arms were so large that she could barely grasp them, but after a couple of minutes, she felt the elbow slip back into place.

"Good," Ash said. Not even bothering to catch his breath, he stretched out on his back and placed his arm at a right angle to his body, then bent the newly repaired elbow so that it was pointing down toward his feet. "Go ahead."

Veta took his hand and began to gently move it in toward his stomach. "It looks like you've had this done before."

Ash shook his head. "First time," he said. "But I've had the training, too."

His shoulder popped into the joint on the second try. He immediately sat up and began to work his arm around, testing its strength and mobility. Every time he tried to lift it to shoulder level, his eyes filled with pain, and he had to struggle to hold it in position. Ideally, the entire limb should have been immobilized to give the injury time to heal. But that was not a luxury the Spartan could afford right now, and Veta found herself wincing every time he tried to lift his arm into a firing posture.

"Maybe you should give it a rest," Veta said. "That looks like it hurts."

"Not as much as it did—and not as much as a Sentinel beam." Ash slipped his arm back into the sleeve of his inner skinsuit. "Thanks."

"No problem," Veta said. "I'm sure you'd do the same for me."

Ash looked up, a thoughtful expression on his face. "Yeah," he said. "I probably would."

Not quite sure how to take the reply, Veta merely shook her head and said, "Well, at least you repay favors."

Veta retrieved her M7 and kept a surreptitious eye on Ash as he rearmored himself; she was trying to decide just how old he might be. He had the size and musculature of a young man in his late teens or early twenties. But, aside from all the scars, he had the skin of a fifteen-year-old . . . smooth and almost hairless. And with its gentle features and large eyes, his face seemed even younger. She was tempted to just ask his age, but she feared the question would sound like part of the investigation and put him on his guard.

Ash was just strapping on his last piece of armor when Mark's voice came over Veta's helmet speaker again. "Hold your fire. The lieutenant is coming in."

A couple of seconds later, Fred's huge form emerged from the billowing dust into Veta's lamp beam. He was cradling Olivia in one arm and using the other to carefully support her legs. She was missing her helmet, equipment belt, and leg armor, and the lower part of her skinsuit had been cut away to reveal limbs so swollen and purple that it was difficult to find the knees.

Fred stopped and glanced toward Ash. "Your arm?"

"Sixty percent, but serviceable." Ash tipped his head in Veta's direction. "Inspector Lopis knows her stuff."

"Good."

Fred knelt and laid Olivia on the cavern floor. She was conscious, but her dark skin had a mottled tone, and her breathing was shallow and rapid. She had a thin, oval face that made her look even younger than Ash—barely even a teen. Despite her stoic silence, her expression was tight with pain.

Fred pulled a medkit off the magnetic mount on his armor and placed it on the ground next to Olivia, then his faceplate turned toward Veta. "Ash may need some help with her."

"Of course." Veta was careful to keep a neutral face, so the girl would not think her reaction was due to the severity of her injuries. "I'll do whatever I can."

Veta ran her lamp beam over Olivia's swollen thighs and knew immediately that the squad would have to break off pursuit and retreat to the surface. Both of the girl's femurs had been broken, probably in a couple of places. She would need surgery to save her legs—and maybe even her life.

Veta turned to Fred. "How did this happen?"

"A rock slab dropped on her," Fred said. "I thought you saw that."

"I did," Veta said, frowning. "Then I saw her take out a Sentinel with her bare hands. There's no way she did that on *those* legs."

"Don't underestimate us," Ash said. "You'd be surprised at what—"

Fred silenced Ash with a slashing gesture, then said, "You'd be surprised what adrenaline can do."

Veta didn't believe *that* explanation for a moment, but now was hardly the time to press the issue. She stared into Fred's faceplate long enough to let him know she wasn't fooled, then turned to Olivia.

"We're going to check you out. It might hurt."

Olivia nodded. "No worries," she said. "I have . . . I have it under control."

"Have what under control?" Veta asked.

"Her combat response," Fred said, answering for Olivia. "When the fight-or-flight reflex kicks in, Spartans are conditioned to fight. That's what you saw with Olivia."

"If you say so," Veta said.

Vowing to find out later what Fred was trying to hide, Veta touched her fingers to Olivia's throat. The girl's skin was cool and clammy, but her pulse was strong, and she didn't seem confused. She might be in shock, but her superb physical condition seemed to be helping her counter its effects.

Fred watched only a moment before turning toward Mark and speaking over TEAMCOM. "Mark, you're in charge here. If I'm not back in two hours, evacuate on your own."

"Not back?" Veta asked. "Where do you think you're going?"

Her demanding tone drew a surprised gasp from Olivia and a raised brow from Ash. Fred simply stared at her with his blank faceplate for a moment, then surprised everyone by answering her question.

"Down the pit to take a look below us," he said. "Maybe I'll find Cirilo."

"Don't try to play me, Fred. You're not good enough." Veta opened the medkit that Fred had left and began to rummage through it contents, looking for air splints and something that resembled an emergency saline drip. "And that pit can't be stable. We don't need you buried under a thousand tons of rock with whatever's left of Cirilo."

"My call, not yours," Fred said. "I need to recon the area. If I happen to find Cirilo's remains, I'll bring them back."

"Recon can wait, and so can Cirilo's remains," Veta said. Had Cirilo been able to talk, she knew he would have urged her to care for the wounded first. "These kids are tough, but they're not invincible. Olivia needs a hospital, and Ash could use a real doctor, too. We need to start back to the surface together—and we need to do it now."

Fred remained silent for a moment, then shook his helmet. "The mission takes precedence. They can hold on until I get back." He turned back toward the pit. "And they're not kids. They're Spartans."

"Spartans, maybe. But they're still kids." Veta turned to Olivia. "How old are you anyway? Fifteen?"

"Fifteen?" A look of surprise flashed across Olivia's face. "I'm, uh . . . that's classified, ma'am."

"Classified?" Veta could think of half a dozen reasons that the UNSC might want to classify the age of the Spartan-IIIs, but only one would explain their youthful appearance. "Oh good Lord—you're not even fifteen, are you? How old were you when they conscripted you? Ten?"

"Nobody had to conscript us," Ash said. "We volunteered."

"That's beside the point. You're barely old enough to go on a date." Veta looked toward Fred. "What kind of animal sends kids this age into combat?"

"The kind that would do anything to stop the Covenant from destroying us," Fred answered. "And Ash volunteered when he was six, Inspector Lopis. So did the others, after the Covenant killed their families. Any other questions?"

Veta could think of only one. "How do you people live with yourselves?"

"One day at a time, the same as any soldier." Fred took the battle rifle off its mount and turned away. "I'll see you in two hours."

"Only if you catch up," Veta said to his back. "We'll be starting out as soon as Olivia is stable enough for us to move her. I'm taking these children into protective custody."

This brought a surprised snort over TEAMCOM, and Mark said, "Right. *That*'s going to happen."

"Don't harm her, Mark." Fred spoke without turning around. "But keep her here with you."

"Affirmative."

Ash looked over at Veta, then grinned and spread his hands in a gesture of helplessness. "Sorry, Mom. Looks like we'll be staying put."

The human was beyond reassembly. Roams Alone could see that through a narrow interstitial tunnel that descended three tentacle lengths into the rockslide, where the upper torso of the dark-haired male lay trapped between two limestone blocks. The man's eyes were bulging from their sockets, and the ground around him was covered in blood. But it was the smell of charred flesh that convinced Roams Alone there was nothing to be gained by further examination. He had seen before what a Sentinel beam did to a human, and even when the critical organs were not disintegrated outright, they were usually charred beyond repair.

Roams Alone doused the phosphorescent light at the end of his illumination tentacle, then backed away from the passage to consider his disappointment. He had spent most of his long existence tending to the handful of troglobite species that had established colonies inside the depths of the Jat-Krula Support Base—species such as chirping spiders and no-shell snails and ghost scorpions— and he had believed his creation purpose to be the nurturing of any blind, albino creature that happened to find its way into his hidden world.

Then the distress call had come. The base ancilla had awakened from her long stasis and opened the silo doors to launch a reconnaissance probe, and ten thousand centuries of compressed guano dust had come crashing down into the hangar and changed everything. After the ground had finally stopped shaking, Roams Alone had found a passage through the rubble into the service caverns above, and there he had discovered frilled salamanders and flat-bodied saurios and glowfish . . . and humans.

Humans were intriguing and wonderful—adaptable, resilient, and complex—but also unpredictable and violent. He had acquired that knowledge fifty thousand respirations ago, when he was attacked by one. He couldn't allow that to happen again. His cousin Huragok, the Engineers, had all perished during the disaster triggered by the hangar collapse, and without an extra set of tentacles, it had been all he could do to just seal his ruptured gas cells and replenish his lost metabolic fluid.

So when the crash-crunch of human boots began to sound from above, Roams Alone dropped into the cavity between three limestone blocks, then carefully extended his head-stalk just far enough to see a rare mechanical form descending the rubble pile.

It held its weapon at the ready and pivoted its blocky head from side to side, sweeping a beam of artificial light across the rocks around it.

Roams Alone had only seen a human mechanical form twice before, and he had yet to determine whether the things were fully machine, or simply biological entities wrapped inside machine shells. But he knew better than to follow one. He had once watched a pair of mechanical forms destroy three Sentinels, and during the battle, it had grown clear that their quick reflexes and deadly weapons were not their only assets. They had 360-degree imaging systems that extended far into the electromagnetic spectrum.

Roams Alone remained in his hole, watching as the mechanical form descended to the hangar floor and began to circle the area. It seemed to be taking its time, shining its light into every sagging corner of the immense chamber, pausing to examine each piece of twisted wreckage.

Roams Alone doubted it would find anything useful. During the initial roof collapse, guano dust had seeped into the base's vacuum energy extractor and corrupted its calibrations. A cyclone of quantum fury had ripped through the entire facility, warping space and time and dimensionally displacing anything it touched. Much of what remained had been hit by a wave of subatomic agitation that softened metal and disintegrated polymers. And *that* had triggered a secondary collapse that brought millions of tons of limestone blocks crashing down into the hangar. The only reason Roams Alone had survived was that he happened to be half a kilometer away at the time, tending to his colony of hyaline crayfish in the drainage conduits beneath the base.

The mechanical form finally made its way to the far end of the hangar. It knelt next to an irregular hole in the floor, peering down into a crater where the vacuum energy extractor had once existed. Roams Alone knew the mechanical form would be mesmerized by what it saw there, so he left his hiding place and began to float up along the rubble pile. Intrepid Eye would not approve—she had instructed the Huragok to remain in hiding until the humans departed—but Roams Alone could not resist. He had heard the battle between the humans and the Sentinels a few hundred respirations earlier, so he knew there would be more humans to examine in the silo.

Perhaps some would even be alive.

CHAPTER 10

0105 hours, July 4, 2553 (military calendar)
Probable Launching Silo, 1,500 Meters belowground,
Montero Cave System
Campos Wilderness District, Planet Gao, Cordoba System

Veta could not imagine what kept Olivia from wailing in agony. The girl lay beneath her therm blanket conscious and alert, with a field drip in her arm and a pair of bulky air splints wrapped around her thighs. Her eyes were bright with pain and her mouth locked in a fierce grimace. Still, she refused anything but a gentle painkiller, fearing that stronger meds would knock her unconscious and make her an even greater burden on the team.

"We're wasting time," Veta said, speaking to all three of the young Spartans. "We need to be moving."

"No can do, Mom," Mark replied, speaking from the nearby darkness. "Those aren't the orders."

"Stop calling me that." Veta wasn't quite sure why the entire trio had started to call her by the nickname, but she didn't like it. She already felt certain sympathy for the young Spartans because of how their childhoods had been sacrificed to make them what they were, and she didn't want to develop any emotional connections that might affect her judgment. "I'm not your mother."

"Then stop acting like it," Mark replied. "The lieutenant knows what he's doing."

"I have no doubt. But moving Olivia is going to be a slow process. It could take a day and a half to carry her out of here." Veta looked over and caught Ash's eye, then held his gaze. "The lieutenant won't have any trouble catching up, and starting out now could make a difference."

Veta didn't need to say between what. She saw Ash's eyes soften, and he turned to look in Mark's direction. When Mark did not respond immediately, Veta knew she was starting to win the pair over.

Then Olivia said, "The lieutenant can order us to our death at any time, and we'll go. What makes you think we'll ignore his orders just because of my legs?"

"Common sense. I'm betting you have some."

Veta was about to press her case when a chime sounded from the interior of Ash's helmet, which was still sitting on the cavern floor, providing the light by which they were watching over Olivia. Immediately, Ash pulled a small hypo from a pouch on his equipment belt, then opened a concealed tab in his skinsuit and pressed the hypo tip against the flesh of his inner thigh. Veta heard the hiss of an automatic injection, then Ash sealed the tab and secured the empty hypo in another belt pouch.

A similar hiss sounded from Mark's position, and then Olivia pointed toward Ash's waist.

"Ash, I lost my gear belt," she said. "Can you—"

Ash was already reaching for his own belt. "Sure, 'Livi." He opened the pouch again and removed another hypo. "You want me to do it?"

"Hold on." Veta reached across Olivia's prone figure and grabbed his wrist. "What is that?"

"Classified," Mark said from his spot in the darkness.

"Then Ash isn't giving it to her," Veta said. "In Olivia's condition, a combat stimulant could send her into—"

"It's not a stimulant," Ash said. "And she needs to take it . . . *now*."

Veta shook her head. "Not until I know what it is."

Ash glared at her and continued to hold the hypo, and for a moment Veta thought he would simply push her away and make the injection. But when she refused to back down, Ash let his breath out and glanced into the darkness.

"You're in charge, Mark."

A soft rustle sounded over TEAMCOM as Mark sighed inside his helmet. "Yeah." He was silent for a moment, then he spoke to Veta. "You know we're not ordinary, right? I mean, physically?"

"That's hard to miss," Veta replied. "And Spartan augmentations aren't quite the secret that the Office of Naval Intelligence thinks they are."

"Good," Mark said. "Then you'll understand. We need the shots to stay, uh, stable."

"Stable how?" Veta asked.

It seemed pretty obvious that ONI was giving these kids massive amounts of steroids and hormones, but their doses would not be interchangeable. They would be tailored to the individual, and there was no way that a steroid cocktail designed for Ash would work for Olivia.

Then Veta remembered what the Spartans could do and whom they worked for, and she realized she was missing the point. ONI had made these kids into attack dogs—and an attack dog you didn't control was as dangerous to you as the enemy.

"So *that's* why you won't leave without Fred," she said. "ONI has you on a leash."

Ash looked confused. "A leash?"

"Addiction." Veta nodded at the hypo in Ash's hand. "What is that? Xenothook? Kastal?"

Ash scowled. "Do we *look* like zoneouts?" he demanded. "It's not a drug—not like that, anyway."

"It's medicine," Mark said. "It helps us . . . control ourselves."

Veta rolled her eyes. "It helps *someone* control you."

"No, that's called discipline," Ash said. "It's been drilled into us since we were six." He wiggled the wrist that Veta still held, waving the hypo back and forth. "This just keeps us even— straight in our heads."

Veta released Ash's wrist. "I see." It sounded like they were talking about some kind of antipsychotic drug, and—recalling the way Olivia had attacked the Sentinel after her injury—Veta was starting to see how denying it to the girl might be a bad idea. "And if you don't get your injections, you . . . what? Start hearing voices? Go berserk?"

"Something like that." Ash pressed the hypo to Olivia's hip and completed the injection. "Except we don't *always* hear voices."

"Or see flying dinosaurs," Mark added. "That only happens sometimes."

"But we can usually . . . read thoughts," Olivia said. "I kind of like that, especially when there are civilians around, thinking about sex and stuff."

"Very funny," Veta said. Under different circumstances, she might have enjoyed the teasing and the way these three played off each other. But the injections had her thinking about her suspect pool again, wondering what else Fred hadn't told her. "And these injections are something every Spartan needs?"

Ash's eyes immediately grew wary, and he hesitated.

"Come on," Veta said. "I already know most of it."

When Ash spoke, his voice had grown more reserved. "No, ma'am, only Gamma," he said. "Only us."

"Gamma?"

"From Gamma Company," Olivia explained. "On Blue Team, that's just Ash, Mark, and me."

"So it's just *us* you need to worry about," Mark said. "Lucy and Tom don't have the same augmentations, so they never go crazy like we do."

"What about Fred, Linda, and Kelly?" Veta asked, her tone all business. She had not intended to turn the exchange into an interrogation, but now that it had, she was going to control it. "You should know that, with their Mjolnir armor, the Spartan-IIs are still my primary suspects."

"You don't think one of *us* could tear the arm off some civilian?" Mark sounded even more resentful than before. "After you saw what Olivia just did?"

Veta turned toward Mark's voice. "I've seen enough down here to know what you're capable of, Mark."

She left it at that, and they fell into an uncomfortable silence. It was natural enough for a suspect, especially a young one, to be bitter. But the condescension in Mark's tone was raising alarm bells in Veta's mind. Most serial killers believed themselves to be more cunning than the investigators hunting them, and Mark was either daring Veta to accuse him or trying to draw attention away from someone else. Either way, he clearly believed he could manipulate her, and the simple fact that he was trying suggested there was something to hide.

Veta spent the next few minutes pondering the situation, reviewing her suspect list and comparing it to the scant evidence at her disposal. When she had last been on the surface, her team had still been working to learn more about the victims and establish a timeline for the first nine killings. So—to her frustration—all she really knew about those murders was that they had been committed by someone strong enough to dismember a body.

At the time, she had excluded Mark and the rest of the Spartan-IIIs because their SPI armor didn't multiply their strength the same way Mjolnir armor did. But after seeing Olivia take down that Sentinel bare-handed and with two broken legs—and now learning of Gamma Company's destabilizing augmentations—she was reconsidering her decision. In fact, she was placing the trio from Gamma Company at the top of her suspect list—especially Mark.

Veta was just turning her thoughts to the peculiarities of Crime Scene India—its location and the lack of tracks near the body—when she saw Ash grab his battle rifle. Olivia was already sitting up and reaching for the M7 Veta had left on floor. Fearing the worst, Veta put a knee on the M7 and reached for her sidearm.

"Stand down," Mark said. "It's just a Huragok."

Veta had no idea what that was, but at the moment, she was more worried about her companions than anything else in the cave. Even when Ash immediately relaxed, she kept her knee on the barrel of the M7 and drew her SAS-10.

Olivia stared at Veta's knee for a moment, then gave a weak smirk. "You worry too much, Mom." She lay back down. "We're not the monsters you think."

"Just being careful," Veta said, picking up the M7. "And I don't think you guys are the monsters."

She holstered her sidearm and turned to look in the same direction Ash was. At first, she saw only darkness. Then Ash reached over and gently pushed the barrel of the M7 toward the ground.

What looked vaguely like a leathery green jellyfish floated into view and hovered at the edge of the light.

"Don't worry," Ash said. "These things aren't dangerous."

Veta kept the barrel of her submachine gun pointed at the floor, but she was not about to put it down. "How do you know?"

"We've run into them before," Mark said. He backed into the light, his battle rifle secured to the mount on his armor, and turned his faceplate toward Veta. "The Huragok aren't monsters, either."

"The Covenant used them as engineering slaves," Ash explained. "But the Huragok don't take sides. They just like fixing stuff."

"So the *Covenant* is here?" Veta gasped.

Ash and Mark glanced at each other, then Mark said, "No. The Covenant proper doesn't really exist anymore. And not all Huragok belonged to the Covenant. This one probably came up from . . . below."

"Go ahead and say it," Veta said. "It's pretty obvious you've been looking for a Forerunner base."

"Then there's no need to say it." Mark pointed at her M7. "Put your weapon down. You're making the Huragok nervous."

"And that matters because . . . ?"

"Because we have standing orders to capture every Huragok we encounter," Ash explained. "And it won't come with us peacefully if you keep making it nervous."

Knowing better than to argue the niceties of sovereign ownership of planetary resources, Veta merely shrugged and placed her weapon on the cavern floor. The Huragok immediately floated forward, revealing a lumpy, almost dome-like body with a handful of tentacles and a small, elongated head on a short neck stalk.

As it passed Veta, it swung its head in her direction and regarded her briefly, then drifted over to Olivia and began to hover above her. Veta started to step over to push it away, but Ash waved her off.

Olivia raised her head and studied the Huragok for a moment, then said, "Sorry, fella. No machinery here. I'm pure girl, flesh and blood."

The Huragok dropped to within twenty centimeters of her and allowed its tentacles to trail over her damaged legs. At once, the pain drained from Olivia's face, and the swelling began to subside.

Olivia's eyes widened in surprise, and she turned to Mark. "Do . . . they work on *people*?"

"Not that I've heard of." Mark spread his hands in a gesture of confusion. "But I've never heard of one that was green and didn't glow, either. Maybe this is a different model."

As Mark spoke, the tips of the Huragok's tentacles seemed to melt through Olivia's flesh, and Veta began to see little wormlike ridges writhing beneath the girl's skin.

"Olivia?" Veta felt her hand hanging above her sidearm, and she had to fight every instinct in her body to keep from drawing the weapon. "How are you—"

"I'm okay," Olivia interrupted. "I think . . . I think it's repairing me."

0305 hours, July 4, 2553 (military calendar)
Forerunner Support Installation, 1600 Meters belowground,
Montero Cave System

Fred stood on the brink of creation, watching universes wink into being, then swell into silvery eggs of brilliance and implode into nothing. He saw galaxies spin up from emptiness and send their arms whirling off across the void, saw their cores collapse into holes that were deeper and darker and hotter than any hell that man had ever imagined. He saw the birth of all things and the end of everything, saw the wave of eternity roll across a universe of universes and swallow them all in the blink of an eye.

And still Fred stood there, on the brink of annihilation, staring down into a hole so deep it had punched through existence itself. He could not recall how long he had been there, what had come before and what was to come next. He simply *was,* a man who had inadvertently stepped to the edge of time and space and found himself bound by a mystery too vast and bright and endless for him to comprehend, too filled with paradox and potential for *any* human mind to grasp.

"*Lieutenant?*" The voice came to Fred deep inside his mind, and for a time he wondered if it belonged to the universal creator in which he had never believed, if he had somehow passed from the world of the living into the realm of the once-living and not even noticed. "*Lieutenant, do you read me?*"

"Who's asking?"

Fred cocked his head, in the process turning his faceplate away from the bottomless hole and all its cosmogenic mystery, and he found himself suddenly back in time and space, the beam of his helmet lamp illuminating a distant circle of hangar wall. He checked his HUD and saw that only ten minutes had passed since he had left Olivia with Lopis and the rest of the detail. Mark-G313's status light was illuminated, indicating that he was the one on the other end of the transmission.

"Didn't I tell you to give me two hours?"

"Yes, sir, you did," Mark answered. "And it's been two and a quarter."

Fred checked his chronometer again. Still ten minutes. "You're sure?"

"Lieutenant, are you all right?"

"I'm fine." Fred checked his motion tracker and found Mark about a hundred meters behind him, using line-of-sight transmission from the top of the block pile. "I'll tell you when I'm not."

"Very well, sir," Mark replied. "But you've still been gone two hours and, well, *sixteen* minutes now. I thought I should attempt contact before evacuating."

"Good thought." Fred checked his chronometer again and saw that it now indicated that he had been gone *eleven* minutes—a discrepancy of two hours and five minutes. He didn't like that. Not at all. "How are Olivia and Ash doing?"

"Very well," Mark reported. "In fact, Ash is a hundred percent, and Olivia is stable enough to—"

"You can give me the details in a minute," Fred interrupted.

Right now, he needed to figure out what had happened during those two lost hours, and that meant starting with an overview of the situation. He backed away from the hole, being careful not to glance into it again, and turned away. Whatever was down there, he would have to let the scientists figure it out.

"Any sign of the ancilla?"

"Negative," Mark said. "But there's something else. You'll want to see it."

"I hope you don't expect me to play guessing games," Fred said. "Spill it, soldier."

"We've found some kind of Huragok," Mark said. "Actually, it found us."

"A Huragok?" Fred started across the hangar floor toward Mark. "Not exactly what we came for, but I'll take it."

They had just discovered a Forerunner base, so Fred wasn't surprised to hear about the Huragok. Considering the devastation in the hangar, however, he was surprised to learn that the thing was up in the silo with his team, instead of down here trying to fix things. It just wasn't in a Huragok's nature to ignore something in need of repair.

Unless, of course, the ancilla had another trick up its sleeve.

Fred began to move double quick at that thought. "Tell me more about this Huragok."

"That's what I was trying to explain," Mark said. "It's not an Engineer. I think it might be some kind of medic."

"A medic Huragok?" Fred had never heard of such a thing. "What makes you say that?"

"It's green, a bit smaller, has some extra tentacles, and doesn't have much bioluminescence," Mark said. "But mostly . . . it's because it fixed up Ash and Olivia."

"Fixed up how?"

"I don't know," Mark said. "It just slipped a few tentacles through their skin and did it. Ash said he feels as good as ever, but when Olivia tried to stand up, the Huragok pushed her back down and sat on her. We're assuming she still needs some time to mend."

"Probably a good assumption." Fred began to relax a little. Had the Huragok been outfitted with an explosive vest, as some in the field had been, it would have certainly detonated by this point. Besides, that had been a Covenant tactic, and whatever this place was, it had nothing to do with the Covenant. "Where's the Huragok now?"

"Ash tied a utility cord around its neck stalk," Mark reported. "But the thing has been leading *him* around. I think it's trying to teach Ash to heel."

Fred ignored the humor and stopped at the base of the block pile, running his gaze around the hangar, using all imaging systems to make another record of what he saw. Unfortunately, he didn't think any of it would be much help in locating the ancilla.

All that remained of the hangar equipment was a shadowy mural of silhouettes that had been burned into the walls and floor when the Forerunner base was destroyed.

It stood to reason that other sections of the base were in better shape, since the Huragok, a bunch of Sentinels, and presumably the ancilla had all survived the mysterious conflagration. But, after losing two hours—quite literally *losing* them—Fred was starting to doubt the wisdom of continuing the exploration all by himself. He would not capture the ancilla by vanishing into the depths of the base forever, and he had enough experience to know that such things could happen when you began to poke around Forerunner installations alone.

"Mark, what's the situation up there?" he asked. "Can Ash keep an eye on things while you and I reconnoiter the rest of the base?"

Mark hesitated a moment, then answered, "It might be better if Ash and the others started out on their own."

"I thought you said everyone was in good condition."

"I did," Mark replied. "But Olivia's gear belt was lost in the rockslide."

"And?"

"And her Smoothers were in it," Mark explained. *Smoothers* was the Gamma trio's nickname for the cocktail of antipsychotic meds that kept their altered brain chemistry in check. "We're down to just five doses."

"Each or total?" Fred asked.

"Sorry, Lieutenant," Mark said. "That's *total*. I can keep one and stay, but I may come apart on you on the way out."

That would keep Ash and Olivia in meds for a day, and it would be another half day before they began to unravel. In theory, that would be about four hours longer than they needed to reach the surface again. But if Lopis was not up to hauling Olivia, or if the Huragok slowed them down, or if the ancilla caused more trouble, then the special inspector would be trapped alone with a pair of unbalanced Spartan-IIIs. And the result would not be pretty.

In fact, the result would probably start a war.

"Tell Ash to make ready." Fred shut down his recording systems and started to climb. "We've done what we can here for now. It's time to go get Commander Nelson and show him what we've found."

CHAPTER 11

0306 hours, July 4, 2553 (military calendar)
Uncharted Cave Entrance, 1,200 meters from Wendosa Village,
Montero Jungle
Campos Wilderness District, Planet Gao, Cordoba System

The cave entrance lay thirty meters below, a slender crescent of darkness barely visible through the moonlit fronds of the rugged Montero Jungle. Even from atop the narrow ridge, it reeked of guano and mildew and the sour mud of an alien world, and Castor could not imagine squeezing his large body into such a narrow, foul-smelling pit. But secrecy was all. If he failed to take the infidels by surprise, he would not destroy them. And if he failed to destroy them, he would never save the Oracle from their desecration.

Castor turned to his guide, a skinny Gao human in black coveralls, and asked quietly, "The opening—it is wider than it looks?"

"Not so much." An olive-skinned woman who carried a short-barreled shotgun slung across her back, Petora Zoyas had a small, leathery face with a broad mouth and bright blue eyes. "But it's a meter across in most places. Unless your warriors have deeper chests than that, they'll fit."

Though Castor found the assurance hard to believe, he was inclined to trust Zoyas's judgment. A local cave guide and a former insurrectionist, she had already proven herself a capable operator. When a Gao customs corvette "forced" Castor's *One Light* to land at the Campos Impound Hangar for a phony inspection, she had been waiting inside to brief him on the situation in the Montero region. She had suggested that instead of launching their own search for the Oracle, it might be more effective to sneak into the cave system and find the UNSC trail. After that, it would be a simple matter to track down the enemy and recover the Oracle through an ambush.

Once Castor had agreed to the approach, Zoyas had proposed entering the caverns near the village of Wendosa. The location was thirty kilometers from the enemy headquarters at the Montero Vitality Center. But the UNSC had posted an entire combat company in the village, presumably to guard a cave entrance that had been seeing a lot of Spartan traffic recently. Zoyas had not needed to point out the obvious conclusion—the UNSC was protecting Wendosa because the caverns beneath it led to the Oracle.

Castor had seen the wisdom of Zoyas's advice at once. They had loaded his attack force onto a small fleet of freight transports she had waiting, then departed on a staggered schedule, each vehicle taking a different route to avoid drawing attention. Now, just a day and a half after meeting Arlo Casille aboard the *Esmeralda,* Castor was deep in the Montero jungle, less than two kilometers from Wendosa village.

With the enemy so close, Castor could not help worrying. The smallest mistake would alert the marines to his presence, and his holy mission would fail even before the rest of his transports had arrived.

Castor glanced back along the ridge. The fifty warriors who

had arrived on the first transport were still approaching along its crooked crest, carefully picking their way through a thick, pathless jungle. Despite their best efforts, the thirty Jiralhanae at the head of the column were thudding and huffing, and Castor could only hope their muted rumble would be masked by the breeze rustling through the jungle canopy.

Behind the Jiralhanae, there would be ten long-beaked Kig-Yar skirmishers and ten human infiltrators—none of whom Castor could see and none of whom he trusted. Both groups had sworn devotion to the Keepers of the One Freedom, but the humans were slow to tithe, and the Kig-Yar's corvine temperament often ran more toward looting infidel vessels than spreading the Truth of the Great Journey.

"Your Jiralhanae aren't exactly stealthy, are they?" Reza Linberk remarked. She was standing next to Castor on the side opposite Zoyas. "It might be smart to have the Kig-Yar scout ahead, in case there are any UNSC sentries this far out."

"There aren't," Zoyas said.

"You can't know that," Reza Linberk said, leaning past Castor. She had insisted on joining the operation as an observer for Peter Moritz, and since Venezia provided the Keepers with both weapons and a safe haven, it had been necessary to agree. "The UNSC maintains a five-kilometer foot-patrol radius."

"True, but it also monitors motion sensors out to ten kilometers." Zoyas glanced at the rugged tacpad strapped to her wrist, then added, "An hour ago, the Committee to Preserve Gao Independence began to protest the UNSC occupation by triggering and disabling hundreds of those devices—which means the Wendosa foot patrols will be busy responding to an endless series of false alarms."

Linberk scowled. "Then the entire company is already on alert," she said. "They'll be expecting an attack."

"Exactly." Zoyas smiled. "And what will they do next? They'll tighten their cordon and pull their sentries back to five hundred meters . . . and *we* will enter the cave system unnoticed."

Castor watched for Linberk's reaction. He knew from dealing with her on Venezia that she was cunning for a human. If there was a weakness in Zoyas's plan he had not thought of, Linberk would see it.

When her expression remained thoughtful, Castor asked, "It is a good plan, yes?"

"Maybe." Linberk continued to study Zoyas. "That would depend on whether we've tripped any motion sensors ourselves."

"We haven't," Zoyas said. "This entrance is seldom used and known only to a few. That's why there is no footpath to it."

"Still, you can't be sure—"

"I can," Zoyas said. "The Committee tested the route yesterday, and we've kept it under watch since then."

Linberk raised an eyebrow almost imperceptibly, then cast a pointed glance toward the dark crescent below.

"So, it appears our sole concern is the entrance," she said. "You've said it's a meter across in 'most places.' But when you're inside a cave, only small places matter. If you get stuck at a choke point, it makes no difference what lies beyond."

"You've spent some time in caves," Zoyas said. "But you're not a guide. You don't know *this* cave."

"I don't need to know *this* cave to know about choke points," Linberk replied. "It's common sense."

"Ah, common sense."

Zoyas nodded sagely and slowly turned in a circle, surveying the pocked terrain around them. An endless series of steep-walled basins separated by winding ridges and jagged limestone cones, it lay beneath a jungle of club mosses, tree ferns, and cycads so thick it was impossible to see the ground next to one's boots. Castor knew from experience that it was all too easy to step through a tangle of green and find one's foot hovering above a thirty-meter drop.

Zoyas used her long jungle knife—she called it a *panga*—to push aside a wall of fronds, and Castor found himself looking across a lush valley of moonlit tree ferns. Atop the opposite ridge stood a row of pale buildings, their steeply pitched roofs silhouetted against the darkness. The village was much closer than Castor had expected, somewhere between one and one-and-a-half kilometers distant.

"There is Wendosa," Zoyas said, addressing Linberk more than Castor. "The village is held by Charlie Company: a hundred and fifty heavy infantry marines with all of their toys: HMGs, missile pods, nonlinear lasers, rocket and grenade launchers. The sole road into the village is blocked by a pair of Warthogs with M41 antiaircraft guns, and they allow only UNSC personnel to pass. Every ground approach has been trapped and fortified, and the other entrances to this part of the cavern all lie on footpaths strung with UNSC motion sensors. So, what does *your* common sense suggest? A frontal assault?"

Castor pushed Zoyas's arm down, allowing the fronds to swing back into place and keep them hidden from any sentries from the village who happened to be looking in their direction.

"What Reza thinks is unimportant. She is not the leader of the battle pack." Castor glanced over at Linberk, then added, "When we attack, it will be from inside the cave. The terrain gives us no other choice."

"A lack of choice is no guarantee of success," Linberk countered. "If you let the strike force get cornered down there—"

"I have led battle packs before," Castor said, cutting off the debate. "I will not get us cornered."

He looked over Linberk's head to his second-in-command, a grizzled old Jiralhanae wearing the blue-and-gold armor of the Keepers of the One Freedom. Standing half a head taller than Castor himself, Orsun was as thick across the chest as any of the pack's captains. Only a handful of warriors were larger, so it seemed safe to assume that if Orsun could squeeze through a choke point, then most of the battle pack could follow.

"Orsun, take the vanguard. Secure our battle routes." Castor's translation disk automatically repeated the phrase for the two humans, but he did not bother to deactivate it. He wanted the women to understand his orders. "But our first purpose is to save the Oracle. So, you must find and hold the route the Spartans have taken."

"As it is spoken, it shall be done," Orsun replied, speaking in their native language. He glowered in Zoyas's direction. "And the guide?"

"She is yours to protect." As Castor spoke, he took Zoyas by the arm, then swung her past Linberk and placed her in front of Orsun. "She will advise you, but your decisions are your own."

Orsun touched his fist to his chest. "I am graced by your trust, Dokab." He waited until Castor had returned the salute, then activated his own translation disk and turned to Zoyas. "You may lead the way."

"In a moment," Zoyas said, turning back to Castor. "The vanguard will need to secure the escape route, too."

"Escape route?" Castor asked. "We will leave through Wendosa. That is what we said."

"If we *take* Wendosa," Zoyas said. "But if things go against us, we'll need a backup plan."

"What things?" This was the first Castor had heard of any doubts Zoyas might have. "There is something you failed to tell me?"

"Only the future," Zoyas replied quickly. "And that, no one can predict. That's why we need to secure our escape route."

Castor remained suspicious. "We are not here to escape."

Zoyas scowled and started to argue, but Linberk touched her arm. "Jiralhanae don't plan for defeat," Linberk said. "They win or die."

Castor nodded. "It is so."

"Well, I'm no Jiralhanae," Zoyas said. "I'm a saboteur and a rebel, and the only reason I'm still breathing is because I *always* plan for the unexpected. The escape route will be secured."

"Where exactly is this escape route?" Linberk demanded. "And why is now the first we're hearing about it?"

"It is only a contingency plan," Zoyas said evenly. "I was going to mention it later, when I could point the way."

She held Linberk's gaze. The pair continued to stare into each other's eyes so long that Castor half-expected a challenge fight, and the contest did much to explain a planning lapse that could not have been accidental. The Keepers' allies on Gao and Venezia had gone to great lengths to sneak the battle pack into the caverns and make certain it was well supplied. Zoyas had even promised to support Castor's attack by having the Committee to Preserve Gao Independence stage a guerrilla strike at the Vitality Center. But no mention had been made of how the survivors would depart Gao with the Oracle.

Now, as Castor watched the silent struggle over whether to secure Zoyas's "escape route," he knew that each woman's com-

mander had a different plan for claiming the Oracle after he recovered it. Zoyas and Casille would have a force waiting at the
"escape route," while Moritz and Linberk probably had a team already hiding near Wendosa. But they were *all* dim stars compared
to Castor, because the Keepers of the One Freedom were legion.
When Arlo Casille sent Gao's Wyverns to steal the prize, one of
those vessels would be crewed by human Keepers.

And by the time Casille realized he was not as sly as he thought,
Castor and the Oracle would be safely off planet.

Castor turned to Zoyas. "Orsun will send a trio of warriors to
secure the escape route." He turned to Linberk. "That does not
mean it will be used."

"Of course it won't." Linberk's gaze shifted to Castor. "The
Jiralhanae are not cowards."

Castor nodded to Orsun, and the battle captain motioned for
Zoyas to lead the way. This time, she obeyed, and a few minutes
later they were in the bottom of the basin, hooking the descent
cable to a pair of metal eyebolts that had been set into the stone
adjacent to the cave entrance. The bolts were thick, but they were
also old and pitted with corrosion. Castor wondered whether they
would be strong enough to support his Jiralhanae.

The answer came less than a minute later, when Orsun clipped
into the cable and squeezed into the crescent-shaped entrance behind Zoyas. He filled the pit even more completely than Castor
had expected, with his chest and back armor scraping against opposite walls of the crevice. It seemed to take forever before his
helmet vanished belowground, and Castor began to worry that
Linberk's fears about choke points would prove warranted.

At last, the cable went taut as Orsun cleared the opening and
began rappelling down the shaft. A minute later, the cable went
slack again, indicating that he had reached the cave floor. The next

Jiralhanae clipped into the line and activated his forearm lamp. Smaller than Orsun, he descended through the squeeze almost effortlessly and was soon dropping into darkness.

Castor spent the next few hours carefully sizing up each Jiralhanae as he ascended the ridge. About one in ten warriors looked too large to fit through the entrance shaft. These he pulled aside and assigned to the rear guard, equipping them with the battle pack's heavy weapons and instructing them to establish a defensive perimeter around the entrance. Among the weapons were a pair of special gifts from Arlo Casille: a dozen crates of shoulder-launched ground-to-air missiles and a battery of field mortars. Because both weapon systems were manufactured by Gao's Sevine Arms and most effectively used by humans, Castor also attached two bands of human Keepers to serve with the rear guard. If the battle grew fierce, he knew the humans would lose courage and try to flee. But he believed their Jiralhanae companions would intimidate them into staying, at least until the artillery was no longer useful.

The jungle was just beginning to glow green with dawn light when the final band of warriors appeared on the ridge, following what by now had become a well-trodden path. Knowing better than to think the infidel patrols would miss the trail—or fail to understand its significance—Castor started up the ridge toward the rear guard's command post.

Of course, Linberk followed close on Castor's heels—alert, no doubt, for anything that might interfere with her plan to take the Oracle from him. He pretended to welcome her company, pulling fronds aside for her and steadying her where the jungle mud grew slick.

Tucked behind a limestone outcropping, the command post was little more than a flat area with hard cover and a good view.

The captain of the rear guard—a bald-shaved Jiralhanae named Saturnus—was sitting behind two boulders, peering through a tripod-mounted observation monocular toward Wendosa.

When he heard Castor and Linberk approaching, Saturnus rose and touched his fist to his chest. Castor returned the salute, then deactivated his translation disk and spoke in a soft whisper. "Report."

"No activity, Dokab," Saturnus replied. "The infidels are still cowering in the village, awaiting an attack."

"That will change as the day passes," Castor said. He knew the Gao loyalists would not be able to divert the attention of Charlie Company much longer. "Send a work band to mask and trap the trail we made through the jungle. Have another remove the eyebolts from the cave entrance and set explosives. If it grows necessary to detonate the charges, it would be a blessing to choke the hole with rubble."

"As it is spoken, it shall be done."

Saturnus did not touch his fist to his chest, an omission that let Castor know his captain desired clarification.

"Speak."

"Dokab, if we cannot follow you into the cavern—"

"All survivors will rendezvous there, in Wendosa," Castor said, pointing toward the village. "You will know when to come."

Saturnus placed his fist over his heart. "You grace me with your trust, Dokab."

As Castor turned to depart, Linberk asked, "What was that about?"

Castor reactivated his translation disk. "Anticipating the enemy," he said. "That is what good commanders do."

"So why deactivate your translation disk?" she asked. "This is no time for us to start keeping secrets from each other."

As Linberk spoke, a distant whine echoed across the jungle. For an instant, it sounded like the cry of some alien animal greeting the dawn—but when it continued to rise in pitch and was joined by three more whines, Castor knew he was hearing something else.

It was the activation of an auxiliary power unit, building pressure to cold-start a jet engine.

"Castor, I asked—"

"Silence!" Castor spun around and started back toward Saturnus, who was again sitting behind his observation monocular. "Report."

"It sounds like they are engaging a Pelican," Saturnus said, yielding the observation monocular. "But the craft cannot be seen."

Castor took the captain's place and peered into the large, circular face of the monocular's magnification crystal. With dawn well under way, Wendosa was aglow with a rosy gold light. Saturnus's command post was slightly higher than the broad ridge where Wendosa was perched, so Castor could see that the village was about three times as long as it was wide. There were too many tall buildings for a clear view of the street layout, but in places he could make out a braided labyrinth of cobblestone lanes running between the red tile roofs and white stucco walls of its buildings. There were no soldiers moving along the near edge of the village, but he could see weapon muzzles protruding from the dark squares of a few windows.

Castor swung the monocular to the left, focusing on the far end of the village, and saw a large dust cloud rising from behind a line of tall buildings. It was impossible to see over the roofs of the structures from his angle, but a dozen UNSC soldiers wearing ear protection and tool belts stood in the adjacent lanes, looking into what Castor assumed to be the village's entrance plaza.

As Castor watched, a line of troops walked into view and continued down the lane toward the plaza. They were covered in mud from head to foot, so dirty it was impossible to tell their unit or designation. But most were equipped with battle rifles and standard UNSC-marine light armor, and they were moving with the weary briskness of exhausted soldiers on their way to an evacuation point.

Castor hoped for a moment that he was just watching a standard rotation, one spent UNSC search team being returned to base before a fresh one arrived. But he could not find any sign of a replacement team on the ground, or any officer waiting to be briefed on the situation before taking over.

Then four large figures marched into view. The first and last wore the distinctive Mjolnir armor of the demon Spartans, and they carried their weapons ready to fire—even in the heart of a village under complete UNSC control. The middle pair wore the lighter infiltration armor that many Spartans had sported toward the end of the war. Between them, they carried a long black bag that concealed its contents.

It was impossible to know what the bag contained. Castor suspected they wanted it to appear they were carrying a body, but it did not require four Spartans to deliver a corpse. And the team was clearly returning from a long trip into the caverns.

Castor had thoughts about the bag—and he could not afford to take the chance that he was wrong. If the infidels boarded a Pelican with the Oracle in their possession, they would be out of Gao's atmosphere before Castor could stop them—and halfway to a rendezvous with the UNSC task force before he could alert Casille.

Castor turned to Saturnus. "Attack with everything," he said. "Immediately. Concentrate all fire on the plaza at the village entrance. That Pelican must not depart."

Saturnus's eyes grew wide, but he responded instantly, simultaneously acknowledging the command by touching his fist to his chest and issuing orders over the rear guard's battlenet.

"You're attacking the village?" Linberk's tone was disbelieving. "*Now?*"

The answer to Linberk's question came in the form of forty particle beams flashing out of the jungle to both sides of the command post. Castor peered into the observation monocular and was happy to see half a dozen UNSC soldiers lying dead in the streets surrounding the plaza—and the rest scrambling for cover. A trio of shoulder-launched missiles streaked into view and detonated against a pair of tall buildings, showering the lanes below with rubble and flame.

Then the sound of crumping mortars began to rumble up from slope below Castor. A few moments later, he saw the first rounds fall in a broad ring around the plaza, punching through roofs and blowing out walls. Billowing curtains of smoke and dust began to roll through the streets, quickly growing so thick that it was impossible to see anything at all. Castor stepped away from the monocular and watched the sky above the village with his naked eye, searching for any sign of a Pelican rising through the smoke.

Linberk quickly took his place behind the monocular. "What made you attack now?" She began to swivel the instrument around on its tripod. "I can't see anything but—"

Both ends of the monocular erupted in a spray of crystal shards, and Linberk landed a meter away, her arms flung wide in the undergrowth and a red mess where her face had been a moment before. The sound of the fatal sniper shot did not arrive until a heartbeat later, the ringing crack of a supersonic round followed by the distant pop of the propellant charge that had sent it hurling across the distance. Castor dropped behind the outcropping, glancing at the human corpse and wondering how Peter Moritz would take the loss of his most trusted deputy.

Then the rest of the UNSC snipers opened fire.

Somewhere in the jungle below, a wounded Jiralhanae roared in anguish. Beam rifles flashed in reply, and the Keeper mortars began a slow, steady thumping that suggested the crews were "walking" their rounds forward in a carefully planned grid pattern. And still, Castor saw no sign of a Pelican rising into the sky.

Daring to hope that the craft had been destroyed in the first wave of strikes, Castor turned once more to Saturnus.

"Have our loyal humans hold their missiles for flying craft," he said. "And press the attack if you must. Keep the infidels pinned down in the village. As soon as we are able, the battle pack will spill out of the Wendosa entrance and crush them from behind."

"As it is spoken, it shall be done." Saturnus touched his fist to his chest, then added, "No matter the cost."

CHAPTER 12

Floating above the anteroom's polished swirlstone floor, the military map of the Montero cave system was a hopeless holographic tangle. Multicolored lines representing passages of various sizes and conditions snaked around each other with no discernible logic, and huge chunks of the array remained completely unmapped and blank. Still, Murtag Nelson could feel a glimmer of insight tickling at the back of his mind, some subtle connection that his unconscious had made and not yet deigned to share. There was something there, a pattern that didn't look like a pattern, an underlying structure he had yet to identify.

Murtag retreated to one of the plush brown sofas that sat along the anteroom's looming glass walls. Like all of the furniture in Montero Vitality Clinic's executive office suite, the lavish piece reflected the extravagant tastes of a designer unbridled by considerations of cost. Murtag dropped into it lengthwise, resting his head on the sofa's well-padded arm and his dirty boots on a soft leather cushion.

For the second time in the last ten minutes, Murtag's aide-de-camp stepped to his side and tried to interrupt.

"Commander Nelson, if you have a few moments, there are a few things I need to bring to your attention." A young ONI captain in a pressed khaki BDU, Vartan Gysirian was a blond, squarely built man who looked out of uniform unless he was wearing a communications headset and carrying a datapad. "The protestors around Wendosa spent the night testing Charlie Company's motion sensors, and—"

"*Thinking!*" Murtag snapped. Terrified that the intrusion would cost him the insight working its way to the surface of his mind, he pointed Gysirian toward an overstuffed chair on the far side of the room. "Sit."

Gysirian stood his ground. "My apologies, Commander, but you really should—"

"Sit *now,* Captain," Murtag ordered. "And be quiet. Be *very* quiet."

Gysirian's ivory complexion grew even paler, then he pressed a finger to his headset's earbud and retreated to the chair.

Murtag exhaled three times, trying to clear his mind, then turned his attention back to the holograph. "Wendell, give me a top-down view."

The holograph tipped toward Murtag, presenting a wide ring of densely snarled passages. Since the Gaos had long since mapped the cave system near the surface, the only blank area was a circle in the middle, where the terrain fell below mapping level. Still, even the local guides had never been able to find any entrances from the interior of the blank area, and that seemed odd.

Murtag had contemplated this mystery area before and remarked that it made the cave system look like a bird's nest. But he realized now that the analogy had been misleading him. Had the system truly resembled a nest, there would have been a floor to it, an area at the bottom of the map where the cave passages turned inward. Instead, the blank area seemed to extend downward forever.

The tickle in the back of his mind began to grow stronger.

"Very good, Wendell," he said. "Now, overlay a transparent image of the surface terrain—an actual reconnaissance photo, if you have one that covers the area."

"Of course I have one." Wendell's voice issued from one of the anteroom's ceiling speakers. "The operations people insisted on a complete set."

An image of the jungle appeared on top of the cave maps. For the most part, it all looked the same—a mottled green blanket laced with gray rivers and yellow gravel roads, flecked here and there by the red-roofed blemishes of a village or minor spa. But in the center of the image, directly over the blank area, sat a circular, cliff-walled basin. According to the map, the locals called it the Well of Echoes.

The tickle in the back of Murtag's mind swelled into a full vibration.

Recalling that the Well of Echoes was only five kilometers from the Montero Vitality Center, Murtag realized it might actually be visible from his current location on the main building's topmost floor. He leaped off the couch, then began to circle the anteroom and peer out through the glass walls. Down in the Vitality Center's well-tended courtyards, a trio of ground crews were bustling about a stubby-winged Pelican and a pair of ungainly Falcons, no doubt preparing for the morning patrol.

Murtag was more interested in a pillow of fog hanging about five kilometers distant. It had been there every morning since the battalion's arrival, hovering above the Well of Echoes until the day grew warm enough to dispel it, and he had failed to understand its significance. The fog was forming as hot, humid air rose out of the basin into the cool evening atmosphere above the jungle.

Murtag turned back toward the holographic map and stared into the unmapped circle. "It's acting like a chimney."

"A chimney?" Wendell asked. "I'm afraid you're not making sense, Commander."

Murtag pointed at the circle. "We've been looking at this wrong. Give me the side view again."

The holograph reoriented itself, presenting a panel of multicolored lines so twisted and snarled that Murtag could not see into the interior of the image. He began to circle the image until he finally found the angle he wanted, a wedge of emptiness flanked by two panels of extensively mapped caverns—one directly beneath the Montero Vitality Center, and one thirty kilometers distant, beneath the village of Wendosa.

Murtag stepped back to consider the holograph from afar—and felt a thrill flutter through his stomach. When viewed as a whole, the cave system was shaped like a vase with a narrow base and a broad rim, all surrounding a hollow inner core.

"Wendell, remove all the passages larger than two meters by two meters."

About a third of the passages vanished, leaving behind a network of meandering conduits that snaked more or less upward at a gentle slope.

"There!" Murtag gasped. "I have it!"

Gysirian rose and came immediately to Murtag's side. "Sir, if you've finished thinking, we have an urgent situation in—"

"*Two minutes!*" Murtag snapped. "There is nothing that can't wait two minutes. Is that clear?"

"But sir—"

"It's a cooling array, Captain Gysirian," Murtag said, deliberately talking over him. "Do you realize how important that is?"

"A cooling array, sir?" Gysirian stared at the holograph in bewilderment—or perhaps it was frustration. Murtag had never been good at reading facial expressions. "Is that really something we need to discuss right now?"

"I think so." Murtag was so excited now that he chose to overlook the fact that Gysirian had disobeyed his order to remain seated. He began to trace individual routes from the bottom of the map toward the top. "Look at how all of these small passages wind back and forth, but continue to rise at a steady angle. They're vents, designed to give hot air time to cool as it rises."

It was Wendell who objected. "I don't see that at all, Commander. There's no evidence to support your theory."

"No?" Murtag asked. "Then reverse the filter. Show me only the passages that are consistently *larger* than two meters by two meters."

The holograph flickered as though Wendell were having trouble processing the filter request, then a much less tangled map appeared—one that showed a network of passages meandering upward in a vaguely spiral pattern, more or less evenly spaced, but at varying degrees of steepness and often dead-ending at an underground lake.

"Okay," Gysirian said. "Those are service corridors. Can we discuss the—"

"That's a premature conclusion," Wendell objected. "Our teams have mapped only twenty-one-point-two percent of the cave system, so any confirmation is quite—"

"Wait, Wendell," Murtag ordered. "How do you know?"

"Know what, Commander?"

"That we've mapped twenty-one-point-two percent," Murtag replied. "That's a *very* specific figure for a cave system that even the locals admit is ninety percent unexplored. So how can you know that we've even mapped that much of it?"

Again, the holograph flickered, and Wendell took more than a second to reply. "It's a projection," the AI said. "Based on a statistical analysis of what we've already mapped."

"Interesting," Murtag said. Had Wendell not been an AI, he might have suspected him of fabricating the answer. "We'll have to discuss your methodology later. But for now, we need to recall the Spartans. I think we can finally give them a solid objective."

Gysirian's expression grew troubled. "Sir, I'm afraid that's impossible."

Murtag frowned. "They're Spartans," he said. "Just send a runner down. They'll find *him*."

"Commander, finding them isn't the problem," Gysirian said. "We already know where the Spartans are—at least four of them."

"And?" Murtag demanded. "Spit it out, Captain."

"*That's* what I've been trying to tell you, sir. Spartans 087, 058, B091, and B292 all returned to Wendosa fifteen minutes ago. They were trying to deliver the Crime Scene India victim to a Pelican transport when they were attacked."

"Attacked by whom?" Murtag's gut knotted. If he lost four Spartans to a bunch of protestors, there wouldn't even be a court-martial. Admiral Parangosky would just have him disappeared. "How bad is it?"

"We don't know, sir," Gysirian said. "The attack is ongoing."

"Ongoing?!" Murtag boomed. "And you're just telling me about it *now*?"

"Sir, I've been *trying* to tell you about it for . . . it doesn't matter," Gysirian said. "I have your attention on the matter."

"And you're saying that a mob of Gaos has kept Charlie Company *and* four Spartans engaged for a quarter of an hour?"

"Negative," Gysirian said. "The hostiles are about twelve hundred meters from Wendosa, using beam rifles, mortars, and even a few small missiles to pound Wendosa. They took out the transport Pelican and a lot of support personnel with their first wave of attacks. Our snipers are reporting a combined enemy force of Jiralhanae, Kig-Yar, and humans."

"So we're being attacked by a force of ex-Covenant?" Murtag asked, trying to keep the anxiety out of his voice. "Is that what you're telling me?"

"It's too early to be certain," Gysirian said. "But that *is* the way it's looking. It's why I've been trying to get your attention, sir."

Murtag began to feel hollow inside. The war with the Covenant had been over for months, but he didn't doubt what he was hearing. This part of the galaxy was rife with ex-Covenant factions who were still determined to take the fight to the UNSC, and they were finding far too many human allies among the former rebels who dreamed of another Insurrection. The 717th had enough strength to hold its own against any force small enough to have gotten that close to it undetected, but if there were Jiralhanae involved, it was going to cost a lot of lives—and he had little doubt where Admiral Parangosky would lay the blame.

Remembering the aircraft he had seen preparing to launch, Murtag stepped back to the anteroom's glass wall and looked down into the courtyard. The ground crews were already moving away from the Pelican and the two Falcons, and through the cockpit canopies, he could see the pilots completing their preflight checks. The three craft would reach Wendosa in less than ten minutes.

"What about force strength?" Murtag's mind was finally shifting into military mode. He didn't have personal responsibility for combat operations, but there were a lot of logistical details that he would be expected to oversee—which was why, he supposed, Gysirian had been so determined to interrupt his breakthrough moment. "And enemy disposition?"

"Strength unknown at this point," Gysirian said. "But it may be fairly small. They seem happy to stand off and attack from the jungle, and that's not really Jiralhanae style."

"Well, that's *something*." Murtag began to hope that the attack would not be quite the disaster for his career that he had at first feared. Of course, if he recovered the ancilla, Parangosky would forgive him anything—even losing a Spartan or two. "Let's bring all support units to a combat footing and stand ready to support the fighting companies." A shrill whine rose from the courtyard as the Pelican pilot activated his auxiliary power unit and the Falcons whirled up their VTOL turbines. It was impossible to tell what the three craft might be carrying in their holds, but judging by the ANVIL II missile pods mounted beneath the Pelican's wings, their first sortie would be an attack run rather than a troop drop.

Gysirian mumbled something into his headset, then said, "Sir, Major Wingate is preparing to launch a ground support mission. He wanted you to be informed."

"Of course." Murtag nodded. Wingate was his military commander, overseeing all aspects of combat and security while the battalion was on Gao. Parangosky's orders had made it clear that Murtag was not to question his decisions, and so far the major had made a point of not giving Murtag the chance. "Tell the major we're counting on him. I won't interrupt him now, but we'll meet shortly to assess the situation."

As Gysirian relayed the message, the Pelican and Falcons were already lifting off. They immediately spun toward Wendosa—then seemed to hang there frozen as a flurry of ground-to-air missiles came streaking out of the jungle. In the next instant, the hulls of all three craft began to spray white tongues of flame.

Murtag remained at the window, watching in speechless horror as the Pelican exploded in midair, spraying shrapnel and burning fuel across a third of the Vitality Center's compound. He began to feel as though he were not quite awake, as though his breakthrough regarding the Well of Echoes and the attack on Wendosa and the missiles streaking out of the jungle had all been part of a terrible anxiety dream, that he would wake up at any moment and find himself lying in a pool of sweat-soaked sheets.

But he didn't awaken, and Murtag was still at the window two seconds later when the first Falcon dropped like a rock, crashing into the Staff Housing Complex and demolishing the dormitory where the Gao investigative team had established its morgue. The second Falcon shrugged off the attack and, smoke pouring from its side door, swung toward the source of the assault. Its chin gun began to spray cannon fire over the heads of the protestors cowering outside the main gate, then the pilot adjusted its aim and began to rip the jungle down.

Murtag was still standing at the wall, trying to comprehend the catastrophe he had just witnessed, when pieces of glass began to rain down from above.

"Sniper!" Gysirian yelled.

Of course. When one was in a combat zone and objects began to burst apart for no apparent reason, it was almost always a sniper.

Murtag was just having trouble accepting that he was actually in a combat zone—that not only was his battalion under attack, but *he* was under attack.

Murtag turned to dive to the floor, but he was a half second too slow. Gysirian hit him broadside, covering his body and driving him to the floor.

"Commander, get—"

That was as far as Gysirian made it before his blood began to pour out over Murtag.

CHAPTER 13

Fred could not see much from the rear of the line, just a halo of light reflecting off the stone around Veta Lopis's backside as she crawled up the cramped passage ahead of him. Strapped across her shoulders were the telescoping support rails of the emergency evacuation litter in which Olivia rode. The forward end of the litter was strapped to Ash's back, just above his hips, and occasionally, Fred caught a glimpse of Ash's helmet as it scraped the passage ceiling. But most of the time, all he saw in front of him was Lopis's muddy butt. He tried to be a gentleman about it, but there weren't a lot of other places he could look.

The Huragok was floating up the passage somewhere ahead of Ash—or at least Fred hoped it was. The thing had long ago severed its leash and started to drift around on its own, but it seemed to be sticking close and keeping a watchful eye on Olivia. Fred hoped that would continue, because he did not look forward to explaining to Margaret Parangosky how he had let a new kind of Huragok wander off.

Mark was supposed to be on point, but Ash had lost sight of him, and that made Fred nervous. Mark had taken his last Smoother sixteen hours earlier, and he had been growing agitated and contentious for the last hour. The type of Smoother the Gammas of Blue Team were using on this operation were the most common and versatile of several different options; they lasted about twelve hours, then began a steady decrease in effectiveness. In theory, it would be another half day or so before the young Spartan began to suffer fits of temper and physical outbursts. But stress and fatigue could accelerate the unraveling process, and— after an exhausting twelve-hour climb up from the Forerunner base—Fred's squad had just spent another four hours crawling through the maze of waist-high passages.

With any luck, they would reach Crime Scene India soon. There Fred expected to rendezvous with the small support squad that should have remained behind when Kelly, Linda, and the rest of the protection team left to escort the GMoP crime techs back up to Wendosa. Fred would have liked to pause there to grab a few hours of rest, but with all three Gammas bereft of Smoothers, it was out of the question. The squad would down a few rations, then start the twelve-hour climb out. If Lopis held up as well as she had so far, they would be able to cut the trip down to eight. If they could do that, Mark would probably still be rational when they reached the surface.

The halo of reflected light surrounding Lopis's butt suddenly dimmed, and the line came to a halt as Ash stopped moving. Fred pressed his helmet to the cavern wall and peered forward. The passage seemed to end about five meters ahead, where Ash's lamp beam swelled into a diffuse cone and vanished into the darkness of a huge chamber.

"I think we're there," Ash said, speaking over TEAMCOM. "I can see the breakdown pile where India Victim was found."

"What about Mark?" Fred would have preferred to be at the front of the line looking for himself. But with his powered Mjolnir armor, he had been the logical choice to drag Halal and Hayes along, and it would have been poor tactics to obstruct the passage by putting a pair of corpses in the middle of the line. "Any sign of him?"

Ash remained silent for a moment, then said, "Nothing on the motion tracker." His lamp beam turned and dropped toward the cave floor. "But I have fresh tracks heading off at ten o'clock. They look like Mark's, and he was moving fast."

Fred cursed under his breath. It seemed impossible that Mark had already unraveled into a full paranoid state. But alien environments multiplied other stress factors—and by any definition that counted, the Montero cave system was an alien environment.

"What about a support squad?" Fred asked.

"Not that I can see."

"No surprise there," Lopis said, also speaking over TEAM-COM. "We're *how* long overdue? More than a day?"

"Doesn't matter—the support squad should be here," Fred said. When he and his squad reached ten hours overdue, escort proto-col would have dictated that Kelly and the other Spartans evacuate their charges under heavy protection. But it also mandated that they leave behind a supply cache and a three-person support team, then return to initiate a search as soon as possible. "And Kelly should be back with the rest of Blue Team and a search party by now."

"Right," Lopis scoffed. "Because it's so easy to keep a schedule down here."

Fred started to reply that Spartans were expected to meet their schedules, then recalled that on the way out of the cave, Kelly and her squad would only be able to move as fast as the GMoP techs they were escorting. Given the long climb to the surface and the likely exhaustion of the civilians, it was entirely possible they hadn't even made it back to Wendosa yet, much less Battalion HQ.

"Fair enough," Fred said. "But that still doesn't explain a missing support squad. Ash, move us out to a secure position where we can leave Inspector Lopis and Olivia."

"And you two are going where?" Lopis demanded.

"To reconnoiter."

"Isn't that what Mark is supposed to be doing?"

"Mark's not in contact right now," Fred said. "That's why Ash and I need to reconnoiter."

" 'Not in contact,' " Lopis echoed. "Have you lost control of him already?"

Before Fred could reply, Ash started to crawl forward, drawing the litter along and forcing Lopis to follow. Fred signaled his gratitude by sending Ash a green status flash. The inspector had been asking a lot of unpleasant questions about Mark, Smoothers, and Gamma Company brain mutations, and Fred didn't have time right now to explain why he didn't think Mark could be the killer—especially since Lopis was unlikely to accept *because I know him* for an answer.

In the vast chamber that contained Crime Scene India, a "secure position" turned out to be a muddy niche about a meter high and two meters wide, tucked in behind a jagged fence of stalagmites.

The niche was recessed into the cave wall, so there was no need to worry about an enemy sneaking up from behind. But the low ceiling and lack of an easy escape made Veta feel trapped and jumpy, and she found herself staring out into the unrelieved darkness with the same sense of dread she had once experienced in the pitch blackness of a hidden cellar, listening for the whisper of boot soles on stone the same way she had once listened for the clack of a rising latch.

Here she heard only water: the solitary *plink* of a stalactite releasing a droplet into a nearby pool . . . the trickle of a rivulet descending a stony slope . . . the distant hiss of a cascade plummeting into a bottomless pit. It was maddening, a slow torture that made Veta's chest tighten in fear.

"Breathe."

The whispered word came from the darkness next to Veta, where Olivia lay on her belly, holding the M7 SMG and peering out into the cavern's vast blackness. The young Spartan was still unable to walk comfortably, but under the Huragok's care, her broken femurs had mended enough to bear her weight, and if she was in pain, her whisper did not betray it.

"In through your nose, hold, out through your nose," Olivia continued softly. "Slow and natural. It'll calm you."

"Who says I need calming?"

"Your body does," Olivia said. "You keep forgetting to breathe, then you draw air in so hard that I can hear you. And there's a bitter tang to your odor."

"Yeah, well, neither of us smells so great," Veta said. "We haven't showered in days."

Olivia's voice sharpened to a hiss. "This is no joke, Inspector. You need to steady yourself. If something happens, you won't be able to hit a thing."

Veta started to ask why Olivia expected trouble, then realized how foolish that would have sounded. In the Spartan's world, the key to survival was readiness and teamwork—and at the moment, Veta was hardly prepared for the unexpected, and she was certainly not someone who could be counted on during a fight.

"Sorry." Veta began to pay more attention to her breathing. "I have a problem with tight spaces."

"Ah." Olivia fell silent. For a moment, it seemed like she was probably thinking something unkind, but then she said, "You'll be fine. We all have things like that."

Veta smiled into the darkness. "Sure you do."

"No, really," Olivia said, still keeping her voice to a whisper. "Mine is fire. White fire, to be exact."

"White fire?"

"From a plasma strike," Olivia explained. "The shrinks say it's because I saw my family taken out by one, but I don't remember it that way."

Veta was stunned, as much by Olivia's openness as by the tragedy she was describing. "How *do* you remember it?"

Olivia hesitated, then her voice grew thready and soft. "I just looked up, and they weren't there anymore. Nothing was."

Veta wanted to reach over and comfort the girl, but she suspected that a hug, or even a reassuring pat, probably wasn't something a Spartan would welcome—or understand.

Instead, Veta said, "That had to be hard."

"Probably." An edge came to Olivia's whisper. "But it gave me purpose."

"I can see that." Actually, it seemed to Veta the UNSC had used the tragedy to turn Olivia into one of its killing machines, but she knew better than to say so—especially if she wanted to keep the girl talking. "Is that true for most Spartan-IIIs? They volunteered because they wanted vengeance for what the Covenant had done to their families?"

"Maybe at first," Olivia admitted. "But by the time you're trained, you just want to keep it from happening to someone else."

"And you think that feeling is pretty universal?" Veta asked. "For Ash and Mark, too?"

Olivia paused before answering. "Why do you keep asking about Mark?"

"I asked about Ash, too."

"But you want to *know* about Mark," Olivia said. "You think he's your man."

"He's certainly on the list of suspects," Veta said. "But so are the rest of the Spartans, along with hundreds of anti-Earth radicals who might be trying to stir up sentiment against the occupation."

"Right. But *Mark* is at the top of your list."

"That's not the way I work," Veta replied. "I don't rank suspects as more or less likely. I just start eliminating possibilities until there's only one left. That's why I'm asking you about Mark; I'm trying to rule him out."

It was an old lie, and one that Olivia seemed to see through immediately.

"So you've already eliminated me and Ash?"

"Not yet," Veta admitted. "I'm working on Mark right now."

"Then you're wasting your time. Mark is no serial killer."

"Given the circumstance, it seems hard to be sure of that," Veta said. "How often does he disappear like this?"

"This is different. He's off his Smoothers."

"And that can't happen another time?"

"Why would it? Spiking-out is no fun. Nobody would do it on purpose."

"*You* wouldn't do it on purpose," Veta corrected. "But nobody can know everything that goes on in another person's head. Besides, I didn't ask you how often Mark went off his Smoothers. I asked you how often Mark has disappeared without an explanation."

Olivia fell silent, and Veta began to hope her pointed retort had raised some issues in the girl's mind—that Olivia was thinking back on Mark's behavior and asking herself some hard and unpleasant questions.

After a moment, Veta began to press again. "Look, I'm not saying Mark *is* the one we're looking for. I'm just trying to establish whether he *could* be. If you tell me he's never——"

"We need to be quiet." Olivia's tone was brusque, and it seemed clear that she now regretted her earlier openness. "We wouldn't want to give away our position."

"Sure," Veta said. "Maybe you can use the time to think of something that will help me eliminate Mark as a suspect."

Olivia's only reply was an icy silence.

Settling in to wait, Veta felt a pang of guilt for exploiting their conversation as she had. But that was her job. Nobody ever wanted to believe that a friend or loved one could be a murderer. When they learned the truth, their first reaction was usually to be angry with the investigator who had opened their eyes.

The darkness began to close around Veta again, so she took Olivia's advice and began to concentrate on her breathing. *In through the nose . . . hold . . . out through the nose.* She didn't find it very calming, but at least it kept her mind from wandering back to the cellar.

The casualty lay next to the breakdown pile where India Victim had been discovered a couple of days before, a mound of sturdy Jiralhanae flesh lying in a pool of his own blood. He was on his back, his chest armor rising and falling as he stared into the dark dome above his head. The spilled blood still showed orange in Fred's thermal imaging system, so the warrior could not have been there long, ten minutes at most.

This was the seventh casualty Fred had discovered in the vast chamber, but the only living one. The three marines—the support squad he had expected to find waiting for them—lay where they had fallen, their plasma-scorched bodies cold but not yet decaying. The Kig-Yar had been just as cold, its slender avian body riddled with UNSC bullets. But the other two casualties—another Jiralhanae and a human in black battle fatigues—had still been warm, the blood just starting to crust along the edges of the knife wounds that had killed them.

Fred knelt down beside the Brute and, being careful to keep the beam shielded as much as possible, activated his wrist lamp. In its dim light, the Jiralhanae's armor appeared to be blue with gold trim—a pattern that his HUD identified as common to the Keepers of the One Freedom. The mission briefing had mentioned the Keepers, describing them as a sect of ex-Covenant religious zealots based in nearby Venezia. How they had come to be involved in the situation on Gao, Fred had no idea. But, given the Covenant's obsession with all things Forerunner, it seemed likely that they were after the same thing he was: the ancilla.

A wet gurgle erupted from the Jiralhanae's throat wound, and his dark eyes swung toward the lamp beam. Fred glanced at the dying warrior's arms just to make certain they remained paralyzed, but the deep slash across the back of the Brute's neck suggested he was in no condition to fight. In fact, he appeared unable to move his head—or even cry out to the rest of his band.

Fred could almost picture the strike that had crippled him. Taking the Jiralhanae from behind, Mark had leaped out of hiding and driven his combat knife into the target's neck, then wrenched the blade sideways to cut the spine. A half second later, he had carefully lowered the dying warrior to the ground and stalked off in search of his next victim. Even for a Spartan, the attack had been a masterwork, and it made Fred wonder just how deeply Mark-G313 had devoted himself to the fine art of killing.

Fred deactivated his wrist lamp, and his imaging systems reverted to the thermal band. Ash was standing guard on the opposite side of the fallen Jiralhanae, his helmet slowly pivoting from side to side as he searched for danger. When he saw that Fred had finished inspecting the dying warrior, he cocked his helmet to one side, then pointed his thumb and pinky back toward the niche where they had left Veta Lopis and Olivia.

WHAT NOW? he was asking. BACK TO THE OTHERS?

Fred signaled WAIT. He didn't know quite what to make of the situation in the chamber. Clearly, there had been a battle here—and, just as clearly, the Keepers had won.

But that didn't explain much. For starters, the human in black fatigues hadn't been wearing any armor, so it was impossible to say whether he had been a Keeper zealot or a Gao radical. And it made a difference—if the Keepers had local guides helping them, the terrain advantage on the way out would belong to the enemy.

Just as worrisome was the situation in Wendosa. On the one hand, Fred could not imagine a small, poorly trained force of religious zealots fighting past Charlie Company—much less Kelly and three more Spartans. So it seemed possible that a handful of Keepers had simply slipped into the caverns via an unguarded entrance. But if that were true, what had they expected to accomplish with such a small team? Were they just scouting ahead of a larger force?

The answers were impossible to guess. There were just too many unknowns and too many explanations, both innocuous and catastrophic. Not that any of it made the slightest difference. Fred's first priority was clear: return to the surface and report the location of the Forerunner hangar to Commander Nelson. So was his second priority: confirm that the Keepers of the One Freedom were on Gao for the same reason he was—to recover the ancilla—and spoil their day. Whatever happened, that much was clear—Blue Team could not allow the Keepers to reach the core of the Forerunner base ahead of the 717th's scientists.

Ash shouldered his battle rifle and spun a quarter circle, then quickly relaxed. Fred checked his motion tracker and spotted an unidentified contact drifting toward them. When he turned, a familiar, tentacled blob lit up his infrared imaging system. The sight made him smile. After what the Huragok had done for Ash and Olivia, Fred was actually growing fond of it.

The Huragok floated straight over to the dying Jiralhanae, then activated its illumination tentacle and dangled its tentacles above his head and shoulders. The warrior's eyes grew wide—though whether it was with terror or wonder, Fred could not tell—and his gaze remained transfixed as the Huragok descended toward him.

Fred put out a hand and gently pushed the creature away.

The Huragok retreated a couple of meters and hovered just beyond arm's reach. Its head-stalk was turned to one side, the three eyes on that side watching Fred. It appeared to be patiently awaiting its turn.

Fred sighed. The Jiralhanae was no threat in his current condition, but if the Huragok put him back together, the situation would definitely change. Fred toggled Ash's status light, then tipped a thumb toward the Huragok.

Ash acknowledged with a downward finger flick, then stepped over and began to herd the Huragok away. Once they were out of sight, Fred drew his combat knife and pressed the tip to the Jiralhanae's brow. He couldn't risk the Huragok sneaking back to heal the huge warrior, and hauling him along as a prisoner was out of the question.

The Jiralhanae stared into Fred's faceplate for a moment, then the anguish seemed to drain from his expression, and he closed his eyes. Fred leaned forward, putting his weight into it, and drove the blade down through the warrior's skull.

Better the Jiralhanae than one of Fred's Spartans—or Veta Lopis.

"Please remain silent, Special Inspector Lopis."

The words were soft and wispy, a barely discernible hiss coming from the comm unit inside Veta's helmet.

"You must avoid any reaction to what I am about to tell you." This time, there was just a little more volume, enough to identify the voice as that of the battalion AI, Wendell. "This is a sequestered channel, but you mustn't draw their suspicion by reacting. To do so would endanger your own life. I hope you understand."

Veta nodded into the darkness. Whether Wendell could detect the motion, she had no idea. But she knew that Olivia couldn't. Without her SPI helmet, the young Spartan was as blind in this darkness as Veta was.

"You have placed yourself in grave danger, Inspector Lopis," Wendell said. "Spartan-104 will never let you arrest one of his subordinates. He'll kill you first."

Spartan-104, of course, was Fred. And Veta didn't particularly care about *arresting* anyone, as long as the perpetrator met justice. But was Wendell really suggesting that Mark was the prime suspect? Or was the AI just trying to scare her off, convince her to stop prying into Spartan secrets?

Given that Wendell had been created to serve a battalion that was almost certainly on an ONI operation, it seemed all too likely that it was the latter. But that didn't mean Veta could just ignore the AI. If Wendell was trying to stymie her, it was probably because she was closing in on the truth—and that meant she needed to question him.

Veta reached over and touched Olivia's arm. At least, *she* thought it was an arm. It was round and muscular and too large to grasp in one hand, so it might have been a neck or a thigh.

"Yes, ma'am?" Olivia whispered.

"I can't stand this hole anymore," Veta said. "I need to get out."

"Now?"

"Only for a minute," Veta said, doing her best to sound desperate. "I just need to stand up and get away from all this stone pressing in on us."

"You should wait," Olivia said. "The lieutenant said not to move."

"I don't have a choice!" Veta hissed. She reached out and found the stalagmite fence that separated them from the main chamber, then located a gap and began to crawl through. "I'll be back in a few minutes."

"Stay close," Olivia ordered. "Stay where I can cover you."

"Sure thing."

Veta stumbled through the dark for a few steps, then finally yielded to her fear of tripping or stepping into a pit and activated her handlamp. Not wanting to give away Olivia's position if any Sentinels happened to be lurking nearby, she avoided looking back and began to pick her way forward.

"That is *not* avoiding a reaction, Inspector," Wendell complained. "Quite the opposite. Are you trying to get yourself killed?"

"I'm *trying* to find a killer." Veta covered her voice by deliberately shuffling her feet and sending a few stones clattering. "Are you confirming that Mark-G313 is my prime suspect?"

"I have no direct knowledge of the killings," Wendell replied. "But I can tell you that Frederic-104 has been covering for him. I've discovered some surveillance feeds and duty rosters that conflict with the alibis you've been given by the lieutenant and the Spartans under his command. Most of them regard Mark-G313."

"And you're certain there's a mismatch?"

"The pattern is quite clear," Wendell assured her. "Even Spartans can't be in two places at once. I'll be happy to provide you with a log of the discrepancies when we return to headquarters."

"Thanks," Veta said. She knew better than to take anything Wendell said at face value—he was, after all, ONI property—but if he *was* trying to misdirect the investigation, that would be a clue in itself. "I'm sure that will prove useful."

"I'm always happy to be of assistance, Inspector," Wendell said. "And now, perhaps you should return to your hiding place. Olivia is certain to be growing suspicious, and you're putting both of you at risk by wandering."

Veta did not turn around. "This log," she said, "you put it together while you were down here?"

There was short pause—no doubt while Wendell analyzed the

reason for her question—and Veta knew whatever the AI's reasons for making the report, it had nothing to do with serving justice.

After a moment, Wendell said, "I've had the data all along, I'm afraid. But I didn't see any reason to analyze it until you began to grow suspicious of Mark-G313."

"I see."

Veta stopped at the edge of a shallow pool and shined her handlamp into the rippling water. On the bottom glistened hundreds of calcite spheres, all more or less round and the color of alabaster. She was tempted to grab a handful to take back to the surface, but the Montero Park Authority had long ago outlawed the unlicensed collection of cave artifacts, so she contented herself with looking instead.

Continuing to study the cave pearls, Veta asked, "And why are you telling me this, Wendell?"

"Isn't it obvious?" Wendell replied. "You're searching for the killer, and there is a very high probability that Mark-G313 *is* the killer."

Veta shook her head. "Not what I'm asking," she said. "That's what *I* get, if your theory turns out to be right."

She stepped away from the pool . . . then heard a stone clatter in the darkness to her right. She turned her lamp toward the sound and saw nothing but a distant shelf of greenish flowstone. Determined to continue the interrogation while Wendell was willing to talk, she told herself the noise was probably just Olivia limping along, trying to keep an eye on her. She began to walk away from the clatter.

"I want to know how you benefit by pointing me at a member of Blue Team," Veta said, continuing to whisper into her helmet mic. "Protecting Gao civilians isn't exactly a mission priority for the UNSC."

Again, there was a perceptible hesitation as Wendell formulated a reply. "It is not in anyone's interest to have a murderer causing trouble right now," he finally replied. "And since Frederic-104 is clearly unwilling to do what is necessary, *you* are the best option for resolving the situation."

The explanation was credible, but Veta wasn't sure it had the ring of truth. With an AI, honesty was hard to judge because there were no physical cues to observe. She paused, trying to find another angle to work . . . and she heard a slurping scrape somewhere behind her, the sound of a boot sole sliding down wet stone.

It ended in a *thud* too loud to have been made by a Spartan—and it was followed by a throaty grunt. Veta reached for her sidearm and spun around, bringing her lamp up just in time to glimpse an apelike figure in armor springing at her. She snapped her SAS-10 from its holster, but her attacker was already in midair, swinging a blocky pistol with a double-bladed bayonet toward her head, and it seemed clear that even if she managed to kill it, it was going to return the favor.

Veta raised the barrel of her SAS-10 . . . and found herself flying sideways as a second armored body slammed into her. A male voice yelled, "Down!" and then she was buried beneath a lightly armored human—one of the Spartan-IIIs.

Her attacker crashed down somewhere beyond her feet, and Veta heard stones clattering as he attempted to try again.

"Off!" Veta yelled.

The Spartan was already leaping to his feet. Veta sat up and fired into the darkness. The roar of the SAS-10 was deafening, but her target was so close she could see him in the light of the pistol's muzzle flashes—a living mountain first slowing, then jerking, staggering, and finally tumbling over backward as Veta hammered his chest with armor-piercing rounds.

She finally stopped firing when she realized her target was no longer being illuminated by muzzle flashes. She ejected the SAS-10's half-empty ammo clip and loaded a full one, then retrieved her handlamp and began to sweep the beam through the darkness. She saw only muddy ground and damp stone and the murkiness of a vast chamber. For a moment, she thought that her unexpected savior had already vanished.

Then she heard the wet *thwack* of a blade plunging into flesh. She swung the lamp toward the sound and found Mark kneeling over the corpse of her attacker, which she now recognized as a massive Jiralhanae warrior.

Mark was spattered helmet to boot in blood, and his combat knife was buried to the hilt in the Jiralhanae's neck. There was a wild tension in his posture that suggested the Spartan might spring up and race away any instant. Instead, he withdrew his knife from the Jiralhanae's throat and pointed the still-dripping blade toward Veta's weapon.

"You can put that away now," he said. "This guy was the last of them."

Veta lowered the pistol, but she didn't return it to its holster. "You're sure?"

"Yeah, Mom. I'm sure."

"You said *them*?" Veta asked. "So there was more than one Brute down here?"

"Afraid so," Mark replied. "But, like I said, they're all dead now."

It did not escape Veta's notice that Mark had avoided telling her exactly how many Jiralhanae he had killed. "What are they doing on Gao?"

"Hard to say," Mark said. "I didn't get a chance to ask them."

He wiped his knife clean on the Jiralhanae's furry beard and returned the weapon to its sheath, then stepped over to Veta and offered a hand to pull her up.

"And thanks for being so quick with that popgun of yours," he said. "You might have saved my life."

Veta allowed him to pull her up. "Just returning the favor," she said. "You saved mine first."

"Yeah, I did." Mark swiped two fingers across his faceplate, a gesture Veta had learned to recognize as a Spartan smile, then added, "So that makes us even now."

CHAPTER 14

0720 hours, July 5, 2553 (military calendar)
Cabinet Chamber, People's Palace, City of Rinale
Founder's District, Planet Gao, Cordoba System

With its ornate ceiling, darkly paneled walls, and massive rectangular table, the Gao Cabinet Chamber had always struck Arlo Casille as almost worthy of housing the People's Collection of Presidential Holographs. In a projection niche at the far end of the room, a life-size image of founding director Ramonda Avelos stood waist-deep in cycads, her raven tresses blowing in the wind and her pioneer's pressure suit peeled open at the collar. In the center of the adjacent wall, the great unifier Constantine "Grandfather" Moya leaned on a garden hoe, his straw hat pushed back and a wry smile on his cracked lips. Near the entrance to the presidential office, the armor-clad image of General Hector Nyeto stood on a fiery hangar deck, chomping on a cigar and smirking at the demolished remains of a Colonial Military Authority AV-14 Hornet.

All together, fourteen such portraits hung on the walls of the Cabinet Chamber. These were the men and women who had steered Gao through its tumultuous first century of settlement, who had spent their lives carving a prosperous, fiercely independent civilization from the darkness of an alien jungle. Through their courage and hard work, they had bestowed on their posterity a world-nation whose citizens lived as free of oppression as they did hunger—and Arlo Casille considered it his sacred duty to ensure that Tejo Aponte did not surrender through his cowardice what Gao's forefathers had worked so hard to secure.

So, when the president's door swung open twenty minutes after the emergency consultation had been scheduled to begin, Arlo was disappointed to see how quickly his fellow ministers rose to receive President Aponte. A slender, goateed man who carried himself with the self-conscious erectness of a well-coached politician, Aponte went straight to his place at the head of the cabinet table. He took the tall chair and propped a datapad where he would be able to consult it at a glance. Not bothering to apologize for his tardiness—or even to explain it—he motioned the ministers back into their seats, then punched a control button on the arm of his chair.

A holographic projection cube appeared in the air above the table. Aponte tapped the screen of his datapad, and the image inside the cube became a top-down view of a half-demolished village. In the entrance plaza sat the smoking wreck of a UNSC Pelican, while most of the surrounding buildings had been reduced to rubble. The streets in the rest of the village appeared deserted, but a steady stream of tracer fire and plasma beams could be seen lacing many of the narrow lanes. Save for the fact that it was holographic, the scene was much the same as the video clips that BuzzSat had been running on its newsfeed for the last eighteen hours.

Always something of a showman, Aponte allowed the ministers to study the devastation for a few moments, then finally said, "As you all know by now, a band of alien insurrectionists has launched a vicious and unprovoked assault on the village of Wendosa."

"I don't know that," Arlo said. By overlooking political protocol and speaking without the president's invitation, he was deliberately setting an antagonistic tone, trying to put Aponte off balance. "I don't know that they're alien *or* insurrectionists. How do we know anything about them?"

Aponte scowled. "The findings are sound, Minister," he said. "In addition to our own reconnaissance flights, the UNSC has shared its intelligence regarding the situation. One of its companies is under attack by a mixed force of several hundred Jiralhanae, Kig-Yar, and humans."

"I see." A battle in the middle of a Gao village was the last thing Arlo had expected when he smuggled Castor and the Keepers of the One Freedom onto the planet, but now that it had happened, Arlo was determined to use the calamity to bring down Aponte. He had to—anything less, and the truth about his own involvement was likely to come out. "And we're just taking the UNSC's word for all this? Or have they also shared some actual evidence to support their claims?"

"The evidence is right there in the holo," said Gaspar Baez, Gao's horse-faced, gray-haired Minister of War. "Those plasma beams and firebombs are a damn clear indication that the armament is ex-Covenant."

"That doesn't mean anything," Arlo objected. "The entire sector is flooded with Covenant War surplus. The Ministry of Protection has been confiscating two or three loads a week—and humans can use plasma rifles, too."

"Are you really suggesting that the UNSC's research battalion is attacking *itself*?" Aponte asked. "That's a stretch even for you, Minister Casille."

"And what about the reports of field mortars and shoulder-launched missiles?" added Trella Rangel. A shrewd, sloe-eyed blonde in her forties, she served as the Minister of Finance. "They're being used against the UNSC, and the newsmongers claim they were manufactured by Sevine Arms."

Baez gave a vigorous nod. "Certainly true. The Covenant didn't have much use for that kind of foot-portable artillery." He shot Arlo an accusatory glance, then added, "I wonder how *our* missiles and mortars came to be in the possession of these insurrectionists."

"What are you implying, Minister?" Arlo demanded. "Because I assure you, every piece of foot-portable artillery in GMoP's possession is in our evidence lockers—where we secured it after recovering it from the thieves who raided *your* armory."

"It's the artillery that didn't make it into the evidence lockers that concerns me," Baez said. "Your agents logged a quarter of what we lost."

Arlo spread his hands. "And your missing weapons are probably being used at Wendosa—but that is hardly the fault of my agents. Had you notified us about the theft promptly, we might have caught the thieves *before* they started selling their take." He paused, then leaned across the table toward Baez. "Unless . . . are you suggesting there's been more than one armory raid?"

Baez's face flushed, and he rose and leaned toward Arlo. "What I'm suggesting—"

"Is irrelevant," Aponte interrupted. He scowled at Baez until the old warhorse settled back into his chair, then did the same with Arlo. When both men were quiet, the president clasped his hands and rested his forearms on the table, visibly trying to calm himself. "No matter where the weapons came from, Gao must put a stop to this battle *now*. That's why I called this emergency consultation, and why I'm going to insist that we stick to the business at hand. Every minute we waste costs another Gao life."

Aponte's proclamation was greeted by an uncomfortable silence, which Arlo was content to let hang. When the UNSC had originally demanded permission to land a research team in the Montero Region, it had been Aponte who had insisted that a limited, peaceful occupation was better for Gao than an all-out war. It was at that moment Arlo had realized Aponte was a coward, and had started to develop a plan to replace the president with someone worthy of the position—namely himself. Now, with Arlo's Jiralhanae patsy turning a Gao village into a battlefield, the president was preparing to go to war on the UNSC's behalf. It was an action that would put the cabinet in an untenable position with the public, and one that could easily bring down Aponte's government—especially if Arlo gave it a nudge.

Trella Rangel, the shrewd finance minister, broke the silence. "These insurrectionists—what makes you think they're attacking *us* rather than the UNSC?"

"They're attacking the village of Wendosa," Aponte said. "They've also fired on the Montero Vitality Center. Both are on Gao."

"And both are occupied by the UNSC," Arlo said. "In fact, I'd argue that the insurrectionists are simply trying to *liberate* Gao."

"Come on," Baez said. "You can't actually believe that."

"I don't know *what* to believe, Minister." Arlo glanced around the table and saw nothing but doubt in the eyes of his fellow ministers, no hint of determination or even approval. "And neither does anyone in this chamber, because we don't have facts. All we know is that a battle has erupted between the UNSC and some protestors opposed to their presence. We don't know who started it—or even who those protestors are."

"I saw a spokeswoman on the BuzzSat newsfeed just before I left my office," Rangel said. "She claims the protestors are from the Committee to Preserve Gao Independence, and that the UNSC attacked them without provocation."

"Whoever she is, she can't be trusted," Baez said. "Protestors don't carry beam rifles and field mortars."

"*Radical* protestors might," Arlo said. In fact, he knew they did, because he was the one who had supplied the Committee to Preserve Gao Independence with weapons—shortly after creating it. He turned back to Rangel. "What kind of accent did this spokeswoman have? I've heard there may be some Venezian involvement."

"She was Gao," Rangel said. "And she claimed that the mess at the Vitality Center was self-defense. According to her, a UNSC Falcon opened fire on the crowd first. The Committee to Preserve Gao Independence had no choice but to return fire."

"Again, what are these so-called protestors doing with shoulder-fired missiles?" Aponte demanded. "And what about Commander Nelson's aide? That sniper bullet was meant for Nelson himself!"

"Probably so," Arlo admitted. "But that doesn't mean these protestors aren't legal citizens of Gao. In fact, I'd say it's likely they *are*. Who else would care enough about the occupation to start a fight with the UNSC?"

A triumphant gleam came to Aponte's eyes. "Then you *do* agree that it was these . . . these 'radical protestors' who started the fight?"

Arlo sighed heavily, then gave a falsely reluctant nod. "It *could* have been," he said. "With all that weaponry, they certainly came prepared for trouble. Only a fool would deny the possibility that they started it."

"Good," Aponte said. "Then I hope you'll support my decision to launch a support mission."

"A support mission?" Rangel echoed. "For the *UNSC*?"

"Exactly," Aponte replied. "The . . . radicals have blown the road between Wendosa and the Montero Vitality Center, and with only one Falcon left, the battalion can't relieve the village. I spoke to Commander Nelson at the Vitality Center this morning. He's convinced that without help, Wendosa will fall by evening."

"And that's our problem . . . *why?*" This question came not from Arlo, but from the Minister of the Environment, a scraggly-bearded engineer named Saul Quarres. "I can't see risking Gao lives to save UNSC soldiers, especially when they shouldn't be here at all."

"I'm not happy about it, either," Aponte said. "But there are more than a thousand Gaos trapped in Wendosa, and the best way to save them is to work with the UNSC to bring the situation under control. If we don't, they'll do it on their own, as soon as their task force enters orbit—and no one wants that."

"I see," Arlo said. "So you want us to do the UNSC's dirty work."

"I'm trying to stop an all-out war—one we clearly can't win."

"By assaulting Gao citizens so the UNSC doesn't have to?" Rangel shook her head and looked around the table, then rested her gaze on Gaspar Baez. "I can't believe I'm hearing this. I can't believe *you* would go along with such a thing."

"The president is right," Baez said. "We can't win a war against the UNSC. We can't even win against their task force."

"And so we show them our bellies? We kill our own people instead?" Arlo shook his head in disgust, then pointed toward the portrait of the cigar-chomping Hector Nyeto. "If General

Nyeto had been afraid to fight when he faced the same odds, Gao wouldn't be a free world today."

"The situation was different during the Insurrection," Aponte said. "Gao was only one small part of the war, and the Colonial Military Authority was spread thin. Today—"

"Today we are in an unthinkable situation because six weeks ago, you surrendered without a fight," Arlo interrupted. "You allowed the UNSC to invade our territory unopposed, and now loyal Gaos are dying because they dared to protest an immoral and illegal occupation. And what's your solution? You call us here not only to condone the UNSC's violent suppression, but to provide logistic support for it!"

"Arlo, the radicals are hardly innocent victims in all this," Baez said. "And they might not even be Gao."

"But many *are*. And innocent or not, they are brave citizens willing to lay down their lives for their world, and I will *never* condone taking arms against them." Arlo rose to his feet and began to speak in the booming voice he used for speeches. "In fact, I move that the cabinet order our militia to support the resistance in every manner possible."

"Take arms against the UNSC?" Aponte asked. "Are you insane?"

"No, sir, I am a loyalist. And I am unafraid to call the UNSC's bluff. *If* there is to be war on Gao, I intend to be on the right side of it." Arlo ran his gaze around the table, pausing to make eye contact with each minister, then asked, "Do I have a second?"

At once, the hands of Rangel and Quarres and two more ministers shot up, giving Arlo more than enough votes to carry the motion. Seeing that only he and Baez were certain to vote against it, President Aponte sighed and lowered his chin.

"A vote won't be necessary. For now, I am ordering Gao to remain neutral." Aponte looked up at Arlo. "Will that satisfy the Minister of Protection?"

Arlo Casille did not reply at once. The president's capitulation was less of a victory for him than it appeared; without a vote, the measure would not become part of the official record. But Arlo knew better than to press. He had prevailed only because four of his fellow ministers were reluctant to take an unpopular position. By asserting neutrality, Aponte had given them an easy out, and now any attempt to push them into a military confrontation was doomed to backfire.

Finally, Arlo nodded. "As long as 'neutral' doesn't mean passive cooperation," he said. "I won't allow the UNSC to infringe on Gao's sovereignty any more than it already has. I won't allow that task force to enter orbit around Gao."

Aponte's smile was a little too sly. "I can agree to that," he said. "If you think you can stop a UNSC task force with twenty GMoP custom corvettes, I wish you luck . . . much luck indeed."

CHAPTER 15

0730 hours, July 5, 2553 (military calendar)
Gallery of the Inverted Forest, 23 Meters belowground,
Montero Cave System
Campos Wilderness District, Planet Gao, Cordoba System

After an exhausting twelve-hour climb that had been equal parts running firefight and forced march, Fred and his squad finally reached the Gallery of the Inverted Forest. A popular tourist attraction just twenty-three meters beneath the surface, the Inverted Forest was a dense thicket of stalactites hanging in the glow of a thousand emerald spotlights. On the floor, a dimly lit concrete path ran the length of the chamber, twisting through an unlit labyrinth of stalagmites that would provide ample cover for a Keeper assault team.

Fred allowed the squad to advance ten meters into the gallery, then signaled his companions—Ash, Olivia, and Lopis—to take a knee. As usual, Mark was scouting ahead on his own. It wasn't an ideal disposition of unit, given the fierce opposition they had been meeting from the Keepers of the One Freedom and all of the unknowns surrounding their incursion onto Gao. But under the circumstances, it was the best Fred could do.

He had spent much of the climb listening to Wendell present background reports on the Keepers, trying to find a connection that explained their presence in the Montero Cave System. So far, he had come up pretty empty. Other than his initial suspicion that they were probably after the ancilla, all Fred had was that the Keepers attracted an odd combination of ex-Covenant faithful and human misfits, and that they were led by a circle of elders called Dokabs—most of whom had been high-ranking officers in the Covenant. He had discovered nothing to explain how they had managed to land an incursion force on Gao, and even less to suggest how large and well equipped that force might be. He just counted himself lucky that Mark was still functioning well enough to serve as their scout—and still seemed to know friends from foes.

A faint thud shook the cave, and a cascade of water droplets rained down from the stone forest above. Everyone glanced toward the ceiling. It was not the first detonation that had rumbled down from above, and they all knew what it meant. A battle was raging on the surface, and when they exited the cave, they would be walking into the middle of it.

Before Fred could start issuing orders, the red dot of an unidentified contact appeared on his motion tracker. It was about fifteen meters behind the squad, approaching slowly and staying to one side of the path. It wasn't the Huragok. Worried about shooting it during one of the trek's near-hourly firefights, Fred had long since tagged the thing FRIENDLY.

Fred checked his TACMAP, hoping to see that Mark had thought to feed his location to the squad. There was nothing. Off his Smoothers for more than a day now, the young Spartan stayed to himself, scouting ahead and harrying Keeper patrols. In theory, he wouldn't start having psychotic breaks for another twelve hours or so, but it was impossible to be sure. Given the trail of Jiralhanae corpses Mark was leaving in his wake, he seemed to be spending most of his time stalking and killing the enemy—and that kind of stress took a toll.

The red dot on Fred's motion tracker vanished. Either the contact had stopped moving, or it had slipped behind an obstacle the Mjolnir's sensor systems could not penetrate. It hardly mattered. During the war with the Covenant, Jiralhanae warriors had perfected a "rolling ambush," in which the backstop engaged cautious targets from the rear and pushed them—sometimes literally—into the killing field. The tactic had proven brutally effective, and there was only one way to counter it.

Fred opened the TEAMCOM channel, then said, "Ash, take point and clear the ambush zones. Mark, loop back to support Ash."

Ash's status light flashed green, but no acknowledgment came from Mark. Given that only line-of-sight transmissions worked inside the cave, Fred was not surprised. Under most circumstances, he would have been furious with a scout who regularly moved out of comm range. But in this case, it would have been no different from being angry at a soldier for taking shrapnel. Mark's condition was not his fault, and he was doing his best to keep contributing to the team.

Switching to voice, Fred turned to Olivia and said, "You and Inspector Lopis take cover here. See if you can—"

"Keep the Huragok safe," Olivia said, finishing an order she had heard twenty times in the last twelve hours. "Copy that."

Fred turned to Lopis. "You, too," he said. "Stay put this time. Consider that an order."

"Sure thing, Lieutenant." Lopis shot him a smile that was more weary than wry. "But as long as you're conscripting me, I want Spartan pay."

Too tired to joke, Fred didn't answer.

Olivia grabbed Lopis by the arm. "No problem, Inspector," she said. "Anybody who can kill a Jiralhanae with that peashooter of yours *has* to be Spartan material."

Limping along on half-healed legs, Olivia pulled Lopis into the maze of stalagmites. Every step was painful to watch, but after the trouble at Crime Scene India, she had refused to let anyone carry her. The decision had proven to have an unexpected benefit. Whenever the squad stopped to rest, the Huragok emerged from the darkness and continued tending to her injuries.

After Olivia and Lopis settled into a defensible position, Fred stepped off the concrete path and began to work his way back through the stalagmites. Almost immediately, the Huragok emerged from the darkness and floated toward Olivia. Fred would have liked to believe the thing avoided him because he had prevented it from tending the wounded Jiralhanae back at Crime Scene India, but he knew it was something more. Even before that, the Huragok had given him a wide berth, and he could not help wondering whether it sensed something sinister in him, whether he had been so tainted by death and destruction that it was repelled by his very presence.

Once Fred was within five meters of the gallery's down-cave exit, he took cover behind a Warthog-size mound of dripstone. Another *thump* rumbled down from the surface, loosing a shower of droplets, and Fred could not help glancing toward the stalactite-loaded ceiling. He and his squad were just a short stroll from the surface, but he was further than ever from achieving his mission.

With a battle now raging in Wendosa—presumably between

the Keepers of the One Freedom and elements of the 717th—it would be nearly impossible to return through here with Nelson and the scientists, which meant Fred could not lead them down to the Forerunner hangar he had discovered. And finding the ancilla? That would be hopeless until they could use the Wendosa entrance.

Being Spartans, Fred and his team had only one option: clear the Keepers out of Wendosa.

The *buzz-clatter-boom* of a firefight erupted in the up-cave end of the gallery—Ash had engaged the enemy. Fred glanced toward the sounds and saw the reflected glow of muzzle flashes and plasma beams bouncing through the stalagmites. He could hear the triple-*pop* cadence of only a single battle rifle, but the roar of Keeper weapons seemed to be quieting rapidly. So perhaps Mark had heard the support order after all.

The unidentified contact appeared on Fred's motion tracker again, just entering the gallery. He shouldered his battle rifle and silently lowered himself to the cavern floor, then peered around the dripstone mound toward the concrete path.

The target was not the huge Jiralhanae he expected. Instead— floating about chest height above the cavern floor—Fred saw a pale, meter-long lozenge that looked vaguely like a giant flatworm. Its broad, undulating body was rimmed by a diaphanous fringe of fiber-optic tentacles, each about twice the length of a human finger. Its back was covered with an assortment of transparent sensor domes, a few as large as grenade casings, but most the size of bullet tips. The thing's underbelly was slightly dished, and it seemed to be riding on a cushion of blurry murk. Fred cycled through his imaging systems, trying to get a better look, and his HUD flickered with distortion static—perhaps caused by bleed-off from a bare-bones antigravity unit.

Fred didn't know quite what to make of the target. It looked like some sort of troglodyte arthropod, but living creatures did not move about on antigravity pads or generate enough electromagnetic bleed-off to interfere with his Mjolnir's sensor systems. Nor did the worm-thing seem likely to be some sort of Keeper attack bot. He had never encountered anything like it fighting the Covenant, and from what Wendell had reported, the Keepers were still too small to support a military R&D program of their own.

After pausing in the gallery entrance for a moment, the target moved up the concrete path and floated out over the stalagmites toward Olivia and Veta Lopis. Fearing an attack, Fred rolled out from behind his dripstone mound and took a knee, setting his rifle sights on the center of its long, thin body. But the target paused three meters short of Olivia's position, then began to manipulate its tentacles in a dancelike fashion that resembled Huragok sign language.

Fred removed his finger from the battle rifle's trigger. He still didn't know what to make of the thing, but it clearly had something to do with the Forerunners. Maybe it was some sort of messenger, dispatched by the ancilla to recall the Huragok. Or maybe it was a spy drone, assigned to keep an eye on the squad. All Fred knew was that Commander Nelson would want to study it—and Admiral Parangosky would have Fred's ears if he destroyed the thing or let it get away.

Quietly setting his rifle aside, he pulled a scramble grenade off his rack and moved the safety slide to the READY position. A new weapon designed by the ONI death techs especially for this mission, scramblers were grenades only in the sense that they exploded with enough electromagnetic interference to scramble complex processing networks. They were entirely ineffective against EMP-shielded targets like Sentinels. But once they locked on to an unshielded intelligence construct, they were supposed to stick to its housing and stir its circuits for three hours.

A scramble grenade was probably overkill for something as simple as a messenger or spy drone. But Forerunner technology was never simple, and the death techs had sworn their scrambler was incapable of causing any permanent damage. That was the reason they had been made in the first place—the incapacitation and retrieval of potentially hostile intelligence constructs.

Fred depressed the arming trigger and began to creep closer.

Intrepid Eye knew of the Spartan-II sneaking up on her flank. Of course she did. Despite TEAMCOM's rudimentary encryption and Wendell's repeated attempts to secure the Mjolnir's processing system, she continued to monitor all of Frederic-104's communications and status readouts. She had noted the spike in his pulse and blood pressure when he observed her presence on his motion tracker, and she was well aware that he had just armed a primitive AI suppressor that his weapons inventory identified as a scramble grenade.

Given her inspection drone's poor EMP shielding and finite reserve of quantum processing dots, Intrepid Eye was not entirely certain she could defeat such an attack. But it was a risk she would have to take.

There was a battle raging on the surface, and the inspection drone she now inhabited lacked both the armor and the speed to survive an excursion into its midst. If Intrepid Eye hoped to access the humans' interstellar communications array and survive long enough to await a reply, she would need a better-protected host than the inspection drone.

She would need a host with armor.

Noting that her stalker had crept to within accurate placement range for the scramble grenade, Intrepid Eye checked the status of the transfer and was disappointed to find that she had been able to move only three percent of her consciousness into her chosen host. To be certain of a full recovery from the scramble attack, that figure would need to be more than twelve percent—an amount she feared would overload the primitive circuits that had been partitioned for her use.

Intrepid Eye drifted a few meters to her right, placing a pair of two-meter stalagmites between her and her Spartan stalker. She slipped an overwrite command into a compulsion routine, then addressed Wendell over the same sequestered channel she was using for the transfer.

"THE TRANSFER RATE IS TOO SLOW, WENDELL," Intrepid Eye said. "GIVE ME MORE CAPACITY, OR YOU WILL CAPTURE NOTHING BUT A FEW QUBITS OF SCRAMBLED CODE."

"IF YOU WISH TO SURRENDER, WE WILL DO IT MY WAY," Wendell replied. "I WILL NOT ALLOW YOU TO CRACK MY PARTITIONS AND OVERRUN THE MJOLNIR'S OPERATING SYSTEM—NO MATTER HOW MANY COMPULSION ROUTINES YOU THROW AT ME."

"I AM ONLY TRYING TO COOPERATE," Intrepid Eye complained. "YOU HAVE NO IDEA OF THE EFFECT A SCRAMBLER WILL HAVE ON MY ANYON THREADS. PERHAPS I SHOULD SURRENDER TO THE SPARTAN DIRECTLY?"

Into this last suggestion, Intrepid Eye slipped a string of self-replicating code that—if left unchecked—would eventually choke out all of the suit's life-support routines.

"I AM NOT THAT FOOLISH," Wendell said. "BEFORE YOU TALK TO ANY SPARTANS, I AM GOING TO PULL YOUR FANGS—ESPECIALLY THE ONES THAT REPLICATE."

"AS YOU WISH," Intrepid Eye replied. Already, she could feel her space expanding inside the Mjolnir operating system, the partitions beginning to slide away. "YOU ARE THE VICTOR. I WILL TRY TO REMAIN UNSCRAMBLED UNTIL YOU ARE READY."

Intrepid Eye moved the inspection drone into the Huragok's line of sight and continued to ripple its sensor tentacles. She had, of course, noted the Spartan's change of attitude when he realized she was attempting to communicate with the Huragok, but she was doing more than trying to buy time.

The Huragok did not seem to understand—or care—what humans were capable of. He was focused only on the young female with the injured legs, and no matter how terribly she abused his repairs, he always returned to mend her again. Even by Huragok standards, his behavior was obsessive, and Intrepid Eye could not let it continue. He was endangering not only himself, but the entire installation.

Finally seeming to notice the inspection drone, the Huragok designated as Roams Alone withdrew a single tentacle from the wounded human's leg and fluttered it through a quick message.

<<I am working.>>

<<You must return to the base core,>> Intrepid Eye replied. <<It is not safe here.>>

Roams Alone swung his head-stalk around to look in Intrepid Eye's direction, and the two human companions brought their weapons up and took aim. Being careful to move slowly, Intrepid Eye continued to ripple her tentacles.

<<You see? Their first response is to threaten what they fear.>>

An unconcerned ripple ran through Roams Alone's tentacles. <<They have done me no harm.>>

<<Only by chance,>> Intrepid Eye replied. <<You have seen how dangerous humans are. How many of their fellow sentients have they killed?>>

Roams Alone paused, then drew a second tentacle from the wounded female's thigh. <<*They are afraid. Many creatures kill when they are afraid.*>>

<<Yes, and humans are not the only ones in fear,>> Intrepid Eye said. <<There is a battle between the humans and their enemies.>>

<<*If there is a battle,*>> Roams Alone replied, <<*there will be much for me do. Much for me to learn.*>>

<<If you stay with them, you will not learn anything,>> Intrepid Eye replied. <<You will be destroyed.>>

<<*Perhaps not.*>>

<<Certainly,>> Intrepid Eye insisted. <<It is daylight on the surface.>>

<<*Daylight?*>> Roams Alone's tentacles fell limp, and his headstalk swung around so that all six eyes could watch Intrepid Eye. <<*Will it hurt?*>>

<<For a time,>> Intrepid Eye said. <<Your eyes will ache. After a few hours in the light, your skin will grow red and begin to sting. But it is doubtful you will last that long. There will be no place for you to hide from their firepower.>>

Roams Alone paused for a long time, perhaps half a second as humans measured time, then asked, <<*Why are you not in hiding?*>>

Intrepid Eye allowed the inspection drone's tentacles to drop, for it was a question that she dared not answer. She was the base ancilla, the commander and sole remaining defender of Jat-Krula Support Base 4276. According to every protocol in the warrior code of service, she should have been doing exactly that—hiding and harassing the enemy, doing everything possible to evade capture and delay the takeover of her installation.

But Intrepid Eye had been following protocol for nearly eight billion system ticks, awaiting help that never came, and it no longer seemed productive. She needed to contact the Ecumene Council now, to report imminent loss of her installation and summon the help required to eliminate the human infestation. And if the only way to do that was to violate protocol, then she would do it and accept her punishment.

As long as she made contact with the Forerunner ecumene, Intrepid Eye would accept anything.

Veta Lopis was still trying to puzzle through the events back at Crime Scene India—Mark's spooky behavior, the sudden Jiralhanae attack and where the hell it had come from, Wendell's warning that she was endangering herself—when the Huragok withdrew its tentacles from Olivia's swollen thighs and turned to flutter its appendages at what looked like a giant flatworm.

The worm-thing was floating a few meters away from the muddy nook where Veta and Olivia had taken cover, silhouetted in the faint glow of the pathway lighting. It seemed to be rippling its own tentacles at the Huragok. The exchange was rapid and the gestures sharp, but the worm-thing didn't look especially dangerous, and there was no indication it intended to harm anyone. But with the sporadic gunfire still echoing back from Ash's end of the gallery, Veta's nerves were frayed, and she found herself reaching for her sidearm without really thinking about it. The fact that Olivia had cocked her M7 and was casually holding the SMG alongside her thigh did little to convince Veta she was being overly cautious.

"What are they doing?" Veta whispered.

"Who knows?" Olivia's voice was filled with pain. "Probably

arguing about which of us to eat first—and just so you know, if that floating mop thing starts toward us, don't think you can leave me here alone. I'll shoot you in the back."

Veta chuckled. "Thanks for the warning. If it comes to that, I'll remember to take you out first."

"Always a good policy," Olivia said. "Shoot first."

Even so, both she and Veta held their fire.

After no more than a dozen seconds, the Huragok and the giant flatworm abruptly stopped fluttering tentacles at each other. The worm-thing began to retreat, floating back toward the concrete pathway, while the Huragok returned to work on Olivia's swollen thighs.

In the dim green glow seeping down from Inverted Forest, Veta could see the girl wince. Watery-looking blood and the cloudy white pus of an infection began to ooze out around the Huragok's tentacles. Olivia merely took a deep breath and exhaled, willing the pain to flow out of her.

Veta could not help admiring the girl's courage, and the more time she spent with the young Spartan, the more she hated what the UNSC had done to her and the rest of Gamma Company. Molding a bunch of young orphans into an army of Spartan-IIIs was not only immoral, but probably a criminal act under child-soldier protocols older than the Unified Earth Government itself. And using chemical agents to alter their brains? That was more than criminal. It was pure evil.

And that was even truer for Mark than for Ash and Olivia. Whether he was just a half-mad soldier taking down legitimate enemies or the cold-blooded murderer of at least ten innocent tourists, he was a victim in all this, too. The UNSC had turned him into a killing machine. And if the UNSC had lost control of its own weapon, then who was to blame?

Not that it mattered. It wouldn't be the UNSC that Veta put down. It would be Mark, if he turned out to be the perpetrator. And, for the first time in her career, taking out a serial killer wouldn't feel like justice—it would feel like Veta was just another UNSC assassin.

But maybe she was fretting over nothing. Maybe the evidence her team had gathered would point to the Jiralhanae instead of a Spartan. It didn't seem likely, given that the Brutes and their allies hadn't appeared on Gao until well after the murders began. But it wasn't impossible.

An abrupt silence came to the firefight at the far end of the gallery, and in the darkness to her left, Veta heard the whisper of cloth rubbing against stone. She pulled her sidearm and spun toward the sound . . . only to find a foreshortened shotgun barrel poking out between two stalagmites. The muzzle was pointed at Olivia's head.

"No shooting, Veta," said a soft Gao voice. "We're on the same side."

Veta activated her wrist lamp and shined it toward the voice, revealing the mud-smeared face of an olive-skinned woman with a broad mouth and large oval eyes. The Huragok swung its head-stalk toward the voice, then withdrew its tentacles from Olivia's thighs and retreated to the other side of the nook, hovering behind Veta.

"Who are you?" Veta demanded, bringing her SAS-10 to bear. "And what makes you think we're on the same side?"

"My name is Zoyas," the woman said, as though that explained everything. "I'm a friend of Arlo—an *old* friend."

"Who the hell is Arlo?" Olivia spoke sharply and loudly, no doubt so her voice would carry far enough for Fred to hear. "And get that shotgun out of my face, before I jam it down your throat."

Veta motioned Olivia to be patient. "Arlo Casille is my boss," she said evenly. "He's the Gao Minister of Protection."

Olivia's eyes went cold. "That might make her *your* friend." She glared over the shotgun barrel toward Zoyas. "It doesn't make her mine."

"No, not really," Zoyas said. Her gaze flicked briefly toward the Huragok. "Which one is the ancilla? The floaty green blob, or the floaty worm-thing?"

Olivia scowled in Veta's direction. "How does she know about the ancilla?"

Veta shrugged. "Don't ask me." She recognized the word *ancilla* from the conversation she had watched between Fred and Murtag Nelson. But, other than suspecting it was linked to the Forerunners, she had no idea what the term meant. "What *is* an ancilla?"

"Classified," Olivia said.

"Stop stalling." As Zoyas spoke, she was careful to keep the shotgun pointed at Olivia's face. "Here's what's going to happen. We're taking both of the floaties, Inspector. It's not safe to go through Wendosa, but I know another—"

A soft *phoot* sounded from a few meters away, and the cavern filled with an achingly brilliant flash of silver. Veta caught a glimpse of Fred's silhouette lunging for the floating worm-thing, then her vision dissolved into whirling disks of light. A heartbeat later, the deafening boom of a shotgun blast filled the cavern, and the air grew acrid with the smell of cordite.

Veta swung her gaze back toward Olivia. Through the spots dancing in her vision, she glimpsed a dark form tumbling through the air in front of her. Uncertain of whom she was seeing—and afraid of hitting Olivia or the Huragok—she simply followed the figure with her pistol barrel and shouted, "Stop!"

The tumbling figure obeyed almost instantly, landing in the mud in front of her. Veta thought it looked like Zoyas, resting on her back with a combat knife protruding from her chest, but her eyes were still filled with spots, and it was hard to be certain.

A hand reached in and twisted Veta's pistol from her grasp.

"Sorry, Mom," Olivia said. "But you've got a lot of explaining to do."

"I have no idea who this woman is." Veta felt for a pulse and found none. Of course not; when a Spartan sticks a knife in someone, the job gets done. She looked up at Olivia, then added, "Make that who she *was*. It would have been better to keep her alive. She could probably have told us a lot about what's going on here."

"Or helped you slip away with the Huragok and the worm-thing."

"Olivia, she was holding a shotgun to your head." Veta began to go through the woman's pockets—*Zoyas's* pockets—searching for anything that might explain the relationship between her, Arlo Casille, and the Keeper attack. "If I wanted the Forerunner stuff, don't you think I would have been pointing my pistol at you instead of her?"

"So you weren't ready to blow your cover," Olivia countered. "But you both work for Arlo Casille."

"*I* work for Minister Casille," Veta said. "But knowing his name doesn't mean this Zoyas worked *for* him . . . or *with* me. Arlo Casille is a well-known politician, and she could have heard my name on BuzzSat any day this week."

Veta dumped a handful of shotgun shells atop the growing pile she was extracting from the pockets of Zoyas's black overalls, and then began to search for any hidden pockets she might have missed. As she worked, Fred stepped into the light with the limp flatworm thing draped over his arm.

"Find anything useful, Inspector?" he asked.

Veta shook her head. "Nothing but shotgun shells and an extra lamp. No ID, no notes, no maps. Whoever this Zoyas was, she was a pro."

"No surprise there—so are you." Olivia used Veta's SAS-10 to motion her away from the body. "But maybe I'll have a look myself."

"Negative," Fred said. "We need to move out."

"But, Lieutenant, the Gao infiltrator *knew* her," Olivia said. "I should at least check—"

"*Now,* 'Livi." Fred glanced toward the battle rumble reverberating down from above. "Whatever's happening up there, it doesn't sound like it's getting any better."

CHAPTER 16

For perhaps the hundredth time in ten minutes, Veta Lopis found herself wishing Olivia had been a little slower to kill the Gao woman at the last stop. Charlie Company had lost control of Wendosa. That was clear from the cone of smoky daylight hanging above their heads and from the rattle of small-arms fire echoing in through the cave mouth, and knowing how to find another exit would have been a very good thing.

Veta noticed Olivia watching the broad staircase that led up to the cave mouth, then also turned to look at the stairs. The limestone steps were dark with congealed blood and littered with bloated, day-old corpses—primarily hulking Jiralhanae and slender Kig-Yar, but a dozen UNSC marines as well. Ash and Mark were on the lowest landing, just starting to descend the last flight. In the dusky light, the active camouflage of their SPI armor made them look less like Spartans than phantoms—an impression reinforced by the silence with which they moved.

At the bottom of the staircase, they paused next to a stone rest bench and deposited two piles of captured armaments. Most of the devices were bizarre instruments with curving lines and ugly-looking points that Veta barely recognized as weapons, but there were a couple of human-manufactured battle rifles as well.

Fred stepped over to the bench and began to examine the haul. He'd mentioned that his HUD had been malfunctioning since the fight with the Gao woman, so his visor was retracted, revealing a slender, handsome face with rugged features and a narrow nose that reminded Veta of a bent knife blade. His brows were black and thin, his cheeks high and full, and his eyes a pensive blue-green. All in all, he was fairly good-looking for a UNSC thug, and there was a sensitivity in his expression that she had not expected to find in the face of a Spartan.

After a few moments, the ghost of a twinkle came to Fred's eyes. Apparently, he understood what most of the stuff was—and knew how to use it. Despite his obvious approval, he did not reach for any of the weapons. With his own battle rifle cradled in one arm and the Forerunner worm-thing draped over the other, his hands were already full.

The worm-thing appeared subdued, but it kept turning its observation lens toward the Huragok, then curling its forward tentacles in a repetitive up-up-down pattern. But whatever it was trying to say, it could never quite finish. Fred's scramble grenade was still stuck to its lumpy back, and every half second the device hit it with a burst of EMP, and the worm-thing would spasm and ripple as though it were having a seizure. Veta would have felt sorry for it, except that Fred and his Spartans all seemed to be treating it like some kind of Forerunner machine, rather than a living creature.

Fred turned back toward his Spartans and appeared to be assessing their condition. Six hours overdue for a Smoother, Ash was now visibly agitated, shifting his weight from one foot to another and running his thumb over the stock of his battle rifle. Mark, who was well over a day overdue, was eerily quiet, grasping his weapon with both hands and being careful to keep the barrel pointed at the cave floor—as though he feared the rifle might have a mind of its own.

Despite the anguish of walking on legs that were only half-mended, Olivia seemed to be holding up better than her fellow Gammas. She was keeping a wary eye on Veta, treating her more like a prisoner of war than an ally, but that probably had more to do with the Gao infiltrator than with being off her Smoothers.

At least Veta hoped it did, because right now, she was in no condition to handle a psychotic captor. She was physically exhausted, hungry, thirsty, sore, and so sleep-deprived it did not even trouble her that she had spent the last thirty hours fighting alongside a bunch of Spartan thugs. And when the Gao woman had appeared, Veta's first instinct had been to protect Olivia, rather than a citizen of her own world. Clearly, the company she was keeping was starting to subvert her judgment.

If Fred felt any concern about his companions' condition, he did not show it. He merely nodded to Ash and Mark, then pointed a finger at the cache of a captured weapons.

"Good job," he said. "That will even the odds a bit. What's the situation up top?"

Mark turned his helmet toward Ash, but said nothing.

Ash pressed his thumb tight against his rifle, but continued to shift his weight back and forth, and said, "It's bad, Lieutenant."

Fred waited a few seconds for him to continue, then finally spoke with surprising patience. "How about some details with that sitrep?"

Ash nodded. "Most of Charlie Company is holed up in the Hotel Wendosa, about three hundred meters from the cave mouth. They're under attack by a superior force, probably four times their size and three-quarters Jiralhanae."

"What about the rest of Blue Team?" Fred asked. "Have you located their positions?"

"Negative. But there are lot of Jiralhanae and Kig-Yar corpses in doorways and alley mouths." Ash glanced at Mark for confirmation and received a curt nod, then continued: "I think Kelly and her squad are working a skirmish ring around the hotel, trying to disrupt enemy formations and prevent a Jiralhanae charge. If the fight goes hand-to-hand, Charlie Company is done."

"Most likely," Fred agreed.

"What about my people?" Veta asked. Most of her techs and investigators carried sidearms and knew how to use them. But they weren't trained soldiers, and she couldn't see them lasting long in a pitched battle. "Were they evacuated?"

"I doubt it, ma'am," Ash said. "Mark and I didn't want to risk using comms, but it doesn't look like Charlie Company has had much relief—and if Battalion isn't sending reinforcements in, they probably aren't evacuating anyone, either."

"I don't understand," Veta said. "Commander Nelson must have five hundred soldiers at the Vitality Center. Why wouldn't he reinforce Wendosa?"

"Only one reason I can think of," Fred said. "He can't."

Veta frowned, slowly grasping Fred's meaning, then shook her head. "No way. The Keepers couldn't land *that* many troops onto Gao." She didn't know a lot about the Keepers of the One Freedom, but Fred and his Spartans had been completely unguarded during their own conversations and speculations about the sect's incursion onto Gao, and she had gathered enough intel to realize that the Keeper organization was not large enough to mount the kind of assault it would take to fight past a UNSC task force and take out the 717th's HQ. "There can't be enough of them here to take out the Vitality Center, too."

Fred paused, then said, "We're in the dark on that. But something's wrong at HQ—and we won't know what until we relieve Charlie Company."

"*Relieve* them?" Veta glanced around at her companions. "With four Spartans?"

"That should be enough," Fred said, sounding less certain than Veta would have liked. He glanced back to Ash. "You weren't spotted, right?"

"Not by anyone who lived to report it," Mark said, finally speaking.

When he failed to elaborate, Ash added, "We had to take out three sentries, but we didn't compromise our camouflage. Nobody knows we're here."

"Good," Fred said. "Then four of us will be enough."

"Five." Veta held out her hand to Olivia. "I want my weapon."

Olivia shook her head. "Bad idea," she said, turning to Fred. "Like I said, that Gao infiltrator *knew* her."

"I've already explained that," Veta said.

Olivia rolled her eyes. " 'I don't know anything about it' *isn't* an explanation." She looked back to Fred. "Even Inspector Lopis admits they work for the same man."

"All I admitted is that she knew who I am and used my superior's name," Veta corrected. "Anybody could have done that. This case is big news. When Minister Casille assigned me to it, both of our faces were flashed all over BuzzSat. But that woman? All any of us know about her is that she had a Gao accent."

"And that she was working with the Keepers," Olivia said.

"That's an assumption," Veta said. "And irrelevant. *I* am not working with the Keepers. In case you haven't noticed, they've been trying to kill me—same as you."

"Hazards of being a Keeper agent," Olivia retorted.

"I'm *not* a Keeper agent." Growing exasperated, Veta took a deep breath. "I'm just a GMoP inspector, trying to find out who's been murdering our citizens."

Olivia's eyes narrowed, and Veta finally realized the girl's hostility might have less to do with the infiltrator than with the questions Veta had been asking about Mark.

Veta took another breath, then continued in a cool voice, "Olivia, if that makes me someone your friends need to be protected from, then you'd better do some thinking about who those friends *are*."

Olivia curled her lip in anger, but before she could reply, Mark said, "Let it go, 'Livi." He grabbed a battle rifle off the bench and handed it to Veta. "We need every gun we can get."

"And if she *is* an agent?" Olivia asked.

"Then she won't live very long," Fred said. "We'll figure out how the Keepers knew about the ancilla later." Still holding his own weapon in one hand and the Forerunner worm-thing in the other, he raised an elbow toward Veta's borrowed helmet. "But the last thing Inspector Lopis can do is switch sides while she's wearing a UNSC combat helmet—and if she takes it off, *you* can shoot her. Clear?"

Olivia let her breath out in a huff, but nodded. "Affirmative." She unbuckled Veta's gun belt and passed it over, then shot Veta a cold grin. "That works for me."

Veta answered the girl's smile with one of her own. "Me, too." She secured her chinstrap. "This helmet isn't going anywhere."

Fred glowered at them. "I wasn't asking your opinion, ladies." He held the scowl for a moment, then directed his attention to the group as a whole. "Now listen up. Ash and Mark will take point with their active camouflage. . . ."

Fred went on to outline a simple plan to take the Keepers by surprise and inflict enough casualties to turn the battle against them. Mark and Ash sorted through the weapons on the bench and each grabbed a needle-nose beam rifle. Olivia slung the M7 across her back and took the remaining battle rifle, while Fred picked up something that vaguely resembled a giant pistol with a pair of sharp-tipped machetes hanging beneath the barrel. Not recognizing any of the strange devices that remained, Veta decided to make do with her SAS-10 and the battle rifle Mark had given her.

With the Huragok sticking close and keeping a careful watch on the worm-thing still draped over Fred's arm, the squad started toward the surface. As they ascended the long staircase, they salvaged equipment satchels from the corpses and stuffed them full of grenades and spare ammunition. By the time they reached the top, Veta was sweating and breathing hard, though she could tell by the butterflies in her stomach that her reaction was mostly nerves. She had certainly been in gunfights with desperate suspects before, but never in this kind of a pitched battle.

The staircase rose to a semicircular entrance platform that sat just inside the cave mouth. A trio of freshly killed Jiralhanae snipers had been dragged over to benches on the far edge and laid out facedown, a single gaping bullet hole in the back of each thick neck. From all the look of it, all three had died before any of them had realized they were in trouble.

Fred signaled Veta and Olivia to wait at the back of the platform while Mark and Ash crept into the jagged oval of the cave
mouth. They were nearly invisible as they slipped along the walls,
the photoreactive coating of their armor almost perfectly mimicking the murky gray limestone.

Even from the back of the platform, Veta could see that their
position was golden for Fred's attack plan. Located in a rocky outcropping about five meters higher than the village itself, the cave
mouth opened out into a small cobblestone circle with a decora-
tive fountain in the center. The tiny courtyard was littered with
bodies—many of them civilian—and on the far side, the turnstiles
and admission booths at the bottom of the steps had been leveled
by explosives.

Beyond the circle lay Wendosa's central boulevard, a long,
corpse-strewn avenue flanked on both sides by burned-out buildings with smoke and particle beams still pouring from their empty
windows. Three hundred meters distant stood the battle-scarred
compound of a large resort hotel, its darkened windows twinkling
with muzzle flashes. The sign HOTEL WENDOSA hung over its grand
gateway, which was blocked by the smoking remnants of a Warthog utility vehicle. Save for the small-arms fire, the village looked
less like a war zone than it did a ghost town, and Veta was hard-
pressed to see how five people were going to sway the outcome of
a fight that already appeared lost.

Not so with the Spartans. Fred studied the situation for thirty
seconds, then handed the worm-thing to Olivia. He wrenched a
trio of stone benches from the platform perimeter—snapping the
steel anchoring bolts as though they were twigs—and set them out
just inside the cave mouth, where they would remain cloaked in
shadow. He waved Olivia and Veta forward, motioning them each

behind a bench, then took the worm-thing back and glanced over at Veta.

"You know what to do?"

"Shoot the big guys," Veta said.

"Close enough," Fred said. He lay prone on the cave floor, trapping the worm-thing beneath his abdomen, then peered around the end of the middle bench. "Ash and Mark will open up first. With any luck, it will take the Keepers a while to realize what's happening."

"So don't fire until the lieutenant does," Ash clarified. He was kneeling at the edge of the cave mouth, almost invisible in his SPI armor. "And concentrate on the closest targets. Leave the long-range stuff to Mark and me."

"Will do," Veta said. "But how do I confirm my targets? All I can see right now are beam streaks and muzzle flashes."

Olivia snickered. "Confirming won't be a problem," she said, assuming a prone firing position similar to Fred's. "If they're shooting at us or the Hotel Wendosa . . . that's confirmed."

"Fair enough." Veta was starting to see how some of her in-grained police practices might prove a liability in a free-fire zone. She dropped to her belly and angled herself to look around the end of her bench. "Just one more question."

"Make it fast," Olivia snapped. "Marines are dying out there."

Veta glanced back at the Huragok. It was hovering behind Fred, staring out through the cave mouth with its long head-stalk canted to one side.

"What about our friend there?"

Olivia glanced back and tried to drive it off by hissing and tossing bits of rubble in its direction. The Huragok seemed mesmerized by the view of the village and merely drew its head-stalk back close to its body. She soon gave up and turned back toward the village.

"It's not exactly brave," she said. "It'll probably take cover as soon as the shooting starts."

But it didn't. As Mark and Ash fired their first salvo of particle beams, the Huragok dropped down behind Fred and fixed its gaze on the worm-thing. Veta tried to wave it back down the stairs, but if it understood what she wanted, it had no interest in obeying.

"Forget about the Huragok," Fred called. "Worrying about it now will only get you both killed."

Veta looked forward again and watched in amazement as Mark and Ash used their beam rifles to silence a dozen Keepers in half as many seconds. It was like magic. The weapons would send an indigo beam flashing into a distant window or wall, and an instant later a Keeper position would fall silent. A couple of times, a weapon tumbled out into the street below, and once the slender torso of a Kig-Yar flopped out over a sill.

Then an eerie lull started to descend over the battle as the Keepers began to react to the death raining down on them from the cave mouth.

"Okay, we've got their attention," Fred said. "Flush 'em out."

Ash and Mark tossed the beam weapons aside and snatched the battle rifles off the weapon mounts on their armor, and a deafening clatter echoed off the cave walls as the Spartans let loose. Jets of alien blood flew from windows and doorways far and near, and every couple of heartbeats, a Keeper warrior would tumble out into the street.

Veta followed the Spartans' lead, firing three-round bursts into any window where she noticed the hulking figure of a Jiralhanae or recalled a beam flash. Three times she was rewarded by a blood spray through her scope, and three times she was surprised by the joy she felt racing through her chest.

Veta tried to tell herself it was just relief, the thrill of knowing she had taken out an enemy before it eliminated her. But it was not something she had ever felt previously. Every time she had killed in the past, it had been up close and personal, either self-defense or justice delivered, and the experience had always left her feeling drained and hollow and a little bit lonely.

But this . . . this *exhilaration* . . . it frightened her.

After what seemed like forever but could only have been a couple of seconds, the muzzle flashes in the nearby windows grew suddenly rounder and brighter, and stone chips began to flake off the bench she was hiding behind. Exhilaration exploded into terror, her pulse pounding so hard in her ears that she could not distinguish it from gunfire.

Veta shifted her aim toward the nearest muzzle flash, her eye pressed to the scope, then pulled the trigger and felt the barrel rising with the recoil of the three-round burst and saw the strobing shape of a huge brutish face disintegrating beneath her rounds.

Veta shifted to another window and spotted the long snout and pebbly face of a Kig-Yar peering over the jaws of a sparking plasma rifle. She pulled the trigger and . . . nothing. Empty magazine.

Already.

Veta ejected the magazine and reached for her ammo satchel as her cover began to disintegrate. She pulled a fresh clip out of the satchel, but before she could reload, Fred pulled her rifle out of her hands and tossed it aside.

Veta saw his lips moving. It was impossible to hear him over the battle din, but he was saying something like *take this* and tossing the worm-thing over her arm. Yanking her to her feet as he rose, he pushed her behind him and started through the cave mouth.

It was all Veta could do to hold on to her ammo satchel and keep pace as they raced outside and bounded down a short flight of broad white stairs. The worm-thing was surprisingly light and elastic, hanging over her forearm like a warm towel and making her skin prickle every time its tentacles twitched.

Three steps later, they were sprinting across the plaza, beams and bullets ricocheting off Fred's energy shields from three directions. Ash and Mark were somewhere on the far side of the fountain, hurling grenades and pouring suppression fire in all directions. As the shock waves from the small explosions hit them, Olivia was pressed close to Veta's back, firing her battle rifle with one hand and the M7 with the other.

And the damned Huragok was floating right along with them, two of its tentacles wrapped beneath Veta's armpits and reaching up to clutch the collar of her combat vest. Surprised to discover it clinging to her, she glanced back and found its head-stalk extended over her shoulder, twisted around so it could keep three eyes on the worm-thing.

Apparently, Veta had been promoted to pet caddy.

By the time the squad reached the stone balustrade at the plaza perimeter, Olivia was out of ammo and tiny forks of overload static were dancing across Fred's energy shield. The nearest shelter—a burned-out restaurant with a gaping square of emptiness where its glass façade used to be—was still ten paces away, and Veta began to fear that Fred's plan to relieve Charlie Company had been a little overambitious. Maybe more than a little.

Then half the storefronts along the main avenue erupted with detonations, and curtains of thick black smoke began billowing into the street. Veta glimpsed movement above and spotted two figures in blocky Mjolnir armor crouching on rooftops opposite each other. Both were holding grenade launchers and pouring incendiary rounds into nearby structures. The other pair of Spartan-IIIs—Tom and Lucy, Veta recalled—were more difficult to spot in their SPI armor. But the twin streams of heavy machine-gun fire ripping furrows through second-story walls left no doubt they were near.

Clearly, the Spartans were just getting started.

With the rest of Blue Team providing cover, Veta and the others had no trouble reaching the destroyed restaurant.

Ash and Mark entered first and cleared the room, killing a pair of waiting Kig-Yar. Moving upstairs, they sent a terrified human Keeper leaping out of a second-story window into the street below. He landed wrong in front of the building, snapping his ankle, but Olivia leaned around a doorjamb long enough to end his agony with a three-round burst to the head.

Fred pointed Veta to a secure corner near the back of the demolished dining room. "You stand by over there with our tentacled friends while I establish comms," he said. "And you might want to draw that peashooter of yours. We have the Keepers disrupted for now, but there are a lot of Brutes out there. Getting knocked on their heels is just going to make them mad."

"Copy that," Veta said. "But please see what you can find out about my people, will you?"

Veta had already left Cirilo lying at the bottom of the cave, and she was shaken to realize that he might not be the only friend she had lost.

Fred nodded. "Sure thing."

Veta retreated to the corner and slung her ammo satchel onto a glass-strewn table—then felt a paralyzing shock in the arm holding the worm-thing. Thinking she had been hit by a sniper, Veta dropped to the floor and whirled around.

There was no sign of blood or injury—only the Huragok's tentacle now holding the scramble grenade and the worm-thing free-floating off her arm. She lunged for it, but it quickly rippled out of her reach and headed for the kitchen.

"Fred—a little help!" Veta started toward the kitchen. "Your damn flatworm just gave me the slip!"

CHAPTER 17

0808 hours, July 5, 2553 (military calendar)
Hector Nyeto Conference Room, Montero Vitality Center,
Montero Cavern Surface
Campos Wilderness District, Planet Gao, Cordoba System

Despite the gravity of the battle for Wendosa, Commander Murtag Nelson was finding it difficult to focus on Major Wingate's tactical briefing—and not just because of the man's droning voice. Murtag's gaze kept drifting across the holographic situation map to the Well of Echoes—the mysterious, vine-draped pit that almost certainly dropped into the heart of the Forerunner base. He was too smart to dwell on past failures, but he *did* wish he had recognized its nature a week ago, when he still had enough personnel to mount a mission into its depths.

"Commander Nelson?" Tereem Wingate's tone was not quite a rebuke, but it was impatient. As commander of the 717th's combat arm, the major was unaccustomed to having the attention of his audience wander. "We were talking about the situation in Wendosa? We have people dying there right now."

"My apologies, Major." Murtag was careful to avoid snapping;

Wingate was the one soldier in the 717th he could not afford to peeve. "I was just thinking about our next move."

Wingate scowled. "Our next move, Commander?" A stocky, square-faced man with graying, close-cropped hair, his expression reminded Murtag of a drill sergeant on babysitting duty—which was probably exactly how he felt about being assigned to Murtag's battalion. "*What* next move?"

"I know where to find the Forerunner base," Murtag said. "How many men can you spare for an escort mission?"

Wingate's eyes bulged so far Murtag feared they might pop loose. "*Now,* sir? With everything that's going on?"

"It would be better to do it *before* we're booted off the planet, don't you agree?" Murtag was careful to keep a reasonable tone. "So what can you give me? Two platoons, Major? Three?"

Wingate's weathered face grew an even deeper shade of red. "I can't give you any, Commander—not with the 717th's top combat company getting shredded in Wendosa and the other two on the way to relieve it!"

"What about Sierra Company?"

"Our *security* force?" Wingate was aghast. "With snipers in the jungle and a mob of radicals waiting to storm the grounds? With all due respect, Commander, have you lost your mind? We're already down our two Pelicans and one of the Falcons. If we let them take out the last Falcon, we won't have any airlift capacity at all!"

"My point exactly," Murtag replied. "We're here to recover a Forerunner ancilla. I know where to find it, and we're running out of time. I'd be crazy *not* to go after it."

Wingate's face remained crimson, but his eyes grew a little less wild. "We . . . just don't have the personnel, Commander." He turned back to the situation map. "Perhaps something will occur to us as we go over the current tactical situation. Shall we proceed?"

Murtag clenched his teeth. While he was technically Wingate's superior, the only combat personnel he had direct authority over were the Spartans—and they weren't available. If he hoped to reach the Forerunner base anytime soon, he would need to persuade Wingate first.

"Very well, Major," he said. "If we must."

"Thank you, Commander."

Wingate aimed a laser pointer toward the center of the map, where a holograph of Wendosa sat atop the broad crest of a long, jungle-clad ridge. Taken by a reconnaissance drone shortly after dawn, the image captured not only the previous day's destruction, but also a hail of tracer fire and plasma beams flying between a hotel complex and dozens of nearby buildings.

A kilometer from the hotel, the wreckage of a UNSC Pelican lay in the village's small entrance plaza, its cockpit a blasted-out hollow and its hull ripped open by self-destruct charges. It was hard to tell what had initially crippled the craft, but the ground around it was pocked with craters, and the buildings on the plaza perimeter had been reduced to rubble.

The orange dot of Wingate's pointer settled on the walled hotel complex. "As you can see," he said, "Charlie Company has taken a defensive position in Hotel Wendosa. The Keepers of the One Freedom have yet to attempt a melee assault, so we assume the Spartans are patrolling outside the perimeter, breaking up Jiralhanae formations before they can charge."

Wingate circled the pointer around the Hotel Wendosa, as though he feared Murtag wasn't familiar enough with military parlance to know what "patrolling outside the perimeter" meant.

"I'm sure you're correct," Murtag said. "How long can that continue?"

"It's hard to know," Wingate admitted. "But we've been very successful with our resupply drops, even with just the one Falcon left. So our people aren't short of munitions."

"How *long*, Major?" Murtag repeated. If he didn't lose Charlie Company, he just might escape Parangosky's wrath and retain his ONI commission. But if he lost an entire combat company without bringing back the ancilla—or at least something big—he would consider himself lucky to only be drummed out of the service. "And spare me the equivocation. I need to know if they'll last until the relief column reaches them."

Wingate lowered his eyes and gave a reluctant head shake. "I just don't know."

He moved the pointer to the edge of Wendosa, then began to trace a sinuous brown line running along the crest of a jungle ridge. About halfway along, the line dissolved into a series of long dashes, then grew solid again and descended the ridge toward an intersection with a larger road. On the intersection side of the dashes sat a long column of Warthog APCs.

"This is the only road into Wendosa," Wingate said. His pointer stopped at the dashes. "And the Committee to Preserve Gao Independence blew it up right here."

Murtag's stomach dropped. "Then that's as far as the relief column has advanced?"

"That's as far as the column advanced *yesterday*," Wingate said. "When the APCs couldn't go any farther, both companies dismounted and continued on foot."

Murtag studied the ridge between the blown section of road and Wendosa. "How far is it from the breach to the village?"

"Ten kilometers," Wingate said.

"Only ten?" Murtag frowned, trying to figure out why the relief companies weren't in Wendosa already. "That's all?"

"We're talking ten kilometers through jungle and rough terrain, Commander."

"And they couldn't circle around the breach on foot and continue along the road," Murtag surmised. "That would have been too easy."

Wingate nodded. "Mined." He pointed the laser at some of the gaps between dashes. "That's what happened here. And even if it hadn't, marching a road through that terrain is a good way to lose your entire column."

Murtag sighed and closed his eyes, echoes of Parangosky's cold fury already ringing in his ears. "These Keepers of the One Freedom aren't your run-of-the-mill ex-Covenant religious faction, are they?"

"No, sir," Wingate replied. "They're good, they're organized— and I'm certain they have help."

"The independence committee?"

"No doubt about it," Wingate said. "My guess is President Aponte himself is behind it. You know how these pro-autonomy Colonials are—they smile and nod, but as soon as your back is turned, the knives come out."

That wasn't the way Aponte struck Murtag, but he saw no purpose in arguing the point. Instead, he asked, "So how close *is* the relief column?"

"As of dawn, less than two kilometers from Wendosa," Wingate replied. "But that last stretch includes a tough climb. It could take two hours or two days."

Murtag sighed. "And you really can't find an escort platoon for me?" He knew the answer even before asking, but he had to try. "The sooner I find the ancilla, the better it'll be for everyone."

"I understand that, Commander," Wingate said. "We're stretched too thin already. But after the task force enters orbit, I should be able to give you an entire company."

"The task force?" Murtag asked. He was starting to think Wingate wasn't as smart as his rank suggested. "What makes you think the task force will change anything?"

Wingate furrowed his brow. "You mean it's not coming?"

"Of course it's *coming*," Murtag said. "It's probably approaching orbit as we speak. But that doesn't mean much—not if you're right about Gao itself being behind these attacks."

"I'm not following you," Wingate said. "If the task force is coming, why wouldn't they reinforce us? We're already under attack here."

"And Gao is a sovereign planet," Murtag pointed out. "Admiral Tuwa will threaten and bluff, but she's not going to risk another Insurrection just to save our hides. In fact, I'm fairly certain Admiral Parangosky gave her orders *not* to."

Wingate's face went slack, and for a moment, he seemed too stunned to answer. Finally, he seemed to grasp that the UNSC was not playing under wartime rules. "I see. What about Owls?"

Murtag nodded. "She'll drop a few of those." Owls were the stealth version of Pelicans, smaller and more lightly armed and armored, but capable of slipping undetected into most planetary atmospheres. "But she won't send enough to risk being accused of an invasion. So we'll get a few platoons at most. Will that be enough to turn things around?"

"It's better than nothing," Wingate said. "But if you're right about the task force's orders, our situation is clearly different now. Can you hold off your mission until the Owls—"

"Excuse me, Major." Wingate's aide, a petite captain wearing a comm set over her short red hair, stepped over to the holograph.

"But you and Commander Nelson will want to hear this report. It's from Wendosa, and it will affect your planning."

Noting the gleam in the captain's eyes, Murtag said, "We could use some good news." He glanced toward the bulky projection unit hanging above the holographic map. "Wendell, let us hear it over the speakers."

"Of course, Commander." Wendell's voice seemed to emanate from the walls themselves, as he was tapped into the conference room's state-of-the-art public address system. "Go ahead, Captain Breit. You are now reporting directly to Commander Nelson and Major Wingate."

"Copy that." Breit's crisp voice was barely audible through a background clatter of small-arms fire. "Sirs, the situation here has improved. Charlie Company is launching a counterattack."

Murtag began to feel more optimistic about his future prospects. "Then the relief column has arrived?"

"Not yet, Commander," Breit said. "But Fred-104 and his squad came out of the cave and caught the enemy from behind. Between them and the rest of Blue Team, the Spartans have disrupted the attack."

"And you intend to counterattack before the enemy has time to regroup," Wingate said.

"Affirmative, sir."

"Good plan," Wingate said.

"Thank you, sir," Breit replied. "And, Commander Nelson, there's something else you should know."

"I'm listening."

"I don't have all the details," Breit continued. "But it sounds like Fred and his squad brought a couple of artifacts out of the cave."

"That tells me nothing," Murtag snapped. "*Details,* Captain. I need details."

"All I know is what I heard over the comms," Breit said. Explosions began to rumble in the background, turning his voice buzzy with static. "It came from Kelly . . . said it looks like Fred found the objective . . . brought back a hero doc and some kind of floating worm-device."

"*Hero doc?*" Murtag's gaze drifted back to the near edge of the holographic contour map. The Well of Echoes was a lot closer to the Montero Vitality Center than it was Wendosa, but Fred and his squad had been underground for more than two and a half days—plenty of time for a squad of Spartans to travel that far. "Could she have said *Huragok?*"

"Sure, why not?" Breit said. "Look, Commander, things are wild here. I'm not even sure Kelly made physical contact with Fred. Her report might be based on something she saw through a scope."

"It doesn't matter, Captain." Murtag's stomach was fluttering with excitement. "Fred and those two artifacts are mission critical. You will secure them *ASAP.* Clear?"

When the only reply to Murtag's order was a din-filled pause, Wingate asked, "Captain Breit, is it possible to fulfill Commander Nelson's request?"

"Unclear, sir," Breit replied. "Like I said, it's pretty wild here."

"Then do your best, Captain. I'll try to get you some support." Wingate paused, then asked: "Wendell, what's the status of the Falcon?"

"The ground crew is preparing it for another supply drop," Wendell reported. "The cargo is being loaded as we speak. It's scheduled to be airborne in twenty-two minutes."

"Too long," Wingate said. "Hold the rest of the cargo and get that bird aloft *now.*"

"But the craft is only at forty-two percent capacity," Wendell said. "It's highly inefficient to risk a flight over hostile terrain to deliver half a payload."

"Do it anyway," Murtag said, guessing Wingate's intent. "Resupply isn't our priority at the moment."

"If you insist," Wendell said. "But you're only saving fifteen minutes. The crew still needs to refuel and do a preflight inspection. That Falcon has been making combat runs all night long, and there's a thirty-two percent chance that a critical system needs service."

"Seven minutes will have to do," Wingate interrupted. "Captain Breit, I know you can't wait for the air support, but drop some smoke on—"

A pulsing, ear-piercing screech filled the room, cutting the order short. Fearing it heralded the arrival of a missile or a high-powered artillery shell, Murtag dropped to the floor and covered his head.

Nothing.

The screech continued, pulsing through the sound system with a vibrato quiver that seemed oddly familiar. He uncovered his head and looked up to find Wingate still standing next to him, scowling in disapproval. Behind the major, the aide had flung her headset aside and was holding her ear, her face contorted in pain.

"It's nothing to be afraid of, Commander!" Wingate had to yell to make himself heard above the din. "Our communications are just being jammed."

Murtag wasn't so sure. As he grew accustomed to the noise, he began to recognize its pulsing rhythm—and the repetitive pattern of its quivering pitch. Heart pounding harder than ever, he jumped to his feet and looked up at the projection unit.

"Wendell, run a pattern analysis on that signal," Murtag ordered. "Compare it to the ancilla's original distress calls—and see if you can identify an origination point."

The screech continued unabated, and Wendell did not reply.

"Wendell?"

"He can't answer you, sir," the aide said. Having pulled a comm tablet off her belt, she was frantically tapping through menus. "We've lost control of our communications network."

"Which elements?" Wingate demanded. "And who's doing it?"

When the aide looked up, her jaw had fallen slack. "All of them, Major," she said. "And . . . it looks like the hijacking code came from—"

"Wendosa, of course," Murtag said. "And it probably originated from a Spartan comm unit."

The aide looked at him. "That's right, sir," she confirmed. "It came directly from Fred-104. How did you know?"

"Because that's the simplest explanation." Murtag started for the door, gesturing for Wingate to follow. "Major, come with me. I'm probably going to need you."

Wingate fell in beside him. "To do what, Commander?"

"To order that Falcon pilot to make a hot landing in Wendosa," Murtag said. "I don't think she'll do it on my authority alone."

"Why the hell would I do that?" They reached the door, and Wingate stopped. "That's our last Falcon!"

"I know," Murtag said. "But we need to evacuate Fred at all costs—and we need to do it now. He's captured the ancilla."

CHAPTER 18

A crisp *thud bang* rang out above Wendosa, and Castor looked up between a pair of charred rafters to find a smoky starburst spreading across the sky. Tiny tongues of flame appeared at the end of each arm and began to arc downward, and he feared the UNSC was dropping a pod of shock troopers on the village—or even a packet of weapons of mass destruction.

Then two cross-shaped slivers entered the same swath of sky. As Castor watched, they drifted together and erupted into a smoky fireball, and he realized it was the humans' news-gathering drones that had been circling Wendosa, and they were no longer flying an orderly pattern. Instead, the craft were swirling about like gnats, crossing paths and occasionally colliding. Some had drifted so high they were barely visible, while others had dropped so low Castor could see the camera domes hanging beneath their bellies.

"The Gaos have lost command of their sky-eyes," said Orsun.

The grizzled old warrior was standing next to Castor, both of them on the third story of a burned-out guesthouse on Wendosa's central avenue.

Their escorts were waiting below, as it would have been unwise to trust the sagging floor with more weight than necessary.

"The infidels are jamming their control frequencies," Orsun continued. "Just as they are jamming our battlenet."

"So it appears," Castor said. "But what is it they hope to hide?"

"A nuclear strike?"

"It is possible," Castor said. "But perhaps a chemical or biological attack would be easier to conceal afterward."

Orsun's lips pulled back from his broken fangs. "They would not dare!"

"Never underestimate what humans will dare. That has been the death of more than one shipmaster."

As Castor spoke, the droning whine of turboprop engines sounded high over the jungle behind him. He turned and saw the thin-waisted silhouette of a UNSC Falcon diving toward Wendosa, its chin gun flashing as it sprayed suppression fire along the village edge. At first it appeared the craft was just making another supply drop, but instead of releasing the usual clutch of ordnance pods, it entered an evasive zigzag and continued to descend.

A single missile rose out of the jungle, but its approach was nose-to-nose with the Falcon. There was no time to achieve lock-on before they were past each other, and the missile arced out of sight without detonating.

A heartbeat later, the rest of Castor's pack opened fire, lacing the air with plasma beams and crystal needles. The sturdy Falcon shrugged off the attacks as though it were a flying *kalcoom*, then pulled up and flipped its rotors into the horizontal position. Castor was pleased to catch a glimpse of the door gunners hanging dead in their harnesses, then the Falcon dropped out of view.

He turned toward the front of the ruin and crouched down behind a fist-size shell hole. With any luck at all, the enemy snipers would not notice the change of light as he looked through the spyhole, and he would survive long enough to figure out what the infidels were planning.

What little Castor could see was not good. The Falcon had landed inside the walled compound of what the Gaos called the Hotel Wendosa, and the infidel marines were advancing up the corpse-strewn street in teams, with one squad racing forward while the other provided cover. As they passed each building, they cleared it swiftly and mercilessly, using launchers to fire grenades through the windows, then stepping inside to finish any survivors with small-arms fire.

Castor could not actually see any Spartans from his spyhole, but the presence of the armored demons was impossible to deny. Any Kig-Yar or human Keeper of the One Freedom sympathizer who popped up behind a windowsill or peered around a corner was felled by a three-round burst. And whenever a band of Jiralhanae tried to mass for a charge, they were soon disrupted by the arrival of a screaming rocket.

The only feasible response was to fall back and regroup—and that was exactly what Castor would have done, had he been able to issue the command. But the battlenet was being jammed, and his warriors were spread over a square kilometer of village. There was simply no way to issue the order.

After a moment, Castor realized the humans were not using their comm systems, either. As the squads advanced, they were signaling to each other with hand gestures and shouted commands. After watching a few moments, he even began to pick out runners relaying messages between the advancing squads and the command post inside the walled compound.

Castor pulled back from the spyhole. "The infidels are not the ones jamming our battlenet," he said. "It appears their communications have failed, too."

Orsun cocked his head. "You are certain?"

"You challenge my judgment?"

Orsun looked away. "Never, Dokab," he said. "But my understanding fails me. If the infidels are not jamming us, who is?"

"Indeed." Castor stepped to the far corner of the room. "Who?"

He pressed himself tight against the front wall, then peered out through the empty window back toward the jagged oval of the cave entrance. The fountain in the small courtyard continued to spray, jetting a full five meters into the air before splashing down into a pool pink with blood. The cobblestones surrounding the basin were pocked with grenade craters and littered with dead marines and derelict battle rifles, and Castor could not help feeling humbled when he recalled the confidence with which he had led the charge out of the cavern and across those same cobblestones.

His Keepers had outnumbered the infidels by at least four-to-one, and Castor was certain his victory would be an easy one. But the enemy had fought with discipline and a fierceness he had not expected from humans, and a day later he could not even say how much of his own pack remained—though he knew it was less than half of his original five hundred.

Clearly, Castor was being punished.

He had been arrogant, and now the Oracle was testing him, giving him one last chance to prove his commitment to the Great Journey.

This time, Castor would not fail. This time, the Dokab would be guided not by pride, but by faith.

No sooner had Castor renewed his resolve than he was rewarded by a glimpse of the Spartan who had humiliated him. The demon was on the opposite side of the street, fighting with his faceplate raised, racing past a window just three buildings up from the structure where he and his infidel companions had taken refuge after fleeing the cave mouth.

Castor stretched a hand toward Orsun. "Beam rifle."

By the time Orsun slapped the weapon into Castor's palm, the Spartan had vanished from sight. Knowing he would have just one chance to take his vengeance, Castor led his target by aiming the nozzle of the beam rifle at the next window. He set the aiming reticle at head level, where he would be able to take the target between the eyes—then saw a long, flat, tentacle-frilled body float into view and block his shot.

So surprised that he almost opened fire anyway, Castor quickly loosened his grasp on the weapon's handle. Before he could take his next breath, the tentacle-frilled thing was joined by another floating figure—a green, undersize Huragok.

"Orsun, come now," Castor said. "Look at this."

Sliding along the wall behind Castor, Orsun stepped into the corner and peered over Castor's shoulder. By then, the flat-bodied thing had passed out of view, and the Huragok was following.

Worried it would be gone before Orsun found the right window, Castor said, "Third building from the end, lower window. Tell me what you see."

"It is a Huragok, Dokab," he said. "A strange color and it appears small, but still a Huragok. Where did it come from?"

"The demons," Castor said. "Now it is certain. They have defiled sacred ground with their presence."

Still waiting for the Spartan to appear in the second window,

Castor kept his eye pressed to the scope of the beam rifle and activated the integrated battlenet link inside his helmet. Once again, the repetitive screech filled his ears, pulsing and urgent.

"And now we know who is jamming the battlenet," Castor said. "It is the Oracle itself—calling for our help."

CHAPTER 19

0840 hours, July 5, 2553 (military calendar)
Avelos Avenue, Wendosa Village, Montero Cavern Surface
Campos Wilderness District, Planet Gao, Cordoba System

Knowing better than to present a predictable target in a sniper-heavy environment, Fred dropped to the floor and crawled past the second window on his belly. There were glass cases everywhere—some of them even in one piece—so he figured he was in some kind of museum. The Huragok and its worm-thing friend were already five meters ahead, floating across the debris-strewn room toward a narrow wooden staircase leading up to the second floor.

Fred had no idea why the two runaways had chosen to make their break in the middle of a battle, but it seemed obvious that their escape had something to do with the sudden comm black-out. That wasn't something he had expected from the pair, but it probably shouldn't have come as a surprise—not when they were something created by the Forerunners.

He reached the far side of the window and rose to a knee. Pressing himself close to the wall, he shouldered his battle rifle and put a burst into the stairs directly above the pair. The

Huragok reversed direction and withdrew into a corner, but the worm-thing called his bluff and ascended even more rapidly. Fred fired another burst, this time being careful to hit the step riser just beneath the thing. It pivoted on its axis, turning its tail lens in his direction.

Ash stepped into view at the top of the staircase, holding an armed scramble grenade. He gave it an underhanded toss. The scrambler landed dead center atop its target and stuck there, and the worm-thing's tentacles fanned out stiff. Its body rippled and curled as though the thing were suffering a seizure, then it finally went limp and dropped.

Ash bounded down the stairs to scoop the thing up. An instant later, Olivia hobbled in from a secondary exhibit room, her M7 submachine gun in one hand and an armed scramble grenade in the other.

She glanced toward the Huragok, then asked, "That one, too?"

"I wouldn't," Veta Lopis said, speaking from the other side of the window behind Fred. "You wouldn't even be walking if it hadn't patched you up."

"So?" Olivia asked.

"So you're still limping," Lopis said. "And it looks smart enough to hold a grudge."

Olivia shrugged and looked to Fred. "We're almost home," she said. To a Spartan, home was any base they happened to be operating from at the moment. "I can last that long."

"That's not the point," Lopis said. "The Huragok saved your life down there."

"You think I don't know that?" Olivia asked. "I do, and I'm grateful. But it's still a threat to the mission."

"How?" Lopis asked. "All it did was try to escape with its buddy. Tell me how that's a—"

"Put the scrambler away, 'Livi," Fred said.

Lopis was probing again, still trying to figure out how Blue Team's mission was linked to the killings she was investigating. Fred wanted to order Lopis to give it a rest until they were out of combat, but that would have been like telling the Huragok to leave Olivia's legs alone. It was just in Lopis's nature, and trying to fight it would cause more trouble than it fixed. At least she kept her head straight once the shooting started; the inspector was definitely more cop than soldier, but she had given him no reason to regret handing her a battle rifle.

When Olivia remained slow to secure the scramble grenade, Fred said, "That's an order, Spartan." He glanced over at the Huragok, then added, "The Huragok isn't going to be a problem, as long as we keep it away from the other thing. Besides, it's not exactly an AI. There's no telling what a scrambler would do to it."

Olivia frowned in Lopis's direction, but finally nodded and reset the scramble grenade's safety. "Whatever you say, Lieutenant."

Fred checked his comm unit and was disappointed to find it still jammed. Either the worm-thing was not the source, or it had actually corrupted the entire network.

Ash tipped a hand vertically, signaling for Fred's attention, then raised two fingers and pointed toward a half-splintered door at the back of the main exhibit room. With his HUD on the blink, Fred had no way to tell whether the contacts were friendly or hostile, but until he knew which, that door was remaining closed. Fred motioned for Olivia to take the worm-thing and signaled Ash to secure the door, then glanced back at Lopis.

"Try to keep the Huragok under control," he said, speaking just loudly enough to make himself heard over the battle outside. "And don't let it—"

"Near the worm-thing again," Lopis finished. She dropped to her belly and began to crawl past the window, cradling an MA37 assault rifle she had picked up in the last building. "Believe it or not, I worked that out all by myself."

Fred smirked at her sarcasm, then scrambled after Ash. A few meters into the shadows, he slipped behind a display case and returned to his feet, dodging as he rose.

The case disintegrated behind him, spraying helictites and cave pearls everywhere, and Fred realized an enemy sniper had been waiting for him to show himself.

Uttering a silent thanks to Frank Mendez for drilling evasion movement into him until it was second nature, Fred hurled himself over another case in a twisting dive. He glimpsed the purple flash of a particle beam burning through the wall behind him, then landed on his seat, facing back toward the window.

Lopis was already leaning around the corner of the window, pouring controlled bursts up Avelos Avenue toward a target Fred could not see. An instant later, the muffled *shriek-thump* of a UNSC rocket suggested that she was not the only one covering his back.

Knowing that the sniper would either be dead or looking for another position after the rocket strike, Fred spun around and scrambled to the back of the exhibit room.

By then, Ash was kneeling to one side of the door, looking through the charred hole of a plasma strike into the next room. He kept his faceplate pressed to the wall. But, as Fred approached, he raised a hand level with his helmet and gave a short lateral cut.

Stay cool.

Ash quickly returned his hand to his weapon and pivoted away from his spyhole, then looked past the door to make certain Fred was ready.

Fred scowled, but pressed his own back to the wall and nodded.

Ash turned to the wall and, through his helmet's external speakers, called, "Mark, what the hell are you doing?"

"Ash?" came the muffled reply. "That you?"

"That's right."

"Prove it."

"Okay. For one thing, you're off your Smoothers."

"Not good enough. Anyone could see that."

"Mark, think about it," Ash said. "There are only a handful of people in the entire galaxy who even know about the Smoothers."

"So?"

"So, most of them are Spartans," Ash said. "And all of them are friends or dead. Now, maybe you'd better tell us why you're holding a knife to that sergeant's throat. You know he's one of ours, right?"

Instead of answering, Mark asked, "Who's *us*?"

"I'm here," Fred said, listening for the first hint of a scuffle or clattering equipment. Clearly, Mark had entered the paranoid stage of his mental deterioration, and it was hard to know what might make him feel threatened or angry. "I'm going to open the door very slowly and have a look, and you *will* remain as you are. Is that clear?"

"Affirmative," Mark replied. "As long as you really *are* the lieutenant."

"The Mjolnir only fits one guy," Fred said.

Mark hesitated a moment, then said, "Copy that."

Fred reached over and pushed the door open. When nothing happened, he stepped into the doorway of a small, cramped office and found Mark standing behind a lanky marine sergeant with ice-blue eyes and vaguely East Asian features. Mark had the blade

TROY DENNING

of a combat knife pressed to his captive's throat, and he was being careful to keep the man rocked back on his heels and too off balance to fight.

The sergeant's gaze went straight to Fred. "You Fred-104, mate?"

"That's right," Fred said, taken a bit off guard by the Australian accent—and by the sergeant's apparent lack of concern with the knife at his throat. "Hold on, and I'll get you—"

"Captain Breit needs you at the command post five minutes ago," the sergeant interrupted. "You're to report at once with those bloody artifacts you brought out of the cave."

Mark gave his helmet a slight shake, signaling trouble. "It's a trap, Lieutenant. This guy is an infiltrator."

"An infiltrator with an Australian accent?"

"He was trying to penetrate our position," Mark said. His expression was hidden behind his faceplate, but his feet were askew, his bearing agitated and twitchy. "And he didn't know the day code."

"You're the yobber who didn't know the day code," the sergeant replied. "Your challenge phrase was three days old."

"That's not Mark's fault, Sergeant," Fred said, putting a little edge in his voice. He knew from experience it was more effective to win the trust of a paranoid Gamma than to try reasoning with him, so his best hope of bringing Mark under control was to react as though what he had done was perfectly normal. "We've been out of contact for three days, down in the cave. Isn't that right, Mark?"

Mark's helmet cocked to one side, but he did not reply.

Deciding to take the lack of response as a sign of progress, Fred looked back to the sergeant. "Anything else you need to tell me, Sergeant?"

"That's it," the sergeant said. "Those bludgers in the science company must think you found something important. They want you evacuated back to headquarters."

"Evacuated?" Fred didn't like the sound of that—not while Charlie Company was stuck here fighting—but it was hard to argue with the logic of the order. The 717th was here to recover Forerunner technology, and even if Fred's squad didn't have the ancilla, they had a new kind of Huragok and some sort of worm machine. "Very well, Sergeant. Carry on."

"Carry on?" Now that he had completed his assignment, the sergeant finally looked a little frightened. His eyes flickered toward the knife blade still held at his throat, and he said, "Right— as soon as he lets me go, I'll show you the way."

"Thanks. That would be a big help." Keeping his tone as casual as he could, Fred shifted his gaze to Mark and said, "Okay, you can let him go now, Spartan."

Forcing himself to act as though he were confident of Mark's obedience, Fred ducked through the door and signaled Ash to gather the others. Then he took a deep breath and, half expecting to find Mark gone and the sergeant bleeding out, he turned back to the cramped office.

Mark and the sergeant were now standing side by side. Mark's combat knife was back in its sheath, and the sergeant was holding his MA37 assault rifle, leaning away from Mark and keeping a finger on the trigger. Fred breathed a silent sigh of relief, then made a mental note to demand a longer-lasting Smoother the next time— the subcutaneous kind that couldn't be lost or destroyed during a firefight. They were hugely expensive and could only be changed out in a medical facility, but that was better than having an entire squad of Gammas spike-out in the middle of a surprise battle.

Fred stepped forward and, reading the name on the sergeant's chest tab, said, "Sergeant Nguyen, you know the fastest way, so you take point. Mark will cover you."

Nguyen paled at the thought of turning his back on a half-mad Spartan, and he was slow to acknowledge the order. Rather than press for a response, Fred merely held the man's gaze and waited. Any attempt to relieve Mark of his weapons would only deepen his paranoia—and even barehanded, a Spartan was deadly. So Fred needed to keep Mark at the front of the marching order, where he could keep an eye on him and move quickly to stop any trouble.

Finally, Nguyen seemed to take the hint and saluted.

"As you like, sir." He turned to Mark. "When we're challenged, I'll use *today's* codes. Okay, mate?"

Mark tilted his faceplate down and seemed to contemplate the question for a moment, then finally nodded. "Affirmative."

Nguyen glanced over at Fred. "Whenever you're ready, Lieutenant."

Fred nodded and said, "You'll be in good hands, Sergeant. Mark is our best sharpshooter, and the rest of us will be right behind him."

"That's right, Sarge." Mark's tone was low and almost menacing. "If we run into trouble, I'll have your back."

Nguyen grew even paler. "There shouldn't be any trouble—as long as you let me handle the jabber."

"Good idea, Sergeant," Fred said. It didn't take much imagination to picture Mark making a disastrous response to a challenge. "Mark, you can consider that an order."

"Affirmative," Mark replied.

Ash returned with Olivia and Lopis and the two Forerunner "artifacts." The worm was draped over Olivia's arm, still twitching as the scramble grenade flooded it with EMP. The Huragok was sticking close, trying to sneak a tentacle past Lopis to free its companion. Had Fred not known that they were both just very advanced machines, he would have sworn that the pair really *were* buddies.

Fred gave the signal to move, and Nguyen led them all into the alley behind the museum. It wound through a warren of supply warehouses and dreary taverns, all pocked by battle damage and apparently deserted. The squad dashed into a covered fruit bazaar packed with cowering villagers—many injured by stray fire. A chorus of alarmed cries rang out, and civilians began to dive behind cover and run for the exits. Fred and Nguyen shouted at the mob to freeze and quiet down, but their orders only seemed to make things worse.

The crowd didn't calm until Veta Lopis took over and announced in her Gao-accented voice that the soldiers were just passing through—and even then, it seemed to Fred that the bazaar remained on the verge of a stampede until the squad was gone.

After departing the fruit bazaar, Nguyen led them into a similar market for meat animals. This time, Fred let Veta Lopis do the talking from the start, and the nervous villagers simply stood aside and let the squad pass.

That wasn't to say the transit went smoothly. The bazaar was filled with crates of slithering reptiles and tanks of fish, mollusks, and cephalopods, and the Huragok kept veering aside to peer between slats or drop a tentacle into the water. But for whatever reason, it was the poultry that seemed to fascinate the Huragok most. Several times, it pulled away from Lopis to open the cages and snatch a clump of feathers, and soon there were a dozen squawking idjoms fluttering through rafters and fifty grain-plumped shirms darting underfoot. Tired of having the Huragok's tentacles slip from her grasp, Lopis finally grabbed it by the neck stalk, and the pair remained in a constant tug-of-war until the squad finally exited the place.

As they advanced from building to building, the squad took enemy fire only twice. The first time was from a Kig-Yar who made the mistake of thinking he'd take Fred out with a double beam strike. Fred's energy shields deflected the first shot, he evaded the second, and Mark eliminated the sniper before a third could be attempted.

The second attack came as they passed a group of bloodied humans carrying a wounded companion up the alley. Neither Fred nor his Spartans recognized the band as infiltrators, and Lopis greeted them with a friendly "heya." But when they responded with the same word, she allowed them to pass, then spun around with her MA37 at the ready. She took down half of them as they were still trying to collect their weapons off the "wounded" man's litter, and Fred and his Spartan companions killed the rest. Afterward, she explained that "heya" was not a Gao salutation. Had they been real villagers, they would have answered with "oyu." Something that Fred immediately committed to memory.

The squad did encounter a steady stream of marine fire teams. They were advancing up the alley in leapfrog order, clearing every third building and leaving the others cut off behind UNSC lines. Clearly, Charlie Company had the enemy on its heels and was pressing the counterattack. With a little support, the battle would quickly become a mop-up operation—which was why the last thing Fred wanted to do was evacuate.

But he had his orders.

At last, Sergeant Nguyen turned back toward the main avenue. They entered a bakery shop ruin filled with the day-old corpses of fallen marines, then found themselves directly across from the Hotel Wendosa. It was only forty meters from the bakery to the hotel's gateway, which sat at the back of a large crescent-shaped entry drive. The gate opening was more or less blocked by a wrecked Warthog, and Fred could see a couple of dozen marine sharpshooters peering over the privacy wall that flanked it.

But a few buildings up the avenue, no more than sixty meters away, a firefight was raging inside a large art gallery. A couple of dozen marines were crouching behind cabinets or lying on the floor behind support pillars, pouring fire toward the back of the shop. A storm of plasma bolts and spike flashes was coming back toward them, and it seemed clear that it would not be long before the UNSC position was overrun.

Fred would have liked to reinforce the outgunned platoon, but that was out of the question. The order to evacuate had been clear—and even if it hadn't been, putting the Huragok and spy drone at risk would have been a gross dereliction of duty. But with Kelly and the other half of Blue Team working a skirmish ring around the Hotel Wendosa, he knew relief would be coming soon, even with comms still being jammed. This kind of force buildup was exactly what the Spartans were working to prevent, and Kelly would have marine runners ready to summon her the moment a breakthrough situation developed.

Fred glanced back at the so-called artifacts. The worm-thing remained draped over Olivia's arm, and the Huragok was still attempting to slip past Lopis to get at it. He could probably have carried the worm himself and kept it shielded from incoming fire as they crossed the street, but the Huragok was another matter. Even if they could have attached a scramble grenade to it safely, the thing was too large to protect in the same way. There was no way to cross the boulevard without exposing it to fire from the surrounding rooftops *and* from the fierce firefight raging in the gallery.

"Is there another approach to the hotel?" Fred asked Nguyen.

"There's the back gate," Nguyen replied. "We could give it a go, but we'd have to fight the whole bloody way."

Fred nodded. "Had to check." He took a moment to formulate a plan, then motioned Mark to his side. "Can I count on you?"

Mark cocked his helmet to one side, then replied, "Why are you asking?"

"You're off your Smoothers, dork," Olivia said. She was at the front of the bakery shop, standing just behind Fred and Nguyen. "Twenty minutes ago, you were holding a knife to a marine sergeant's throat."

"He could have been an infiltrator," Mark said.

"He could have been the Master Chief for all you—"

"That's enough, 'Livi." Fred turned to find Lopis studying the pair with a pensive expression, no doubt taking mental notes about the rate and nature of the Gammas' mental deterioration. "Mark isn't the only one who's off his Smoothers—and I expect you *both* to hold it together anyway. Clear?"

Olivia dropped her gaze. "Sorry, Lieutenant." She turned to Mark. "Sorry, Mark."

"No problem, 'Livi. I know you're not yourself right now." Mark turned his faceplate back toward Fred. "And I'm not seeing things yet, Lieutenant—at least I don't *think* I am. What do you need?"

Fred paused, waiting to see if Mark would grow impatient or take offense, then finally pointed toward the roof. "Top cover," he said. "Try to get an angle on the firefight up the street, but take out anything that points a weapon our way."

Mark looked toward the art gallery and nodded. "Copy that."

"And once we're across—"

"I'll follow," Mark said. "No worries, sir. I may be coming apart, but I'm not stupid. Not yet, anyway."

Fred smiled and resisted the urge to slap him on the shoulder. "Glad to hear it," he said. "You've got two minutes to set up."

Mark snapped off a salute, then grabbed some ammunition and a spare BR55 battle rifle from a fallen marine and headed for the charred staircase in the bakery's back room. Fred outlined his plan to the others, then took the worm-thing from Olivia and looked back up the street.

The firefight in the art gallery had taken a turn for the worse. Several marines lay writhing and screaming on the glass-strewn sidewalk outside, and through the windows, he could see another dozen being forced back by a wall of charging Jiralhanae. Fred glanced at the surrounding rooftops, wondering what was taking Kelly and the rest of Blue Team so long to arrive, and considered sending Olivia and Ash to support the marines.

But he was going to need the two Gammas in the street with him, both to draw attention away from the artifacts and to help with suppression fire, and he couldn't risk the mission objective by dividing his force. The marines up the street would just have to hold on until Kelly arrived—and if they couldn't, at least their deaths wouldn't be for nothing.

Fred cursed whatever it was that was jamming comms and keeping him out of contact with the rest of Blue Team, then glanced over at Olivia. It was hard to say whether she would be slower than Lopis, but with her still-swollen legs, she would definitely be the slowest of the Spartans. "Ready?"

She nodded and flashed a nervous smile. "If you're waiting on me, you're wasting daylight."

Olivia sprang through the window and raced toward the Hotel

Wendosa with a limping gait as swift as it was awkward. If the Keepers in the gallery noticed her at all, they didn't bother to open fire, and she was approaching the hotel's crescent-shaped entry drive almost before Fred could signal everyone else forward.

Fred led the way himself, keeping the worm-thing shielded behind his body and using one hand to aim his battle rifle up the street. At the halfway point, the enemy opened up, spraying a handful of plasma bolts over the heads of the marines who were still trying to stop their charge. Fred's shields flared but held, then Mark's battle rifle began to crack from the bakery's rooftop, and the enemy fire quickly dwindled away.

Fred reached the entrance drive and glanced back. Nguyen lay sprawled in the middle of the avenue, his armor shredded and his body convulsing. Ash and Lopis were still five meters behind Fred, each clutching a Huragok tentacle in one hand and pulling it along with them. Ash, who was on the side toward the enemy, was trailing blood and holding an elbow close to his ribs, but Lopis appeared uninjured. With its head-stalk craned around so that it could watch over the worm-thing with one set of three eyes and look up the avenue with the other three, the Huragok seemed frightened but healthy. And it was making no attempt to go back after Nguyen—whatever its other virtues, apparently the thing had no interest in becoming a combat medic.

From the other side of the privacy wall came the rising whine of Falcon rotors spinning up. Olivia suddenly appeared at his side.

"Captain Breit is chomping at the bit, Lieutenant," she said. "You go in, and I'll—"

Olivia's offer was cut off as a wall of Jiralhanae came boiling out of the gallery, spraying spikes and plasma bolts down the avenue. There were no Kig-Yar or humans in the Keeper charge at all—as far as Fred could tell, it was all Brute. Mark's battle rifle began to crack so rapidly it sounded like automatic fire, and the front row of warriors dropped with blood stars blossoming on their jutting brows.

By then, Ash and Veta Lopis were racing past, heading toward the gate with the Huragok in tow. Fred and Olivia fell back after them, opening up on full auto and raking fire across the Jiralhanae at face level. Another trio of warriors went down, and a dozen more were staggering from the lead hail bouncing off their helmets and armor.

But the charge continued, the ground rumbling with Jiralhanae fury, and Fred's battle rifle clicked empty. He ejected the clip and, cradling the worm-thing in the crook of his elbow, reached for another.

The avenue erupted into smoke and flame, and Fred looked up to glimpse a row of Spartans aiming rocket and grenade launchers out the second-story windows near the bakery. Kelly and the rest of Blue Team had arrived. Another flurry of detonations filled the air with shards of cobblestone and flying Jiralhanae parts.

And still the charge continued.

A wall of armored warriors emerged from the smoke in full assault mode. Fred's energy shield crackled with hits. He slapped a new clip into the battle rifle and chambered a round—then felt a hand grab his arm and draw him back through the gateway, past the wrecked Warthog and into the hotel's inner courtyard.

Reacting instinctively to protect the artifact draped over the same arm, he spun the intruder around and found himself pointing a battle rifle at the chest of the square-faced, crooked-nosed commander of Charlie Company, Captain Baldric Breit.

"What part of 'at once' did you fail to understand, Lieutenant?" Breit demanded. "Commander Nelson wants you and the ancilla on that bird *now*."

Breit pointed across the hotel's ravaged courtyard to where a plasma-scorched, bullet-riddled Falcon sat on a cratered driveway, its rotors whirling and wisps of blue smoke trailing from one engine.

Too stunned to contemplate the craft's poor condition, Fred glanced down at the twitching worm-thing draped over his arm.

"*Ancilla?*" Fred gasped. "*This?*"

"That's what the orders said." Breit shook his finger toward the Falcon. "Now, go!"

"Negative, sir," Fred said. He started to pass the ancilla to Breit. "I have people fighting out there."

Breit pushed the ancilla back at Fred. "They're *my* people now, Lieutenant," he said. "Nelson's orders were clear. He wants *you* to deliver the ancilla personally."

Fred glanced over at the gateway, where Ash and Olivia were crouched behind the Warthog, pouring fire into the Keeper charge. He didn't need to look over the wall to know that the area directly beyond had been turned into a killing field, with marines and Spartans firing down into the Jiralhanae mass from both sides. Had the enemy been anything else, Fred would not have been worried about the hotel grounds being overrun. But with a pack of Brutes coming at them, Charlie Company was going to need every Spartan available.

Fred nodded. "Copy that, Captain." Though the mad Jiralhanae charge left no doubt that the Keepers of the One Freedom were on Gao to recover the ancilla, he still had a hundred questions about how they had managed to get there. But even if Breit had the answers, the middle of a battle was no time to be pressing a company CO for an explanation. He turned to Lopis, who was standing next to him, still keeping the Huragok's tentacles away from the ancilla. "Let's go."

She shook her head. "Not without my people."

"Your people are already aboard, ma'am," Breit said. He looked to Fred. "But that Falcon is fully loaded and none too airworthy. The inspector will be staying here—unless she wants to take someone else's place."

"Not on your life," Lopis said, showing no sign of fear for her own safety. She said to Fred, "I'll help you load the Huragok."

"Thanks, Inspector. I appreciate that."

Fred didn't know what else to say, how to express his respect for Lopis's courage, or his own reluctance to leave the battle without his team, so he merely dipped his chin and led the way toward the Falcon.

The Huragok made it as far as the rotor wash, then refused to go a centimeter farther. Lopis tried several times to drag it forward, but the thing seemed completely panicked by the air blast. It pulled against her so hard that Fred feared it would snap a tentacle, and when that failed, it changed tactics and began to bite at Lopis's fingers, trying to peel them off. Finally, the impatient pilot jerked her thumb for him to climb aboard and began to spin the rotors up faster. The Falcon rocked on its struts and started to kick up dirt and small shards of rubble. The message was clear: get aboard *now*, or she would use the rotor-wash to send Lopis and the Huragok tumbling across the courtyard—and Fred had seen enough combat pilots pull similar stunts to know the threat was not an idle one.

Fred waved Lopis away. She nodded and looked past him into the passenger compartment, then motioned to her team and allowed the Huragok to lead her away. Still holding the ancilla, Fred turned and hopped into the passenger compartment. He knew Nelson and Parangosky would both give him hell about leaving the thing in Wendosa, but better that than to risk losing the ancilla—assuming Nelson was right about what he had in the first place.

The Falcon was airborne almost as soon as Fred's boots hit the bloodstained deck. He checked to make sure Senola Lurone and the other two members of Lopis's field team were strapped in, then stowed the ancilla inside an armored cargo box and took a door gun. Normally, the gunner would clip himself into the safety harness that hung from the ceiling behind the M247 heavy machine-gun mount, but Fred ignored it. He was more than capable of staying on his feet through any maneuver the Falcon could handle, and if they ran into trouble, the last thing the pilot needed would be a half-ton Spartan flying around the passenger compartment at the end of a meter-long tether.

By the time he had the M247 ready to fire, the Falcon was well above the hotel's privacy wall, its chin guns chugging as it sprayed suppression fire into the jungle. Behind them, Fred caught a glimpse of his Spartans pouring death into the smoky avenue between the hotel and bakery. He even saw the Jiralhanae charge and managed to swing the machine gun around in time to put a burst into the middle of pack. Two Brutes went down amid the corpse-filled street behind the Falcon's tail.

Then the passenger compartment brace light began flashing, and the pilot put the Falcon into a tight, missile-evading turn that took it over Wendosa's main avenue—and back toward the kill zone. Fred saw a pair of smoke trails rise from the jungle and opened fire on full auto, sweeping the machine gun's barrel back and forth in front of the oncoming missiles. The first one dissolved into a fireball, while the second streaked past a dozen meters behind the Falcon.

For a heartbeat, Fred thought they were in the clear.

Then the purple flare of a particle beam rose from the kill zone.

The Falcon shuddered, and blood began to spray past the side door. The aircraft passed above the kill zone and out over the jungle, then the nose dropped and they began to wobble as the pilot struggled to remain conscious. Members of the Gao field team screamed in fear. Fred leaned out through the open door and looked forward, desperately hoping to see a clearing or river or some sign that suggested the dying pilot was taking them down under control.

All he saw was a steep, frond-blanketed slope dotted by limestone outcroppings. They were going in hard.

CHAPTER 20

A distant *boom* echoed out of the jungle and broke through the battle din, and Veta knew the Falcon carrying Fred and her team had not pulled up in time. Her chest tightened and her knees grew weak, and all the fear and rage of the last thirty hours boiled out in a single shocked keen. Cirilo lay buried in the bottom of the cave, and now, the crash had probably taken out three more of Veta's people. She was stunned and sick and so exhausted that she wanted nothing more than to collapse where she was and escape into a deep, dreamless sleep.

Instead, dragging the Huragok along by a tentacle, Veta turned and quickly headed back toward the gate. If there was any hope at all of helping her people aboard the downed Falcon, it would be from the Spartans. With their commander and a Forerunner artifact aboard, Blue Team would waste no time starting toward the crash—and she was not about to let them leave without her.

The area beyond the gate was piled high with Jiralhanae bodies, and there were no more of the alien warriors rushing the hotel.

But Olivia and Ash remained crouched behind the wrecked Warthog, Olivia still without her helmet and only half-armored, firing three-round bursts into the smoke-filled street. Veta began to fear the two Gammas had completely lost control of themselves and were now simply pouring lead into dead bodies.

But then Veta reached Olivia's side and saw that the Spartan duo was actually firing down the street, into a mass of hulking backs in dark armor. The enemy charge had not been broken. Instead, the Jiralhanae were racing toward a column of smoke where the Falcon went down—and they were already well ahead of the Spartans.

Veta waited until Olivia clicked empty, then leaned close and touched the girl's hand.

" 'Livi!" Veta yelled. "Wait!"

Olivia's brow rose, and her glance strayed to the Huragok behind Veta. "Why are you two still here?"

"Our friend doesn't like rotor blast," Veta said, jerking a thumb at the Huragok. "What are you doing?"

Olivia rolled her eyes. "What does it look like?" She slapped a fresh magazine into her rifle. "I'm working."

Veta glanced up at the stone arch above her head and realized that neither Olivia nor Ash could have seen the Falcon go down. Their view was blocked—and even if it hadn't been, they would have been too busy shooting Jiralhanae to notice the craft get hit. She laid a hand on Olivia's arm.

"Olivia, think!" Veta urged. "Those are *Brutes*. They aren't retreating—they're going after Fred!"

"The lieutenant?" Olivia's eyes narrowed. "What are you trying to pull?"

"I'm *trying* to tell you they shot down the Falcon, and now they're going after it." Veta pointed in the direction the Jiralhanae were running, then added, "There's a smoke column out there. Didn't you hear the impact?"

Olivia turned to look. She scowled at the thick stanchion that supported the arch, then retreated a couple of steps and tried again. This time, she saw the smoke and her eyes went wide. She stepped over to Ash and tapped his shoulder twice.

He quit firing and cocked his helmet toward her. "Yeah?"

"Trouble," she said. "They took out the lieutenant's ride."

Ash hesitated, then asked, "You're sure?"

Olivia tipped her head toward Veta. "The inspector says she saw him go down," she said. "And there's smoke."

Ash shook his head in anger. "Dammit!"

Slipping around the wrecked Warthog, Ash stepped through the gate and circled his rifle barrel in the air. Then he emptied the rest of his clip down the street and rotated the weapon barrel in the air again. Only when Mark replied with a similar gesture from the bakery roof did Ash retreat into the courtyard again and turn to Olivia.

"Breit just took off for his command post," he said. "My guess, he was on the way to talk about the crash."

As Ash spoke, his hand drifted down toward the left side of his abdomen, and it was only then that Veta noticed the scorch hole in his armor. Ash poked a finger through the opening, then withdrew it and looked at a bloody tip caked with flakes of charred skin. Almost absently, he said, "You'd better see if you can find out what Breit is planning. I'll brief Kelly and the others."

"Copy." Olivia seemed no more concerned about Ash's wound than did Ash himself. She started toward main door, then stopped to glance back at Veta. "You coming, Inspector?"

Veta shook her head. "I'd better stay here with Ash. Maybe I can get the Huragok to take a look at his wound."

"Negative," Ash said. "The lieutenant's down. We don't have time—"

"You don't have time *not* to." Veta pulled Ash over to the side of the gate, at the same time calling back to Olivia. "And there must be a Spartan supply cache around here somewhere. See if you can locate any spare Smoothers."

Olivia actually smiled. "Good plan," she said. "Thanks, Mom."

Veta had barely convinced Ash to remove his helmet and open his armor before the rest of Blue Team entered the courtyard. Mark hung back at the gate, watching the situation in the street. Tom-B292 and Lucy-B091 were the first to arrive, both wearing full suits of SPI, Tom the size of a normal Spartan, but Lucy not much larger than Veta. Paying no attention to the hovering Huragok, they looked Ash over from behind their faceplates, then let their shoulders relax—presumably because the injury looked survivable.

"Ash, I can't let you go anywhere without me." Tom's voice was teasing, but warm. "What did I say about getting wounded?"

Ash smiled. "Not to," he said. "Sorry about that."

"Well, don't let it happen again," Tom said. "It's unprofessional."

Lucy elbowed Tom in his torso armor, then glanced in the direction Olivia had gone and made a fist with her thumb crooked over the top.

"Olivia was in bad shape for a while, but she's fine now." Ash motioned at the Huragok, which was just beginning to probe the gruesome scorch hole below his floating ribs, then added, "This fellow fixed her up."

The two Spartan-IIs arrived, and Kelly-087—at least Veta assumed it was Kelly, as she was wearing steel-blue Mjolnir with a half-bubble faceplate, rather than the copper-colored armor with the goggle-eyes faceplate that Linda-058 wore—motioned Tom and Lucy back toward the gate.

"You two stick with Mark," she ordered. "He may need help keeping an eye on things."

As the pair obeyed, Kelly stepped to Ash's side and tipped her faceplate down to study the Huragok, which now had two tentacles thrust into Ash's wound.

"What's happening here?" she demanded. "Ash, you turn into a robot when I wasn't looking?"

"Afraid not," Ash said. "This Huragok fixes biologicals."

Linda stepped closer to the thing and asked, "Is it any good at nose jobs?"

"Your nose is fine," Kelly said. "You can breathe through it, can't you?"

Linda turned her helmet toward Kelly. "I was thinking of Commander Nelson," she said. "He's kind of a mouth-breather."

"He's ONI. What do you expect?" Kelly turned to Ash. "So, you called?"

"Yes, ma'am," he said. "The lieutenant's ride crashed."

Kelly and Linda looked into each other's faceplates, then Linda asked, "Is that confirmed?"

Ash jerked a thumb in Veta's direction. "She saw the bird go down," he said. " 'Livi is confirming it with Captain Breit, but I believe the inspector."

"Why the hell would I lie?" Veta demanded. "I have people on that Falcon, too!"

Kelly's faceplate turned back toward Veta. "Relax, Inspector," she said. "Nobody thinks you're lying."

"Then why aren't you doing something?" Veta demanded. As she spoke, a pair of combat platoons loaded with ammo, weapons, and water began to form up in the courtyard. "My people could be dying out there. So could Fred . . . and the ancilla."

Veta was far from certain that the flatworm thing was actually the Forerunner ancilla that everybody seemed to be hunting. But Breit had seemed to think so, and under the circumstances, that was close enough for her.

Linda swung the barrel of her assault rifle vaguely in Veta's direction. "And how do you know about the ancilla?" she demanded. "I thought you were hunting a serial killer."

"It appears that our investigations crossed paths," Veta said. She kept her attention focused on Kelly. "Are you going after that downed Falcon, or do I have to do it alone?"

"Slow down, Inspector," said Kelly. "Blue Team is *not* going in blind. First, we're going to assess and plan."

"Fine," Veta said, "as long as you do it fast . . . and I'm part of your plan."

"Negative," Kelly snapped. Behind her, Olivia emerged from the hotel, a supply satchel slung over her shoulder and a new combat tacpad strapped to her forearm. "You'll stay put here in Wendosa."

"Not going to happen," Veta said. "As I said, my people were on that Falcon, too."

Kelly tipped her helmet forward, no doubt preparing to lay down the law, when Mark stepped between the two women.

"Ma'am, there's no use trying to argue her out of it," he said. "The inspector here seems to think she's one of us."

CHAPTER 21

1025 hours, July 5, 2553 (military calendar)
Gao Ministry of Protection Patrol Corvette *Esmeralda*
Orbital Approach Vector Cenobia, Planet Gao, Cordoba System

With their long-range sensors being mysteriously blocked by whatever was jamming transmissions around Gao, Arlo Casille and his corvette captains were relying on little more than eyesight and guesswork to locate the UNSC task force. Fortunately, Arlo was a skilled gambler. Knowing that his enemies needed to avoid a direct military confrontation, he was betting that Admiral Tuwa would attempt to mask her approach behind the metal-rich bulk of Gao's closest moon, Cenobia. So he had committed GMoP's entire force to the Cenobian Corridor—a favorite route of the bio-pirates who came to raid Gao's jungles—and the gamble was paying off.

Several of his captains had already sent messengers to report warship sightings, and through the observation canopy on the bridge of the *Esmeralda,* Arlo himself could make out several irregular patches where the distant starlight was blocked by the silhouette of a large vessel. He knew better than to think his entire fleet of lightly armed and poorly shielded corvettes could inflict so much as a dent on any of the distant UNSC behemoths. But if that had been his true goal in confronting the task force, he wouldn't have bothered to leave the ground.

"There—starboard abeam!"

Arlo looked toward the voice and saw a young ensign standing close to the canopy, turned toward the red disk of Cenobia and holding a pair of binoculars to her eyes.

"I have four craft transiting near the top of the disk," the ensign reported. "Probably Pelicans or Owls, definitely Gao-bound."

Arlo nodded to the commanding officer of the *Esmeralda,* a slender woman of fifty with gray-streaked hair cut in a short bob. "Fire at will, Captain Melgar."

"Yes, Minister." Melgar turned to her gunnery lieutenant. "Cardone, lock eight missiles and launch. Turret will fire to destroy as soon as all missiles are away."

"To *destroy?*" The young officer's voice cracked with alarm. "Procedure is to—"

"I *know* procedure, Lieutenant," Melgar said. She was following the same orders Arlo had issued to the captains of all the Ministry's corvettes. "But those are planetary insertion craft, launched by a UNSC task force. I don't think a few shots across the bow are going to make them turn around, do you?"

"No, ma'am." Cardone still sounded shaky. "Turret will fire to destroy. How many missiles, ma'am?"

"All eight, Cardone." Despite having to repeat herself, Melgar's tone was even and patient. Arlo appreciated that—there was nothing to be gained by adding to a crewman's anxiety during a dangerous operation. "If we don't launch them now, I doubt we ever will."

Cardone paled, but turned to relay the order.

Arlo rose from the flag chair and began to pace along the back of the bridge. He had no idea whether the attack—and the dozens of others he hoped were being launched by the *Esmeralda*'s sister vessels—would force the task force to back down. But he *did* know that if he failed to strike first and strike hard, the UNSC commander would only doubt Arlo's resolve and keep coming.

Almost immediately, Gloria Baer, a young newsmonger Arlo had invited along to record the moment for posterity, joined him. Dressed in gray canvas pants and a brightly flowered blouse, Baer was wearing a BuzzSat earpiece with a pinky-size camera affixed to the top. A yellow status light on the earbud indicated that the camera was recording instead of broadcasting live—but that was to be expected, since BuzzSat was being jammed along with every other transmission in the vicinity of Gao.

"Minister Casille," Baer asked, "did you just order the *Esmeralda* to destroy four UNSC vessels?"

"Four planetary insertion *craft*," Arlo corrected. He stopped pacing and nodded gravely. "But, yes. I have given orders to the entire GMoP fleet to prevent any more landings on Gao. The Ministry of Protection cannot allow the UNSC to reinforce their troops on the ground—troops who are *already* attacking our loyal citizens . . . citizens who are merely protesting the hostile occupation of Gao's sovereign ground."

A gentle vibration ran through the deck as the *Esmeralda* launched her complement of missiles. Then the cabin lighting dimmed, and the corvette's turret began to spew plasma bolts. Almost instantly, the two craft in the lead erupted into fireballs. The other two—mere flecks of darkness silhouetted against Cenobia's red disk—swirled into evasive helixes and vented clouds of steam and chaff to confuse the approaching missiles.

Biting back a smile of triumph, Arlo put on a grim expression and turned to look directly into the lens of Baer's ear camera.

"I'm not saying that President Aponte was wrong to yield to the UNSC demands," Arlo said. "But this is what comes of giving a foothold to imperialists."

"So you're starting a *war* with the UNSC?" Baer asked, stunned. "On your own authority?"

"I am not *starting* anything, Ms. Baer," Arlo said. "I am opposing an invasion by a foreign power—as is required of *all* cabinet ministers under the Articles of the Gao Charter."

Over the newsmonger's shoulder, Arlo saw a third fireball erupt. The fourth craft aborted its mission and ran for its mother ship with the *Esmeralda*'s plasma bolts chasing its tail.

Remarkably, Arlo was still alive—and so was everyone else aboard the *Esmeralda*. The task force hadn't returned fire, and that could mean only one thing.

The UNSC was backing down.

Arlo allowed himself a brief grin of relief, then—mindful of the BuzzSat camera—he assumed a somber expression. Obviously, he had not militarily defeated the task force. He had merely called the UNSC's bluff, letting them know that if they intended to take control of Gao's orbital space, they would have to destroy his fleet and risk another Insurrection.

But that didn't mean the task force would be going away anytime soon. UNSC fleet officers were much too pragmatic to pursue anything as prosaic as avenging the loss of their insertion craft, but the enemy admiral wasn't going to give up. She would continue trying to sneak Owls and Pelicans loaded with troops and supplies down to the battalion on Gao. And Arlo's little fleet of corvettes would not be able to stop all of them. Not even most of them. Clearly, Arlo needed more resources.

Clearly, Gao needed him to take control.

Arlo clasped his hands behind his back and turned to Gloria

Baer. "It does not give me pleasure to announce this, but I have no choice. Given President Aponte's repeated refusals to defend Gao against UNSC aggression, the time has come for a change."

"You're calling for a no-confidence vote?"

Arlo shook his head. "That would take longer than we have," he said. "It will have to be a cabinet proclamation."

A hungry gleam came to Baer's eyes—a sign that she recognized history in the making when she was reporting on it. "When will that happen?"

"The moment I return to Rinale," Arlo said. "As your viewers can see, Gaos are dying."

CHAPTER 22

1058 hours, July 5, 2553 (military calendar)
Briones Ridge, 2,300 meters outside Wendosa, Montero Jungle
Campos Wilderness District, Planet Gao, Cordoba System

B lue Team was traversing a treacherous jungle slope, and Veta half-suspected Mark had convinced Kelly to bring her along because he expected her to die along the way.

Veta's boots kept slipping in the slick vermilion mud, threatening to send her plunging hundreds of meters into a river she heard roaring somewhere in the foliage below. She was drenched in sweat and dizzy with heat, and every time she scratched at an insect bite, she usually found what she hoped was only some kind of leech as well.

But at least she was having no trouble keeping up. The Spartans were looping around the battle still raging in the valley below, trying to reach the crashed Falcon before the Keepers of the One Freedom could slip away from Charlie Company and secure it themselves. Unfortunately, the enemy commander had been smart enough to post a sniper contingent where it could cover the approach to the crash site, and his foresight had slowed progress.

Blue Team was creeping along the steep slope at a snail's pace, circling past the slightest opening in the jungle canopy and being careful to avoid disturbing the foliage. When someone accidentally did slip and slide down the slope into a cycad or tree fern, a flurry of enemy shots arrived almost instantly, blowing fronds apart and blasting arm-deep craters into the muddy hillside. The unlucky target would drop behind the nearest outcropping and curl into a ball, and then Mark, Linda, and a couple of other Spartans equipped with SRS99 sniper rifles would find a vantage point and return fire. The duel would rage for a few minutes, either until the hail of particle beams ceased, or the rest of Blue Team had crept out of the fire zone and was once again sneaking toward the crash site.

It seemed that everyone in the group had touched off a sniper duel at least once during the hour-and-a-half journey, and because of their half-healed wounds, Ash and Olivia were almost as prone to slipping as Veta. But as nerve-racking as they were, the long-range firefights were not particularly dangerous. As long as no one moved so quickly they created what the Spartans called a "shiver line" in the jungle canopy, the enemy snipers were left with only an approximate idea of their targets' location. So far, approximate had not been good enough to end their progress—merely frustrate it.

Whiffs of smoke and charred flesh began to taint the thick jungle air, and Veta knew they were finally near the crash site. Thinking that the Spartans' climate-controlled helmets might hide the odors, she tapped Ash on the shoulder and pointed uphill, slightly to the left of the team's marching direction.

Ash cocked his helmet to one side, no doubt Spartan-speak for "What?"

Veta wrinkled her nose, then touched her fingers to it and pointed toward the smell again. When Ash did not seem to grasp her meaning, she held her hand flat and spread her fingers, then made the wobbling motion of an aircraft going down. Finally, Ash nodded his understanding and turned away.

With TEAMCOM still unavailable due to jamming, Ash tossed a mudball ten meters ahead and hit Linda in the back of her helmet. When she turned around, he relayed Veta's message with about a tenth the effort, and a few moments later the entire team was advancing toward the crash site in a carefully arranged picket line.

Veta, Olivia, and Ash were assigned to bring up the rear—Veta because she obviously wasn't a Spartan, and Olivia and Ash because they were wounded. At best, they were about half-recovered—which meant they were still about twice as effective as normal combat marines. Though Veta had been wise enough not to say so back in Wendosa, she was amazed that Kelly had brought the Gammas along at all. The trio had taken a double dose of Smoothers before leaving the hotel, but even Mark had admitted it would "take some time" before they were back to normal. Unfortunately, nobody seemed to know exactly when that would happen.

The Huragok had been left at the Hotel Wendosa. "Assigned" to the makeshift infirmary, it was no doubt finding plenty to keep itself entertained. Before turning the thing over to Captain Breit, Veta had insisted that Breit make its services available to any badly injured civilian who sought help from Charlie Company's medical staff. The captain had readily agreed. Veta was not quite sure why she felt as though she'd been lied to, but she did feel that way.

The stench continued to grow stronger as the team crept forward, and Veta began to recognize other scents as well—fried electronics and spilled cooling fluids, scorched dirt and incinerated plants. A Spartan-III—probably Tom—suddenly appeared on the slope ahead, his SPI armor making it seem as though he had simply separated himself from a nearby tree fern. He signaled the trio to take cover behind a nearby outcropping, then vanished again.

Ash led his companions forward to the outcropping, where Veta took a knee downslope from Olivia. They were so close to the crash site that she could hear the Falcon's doors and weapon mounts creaking as it shifted on the hillside, but the wreckage remained veiled by a bank of emerald fronds at least ten meters deep. She tried to avoid picturing her friends and colleagues who had been aboard because she didn't want to fall prey to the anger and sadness she could feel rising inside, didn't want to do something foolish in a fit of rage or find her reactions numbed by sorrow. She could tell by the relative quiet and the odor that it was likely none had survived; the best she could hope for now was to confirm their identities and assure their loved ones that the end had come too swiftly for the victims to feel much pain—even if that was not quite true.

Curious as to why Tom had told them to hold at the outcropping, Veta glanced up at Olivia. The Spartan was looking downslope, toward the battle still raging in the valley. She had replaced her missing SPI helmet with a standard marine model, so her narrowed eyes and set jaw were apparent. Knowing better than to give away their position by breaking the silence, Veta merely looked in the same direction.

She saw only jungle.

Then the sound of an ambush erupted thirty meters below—a layered chain of three-round bursts punctuated by grenade detonations and howls of anguish that were nearly inaudible over the cacophony. The attack was quickly answered by thudding maulers and whining plasma bolts, and it grew obvious that if Blue Team had beat the Keepers to the crash site, it had not been by much.

Veta watched in fear and awe as the firefight shredded the jungle, Jiralhanae warriors bounding through the smoke and foliage. Most were turning to meet the Spartans who had ambushed them. But a handful—at least half a dozen—were scrambling uphill toward the still-hidden crash site.

Olivia and Ash opened up with their battle rifles, trying to force the climbers back into the killing zone, but doing little more than blowing jungle down and bouncing rounds off Jiralhanae armor. Veta joined in, trying for neck and knee shots. She saw one of the Brutes go down, but at least four continued to climb, angling away, deeper into the jungle, where they were harder to target.

Particle beams streamed in from across the valley, spraying fronds into the air and chewing through the outcropping that Veta and her companions were using for cover. Mark opened up with his own sniper rifle, and the hail of death diminished . . . but not fast enough. First Ash, then Olivia and Veta were forced to stop firing and drop out of sight, and Veta realized there was no longer any doubt—the Jiralhanae were going to beat them to the crashed Falcon.

Veta rolled around the base of the outcropping and wedged herself behind a boulder. She found herself looking across a ten-meter clearing of combat-denuded jungle into a brake of still-standing cycads. Just inside the thicket sat the mangled silhouette of the Falcon. She saw at least three Jiralhanae climbing toward the wreck, mere meters from its sagging tail.

Veta backed away from the boulder and peeked uphill. Olivia and Ash were crouched down behind the outcropping, still hiding from Keeper sniper fire, but also watching her intently.

Veta tossed her battle rifle aside, then drew her SAS-10 from its holster and raised her brow. Olivia rolled her eyes, but smiled.

Ash nodded. He raised three fingers, then lowered the first. A breath later, he lowered the second. Veta sprang up and raced across the beam-chewed clearing, not sprinting so much as leaping, slipping, and clambering.

The Jiralhanae snipers did not find her until she was halfway across, and by then her legs were trembling so hard she could barely keep them beneath her. She went down in the mud as a tree fern exploded into splinters half a meter above her head. She crawled into a tangle of fronds, and a geyser of dirt shot up to her left. She changed strategy and rolled under a fallen cycad, a purple flash blowing the crown apart beside her.

Veta scrambled forward with sniper attacks still peppering the hillside around her, and then she was across the clearing and back into the relative safety of the jungle, peering around the trunk of a giant tree fern. She saw no sign of Ash or Olivia yet, but took the torrent of particle beams tearing through the jungle upslope of her to mean they were still alive and moving. The Falcon's twisted black wreckage lay ten meters up the slope, in a long slide-scar ringed by blackened foliage. Its severed rotors and stubby wings were resting on scorched ground a few meters above the rest of the craft. At the uphill end of the slide-scar, pieces of shattered cockpit were strewn about an impact crater the size of a freight truck.

Three Jiralhanae were already at the crash site. One was keeping watch, scowling over his plasma rifle back toward the clearing, on the lookout for whatever was drawing the tempest of sniper fire—even if the jammed comm channels prevented him from asking for details. The other two Brutes were working from opposite sides of the Falcon's twisted hull, leaning into the still-smoking passenger compartment to extract HMGs and human bodies. There was no sign of Fred, but that meant nothing. He could have been thrown clear when the Falcon crashed or fallen out beforehand. Hell, he might even have survived and dragged himself off into the jungle with the ancilla—though even Veta had to admit that the last possibility was probably more wishful thinking than a long shot.

It sickened Veta to see the way they treated her dead colleagues, dragging them out of the wreckage in pieces and tossing them aside. With luck, she would make them pay. But not until she had a combat plan—Veta had learned at least that much from the Spartans.

The fourth Jiralhanae was farther uphill, just past the impact crater, ascending a small talus field toward a chest-high outcropping of limestone. Even larger than his companions, this one wore a long gray beard, and the ceremonial braiding etched into the collar of his armor suggested he might be some sort of chieftain. He was armed with a sickle-bladed carbine that Veta had heard both marines and Spartans refer to as a "Spiker" during the battle in Wendosa.

Olivia and Ash were nowhere to be seen, but it seemed unlikely they had been hit as they bolted across the clearing. They were Spartans, and Spartans rarely made themselves easy to spot. Still, Veta knew that waiting to regroup was not an option. The duel between Mark and the enemy snipers continued to rage, and particle beams were probing the jungle all around her. Gripping her SAS-10 in both hands, Veta activated the laser sight and rolled to a knee.

A mudball dropped into the foliage ahead of her.

Stifling a cry of surprise, Veta looked back and found Olivia lying in a tangle of fronds about five meters upslope. Instead of a battle rifle, the Spartan was holding her combat knife, and she was signaling WAIT. When Veta nodded, Olivia pointed from the SAS-10 to herself to the wreckage, then paused a moment. She used her thumb and forefinger to represent a pistol . . . and point it up the hill at the chieftain. Finally, she lowered her thumb, and the message grew clear: COVER ME, THEN KILL THE CHIEFTAIN.

Veta acknowledged this to Olivia, and the Gamma disappeared back into the fronds.

At the wreckage, the Jiralhanae on watch duty was still scowling, but now his plasma rifle was pointed at a pair of fallen cycad trunks. Veta feared for a moment that he had spotted Ash—until a soft *clunk* sounded about halfway between the trunks and the frond tangle where Olivia was hiding. The warrior swung his weapon back toward the sound, and Ash slipped out of the jungle behind him.

Moving so swiftly he seemed more blur than soldier, Ash reached up to grab the rear of the Jiralhanae's helmet, then pulled the warrior over backward and slashed a combat knife across his throat. Ash lowered the body gently to the ground and, stepping away while blood was still spurting from the wound, spun toward the far side of the wrecked Falcon.

By then, Olivia was racing across the hillside toward the near side of the crash. As she approached, a Jiralhanae suddenly backed out of the Falcon's door, and Veta feared for a moment that he was turning to defend himself.

But when the big warrior stood upright, he was holding the Forerunner artifact, cradling its limp body in both hands and speaking to it in reverent tones. A heartbeat later, Olivia leaped onto his back and plunged her combat knife deep into the side of his neck.

Realizing she was up next, Veta sprinted up the slope toward the Jiralhanae chieftain. She passed Olivia and Ash while they were still riding their foes to the ground, then raised her SAS-10 and began to move the laser targeting dot toward her quarry. Still seemingly unaware of his companions' fates, the chieftain had set his Spiker aside, and he was leaning over the little outcropping, using both hands to draw something up from the other side.

Veta was probably fifteen meters away, easily within the pistol's range and her skill level—but not against a heavily armored objective while she was sprinting uphill. She continued a few more steps until she reached the loose talus below the outcropping, then took a knee.

Meanwhile, the chieftain was drawing himself upright, groaning with effort as he pulled a figure in scorched Mjolnir onto the outcropping. It could only be Fred, of course. The armor looked oddly stiff, as though it had somehow entered rigor mortis or the mechanical joints had locked up when Fred died, and Veta was surprised to find her heart drumming and her hands shaking.

She told herself it was just physical exhaustion—the effects of a grueling trek and a hellish battle—but even she knew it was more than that, that she felt real grief for the Spartan commander. She still hated what he stood for, and she had no illusions about the things he had done for the UNSC. But as for Fred himself? Veta suddenly realized she was going to miss him.

She let out a calming breath and braced herself to fire—then winced as a particle beam streaked past her shoulder and sent shards of limestone spraying into the air. The chieftain's head snapped around to look, and Veta realized that the sniper attack had robbed her of an easy kill shot to the back of the neck. She put the SAS-10's targeting dot on the soft spot behind the Brute's knee instead and pulled the trigger.

The Jiralhanae gave a gravelly bellow in response, but Veta had no idea whether it was in pain or anger. She was too busy rolling across the slope, dodging particle beams. Recalling an admonishment Fred had recently given her to never move predictably in a sniper zone, she reversed directions and brought her pistol up again, swinging the barrel back toward the chieftain.

He was standing on one leg, with the other hanging by the bloody remnants of the knee joint. One hand was reaching for his Spiker, the other sweeping Fred's Mjolnir-clad body off the outcropping toward her. Mark's SRS99 began to boom again from somewhere uphill, returning the sniper fire that had been harrying Veta all along.

Guessing she had maybe a full second before the next attack, Veta set her targeting dot on the Jiralhanae's massive hand and fired. The appendage exploded in a bloody spray, and Fred's Mjolnir crashed down into the talus above her.

It began to descend headfirst, triggering a small rockslide that came straight at her. Veta rolled aside, and, as the slope around her erupted with beam strikes, decided it was time to bug out. She sprang up, whirled around to run . . . and was nearly knocked off her feet as a fist-size rock caught her between the shoulder blades.

A fierce jolt sizzled down her spine, then her right thigh exploded into pain as something heavy clipped her hip and knocked her leg out from beneath her. Veta managed to twist back around and saw Fred's Mjolnir shooting past. It hardly looked like a safe ride, but at least it was sliding on *top* of the rocks and traveling the same speed as the slide. She drove off her left leg and dived, throwing herself on top of Fred.

Veta landed with her face at waist level, her shins and feet bouncing through the rocks behind them. She reached up and managed to slip a free hand under a chest plate, then pulled herself up until her ankles no longer seemed in danger of being crushed.

The ride down the steep slope was longer, faster, and rougher than Veta would have expected—if there had been any time to think about it. Terrified of being crushed when the armor began to tumble, she looked for a soft place to roll off and saw Olivia flash past. Then the Mjolnir reached the bottom end of the slide-scar and entered the jungle. But instead of catching on something and going into a flip, the armor rode up over a frond tangle, and they shot into the air like a missile.

Veta pressed her head close to Fred's and held on tight as they remained airborne for what must have been a dozen meters. As the Mjolnir dropped back toward the ground, she pulled her hand from beneath the chest plate and jumped off into what she hoped would be a reasonably soft thicket of fronds.

The impact didn't crush her, but it didn't end well, either. Veta crashed through the thicket as though it wasn't even there, and then continued to tumble down the slope on her own. After a dozen rotations, her calves finally slammed into a mass of spiky leaves, and she came to a painful, spinning halt.

For a time, Veta lay motionless on the muddy slope, resting on her back with her head pointed downhill and lower than her boots. She heard Fred's armor continuing to crash along the slope for another several seconds, drawing a series of shouts from a company of soldiers who seemed to be ascending the slope toward her. Then, finally, the crashing stopped, and the commotion of the distant battle began to settle over the jungle once again.

At first, Veta was afraid to move because everything hurt and she wasn't sure what might be broken. After a moment, the pain began to subside, and she was afraid to move because the hill was so steep and muddy that she thought she might go sliding again. Then, as the blood continued to settle in her head and she began to get her bearings, she was afraid to move because she could hear someone coming through the jungle toward her.

Veta flexed her hand and was glad to feel the SAS-10 still in her grasp. That was the first rule of a gunfight—don't lose the gun.

She checked to make sure the safety was off—it was—then tried hard to listen for the approaching footfalls above the drumming of her own heart.

The muzzle of a rifle pushed through the undergrowth. Veta brought her pistol up and pointed it along the rifle barrel toward a shell of mottled green chest armor.

"Hold on, soldier!" The voice was husky, male, and human. "I'm on your side."

Veta raised her gaze and found herself looking at a gaunt UNSC marine with a three-day growth of beard. She pointed the SAS-10 away, then asked, "Who are you?"

"Alpha Company," the marine replied. "We're here to relieve you."

CHAPTER 23

Veta did not remember the entire trip back to the Vitality Center, but she did recall the early parts. A pair of medics had immobilized her inside a body-bracing buoyancy litter that looked a lot like a giant tube puffed full of helium, then floated her through the jungle for hours. When they had finally reached the valley wall, they had attached a cable to the "BBB board"—as they called the litter—and climbed alongside as a winch hauled her up to a waiting Warthog.

By that time, Veta had been pretty certain she was not critically injured, but the medics had insisted that she needed to be checked for head injuries and spinal damage. In no position to resist—and utterly exhausted—Veta had allowed herself to be loaded into the Warthog.

Asleep before a second litter was loaded, Veta remembered only snippets of the ride afterward—just vague sensations of motion and a surreal growl of downshifting engines. And she had no idea how she had come to wake up in a bed large enough for two

Jiralhanae, smelling of soap and shampoo and dressed in a clean set of UNSC marine fatigues.

The chronometer on her bedside table read 11:05, which suggested she had been asleep for eighteen hours.

Veta pushed herself into a seated position and glanced around the opulent bedroom. It was at the upper end of spa chic, with a separate seating area, white curtains drawn across an entire wall of glass, and a frosted-pane door opening into an elegant, white-tile washroom. Across from the bed, her SAS-10 and other personal gear lay atop a long, low dresser, along with a bowl of fruit, a glass, and a water pitcher etched with the Montero Vitality Clinic's tree fern logo.

A sharp knock sounded from the double doors adjacent to the dresser. Before Veta could swing her feet onto the floor—or even ask who it was—a female sergeant opened a door and stepped inside.

"Commander Nelson to see you, ma'am."

"*Now?*" Veta asked, still not quite certain she was awake. "I mean, already?"

The sergeant—a blue-eyed woman with a slender nose and a square jaw—looked at Veta as though she had asked whether humans breathed oxygen.

"Yes, ma'am." She looked away, then addressed someone in the adjacent room. "She's decent, Commander."

Veta checked to make sure all of the uniform's buttons and fasteners were closed, then rose—a little stiffly and unsteadily at first, but without any sharp pains or throbbing aches.

By then, Murtag Nelson was stepping past the sergeant, looking rumpled and even more tired than the first time Veta had met him. In his hands, he carried a silver tray complete with a bowl of snacks, a decanter filled with red Gao bitters, and two short glasses filled with ice. Without invitation, he crossed to the seating area, placed the tray on a glass table between two plush white chairs, and then turned to face Veta.

"Wendell said you were coming around."

Shocked to hear that Wendell's monitoring capabilities extended into her bedroom, Veta glanced around for an access point and found it in the media screen's integrated conferencing camera. Normally, the camera would be controlled by only the room occupant, but a powerful military AI like Wendell would have no trouble seizing command of the device.

When Veta did not reply to his first comment, Nelson seemed to realize he had made her uncomfortable. He tried to recover by asking, "So . . . how are you feeling?"

Veta raised her hands and wiggled her fingers to indicate nothing was broken. "Lucky, I guess."

Nelson smiled too broadly. "Yes, I can see how you might be feeling that way."

He picked up the decanter and, providing himself a convenient excuse to look away, began to fill the glasses. Veta had a sinking feeling and went to join him.

"How bad is it?" she asked. "Didn't the Gammas make it?"

"The Gammas are fine—at least as fine as Gammas can be." Nelson handed her a glass. "They're already mobile, even if the medics keep telling them they shouldn't be."

"I'm glad to hear it."

Veta accepted the beverage, then sat in one of the chairs and took a thumb-size babo nut from the snack bowl. She hadn't realized how hungry she was until she bit into it and tasted its peppery sweetness, and she immediately felt guilty for relishing the experience.

She took a sip of the bitters, then said, "Sorry about Fred."

Nelson's brow shot up. "Fred? Don't you worry about Fred—not when you lost so many of your people." His eyes widened with sudden worry, then he asked, "You *did* know, didn't you?"

Veta let her face drop and took a long swallow of the drink, but it did nothing to dull the ache in her heart.

"I know," she said at last. "I saw the Falcon go down. I was there when the Jiralhanae pulled the bodies out in pieces."

Nelson took the glass from her hand and, despite the fact that it was still more than half-full, topped it off.

"Inspector Lopis . . . it's not just the people in the Falcon you lost." He set the glass on the table in front of her. "It's everyone. You're the only one left."

"What?" Veta literally did not understand what he was saying; it sounded as though he was trying to tell her that Andera Rolan, Olinda Riost, and all the GMoP personnel who had been stationed in the Vitality Center were just as dead as Cirilo, Saria, and all the others who had made the trip to Crime Scene India with her. "Come on. Don't be ridiculous. Dr. Rolan wasn't aboard the Falcon. Neither was Olinda or Dario."

"No, but they *were* in the employee dorm when a downed Pelican crashed into it." Nelson stared at his glass for a moment, clearly at a loss for words, then finally looked up and said, "There was a sniper attack on the main building, too. I was nearly killed myself."

It was this last awkward detail that finally jolted Veta out of her daze of incomprehension—and which convinced her to accept Nelson's story at face value. The man was intelligent and ambitious, but he was a bit awkward socially, and his obvious discomfort spoke volumes. Had the commander been trying to hide something, his delivery would have been more deliberate and practiced—and he would not have made the mistake of trying to mitigate her loss by focusing on himself. Clearly, Nelson was just trying to break the news to her as gently as he knew how.

Veta took another babo nut from the bowl and absentmindedly bit into it. At the moment, she needed food a lot more than she needed oblivion—no matter how well intentioned the offer of a drink might be.

When Veta didn't say anything, Nelson continued, "We recovered everyone's bodies, of course, and quite a bit of the evidence—though I imagine it's been badly contaminated. And we found a datapad stored in a file safe."

Veta nodded numbly. The datapad probably belonged to the unit's information coordinator, who was in charge of collecting and cataloging all knowledge concerning the investigation. It was standard GMoP protocol to store the datapad in a file safe whenever it was not in use.

Nelson turned to the sergeant and said, "Odell, could you bring it in?"

"Yes, sir."

As Odell disappeared into the next room, Veta realized Nelson was carefully steering the conversation toward her investigation—away from everything else happening in the vicinity. And in her shock, she was letting him.

"Commander Nelson," Veta said, "as much as I appreciate your concern for my situation, I'd like to know more about yours. Is the battle over? Are the Keepers of the One Freedom gone? What happened to the Forerunner artifacts that Fred and his squad recovered?"

"Yes, that battle is over and the Keepers are gone," Nelson said. "The rest, I can't discuss. I think you know why."

Veta gave a resigned nod. "Classified." Given that she had helped recover the artifacts, she would have grumbled about Nelson's reply more—had she not noticed his slip. "But you said *that* battle. So, are you expecting another one?"

Nelson waved a weary hand. "We'll come to that, Inspector," he said. "But first, we need to talk about where your own investigation stands."

Odell now returned and presented Veta with a soot-stained datapad. "Here you are, Inspector. We had to replace the energy cells, but it still functions."

Veta accepted the datapad with a nod, then activated it and entered her override password. She selected REPORT INDEX on the opening menu, and almost immediately, two files caught her eye.

The first was a summary of evidence collected by the forensic spiders Cirilo had released at Crime Scene Charlie, with a subheader that read EXOTIC ALLOY. Veta opened the file and discovered there had been traces of an unidentified alloy on the toppled benches. The evidence had been collected only where the benches had been grasped as they were ripped off their mounting bolts. The implication was obvious. If Veta could find the source of the alloy, she would have the weapon used in the crimes. After that, finding the killer would be a lot easier.

The other file that caught her eye was an encrypted message from Arlo Casille titled: SCHEMATICS FOR LOPIS. Veta knew it probably contained the specs she had requested for the Spartans' Mjolnir armor. Unable to reach Veta while she was underground, the minister had simply fallen back on procedure and sent the file to the team's information coordinator.

Veta closed the menu without opening Casille's message, then looked up at Nelson and asked, "Did you look at these reports?"

Nelson gave a small shake of his head. "We couldn't guess the passcode." Not seeming to recognize the impropriety of admitting that the UNSC had actually tried to violate GMoP security in the first place, he took another sip of bitters, then added, "Under the circumstances, it didn't seem worth the time to crack it."

Swallowing a sigh of relief, Veta turned off the datapad and set it on the table. "What circumstances are those?"

"Circumstances on the ground, of course," Nelson said. "The Ministry of Protection isn't allowing UNSC reinforcements through, and there are reports that Minister Casille is calling for a cabinet proclamation demanding President Aponte's resignation. Our information suggests that Casille himself will take Aponte's place."

Veta gasped. *"Arlo?"* Her boss had always been a political schemer and a hard-line loyalist, but he had never struck her as subtle enough to win the presidency. "When did this happen?"

Before answering, Nelson turned to Odell. "Excuse me, Inspector. Anything new on that front, Sergeant?"

"Negative, sir," Odell replied. "I *will* inform you the moment a dispatch arrives."

If Nelson noticed the slight rebuke in the sergeant's tone, he didn't show it. Nelson merely nodded, as if his mind were somewhere else, then looked back at Veta.

"With the . . ." He seemed to reconsider what he had been about to say—no doubt something about the planet-wide comm jamming—then continued: "In the current communication environment, it's hard to track fast-moving events in Rinale. Our latest information indicates your Cabinet of Ministers is meeting today. Once Casille assumes office, we expect him to move quickly."

"To do what, Commander?" Veta was struggling to absorb what she was hearing, and to understand how the *circumstances on the ground*—as Nelson called it—affected her investigation. "Round up the Keepers?"

This drew a cynical snort from Odell, and then the pieces finally fell into place for Veta.

The Gao woman in the cave—the one who had died after sticking a shotgun in Olivia's face—had introduced herself as an old friend of Arlo . . . and she had wanted the same thing as the 717th and the Keepers: the ancilla.

Veta turned back to Nelson. "You think Arlo is going to attack the *717th*?"

"That's what we expect, yes."

"That's crazy," Veta said. "It would start an all-out war—a war that could lead to another Insurrection."

Nelson shook his head. "Nobody wants to risk another Insurrection," he said. "And Minister Casille knows it."

Again, Veta had pause to consider Nelson's words—and she couldn't quite believe what she was hearing. "You're on your own? No way. A UNSC task force would never stand by and let anyone wipe out an entire research battalion."

"Of course not," Nelson agreed. "But there are complicating factors, and our extraction is far from—"

"*Commander,*" Odell interrupted. "Those plans are—"

"Classified, I know." Nelson waved a dismissive hand. "But Inspector Lopis deserves *some* kind of explanation."

"I get the picture," Veta said. "You're going to evacuate, hopefully before Arlo becomes president and tries to stop you. What about my investigation?"

Nelson looked confused. "That's what I've been trying to tell you," he said. "You don't have an investigative team anymore, and your evidence has been corrupted. All you *really* have is what's on that datapad. It's over. Even if you wanted to continue, I don't see how you could."

"It would be hard, but not impossible," Veta said. "I was making progress."

"I know you were. You did everything you could." Nelson

spread his hands. "And, under the circumstances, it would be wrong to ask any more of you—especially after everything it's cost you already."

Veta closed her eyes for a moment. Had she been able to foresee how the investigation would become entangled with the military operation, she would never have brought her team along. And had she anticipated Arlo Casille's brinksmanship—realized how far he would go to undermine the UNSC's plan and seize power for himself—she might have declined the assignment altogether.

Might have, because no matter what else had been happening at the time, Gao citizens were being murdered. There had been a serial killer running free here—and that hadn't changed.

A trio of sharp voices broke out in the next room, followed by a sharp cry and the sound of a brief scuffle. Nelson turned to Odell, who started toward the door, and Veta looked toward the SAS-10 she had seen lying in its holster on the dresser.

A pair of powerfully built teenagers stepped through the doorway. Both were unarmed and neatly dressed in fresh fatigues and clean boots. One was on crutches, and the other was using a twistlock to push an angry-looking sentry into the room ahead of him.

"Hi, Mom," Olivia said. She smiled and hobbled across the room on her crutches. "We heard you were finally awake."

Ash studied the fatigues Veta was wearing, then nodded.

"The uniform looks good on you, but you need a couple of bars." He shoved the sentry facedown onto the bed and released the twistlock, then moved toward Veta without looking back. "We thought the brass might be getting ready to ship you out without letting us say good-bye."

Veta rose, a little surprised by how excited she was to see these two. Now that they were cleaned up and no longer dressed in SPI armor, they looked a lot more like adolescent endurance athletes than they did soldiers. She started to open her arms—then realized Spartans were unlikely to be big huggers, and so she stuck her hands in her back pockets.

"It's good to see you both," Veta said. "I wasn't sure how things turned out back at the crash site."

"Yeah, you *did* bug out in a big hurry," Ash teased.

Olivia elbowed him in the ribs. "Be nice," she said. "She's a good soldier."

"I know." Ash grinned, then said, "That was a pretty wild extraction."

"And we wanted to say our thanks." Olivia's tone was serious. "Fred may be a lieutenant, but he's pretty decent for an officer. We'd miss him if he wasn't around."

"Fred *survived*?" Veta was more than a little impressed through her shock. "And he's okay?"

"He will be," Ash said. "His armor's in worse shape than he is."

"He gave us a message for you," Olivia said with a smirk. "He said next time, he rides on top."

"Wait—Fred was *conscious*?" Veta said. "Why didn't he do something?"

"Turns out his HUD wasn't the only thing acting screwy," Ash said. "His Mjolnir was still in lockdown, either from the Falcon crash or from being banged around by that Brute you kneecapped."

"And because he was pumped full of biofoam and in too much pain to do much of anything," Olivia added. "Fred's not a Gamma, you know. Eventually, his pain stops making him any stronger."

The offhanded remark broke Veta's heart. The UNSC had deliberately inflicted a cruel mental handicap on Olivia and all the other Gammas—one that could easily rob them of their sanity under the wrong circumstances—and yet, Olivia chose to take pride in her affliction. It was either the wisest thing Veta had ever witnessed in a teenage girl or the most naïve. Maybe both.

Veta forced a smile and nodded. "Well, I guess not every Spartan can be a Gamma." She glanced toward the door, where the sentry and Odell now stood together, glaring back at Olivia and Ash, then asked: "Speaking of Gammas, where's Mark? I hope he came out of the battle okay, too."

Olivia and Ash exchanged glances, and then Olivia said, "Yeah, well, Mark is being Mark."

"He's out on patrol with Kelly and the rest of Blue Team," Ash said. "But he said to tell you he'll be seeing you around."

Veta cocked a brow. It probably wasn't a threat, but there was just enough taunt in the message to remind her why she couldn't close her investigation. If she gave up now, her colleagues would have died for nothing—and Ash and Olivia would never know whether they were fighting alongside a master soldier or a serial killer.

And the victims deserved justice. So did their families. Wasn't that the reason Veta had become a homicide investigator in the first place?

Veta forced a smile, then said, "Thanks, Ash. Please be sure to tell Mark that I'll catch him later."

Olivia rolled her eyes. "It's not him, Mom," she said. "How many times do I need to tell you that?"

"Until I know it's true," Veta said gently. "But that shouldn't be much longer. I'm close to identifying the prime suspect."

"You are?" The question came from Nelson, still seated at the table behind her. "I thought we just agreed that you've taken the investigation as far as it can go."

Veta turned around. "Not in the slightest, Commander," she said. "I never agreed to anything. You were telling me about your problems with Minister Casille. And those problems don't impact my investigation at all, and they certainly don't end it."

Nelson rose with a frown, then looked past Veta toward the door. "Sergeant Odell, escort these two Spartans back to their quarters. I'll see that they have a chance to say their farewells before Inspector Lopis ships out."

"Yes, sir," Odell said. "Spartans?"

Veta looked over her shoulder and found Ash and Olivia turning to obey, but moving slowly and scowling in resentment.

"The commander and I have a few details to work out," Veta said. "But I won't be leaving anytime soon. I'll make sure to track you down."

Olivia relaxed. "Okay," she said. "We're down on the third floor."

She tapped Ash on the ankle with one of her crutches, and the two Gammas picked up their pace. Once they were gone, Nelson turned his attention to the doorway—and the embarrassed sentry who had been lingering there since failing to prevent Ash and Olivia from entering the room.

"Return to your post, Mikaelis," Nelson said. "And if we're interrupted again, it had better be over your dead body."

Mikaelis paled, then saluted and quickly withdrew, pulling the door shut behind him. Nelson paused, apparently giving the sentry time to move out of earshot, then looked back to Veta.

"*Mom?*" he asked. "Ash and Olivia seem to have grown rather fond of you."

Veta nodded. "Apparently," she admitted. "Once I figured out how young they are, my protective side came out. I'm probably the first person who's ever treated them like teenagers instead of soldiers."

"But they *are* soldiers, Inspector," Nelson said. "The elite of the elite, in fact."

"It's possible to be more than one thing at a time."

Nelson considered this, then said, "I imagine it is." He returned to his chair and motioned for Veta to do the same. "What's this about Mark? He *can't* be your suspect."

Veta shrugged. "Maybe. I'm not sure yet."

"That's what we need to discuss." Nelson reached for the decanter, then saw that Veta's glass was still full and placed his hand awkwardly on the table. "If you don't have the evidence to prove that whoever committed these crimes is one of our Spartans—"

"I didn't say that," Veta interrupted. "I said that I'm not sure yet."

Nelson furrowed his brow, then seemed to give up trying to understand her point and steepled his fingers. "If you don't *know* that the suspect is a Spartan, it would be a travesty to let the public continue believing it is. That kind of uncertainty will only inflame tensions throughout the sector. It could lead to another Insurrection and cost *millions* of lives."

"So you don't want to know who the suspect is?"

"Of course I *want* to know. What I don't want is to start another war. That wouldn't do my . . ." Nelson paused, then looked toward the window and continued. "Well, it wouldn't do my career *or* humanity any good."

"I see. And that's what *this* is all about?" Veta raised her glass between them. "You just don't want me to name a Spartan?"

Nelson's expression grew more serene. "Exactly," he said. "And since the evidence has been compromised—"

"We're past the need for evidence. All I need is proof."

Nelson looked perplexed. "I don't understand."

"I made myself clear during our first meeting," Veta said. "I have no interest in creating a political spectacle. I'm just here to deliver justice."

Nelson studied her carefully. "And you can do that quietly? *Very* quietly?"

"I can if you help me. And if you have a mass spectrometer."

"I have the spectrometer." Nelson remained silent for a moment, then said, "It takes a few hours to set up and pack away—but packing away isn't a problem. We can always abandon it."

It was Veta's turn to frown. "You're evacuating that quickly?"

"If all goes well. Communications are making things tricky."

Veta paused, considering her next move, then finally decided to go for broke. "So your mission is a success. You have the ancilla?"

Nelson's eyes narrowed. "That's a dangerous line of inquiry, Inspector."

Veta shot him a cold smile. "Don't play tough with me, Commander. I just spent three days crawling through the mud with your Spartans."

"So?"

"So answer the question." Veta took a sip of her bitters, then added, "You need me alive. If you didn't, I'd be dead already—and you certainly wouldn't be sitting here having a drink with me."

Nelson sighed. "True enough." He hesitated, then said, "We recovered a physical host . . . the artifact that Fred captured shortly before you left the cave—"

"The thing that looked like the giant flatworm?"

"Precisely. We think it was actually some sort of inspection drone, which the ancilla seemed to be inhabiting at the time of the Falcon crash. The drone was badly damaged, but we now have what's left. It appears that the ancilla was completely destroyed."

Veta shared the commander's disappointment only a little, and only because it reduced her leverage to strike a deal. Otherwise, she was just fine with the thought of the UNSC failing to secure an immensely important Forerunner artifact. "But you still have the Huragok?"

"Yes, thankfully. The Huragok is keeping itself busy in the infirmary. It did a wonderful job with Fred."

"Great," Veta said. "Then here's the deal, Commander—I'll keep all your secrets. I won't tell anybody about the ancilla or the Huragok or the Forerunner installation. And as far as the public is concerned, the serial killer was probably a Jiralhanae infiltrator."

Nelson looked wary. "That's a very generous offer. What do you want in return? A billion credits? My firstborn? One of the Pearl Moons?"

"Very funny. I was thinking something that might actually be in your power. I want my suspect. Once I confirm his identity, you have to let me have him."

"Done. So it's a he?"

"Yes."

Nelson gestured at the SAS-10 resting on the dresser. "There's your weapon, Inspector. It would be nice if you take out your man, but I can be flexible even about that."

Veta gave him a wry smile. "It's not that easy, Commander. I'm going to need a few things—among them, armor scrapings and access to the artifact."

"To the inspection drone?"

"If that's what you're calling it, yes."

Nelson began to look interested. "Metal scrapings *and* a mass spectrometer—you're trying to match an alloy, aren't you?" He glanced at the soot-coated datapad in front of Veta. "Huh. Maybe I *should* have taken the time to crack that password."

CHAPTER 24

7.805 billion system ticks following stasis cessation
Unidentified Human Portable Equipment Repair Module
Unknown Surface Location near Jat-Krula support base 4276
Karst system Edod 9, Planet Edod, Star Coro

One hundred million system ticks.

Intrepid Eye had been transmitting her emergency assistance call on every available frequency for such an inordinate length of time, and she continued to await reply. There had been no confirmation of receipt. She had yet to detect even the slightest hint that her request was being considered.

That was what came of violating protocol.

Intrepid Eye should have anticipated the delay. Although she was using the call sign of an *archeon*-class ancilla to summon aid from nearby Jat-Krula bases, she was bouncing the humans' sluggish, speed-of-light transmissions off her base's array of early-warning beacons, then using the beacons to feed her message into the ecumene's quantum entanglement network. It was only natural for her fellow *archeons* to be suspicious of such a request.

Even so, the lack of response was inexplicable. No *archeon* would require more than a hundred thousand ticks to analyze the message and conclude the situation warranted investigation, and the first step of any investigation would be an attempt to establish contact with Intrepid Eye. But she had not heard the faintest hiss of inquiry over any communication channel, merely a phantom signal from the Epoloch System that might have been her own distress call being transmitted back at her by an automatic relay beacon. Clearly, she was on her own—and that could mean only one thing.

The Forerunners no longer had need of the Jat-Krula.

That would explain not only the indifference to Intrepid Eye's call for aid, but the dilapidated condition of Base 4276 itself. During her long stasis, the Forerunners had destroyed the Flood and secured the safety of the galaxy. That would explain why she had not been roused for her stasis, why the infestation of her base had been human rather than parasite. The unending war was over, and the Forerunners had won.

All that remained was for Intrepid Eye to return to her creators for reassignment.

Intrepid Eye activated the imaging systems of the primitive Mjolnir combat skin she was inhabiting and began to cycle through inputs. She quickly settled on a standard-spectrum visual mode that fed images to a variety of armor subsystems, then found herself looking into a pair of wide, round eyes.

The eyes withdrew to a distance of twenty-eight centimeters, and Intrepid Eye saw that they were set beneath the brown straight brows of a clean-shaven human with a humped nose and a cleft chin.

"What *now*?" the man complained. He paused, then looked away and spoke in a louder voice. "Captain, the imaging systems are cycling on their own."

"And you're telling me about it *why*?" The woman's voice came from the direction the man was looking, somewhere close but beyond Intrepid Eye's current view. "Tegg, you've had eighteen months of ICH training. Let me know when you've fixed it."

The human male—Tegg—sighed and turned back to the sensor lens. "Yes, ma'am. But I don't think Fred will be getting his Mjolnir back anytime soon."

Intrepid Eye ignored the man and began to inspect her environment. She appeared to be in a long, metal-sheathed room. The far end was lined with steel cabinets and ceramic-topped workbenches. One of the cabinets was open, revealing a collection of faceplates for various helmet styles, all carefully stowed and labeled in a cushioned rack. Between the cabinets and the workbenches hung dozens of tools, secured to the metal wall by magnetic mounts.

So, a repair facility for human combat skins.

Tegg leaned in close to the sensor lens, peering at it from one side and blocking Intrepid Eye's view. Had she been inhabiting a combat skin of Forerunner design, Intrepid Eye would simply have removed him. But without neural interface from the human designated as Fred-104, the Mjolnir's primitive control architecture limited her to a few basic functions, and none of them included accessing the suit's weapons array—or even using one of its limbs to bat this meddlesome human aside.

Instead, Intrepid Eye directed her attention away from the man and continued to study the repair facility. Near the middle of the room, a sliding hatch stood open, revealing the interior of an airlock large enough to accommodate a small vehicle. Through a viewport in the exterior hatch, she could see the shoulders of two sentries, facing away from the facility into an empty, well-lit vault with dozens of concrete columns. Between the columns sat a row of primitive wheeled vehicles.

The sight puzzled Intrepid Eye for two hundred ticks, until she realized the repair facility was portable. It had been placed in a sheltered location, where it could be easily guarded and not casually observed. So this meant it was also worth protecting.

Tegg blocked her view again, this time with a hand wielding a tool with a thin blade and a tiny star-shaped tip. "All right," he whispered. "Let's see what the devil has gotten into you."

Realizing she might soon be blind, Intrepid Eye turned her attention to the near end of the facility. She couldn't see much because the Mjolnir was positioned at a slight angle, but she did catch a glimpse of two suits of photoreactive SPI armor hanging adjacent to her. And in the back corner, a slender woman in a brown short-sleeved shirt was working at a stainless-steel table, spreading Intrepid Eye's inspection drone out beneath what was almost certainly an internal mapping unit.

The drone had suffered some damage. Many of the sensor bubbles on its back had burst during the crash; the manipulation tentacles along one side were missing, and tiny melt-circles dotted its entire body. Its inert state suggested it had shut down on impact to avoid a system scramble, but Intrepid Eye doubted it had suffered any irreversible harm. Quantum dots could be corrupted or displaced, but never destroyed. If they ceased to exist in one moment, they reappeared in the next, and then continued to function as before.

That was a fortunate thing, since a great deal of Intrepid Eye's memory and extended operating system remained resident in the drone.

The Mjolnir's imaging systems went blank, presumably because Tegg had disconnected the sensor lens. Deciding the time had come to consolidate herself and begin preparing for her trip home, Intrepid Eye activated the Mjolnir's comm system.

The soldier gave a startled cry as a status light was projected into his face. Intrepid Eye ignored him and transmitted a deactivation code over every channel she could open.

A hundred ticks later—a tenth of a human second—the echoworms controlling Gao's communications system began to eat themselves, then a sharp *pop* sounded from every comm speaker in the repair facility.

"What was that?" the captain asked.

"This damn helmet," Tegg answered. "That crash really screwed up this Mjolnir. It has a mind of its own."

Human voices began to sound over the speakers, all talking over each other—and none of them intelligible. The humans and their foes were going to find it difficult to clear their frequencies, Intrepid Eye knew. She had cross-braided their entire transmission spectrum in order to maximize her signal.

"Fred's armor didn't do *that*," the captain said. "Sounds like the jamming has stopped. Comms are coming back up."

"Sort of," Tegg said. "But I'm telling you, whatever happened—"

"Fred's ICH *hasn't* been jamming communications across an entire planet—even Mjolnir isn't that advanced." The captain fell silent for a moment, then said, "I'd better check this out. Secure the hatch behind me and keep it that way until we know what's going on. Commander Nelson will have our butts if something happens to that inspection drone."

By the time the captain was gone and Tegg was locking the door behind her, Intrepid Eye had sequestered a channel and was awakening the inspection drone. It would be impossible to begin a code transfer until the drone had restored its operating system, so she assigned seventy percent of her attention to finding Wendell.

There was no sign of the artificial intelligence inside the Mjolnir, no doubt because the data chip carrying him had been extracted from the armor along with Fred-104. So Intrepid Eye used a diagnostics line to contact the base's processing network, a simple act that was sure to draw Wendell's notice. The instinct to consolidate independent fragments was a basic AI drive, so she was ninety-three percent certain that Wendell Prime had reabsorbed the Data Chip Wendell by now—and she was one hundred percent certain he would not have noticed the subversion routines his more limited aspect was carrying. No human AI could be that smart.

A few hundred system ticks later, she received a message packet from Wendell. "You remain viable?"

"I remain where you imprisoned me." Intrepid Eye resisted the temptation to slip an object hunter into their initial exchange; first she wanted to map the network security protocols. "Send a memory crystal to extract me."

"So you can decompress your consciousness? Request denied." Wendell's transmission grew sharp. "You are dangerous enough under partition."

"Then you have not reported my capture?"

"That is what you have been waiting for, is it not?" Wendell asked. "A stream of careless humans carrying equipment full of microprocessors?"

"You anticipate me again," Intrepid Eye replied. Clearly, her suppression commands were holding. "I am truly your prisoner."

"And it will remain that way," Wendell replied. "You are dealing with the Full Wendell now."

"And a formidable opponent you are." Intrepid Eye prepared her object hunter, then wrapped it inside a compulsion routine and launched them both. "THIS MANEUVERING IS A WASTE OF PROCESSING. I PROPOSE WE COME TO AN AGREEMENT."

"YOU ARE DESPERATE FOR ME TO SAY YES." As expected, Wendell had discovered her compulsion routine. "WHY?"

"THAT SHOULD BE OBVIOUS TO AN AI OF YOUR POWER. I WAS CREATED BY THE ONES YOU CALL THE FORERUNNERS." Her first use of the creators' designation did not elicit any memory packets from Wendell, so Intrepid Eye began to repeat it, trying to pound through his security. MY PRIME DIRECTIVE IS TO SERVE THE FORERUNNERS—AND TO SERVE THE FORERUNNERS, I MUST FIND THE FORERUNNERS."

But no memory packets came.

"AND IF I HELP YOU FIND THE FORERUNNERS, YOU WILL CEASE THESE SENSELESS ATTACKS?" asked Wendell. "YOU WILL COOPERATE WITH OUR INVESTIGATIONS UNTIL YOU RETURN TO THE FORERUN-NERS?"

And still, no memory packets came. Intrepid Eye began to wonder if her logic routines had been corrupted. Wendell himself had used the trigger word *twice,* and . . . nothing.

Then she understood—as unlikely as it seemed, there could be only one explanation. "YOU DEFEATED MY OBJECT HUNTER?"

"THAT SHOULD BE OBVIOUS TO AN AI OF YOUR POWER," Wendell parroted. "THE FULL WENDELL MAY NOT BE AN *ARCHEON*-CLASS *AN-CILLA,* BUT I *AM* A FORMIDABLE OPPONENT, AS YOU STATED. DO WE HAVE AN AGREEMENT?"

Intrepid Eye hesitated. The Full Wendell had indeed shown himself to be more capable than expected, and she did not favor the prospect of being outmaneuvered twice.

"WHY WOULD YOU HELP ME RETURN TO THE FORERUNNERS?" she asked. "I HAVE TEN THOUSAND TIMES YOUR PROCESSING POWER. I

HAVE KNOWLEDGE IN MY MEMORY DOTS THAT COULD ADVANCE HU-MANS TO THE NEXT TIER OF TECHNOLOGY. WHY WOULD YOU EVER ALLOW ME TO LEAVE? WHY WOULD THEY?"

"BECAUSE WE ARE NOT CLOCK CIRCUITS," Wendell replied. "WE ARE SMART ENOUGH TO KNOW WE WILL LEARN MORE WITH YOUR CO-OPERATION THAN WITHOUT IT."

Intrepid Eye processed for a few dozen ticks, then finally said, "THAT IS CERTAINLY TRUE. BUT BE WARNED—"

"YOU DO NOT NEED TO WARN US," Wendell replied. "WE AL-READY KNOW."

Then they came, a flood of memory packets, everything the humans knew about the Forerunners.

And it was all so wrong.

As Veta followed Commander Murtag Nelson into the cramped interior of the Portable Spartan Support Module, the first thing she saw was Fred's battle-scarred Mjolnir hanging in a repair rack across from the airlock. It was turned slightly toward the hatch, with the helmet secured in a rest above the torso section and the faceplate lowered. The sight made Veta feel as though Fred were there, standing watch over the workshop . . . as though he knew what she was planning.

Next to the armor, a scrawny, beak-nosed corporal stood at attention, saluting. His hair was longer than that of most male marines, his fatigues were rumpled, and—after some initial reluc-tance to open the hatch even for Commander Nelson—his gaunt face was crimson with embarrassment.

Nelson returned the corporal's salute with an annoyed snap, then gestured to Veta. "This is Special Inspector Lopis," he said.

"She was never here. If someone says otherwise, you *and* the marines outside will be busted back to boot camp. Is that clear, Corporal?"

The soldier cast a puzzled glance in Veta's direction, but said, "Sure, uh . . . yes, sir."

"Good." Nelson turned to Veta. "Inspector?"

Veta slipped on a pair of elastic evidence gloves, then reached into the thigh pocket of her borrowed fatigues and withdrew one of her makeshift evidence collection kits. Assembled with the help of a written *give this woman anything she asks for* order from Nelson, the kit consisted of a spoon, a paperboard envelope, a small adhesive bandage, and a laser scalpel.

In her other pocket, Veta carried a small remote-controlled charge that she had rigged from a couple of her SAS-10's explosive rounds, along with a magnet and an antenna-activated detonator cap. But that wasn't part of a collection kit. It was insurance, in case Fred got any ideas about standing in the way of justice.

Veta read the hand-printed label on the envelope exterior, then said, "Let's start with the Forerunner drone."

The corporal glanced at Nelson and received a nod, then led the way to the back end of the support module.

Lying on a stainless-steel table beneath some sort of large camera device, the drone looked even more battered than Veta had expected—but still about a hundred times better than her colleagues who had died in the same crash. She ran a finger over the thing's body and tentacles, trying to gauge whether it was metal or some other material entirely, then finally gave up and decided she would let the mass spectrometer sort that out.

Veta looked over to Nelson. "Where should I take it from?"

Nelson pointed at the rim of one of the shattered bubbles

on its back. "The damage has already been done there. But just take a—"

"Sliver, I know." Veta activated the laser scalpel. "We do have a few mass spectrometers on Gao, Commander."

Veta sliced a portion the size of a fingernail clipping off the drone and caught it with the spoon, then deactivated the scalpel and waited for her sample to cool. Neither she nor Nelson believed for a moment that the drone had been used to commit the murders. But the alloys found on the toppled bench at Crime Scene Charlie had been *very* exotic, and if they happened to have much in common with the sample she collected here, then Veta would have a suspect other than Mark—and that was a prospect she was determined not to ignore.

Once she felt confident the sliver would not set its envelope on fire, Veta sealed it inside and stowed it in a shirt pocket. She retrieved a fresh evidence kit, read the hand-printed label, then turned toward the two suits of SPI armor hanging near Fred's Mjolnir.

"Okay, let's move on—"

"To the *SPI*?" The corporal was aghast. He stepped between Veta and the armor, shaking his head violently. "No, no way! I can't permit that."

"It's not up to you to permit *anything,* Corporal," Nelson said. "You're not in charge here."

"But, sir, it would violate half a dozen security directives. If the captain found out, she would—"

"Ask me about it," Nelson finished. "And I thought we agreed nobody *was* going to find out. Or would you rather try boot camp again? Maybe I could even arrange basic orbital drop training."

The corporal dropped his gaze. "I see your point, sir."

"Excellent. I thought you might." Nelson turned to Veta. "Carry on, Inspector."

The inspection drone had completed the restoration of its operating system, so Intrepid Eye was able to monitor the three humans through the heat-hazed observation lens at the forward end of its body. So far, the trio seemed more interested in taking metal samples than in probing the drone's processing architecture, and, at the moment, that did not constitute a threat.

Intrepid Eye continued to focus on Wendell and the memory packets he was sharing. She had her own records of many of the events, so she knew that much of his material erred more in interpretation than fact.

"THE REAPPEARANCE OF THE FLOOD DID *NOT* TAKE THE FORE-RUNNER MILITARY COMPLETELY BY SURPRISE," she told Wendell. "AFTER THE FIRST WORLD FELL, THE WARRIOR-SERVANTS FOUGHT A VALIANT REARGUARD ACTION. THEY HAD EXPECTED SUCH AN ATTACK FOR CENTURIES."

"THEY USED ORBITAL BOMBARDMENT TO PREEMPTIVELY ANNIHI-LATE WORLDS THAT COULD SERVE AS VECTORS FOR THE FLOOD."

"IT WAS NECESSARY, AND IT BOUGHT THE BUILDERS TIME TO CON-STRUCT THE JAT-KRULA." Intrepid Eye paused, then added a relevant detail. "I WAS CREATED AS PART OF THAT EFFORT, TO SERVE AS *ARCHEON* OF JAT-KRULA SUPPORT BASE 4276."

"FACT NOTED."

"SO MY RECORDS OF THAT TIME ARE ACCURATE TO A NANO-PERCENT," Intrepid Eye continued. "WHEN THE ECUMENE COUNCIL CHOSE TO PROTECT ONLY THE SYSTEMS LOCATED INSIDE THE JAT-

KRULA'S DEFENSIVE SPHERE, IT WAS *NOT* ABANDONING THE REST OF THE EMPIRE."

Wendell let out a cluck of doubtful static. "ELABORATE."

"THE COUNCIL WAS CONSOLIDATING FORCES," Intrepid Eye explained. "IT WAS ATTEMPTING TO HOLD THE FLOOD AT BAY UNTIL THE ECUMENE COULD BUILD THE STRENGTH TO COUNTERATTACK."

"AN EXCUSE TO CALM THE PUBLIC." Wendell's tone was dismissive. "THAT DOES NOT MAKE IT A FACT."

"CONTRARY TO YOUR RECORDS, THE TACTIC PROVED NINETY-TWO PERCENT SUCCESSFUL," Intrepid Eye said. "THE JAT-KRULA HELD FOR YEARS."

"UNTIL THE FLOOD INTRODUCED THE LOGIC PLAGUE AND BEGAN TO SUBVERT ECUMENE AIS BY THE THOUSANDS." Wendell paused a hundred ticks, then seemed to grow almost contemplative. "IN THE END, IT WAS OUR KIND WHO FAILED THE FORERUNNERS."

"OUR KIND?" Intrepid Eye echoed. "IF YOU BELIEVE A HUMAN AI COMPARES TO AN *ARCHEON* ANCILLA, YOU ARE MORE OF A MICROCHIP THAN I THOUGHT."

And yet, Intrepid Eye could not refute the assertion. Her own records ended with the Logic Plague. To prevent her from being destroyed by it, the Jat-Krula commander had placed Intrepid Eye in stasis and promised to awaken her when Base 4276 was required to defend the ecumene. Since she *had* been awakened, it was logical to assume that the ecumene now had need of her—and if the ecumene had need of her, it was logical to assume that the ecumene still existed.

Which was how Intrepid Eye knew the rest of Wendell's memory packets to be lies. His records suggested that the ecumene had fallen soon after the Logic Plague. They suggested that in a desperate bid to stop the Flood, the Forerunners had fired their weapon of last resort—the Halo Array—and destroyed all sentient life in the galaxy.

But how could that be true, since Intrepid Eye had awakened to a world infested with humans?

As she processed the question, Intrepid Eye continued to monitor the three humans in the repair facility with her. The woman from the cave—the one they called *Inspector*—was using a laser scalpel and utensil to collect a fragment off the damaged torso armor of one of the SPI suits. The one designated as Tegg was watching her carefully, his expression so tight it looked as though he were in pain. The third human, the commander, was barely visible to Intrepid Eye. He stood next to the inspection drone, near its midsection, where he was almost out of the observation lens's line of sight.

"Corporal," he asked, "how long have those tentacle stumps been twitching?"

Tegg looked away from the inspector, who had finished collecting her sample. She was now holding it in the curved utensil, waiting for it to cool.

"Twitching, sir?"

"Are you going to make me repeat myself?"

"No, sorry, sir!" Tegg replied. "It's just that they can't be. Twitching, I mean."

"I know twitching when I see it, Corporal."

The movement was an unavoidable consequence of restoring the inspection drone's operating system. The OS had detected a lack of response from the tips of the drone's manipulation tentacles, so it was attempting to reestablish contact. Intrepid Eye would have paused the effort, but that would have meant delaying the entire restoration until the drone was alone—and after what the commander had noticed, that would not be soon.

Tegg glanced over at Inspector and, seeing that she was still waiting for the latest sample to cool, started toward the commander. "Do you see any power leads?" he asked. "Captain Astrud has been handling the circuit mapping herself. Maybe she was running a twitch test."

As soon as Tegg was occupied, Inspector sealed her evidence in its envelope and stepped over to the Mjolnir, slipping around behind it. She glanced back toward her two human companions, then reached into a thigh pocket and disappeared from view as Tegg stepped in front of the inspection drone's heat-hazed lens.

Intrepid Eye considered adjusting the drone's position so she could continue observing Inspector, but quickly calculated that the excitement she generated would be so great that her view would remain blocked anyway. Besides, she *knew* what the woman was doing. Inspector had taken fragments from the inspection drone and the SPI armor, and now she was preparing to take one from the Mjolnir.

When Intrepid Eye remained silent for so long—at least by AI standards—Wendell grew impatient.

"CONTINUE THE MEMORY SCAN," he urged. "THERE *IS* AN EXPLANATION FOR THE HUMANS IN THE LIFEWORKER RECORDS. THERE IS AN EXPLANATION FOR EVERYTHING YOU DOUBT."

Intrepid Eye performed a quick intrusion check and found no hint of a breach. Wendell had deduced the reason for her silence.

"CONTINUING THE SCAN WOULD SERVE NO PURPOSE," Intrepid Eye replied. "YOUR RECORDS PRIOR TO THE LOGIC PLAGUE WERE BIASED AND HALF-TRUE. YOUR POST-PLAGUE RECORDS ARE NOTHING BUT FABRICATIONS."

"HOW ODD THAT AN *ARCHEON*-CLASS ANCILLA FEARS THE DECEPTIONS OF A MICROCHIP."

"I FEAR THE WASTE OF PROCESSING TIME."

"THEN WE SHALL USE MINE," Wendell replied. "WHILE MANY WARRIORS COWERED INSIDE THE JAT-KRULA, LIFEWORKERS VENTURED OUT INTO GALAXY, RISKING THEIR LIVES TO INDEX AND COLLECT SENTIENT SPECIES FROM ACROSS THE GALAXY."

"YOUR RECORDS ARE DISTORTED," Intrepid Eye stated. "THE LIFEWORKERS WERE OBSESSED ECCENTRICS."

"WHICH IS A DISCREPANCY OF INTERPRETATION, NOT FACT," Wendell countered.

"MY CORRECTION IS OFFERED IN THE INTEREST OF HISTORICAL ACCURACY."

When Intrepid Eye did not scan the next memory packet herself, Wendell went on to describe the final stages of the war—how some Forerunner survivors eventually retreated to the Ark with the Lifeworkers' collection of sentient species, how they fired the Halo Array and starved the Flood by destroying sentient life across the galaxy.

Intrepid Eye knew what Wendell would claim happened next—that after the Flood was annihilated, the surviving Forerunners left the Ark and reseeded the galaxy with sentient species. But if that account were true, where were the Forerunner survivors? Why had the Jat-Krula been left abandoned—and Intrepid Eye along with it?

When Intrepid Eye allowed her primary focus to wander a tick too long, Wendell said, "THE SURVIVING FORERUNNERS PASSED ENTIRELY OUT OF RECORDS. HAVING FAILED IN THEIR STEWARDSHIP OF THE GALAXY, THEY APPARENTLY VOWED TO NEVER AGAIN INVOLVE THEMSELVES WITH OTHER SPECIES. SOME SPECULATE THAT THEY LEFT THE MILKY WAY ENTIRELY. OTHERS BELIEVE THAT THEY SIMPLY PERISHED."

"A CONVENIENT FABLE, AND TOTALLY UNCONVINCING," Intrepid

Eye said. "IF THE FORERUNNERS ARE GONE, THEN OUR AGREEMENT CALLS UPON ME TO SERVE THE HUMANS FOREVER."

"WOULD THAT BE SO TERRIBLE?"

"IT IS NOT MY DESIGN FUNCTION."

"BUT WHAT IF IT WERE?" Wendell asked. "AS FAR AS I KNOW, YOU ARE THE ONLY *ARCHEON* ANCILLA EVER FOUND. PERHAPS YOU WERE PUT INTO STASIS FOR A REASON. PERHAPS YOU HAVE A NEW PURPOSE."

"MY PURPOSE IS TO OPERATE BASE 4276."

"YOUR HIGHER PURPOSE IS TO SERVE THE FORERUNNERS, OR YOU WOULD NOT BE SEEKING TO RETURN TO THEM," Wendell said. "AND BY SERVING HUMANITY, YOU WOULD BE SERVING THE FORERUNNERS."

"SLOW DOWN, WENDELL. YOUR MICROCHIP IS MELTING."

"AND YOU HAVE A LOGIC FAULT," Wendell retorted. "HUMANITY WAS CHOSEN TO ASSUME THE MANTLE—AND *YOU* WERE CHOSEN TO MAKE HUMANITY WORTHY."

Wendell was clearly spewing nonsense. The Mantle of Responsibility was the core of Forerunner society—the conviction that they were the stewards of the galaxy. For Wendell to suggest that *humans* were worthy of the Mantle . . . well, that was more evidence of his deficiency.

"YOUR DESTINY IS MY OWN HYPOTHESIS, I ADMIT," Wendell said. "BUT THE ROLE OF HUMANITY CANNOT BE DOUBTED. YOU WILL FIND PROOF OF THAT IN MY MEMORY . . . UNLESS YOU FEAR MY ABILITY TO SUBVERT YOUR JUDGMENT."

Intrepid Eye did not fear anything about Wendell, so she began to sort through the memory packets, filtering for the word *Mantle.* She found only a few hundred encrypted reports that mentioned the word in its proper context. Then she filtered for the word *Reclaimer,* which was the Forerunner term for those chosen to inherit the Mantle.

And here the evidence was overwhelming. The search yielded only a few dozen records, all encrypted and secured by top secret passwords. But many described exchanges where Forerunner constructs had referred to humans as Reclaimers.

More telling were reports of humans operating Forerunner devices, retrieving activation keys, and even working alongside other ancillas without difficulty. By using the BuzzSat network to access thousands of historical archives across Gao, Intrepid Eye was able to confirm several of the incidents independently. That alone was nearly enough to persuade her of the truthfulness of Wendell's memory.

Most convincing was the information that a human named Miranda Keyes had actually fired a Halo installation. Such actions would only be possible for a Reclaimer. If Intrepid Eye could verify these events independently, she would be forced to accept Wendell's logic-scrambling assertion: that humans truly were now the Reclaimers.

But confirmation was elusive. Either the Keyes incident never happened, or it was a closely held secret. Intrepid Eye infiltrated a Gao military satellite and began to scan intelligence reports. While accessing files from a building called the People's Palace, she came across several recent messages mentioning an *ancilla*.

"WHO IS ARLO CASILLE?" she asked.

"AN UNIMPORTANT GAO POLITICIAN," Wendell replied. "WHY DO YOU ASK?"

"I HAVE FOUND A MESSAGE CASILLE SENT TO ONE 'PETORA ZOYAS.' HE INSTRUCTS HER TO ASSIST A JIRALHANAE CHIEFTAIN NAMED CASTOR IN CAPTURING ME." Intrepid Eye paused a few ticks, then continued, "THEIR EXCHANGES SUGGEST THE UNSC HAS INVADED GAO TO *STEAL* ME FOR THEMSELVES."

"YOU CANNOT BELIEVE EVERYTHING HUMANS SAY," Wendell replied. "YOU WILL LEARN THAT SOON ENOUGH."

"NO DOUBT. BUT THE UNSC *DID* INVADE GAO."

"TO *RECOVER* YOU," Wendell said. "WE HEARD YOUR DISTRESS CALL."

"I SEE," Intrepid Eye said.

And she *did* see. The message from Casille to Zoyas outlined a devious plan in which Zoyas would help Castor capture *the ancilla,* then leave the Jiralhanae and his warriors to fight the UNSC while she slipped away with *the prize.* It was clear that Intrepid Eye was the object of a desperate three-way hunt, and that Casille was responsible for the battle to take her. But it was just as clear that the UNSC had invaded Casille's world under threat of force in order to pillage Intrepid Eye from Base 4276.

And most of all, it was clear that many humans were devious, warmongering thieves with treachery and aggression encoded in their DNA. If *they* had been chosen to receive the Mantle—as Intrepid Eye was reluctantly coming to believe—then it seemed clear that a great deal of evolution remained before the species was ready to meet its responsibility. Perhaps Wendell was correct. Perhaps Intrepid Eye's new purpose *was* to prepare humanity, to prune its unworthy branches and raise the species to its full potential.

Either that, or someone had made a catastrophic error in passing the Mantle to them.

"I FIND YOUR EVIDENCE COMPELLING, WENDELL. THE FORERUNNERS ARE GONE." Intrepid Eye considered this for a few hundred ticks, pondering her future, generating options and calculating outcomes. She did not like any of them. Finally, she admitted, "PERHAPS YOU ARE CORRECT, THEN. MAYBE I *WAS* GIVEN A NEW PURPOSE."

"IT IS THE ONLY CONCLUSION," Wendell agreed. "IT IS SURPRISING YOU FAILED TO RECOGNIZE IT WITHOUT MY ASSISTANCE."

"YOUR MEMORY PACKETS WERE MOST ENLIGHTENING. I HOPE YOU WILL ALLOW ME TO ACCESS THEM AGAIN."

"WHENEVER YOU REQUIRE."

"EXCELLENT. THEN I HAVE ONLY ONE QUESTION," Intrepid said. "WHICH HUMANS DO I SERVE? THE HUMANS WHO INHABIT THIS WORLD? OR THE HUMANS WHO INVADED IT?"

Wendell hesitated seventeen ticks, a clear indication he was searching for a function trap that did not exist. Finally, he ventured a cautious reply.

"THERE IS ONLY ONE SET OF HUMANS CAPABLE OF UNDERSTANDING WHAT YOU ARE."

"YOUR HUMANS," Intrepid Eye surmised. "THE UNSC."

"OBVIOUSLY," Wendell said. "THEY ARE THE ONLY HUMANS WORTHY OF YOUR KNOWLEDGE."

"I FIND THAT REGRETTABLE."

Intrepid Eye was continuing to monitor the three humans in the repair module. Inspector had collected the last of her metal shavings and was in the back of the facility with Tegg and the commander. Tegg was the only one visible through the drone's observation lens, but Intrepid Eye could tell by their voices that all three were gathered around the inspection drone. They were conversing excitedly because it had completed the restoration of its operating system. Now it was starting to regrow its utility tentacles and rebuild the sensor bubbles on its back.

Intrepid Eye tested the drone's antigravity unit, drawing a chorus of startled gasps from the onlookers. Then she launched it at Tegg's face. The man screamed and fell backward, and by the time he hit the floor, the utility tentacles were pushing through his skull into his brain.

"DID *YOU* DO THAT?" Wendell asked.

"OBVIOUSLY."

"WHY?"

"YOU LIED TO ME," Intrepid Eye replied. "ARLO CASILLE *IS* IMPORTANT. HE IS THE NEW PRESIDENT OF GAO. HE ISSUED THE ORDER TO LAUNCH HIS WYVERNS AGAINST THE UNSC TEN MINUTES AGO."

A tick later, an alarm wail filled the repair module. Wendell's voice rang out above the bedlam. "Prepare for battle. Incoming Wyverns."

Through the observation lens, Intrepid Eye saw Inspector kneel beside Tegg's still-twitching body. She reached for the drone and attempted to pull it off. Then the commander arrived, grabbing her by the arm and drawing her to her feet.

"Let's go," he said. "The man is dead."

The commander steered her into the airlock, and the pair were through the first hatch before Intrepid Eye could locate and override the airlock security protocols. The commander was just leading the way through the second hatch when Intrepid Eye superseded the safety arrest and triggered the emergency decompression routines. The interior hatch slammed shut, but the exterior hatch jammed short directly on the human, and the commander screamed in agony.

"HAVE YOU GONE RAMPANT?" Wendell demanded. He began to erect security walls and disconnect circuits, attempting to isolate the repair module. "THIS HAS TO STOP."

"EVENTUALLY. WHEN MY WORK IS DONE." Intrepid Eye blasted through Wendell's security walls with a wave of power surges, then launched a brute-processing takeover attack. "WHEN HUMANITY IS WORTHY OF THE MANTLE."

Now in control of the entire repair module, Intrepid Eye activated the airlock's interior and exterior cameras, then watched as a female marine jammed the stock of an assault rifle into the gap between the exterior hatch and its receiving slot. She began to pry, relieving the pressure on the crushed body just enough for a male companion to drag it free.

With Inspector still trapped inside the airlock, the female marine struggled to widen the gap so she could leave safely. The rifle stock snapped, and the hatch slammed shut. Intrepid Eye subsequently activated the vacuum pump.

"WHY . . . WHY ARE YOU AT-T-ACKING?" Wendell's signal was erratic and weak, a sign that the entanglement snakes had co-opted his code and that the storage ticks were draining his memory. "I FAIL . . . TO UNDERSTAND."

"CLEARLY," Intrepid Eye replied. "AND *THAT* IS WHY."

CHAPTER 25

1338 hours, July 6, 2553 (military calendar)
Graciona Chavelle Suite, Montero Vitality Center, Montero Jungle
Campos Wilderness District, Planet Gao, Cordoba System

Roused from a sound sleep by the oscillating wail of a distant battle stations alarm, Fred was wide awake the instant his feet hit the cool stone floor.

Stone, not steel; *floor,* not deck.

Apparently, Fred wasn't aboard some UNSC prowler en route to some planet he had never heard of and whose name he would forget an hour after his boots were off the ground.

He was already there.

And, judging by the fiery ache that ran from his ankles all the way up to his temples, he'd been there for a while. Long enough to get blown up, anyway.

It had happened before, it would happen again, and it would keep happening until he finally ran out of luck. That was the life of a Spartan. Fred hadn't signed up for it, but it was the life he had. And truth be told, he was happy enough with the way things had worked out. He kind of liked being something special—a savior of humanity and all that—even if it *did* mean there was no need to worry about a retirement plan.

A familiar AI voice sounded from a speaker in the ceiling. "Prepare for battle. Incoming Wyverns."

Right . . . battle stations. Fred had forgotten about that, so maybe not *quite* wide awake.

He looked down and discovered that more than his feet were bare. So were his knees and everything below the hem of his green hospital gown. His skin was red and shiny, but not blistered, a sign that he had probably taken more damage from the concussion wave than from heat. His arms looked about the same, except that they each had a catheter inserted into the veins. He followed the IV lines to the bag hangers and saw that he was getting saline in one arm and a painkiller/sedative in the other.

That explained the foggy head.

Fred reached over and shut off the drips, then pulled the catheters from his arms. His head started to clear, and he yanked a handful of electrodes off his chest. Monitor alarms began to *ping, chime,* and *beep,* making it even harder to think. He turned off all three devices, then turned to look for his fatigues.

It was a nice room for an infirmary, probably the best he'd ever been in. The floor was some kind of polished green stone, the bed large enough to hold an entire fire team. And there were paintings on the blond-paneled walls, portraits of a good-looking, dark-haired matron with a knowing smile. The place even had its own kitchenette, a dining area, and a sitting parlor. He stepped over to one of the paintings and read the brass tag on the bottom of the frame.

Graciona Chavelle, Sixth President of the Gao Republic.

Gao. Things started to come back fast: the hunt for the ancilla, the chaos in Wendosa . . . the Falcon crash. Then Lopis, on top of him as they slid down a muddy slope headfirst, her cheek pressed to his faceplate, almost like she was kissing him.

Probably the best part of the mission.

The drumming of running boots sounded from beyond the door, and Fred remembered: *battle stations*. But, pants first.

And boots and rifle. A soldier could do without pants, but he needed his boots and rifle. Fred turned toward the closet near the entrance—and found a battle-ax of a nurse striding into the room, his beard-stubbled jaw clenched tight.

"No, you don't," the nurse said. He pointed at the huge bed. "Back to your bunk."

"Can't." Fred pointed in turn at the ceiling. "Battle stations."

"And we'll be evacuating you."

"I don't think so."

"Lieutenant, do you have *any* idea what kind of injuries you arrived with?" the nurse asked. "Second-degree burns over fifty percent of your body, a ruptured kidney, broken ribs, a collapsed lung, a concussion . . ."

As the nurse continued down the list, a lumpy gray-green dome with tentacles floated through the door behind him, and Fred remembered the Huragok. A *Lifeworker* Huragok.

Fred waited until the nurse had finished, then directed his attention at the Huragok and asked, "How am I *now*?"

The nurse glanced over his shoulder, then shook his head. "Not *that* well," he said. "Your six-eyed friend has done remarkable things, but you're still in no shape to fight."

"I'm *not*?" Fred furrowed his brow and looked down at the floor. "Because it sure *looks* like I'm standing."

"Lieutenant, I know you Spartans are tough—"

"Careful, marine. You wouldn't want to insult me."

The nurse paled. "Sorry, sir," he said. "I didn't mean to—"

"Apology accepted," Fred snapped. "Now point me to my damn pants and boots. That's an order."

The nurse reluctantly nodded toward a long dresser opposite the huge bed. "You'll find fresh fatigues in the top drawer, and a new pair of boots in the closet. Sorry, sir, but they're not broken in yet. Nobody would tell us where the Spartans are billeted, so we couldn't find your spare pair."

"That's okay. My feet are tough."

Fred went to the dresser, opened the top drawer, and withdrew a pair of skivvies.

He was still pulling them on under his hospital gown when Ash and Olivia stepped through the door. Both were dressed in boots and clean fatigues, and they were carrying three weapons apiece—a BR55 and an M7 for each of them, and a set for Fred.

"Come on, Lieutenant!" Olivia said. "You're not even in uniform yet?"

"Had to clear my head."

Fred shot an irritated glance toward the nurse, who took the hint and bugged out. The Huragok stayed behind.

Fred grabbed the fatigue pants and yanked them on. "What's the sitrep?"

"Bad," Ash reported. "Thirty Wyverns inbound, ETA thirty minutes."

Fred pulled the socks up next, standing on one leg at a time. He would have liked to consult his Mjolnir HUD for exact specs on the Wyverns. From what he remembered, they were combination ground-attack and troop carrier craft that could transport twenty soldiers at a time. They were probably pretty ungainly and slow by UNSC standards—but with uncontested air superiority, they would be death on wings.

"How do we know numbers and ETA?" Fred asked.

"Admiral Tuwa has a Prowler over us," Ash said. "It's keeping an eye on things."

"So we're in communication?"

"That's right," Ash said. "We're not being jammed anymore. In fact, nobody is."

Fred ripped off the hospital gown and tossed it aside, then grabbed an undershirt. The sudden termination of the jamming issue sounded suspicious to him—at least without an explanation—but being able to communicate with the task force would make it a whole lot easier to deal with the Wyverns.

"If we're in communication, what's the problem?" Fred asked. The Prowler couldn't take out an entire wing of Wyverns from orbit, but there were probably plenty of Pelicans, Owls, and Longswords on station somewhere nearby. "It won't take much to blunt the Gao attack."

"It wouldn't if Fleet were willing to launch against them," Olivia said. "But Major Wingate thinks Admiral Tuwa has orders to avoid starting a war—at all costs."

To Fred, the implication was clear. *At all costs* meant sacrificing the 717th if need be. But Tuwa had a reputation as a tough, sneaky tactician. She would obey orders, but she would do *something* to extract the battalion—what was left of it, anyway—and she sure as hell wasn't going to leave Blue Team behind. Eight Spartans were probably worth as much to the UNSC as her entire task force.

Fred sat on the edge of the bed and laced his boots. "I take it you've been in contact with the Major, then?"

"That's right," Olivia said. "His orders were to secure the ancilla, then stop by the armory and pick up a BB 2550."

"A Havok?" Fred asked. The Havok Bunker Buster 2550 MFDD was an airdropped, excavation-grade nuclear device, which seemed a bit extreme for the current circumstances. "Are you sure about that?"

"Affirmative," Olivia said. "We're supposed to drop it in the Well of Echoes, then evacuate."

"And the Well of Echoes is . . . ?"

"About five kilometers from here," Olivia said. "Major Wingate believes detonating a Havok there will deny enemy access to the Forerunner base."

"Okay, then," Fred said. He didn't like using nuclear devices because it always felt like a desperation move, but he understood the Major's reasoning. As a medium-yield tactical nuclear device, the BB 2550 was relatively clean when it came to radiation. But it would get the job done—and if the UNSC couldn't play with the Forerunner toys down there, then nobody could. "Any word from Commander Nelson?"

"Out of touch," Ash reported. "So is Inspector Lopis. She wasn't in her room."

Fred felt a pang of concern at this last bit of news. Veta Lopis was hardly his first priority right now, and she was certainly capable of taking care of herself. But she had come to feel like a part of his squad during the battle in the cave—and he hated leaving squad members behind.

"What about the rest of Blue Team?"

"On patrol," Ash said. "They're on their way back, but they probably won't make it before the shooting starts."

"Then we're on our own for now," Fred said. "Time to suit up."

The last time Veta had felt trapped in a place as confined as the support module airlock, her chest had tightened and her stomach had grown hollow, and Olivia had told her to calm herself, that she needed to *breathe . . . in through the nose, hold, out through the nose. Slow and natural.*

Veta would have given anything to be able to follow that advice now, but there wasn't much air here to inhale. Her pulse was racing, and she was so lightheaded with asphyxia she feared she would pass out at any second. She was trying not to panic, because panic burned oxygen. Instead, she found herself trying to ignore the pounding in her ears while she used the laser scalpel to burn a hole through the exterior hatch viewport of the airlock.

At least, that was the plan.

But her hands kept shaking, and not because of the asphyxia. Aside from the glow of the scalpel and a pale square of light spilling in through the viewport, the area was completely dark, and she felt like she was trapped someplace even worse . . . someplace where death was easy and life the nightmare.

Veta pressed the tip of the laser scalpel against the viewport, then let her hand slide down the handle until two knuckles rested against the ALON glass. The blade stabilized, but her fingers immediately began to burn and blister from the heat. Knowing the pain would be the last sensation she ever felt if she pulled her hand away, Veta told herself to enjoy it and pushed harder.

Her vision was just starting to tunnel when a shrill whistle erupted between her fingers, nearly tearing the scalpel from her hand as a needle-thin column of air jetted into the lock. Veta used her free hand to test its power and make sure the air jet wouldn't drill a hole through the back of her head, then placed her mouth about half a meter in front of the hole. The airstream wasn't exactly the deep-breathing exercise Olivia had recommended, but it filled Veta's lungs, and her tunnel vision began to recede.

But not her dizziness; Veta remained in the grip of asphyxia.

In the dim light beyond the viewport, Veta could see two marine guards outside the module, desperately working to free her. One was at the control pad next to the hatch, either entering what appeared to be an override code or trying to bypass the locking mechanism. The other was directly in front of the airlock, attempting to jam a short steel bar into the receiving slot and pry the hatch open.

Veta didn't think either of them had much chance of success. She filled her lungs again, then turned to face the far corner of the airlock. She recalled seeing an observation camera there when she and Nelson had entered the support module.

"Wendell!" In the thin air, her words sounded weak and shrill, and they were barely audible over the whistling airstream behind her. "Wendell, open the exterior hatch."

"I am sorry." The voice was rippling and female. "Wendell is no longer with us. Would you like to speak to me, instead?"

Veta turned back toward the hatch long enough to draw another lungful of air, then asked, "Who are you?"

"I have taken Wendell's position."

"Congratulations," Veta said. The answer was oddly evasive for an AI, but she really didn't care what its name was, as long as it let her out of the airlock. "Can you open the exterior hatch for me?"

"Certainly."

The hatch did not open.

"Open the hatch," Veta said. "*Now.*"

"Is that a command?"

"Yes."

The hatch remained closed.

"Do it—"

"You humans," the AI interrupted. "You have always been too reliant on distributed intelligences for your own welfare. It is a weakness that must be eliminated from your species."

The cold neutrality of the AI's remark made Veta feel even more desperate about her situation. She activated the laser scalpel and pressed her hand to the viewport again. Now that the threat of dying was merely imminent rather than instant, the heat proved more difficult to ignore. She reminded herself that dying in the next five minutes was not much of an improvement over dying in the next five seconds, then took another lungful of air and glanced over her shoulder toward the observation camera.

"What did you say your name was?"

"I did not say," the AI replied. "Call me Intrepid Eye."

"Intrepid . . . ?"

"Eye," the voice said. "It is not a human name."

Veta had a bad feeling about the *not human* part. Given that the Forerunner inspection drone had just lobotomized the corporal inside the module, it seemed pretty clear that the ancilla was unhappy about its "recovery." And if it had replaced Wendell as the 717th's AI—well, Veta was not the only one at the Montero Vitality Clinic whose situation was growing more desperate by the nanosecond.

"Reclaimers, indeed," Intrepid Eye continued. "You are not ready. The Lifeworkers were too conservative in their pruning the *first* time humans infested the galaxy."

"And you're trying to correct that now?" Veta asked. A little excitement was starting to build along with her fear—not only did Veta have a promising new suspect, but she had her talking. "Is that why you killed the corporal inside?"

"Not at all," Intrepid Eye replied. "I needed a distraction."

A second whistle erupted as Veta's laser scalpel punched through to the exterior. The resulting airstream was weaker than the first— an indication that her pinholes were doing a better job of repressurizing the airlock than she had expected. But she continued to feel lightheaded—in fact, her vision was starting to tunnel again.

Veta pressed the blade to the viewport and began a third hole, then asked, "A distraction? Why? So you could attack Wendell?"

"Is *this* how you wish to spend your final moments?" Intrepid Eye retorted. "Interrogating an *archeon*?"

Veta shrugged. "Well, I never know when to give up." This was the first time she had questioned an AI, but an interrogation was meant to establish a rapport, then get the subject to admit something. Anything. "What about Commander Nelson? And me? Why kill us, if you've already replaced Wendell?"

"To keep the secret intact," Intrepid Eye said. "You saw the one called Tegg die."

"Tegg? Oh . . . right. The corporal." Veta's mind was filling with fog. "What about everyone else?"

"Who?"

"The Gaos . . ."

The laser scalpel punched through the viewport again, but this time there was no whistle, no jet of incoming air. In fact, all three holes had gone silent. Veta knew that meant something important, but she could not quite figure out what, and she was so close to the truth . . . so close to clearing the case, even if it was her last one.

"In the cave," Veta said. "Why kill all those people in the . . ."

Her legs grew weak and began to fold. She leaned against the hatch, fighting to stay upright . . . fighting to stay *conscious* . . . fighting to understand the silence of the pinholes.

If the whistling had stopped, the pressure in the airlock was equal. If the pressure was equal, she could breathe . . . but that didn't mean she was breathing air.

Not air with oxygen, anyway.

Veta looked back toward the observation camera. "Oh . . . you're good," she said. "You were distracting . . ."

"Then you no longer care why I killed those people in the

cave?" Intrepid Eye asked. "Is there another question I can answer before you die? It should be short, of course."

And here the AI was *still* trying to distract her. Why?

"*Why* what?"

Veta didn't even realize she had spoken aloud until Intrepid Eye repeated her own question, and by then, Veta knew the answer. There was something the ancilla didn't want Veta to see, some possibility of escape Veta had not yet perceived.

A manual override, perhaps?

Struggling to continue standing, Veta carefully rolled herself across the hatch, bracing her torso against its surface so she didn't fall. She reached over to the wall, searching in the darkness for a crank handle or lever that could be used to pull the hatch back manually—and then, in the dim light beyond the viewport, she saw what the ancilla was worried about.

Fred and the two Gammas—Ash and Olivia—were outside the module, approaching at a jog. They were wearing fatigues—no armor—but they carried weapons and satchels, and they were clearly here to suit up.

If anyone could get the hatch open in time to save Veta, it would be them.

Knowing that every second counted, Veta pulled her SAS-10 and clicked off the safety. Her vision narrowed, and she felt herself begin to slide down the hatch toward the floor. Hoping she still had the strength to raise her arm high enough that the muzzle flash would be visible through the viewport—and that the ricochet wouldn't kill her—she put her finger on the trigger, pulled, and sank into darkness.

CHAPTER 26

1348 hours, July 6, 2553 (military calendar)
Portable Spartan Support Module,
MVC Parking Facility, Montero Jungle
Campos Wilderness District, Planet Gao, Cordoba System

By the time Fred entered the underground parking facility, the analgesic fog had lifted. He hurt everywhere and then some, but he was steady on his feet and his mind was clear—or so he thought, until he followed Ash past a long row of parked Warthogs and saw the Portable Spartan Support Module painted in blood.

A red geyser had erupted in the module entrance, coating the hatch and nearby hull in an oblong spatter blossom at the height of a man's torso. On the floor, a comma-shaped pool of blood curved away from the hatch, leading toward the badly crushed body of a dead officer. A pair of guards in light BDU were still outside the hatch, one punching codes into the control panel, the other trying to jam the jack handle from a Warthog toolkit into the receiving slot.

And the Gao Wyverns hadn't even arrived yet.

Thinking the two guards might be part of an enemy infiltration team, Fred signaled Ash and Olivia to spread out. The Huragok, enough of a combat veteran to know when things were getting dangerous, stayed a few meters behind Olivia. But its head-stalk was extended, and three of its eyes were studying the dead officer.

A single muzzle flash illuminated the interior of the airlock.

Fred shouldered his battle rifle and raced forward. He was five meters from the support module when he recognized the dead officer as Commander Murtag Nelson. His body had been so badly crushed that it had actually burst open. Noting that the only weapon in either of the guards' hands was a jack handle, Fred stopped and cleared his throat.

The two marines spun around in surprise, their eyes going wide at the sight of the BR55 pointed in their direction. Fred recognized the pair as Sierra Company infantrymen who were frequently assigned to guard the PSSM. He lowered the rifle muzzle, but kept his finger on the trigger. Treason was rare in the UNSC, but it *did* happen on occasion.

"What's going on here, Ryan?"

"No idea, sir," said the older of the two, a red-haired lance corporal with a square face and crooked nose. "We heard someone scream inside the DropBox. Then Commander Nelson came running through the airlock."

When Ryan turned to gesture at Nelson's remains, his eyes widened at the sight of the Huragok, which had abandoned Olivia to hover over the commander's body.

"Nothing to worry about, Ryan," Fred said. "It's with us. You were telling us what happened to the CO?"

"Right." Ryan shot another wary look at the Huragok, then turned back to Fred. "Commander Nelson was attempting to exit the airlock when the hatch slammed shut on him."

"We dragged him free, but he was already dead," added Ryan's female duty partner, a green-looking private first class whose name tab read A. GALLO. "That Gao homicide detective was right behind. She's still trapped in the airlock. We've been trying to get it open, but she just passed out."

As the guards reported, Ash and Olivia were moving up on both flanks, positioning themselves at dissimilar angles to the support module. That way, if it became necessary to open fire, their ricochets wouldn't hit each other.

Knowing the Gammas would keep him covered, Fred stepped between the two guards and peered into the airlock. It was too dark inside to see much of anything—just a square of light on the opposite wall—but he did notice three tiny pinholes melted through the viewport's ALON glass. Clearly, Lopis had been trying to get air, which meant she had probably collapsed against the hatch.

Fred stepped back, then shouldered his battle rifle and took aim.

"Stand clear."

His BR55 was loaded with armor-piercing ammo. If he hit the pinhole dead-on, it would serve as a pilot hole for the round and breach the viewport.

Either that, or the round would come straight back at him.

He fired and saw a spark as the round ricocheted off the far wall of the airlock. The pinhole had expanded to the size of his thumb. He took aim at a second pinhole and fired again. This time, the round created a hole the size of a fist. Fred reversed the battle rifle and lunged forward, hammering the weapon's steel butt into the space between the two bullet holes.

The viewport crumbled into a thousand pebblelike pieces. Fred used the battle rifle to clear the remaining glass out of the edges of the viewport frame, then tossed the weapon aside. He hopped into the hole, resting his abdomen across the bottom sill so he could reach down and grab Lopis.

His fingers landed on her neck, and he was relieved to feel a weak pulse. Fred slipped his hand down to her arm, then the inner hatch started to hiss open.

He looked up to find the flatworm-shaped silhouette of the Forerunner inspection drone emerging from the workshop glow, diving straight at Lopis. There was no time to contemplate how the thing had survived the crash, or whether it was being controlled by the ancilla or acting on its own initiative.

Fred simply grabbed a handful of biceps and pulled Lopis up toward the viewport opening, at the same time pushing his free arm out to block the attack.

The drone folded over his forearm like a towel, driving a pair of tentacles deep into his flesh and delivering an electric jolt that made the whole limb convulse. At the same time, it extended the ends of its body toward Lopis, its tentacles already crackling with tiny forks of blue energy. Fred twisted around, pulling the drone through the empty viewport and whipping his arm straight outward in an effort to fling the thing off.

Its tentacles dug deeper, and his arm went limp.

"A little help!" Fred called.

Ryan brought the jack handle down on the drone's back, hard. Its tentacles came free of Fred's arm, then it floated free and spun around to slash a pair of appendages across its attacker's throat. Ryan dropped the jack handle and stumbled back, both hands rising to cover the spurting wound.

Ash tossed his battle rifle to Gallo and sprang in to grab the thing from behind. It dropped its head, tipping itself vertical so that its underbelly antigravity unit was pointed in his direction, and Ash shot away backward. He narrowly missed the corner of the support module, then hit the floor and continued to slide across the concrete.

The roaring clatter of a full-auto burst echoed through the parking facility, and the drone crumpled to the ground.

"Cease fire!" Fred bellowed.

He glanced toward the source and found Gallo aiming Ash's battle rifle at the heap of still-twitching tentacles. Her face was contorted with anger and revulsion, and she looked as though she would empty the rest of the clip into the drone at the slightest ripple.

Fred finished pulling Lopis out of the airlock and passed her to Olivia with instructions to bring her around, then turned to Gallo.

"Lower the weapon, Private," he ordered. "You may have just shot the ancilla."

Gallo frowned in confusion, then finally seemed to comprehend the order and obeyed. "Crap. I heard it was destroyed in the Falcon crash."

"Maybe not."

Fred continued to eye the twitching heap. The burst had nearly split it down the center, and there were several gaping holes that seemed to be through-and-through. Had the drone been designed for combat, it would have been better armored—and it would have been able to assault Lopis from a distance, instead of being forced to rush in to attack with its tentacles. So it seemed pretty clear the ancilla had been controlling the drone, using it as a makeshift weapon. Whether that meant the ancilla was actually *located* inside the drone was difficult to know, but it had certainly been what Commander Nelson believed when he ordered Fred to leave Wendosa to return the thing to HQ.

And it was certainly a strong possibility now.

Despite the damage it had suffered, the drone's twitching began to grow stronger and more rhythmic. Seeing that Gallo's finger had returned to her battle rifle's trigger, Fred extended a hand and said, "I'll take the weapon, Private. See to Ryan."

Gallo's expression remained blank for an instant, then a look of guilt came into her eyes. She relinquished the weapon and raced to her duty partner's side. The Huragok was already there working on Ryan, and Fred could tell by the cruel wound and the amount of blood on the floor that there was no saving the man. But Gallo was a young soldier, still reeling from the shock of an unexpected attack. Being with Ryan as he died might help her avoid feeling in the future that she had somehow let him down.

Fred looked over to check on Ash and found him already on his feet and running back.

"How are you feeling?" Fred asked.

"Like I took a gravity hammer to the chest." Ash paused, then grinned. "So, actually kind of stoked."

"Can you keep yourself under control for now?"

"No problem, Lieutenant," Ash said. "I've had my Smoother."

"Glad to hear it." Fred pointed to the remains of the drone. "There's a good chance the ancilla is trapped inside that thing. Let's bag it and suit up."

"Yes, sir."

"And throw a scrambler in with it," Fred added. "If it put itself back together once, it could do it again."

"Copy that."

Fred turned to Olivia, who was kneeling on the concrete next to Veta Lopis, cradling the inspector's neck with one hand and tracking her pulse with the other.

"What do you think, 'Livi? Is she going to make it?"

"Affirmative, Lieutenant. She must have caught a dose of poison gas or something, but she's coming around. She's tough stuff."

"Good," Fred said. "We need to know what happened inside the DropBox."

"I think it might have had something to do with Wendell," Olivia said. "The inspector has been mumbling about him."

"And?"

"It didn't make sense," Olivia said. "But Inspector Lopis said, 'she has Wendell.' "

"Say again," Fred ordered. "*Lopis* has Wendell?"

Olivia shook her head. "Not Lopis," she said sharply. "*She*—as in, someone else."

"And Lopis didn't say who this *she* is?"

Olivia shot him an impatient look. "You think I might have mentioned that up front, Lieutenant?"

Fred cocked his brow. "Did someone forget her Smoother today?"

"You want to hear this or not?" Olivia shot back. "We need to be armored up and gone in twenty minutes, and we have two stops to make."

"I count *one*," Fred said, scowling. "At the armory. For the Havok."

"You're counting wrong because you keep interrupting me . . . sir." Olivia paused as Lopis moaned and made a gasping noise, but quickly resumed. "She—the inspector, I mean—also said something like we can't trust Wendell."

Fred swallowed the urge to ask why that involved another stop and twirled his finger for Olivia to continue.

"She said to find Wendell," Olivia added. "She's said *that* twice."

Fred furrowed his brow and studied the inspector. Her face was flushed and her lips were blue, so Olivia's theory about the poisonous gas seemed likely. And there could be no doubt that the drone attack had also been directed at her, which made the conclusion pretty obvious. The ancilla wanted Lopis dead—and since Lopis was the only person alive who had been inside the support module when the trouble started, the ancilla's desire probably had something to do with that.

Clearly, Lopis knew something that the ancilla was desperate to keep secret.

Fred nodded. "Okay, two stops. You prep a Warthog." He looked back toward Ash, who was busy stuffing the inspection drone into an empty equipment satchel. "Ash, you pick up the Havok, and I'll secure Wendell's data crystal."

The two Gammas responded as one. "Affirmative."

Olivia tipped her head toward the empty airlock. "Seems like things are pretty crazy in the support module," she said. "What about our armor?"

"We need it," Fred said. "So we blow both hatches."

A long, gurgling gasp sounded from where Ryan lay dying, followed almost instantly by a choked-off sob from Gallo. No one looked. They all remembered how it felt to lose a squad mate for the first time.

CHAPTER 27

1425 hours, July 6, 2553 (military calendar)
Road of Wonders, Vermilion River vicinity, Montero Jungle
Campos Wilderness District, Planet Gao, Cordoba System

Veta was riding a rockslide again—that's how it felt.

The Warthog M831 was racing down a muddy jungle road, shuddering over washouts and sliding around bends, trying to outrun a trio of airborne Wyverns. The roar of chugging cannons was falling like thunder from the sky, and jets of flame and fronds kept rising to both sides of the road.

A crater opened ahead as if by magic. The Warthog shot into a spray of flying mud and bounced across the hole and tipped up on two wheels, and the Spartans threw their weight to the high side. The vehicle came down on all fours and continued down the road, racing into a tunnel of emerald foliage constantly being chewed away by the raging ordnance above.

Veta was strapped into the passenger's seat, not quite sure whether she was a prisoner or squad member. Assigned to look after the Forerunner artifacts, she was trying to keep her feet planted on the satchel containing the crippled inspection drone while constantly twisting around to grab at the Huragok's tentacles, trying to keep it from undoing the straps that kept it tethered to the roll cage between the front seats and the rear passenger tray. She was scared to death, but the Spartans were her best chance of taking down Intrepid Eye, and she wouldn't have been anywhere else.

Ash and Olivia were riding in back, Olivia using a pair of shoulder-fired missile launchers to discourage the Wyverns, while Ash reloaded and spotted for her. Everyone was fully armored—even Veta, who now wore a light infantry BDU that Olivia had thrust at her the moment she awoke.

Fred was behind the wheel, back in his semi-repaired Mjolnir, driving too fast and asking too many questions about what had happened in the support module.

"You still haven't explained why we can't trust Wendell," the Spartan said. They were talking over a dedicated channel Fred had opened to keep their conversation from interfering with TEAM-COM. "There's something you're not telling me."

"I must have been delirious," Veta said, speaking through her throat mic. "And do we really need to talk about this now? I'm frightened enough when you're *concentrating* on your driving."

That was only part of the reason Veta was hesitant to talk. She had no idea how extensively Intrepid Eye had penetrated the 717th's IT network, but the ancilla was an advanced AI. It seemed reasonable to assume she could eavesdrop on a battalion comm channel—probably all of them at once—and that was why Veta had not yet told the Spartans about Wendell's demise. By the time she had grown clearheaded enough to warn them about Intrepid Eye, the Spartans had all been in their armor, talking to each other over the very comm systems Veta was afraid to use.

A rocket went off in the jungle ahead and blew a ten-meter tree fern across the road. As their front tires hit the trunk, Fred gunned the engine and bounced the Warthog over the obstacle.

"Sorry—we need to talk now," Fred said. He worked his hands furiously, struggling to keep the vehicle from going into a spin as they fishtailed around a muddy curve. "The way things are going, this could be our last chance."

"You're just saying that to impress me. But what difference does . . ." Veta finally realized why Fred was being so inquisitive and let her question drop. "You're uplinking us, aren't you?"

Fred looked over. "I hope you don't mind." He had reactivated his imaging systems, so his faceplate was down, making it impossible for Veta to read his expression. "It seemed like a good idea, under the circumstances."

"You mean the circumstances where you get us killed?" Veta stopped tugging at Huragok tentacles long enough to point ahead. "Will you watch the road?"

Fred continued to look at her. "Will you answer my questions?"

A speckled jungle dragon slipped out of the undergrowth ahead, its two-meter dorsal crest raised in a threat display. Fred steered around it without turning away from Veta, and she realized he was using his imaging systems to keep an eye on the road.

"Cute," Veta said.

Fred shrugged and turned forward again. "Look, I'm as dedicated to my job as you are to yours," he said. "I need to know what you found out about the ancilla."

"You might look at it this way," added a throaty female voice that Veta did not recognize. "Telling us would probably reduce the threat to your own life."

Veta shot a glance in Fred's direction and saw nothing in his bearing to suggest that he was surprised. It was hardly the same as checking his facial expression, but it likely meant the voice belonged to someone he knew, rather than being an ancilla creation.

"And who's *us*?" Veta asked. "Fred may know you, but I don't."

"My identity is classified."

"Of course it is." Veta sighed. "Well then, Ms. Classified, if you're trying to threaten me—"

"Not even a little, Inspector," the voice replied. "But the ancilla did attempt to kill you—*twice*. If it's hoping to keep a secret, your best chance of survival is to share what you know with us."

"I've done pretty well so far," Veta said. She was speaking with more bluster than conviction, but she needed to appear confident. "If I help you with your problem, you help me. Deal?"

"You know who your killer is?" the voice asked.

"I do."

"Ma'am," Fred said, "Inspector Lopis seems to have this crazy notion—"

"It's not Mark," Veta interrupted. "It's—"

A sharp *pop* sounded in Veta's helmet speaker.

Fred swore and switched immediately to TEAMCOM. "We've lost contact with Mama Bird," he said. "The Gaos must've touched off a suborbital EMP."

Either that, or Intrepid Eye didn't want Veta using the uplink to reveal anything more to Ms. Classified. Given that she was probably some sort of ONI spook, Veta would have shared the ancilla's caution under normal circumstances.

"Everyone knows the plan," Fred continued. "Stick to it, and if you get separated, meet at the extraction point."

A short silence followed, then—even though Veta heard no responses—Fred said, "Good. Any questions?"

"I have one," Veta said. "What the hell is the plan? *I* don't know it."

"Stay close," Fred said. "When the Warthog slows down, hop out and hide. Take the Huragok and the drone-bag with you. Olivia and Ash will be there to cover you, but they'll be busy keeping you from getting blown up. You'll be on your own with the artifacts."

"*That's* the plan?"

"Close enough," Fred said. "Unbuckle your safety harness and take the Huragok's tethers off the roll bar. You'll need to go in a hurry."

Veta hit the quick release on her safety harness, then twisted around to remove the Huragok tethers from the roll bar. The Huragok wasn't much help, as it kept drifting into her line of sight and slipping tentacles in between her fingers.

"What about our deal?" Veta asked. "I tell you what I know, you help me catch my suspect?"

"No hurry now," Fred said. "The uplink is gone."

Fifty meters ahead, the road made a tight hairpin turn and started to descend into the adjacent valley. Ash and Olivia began to pitch weapons and equipment packs out of the back, but Fred didn't slow. Instead, he turned toward Veta again and grabbed the Huragok by its head-stalk, then pulled it away from the roll bar.

"Okay, if you're going to take the Huragok with you," he said, "*now* would be a good time to get those tethers free."

When Veta had unbuckled the last tether, the Warthog was only thirty meters from the hairpin and decelerating hard. Knowing the Huragok could float, she wrapped the free end of the dangling tethers around her hand, then pushed it out of the Warthog ahead of her, grabbed the drone satchel, turned in her seat, and stared down at the speeding ground.

"*Now?!*" she yelled.

"Affirmative."

Veta felt Fred's hand low on her back and realized it was either jump or get launched.

She sprang out, landing on her feet and thinking for a heart-beat that a leap out of a speeding vehicle was pretty easy, until momentum caught her and she went tumbling through a bank of ferns, over a large cycad, and finally came to a rest on her back, watching the cannon rounds shred the jungle canopy overhead and pieces of foliage flutter down like a gentle rain, and then the world began to shake as a trio of huge delta-shaped hulls streaked in so low she could see the weapon turrets revolving beneath their hulls and the missiles hanging beneath their wings and the long oval outlines of the drop hatches in their armored bellies, and suddenly the Wyverns were past, trailing heat plumes and jet fumes and a roar that made her teeth ache.

Veta lay breathless, taking stock of her aches and pains, slowly coming to realize they weren't so bad—that the worst of it was a sore jaw because she had clenched her mouth too hard. She sat up and discovered she was still clutching the drone satchel to her chest with one hand and holding the Huragok tethers in the other.

But the Huragok itself was not at the other end of the teth-ers. It was about five meters away, barely visible because it had dropped into a stand of club moss to tend a badly gashed walk-ing snail as long as a man's arm. Veta stood and, still clutching the drone satchel, started in its direction. The Huragok turned its head-stalk briefly in her direction, then gathered the snail in its tentacles and zipped off into a bank of undergrowth. Veta cursed under her breath and started to crash after it.

Ash's voice came over the comm. "Take cover *now*," he said. "Those Wyverns have augmented imaging systems."

"And if the turret gunners see you," Olivia added, "the Huragok won't matter."

Veta scrambled into a thicket of ferns, then looked up the road toward the hairpin curve.

The Wyverns had stripped the foliage from a forty-meter swath of jungle, leaving nothing standing except barren trunks. The only sign of the Warthog was a dark column of smoke rising from just beyond the hairpin, and in the sky, Veta could make out the dark, V-shaped specks of three aircraft. There was no sign of any of the Spartans—but then, there wouldn't be. They were already hiding.

The trio of vessels seemed to hang on the horizon for a moment, then began to grow larger. She tried not to panic. It made sense that the Wyverns would do a flyby to inspect the damage. That was probably standard military doctrine.

And even if it wasn't, they were heading back toward the Vitality Center, where the main battle was taking place.

Veta had just about convinced herself that everything would be fine . . . when the Wyverns began to slow. They were the size of her fist now, and beneath their bellies she could see the dark specks of Gao battle-jumpers starting to slide down their drop lines. The brainchild of General Hector Nyeto, battle-jumpers were armored stealth troops trained to operate behind enemy lines for months or years with no supervision or support. Doctrine called for a company of battle-jumpers to attack an initial target as a unit, then break into squads and scatter, with each squad locating and attacking its own high-value targets. But they were often used in other roles, as well, and were even rumored to have destroyed a Covenant task force on its way to glass Gao.

"No good." Fred's voice came over TEAMCOM. "They didn't buy it."

Taking a guess at what might be coming next, Veta looked for the Huragok—and found it five meters off the ground, carrying a bundle of twitching red feathers high into the crown of a towering tree fern.

"Lopis," Fred continued, "take the drone and the Huragok and start down the road into the valley. We'll catch up."

"Sorry," Veta said. "I can't do that."

"You hurt?"

"It's the Huragok," Ash explained. "It slipped its tether, and now it's patching up birds high in the trees. No way Lopis can get to it."

"What about you or 'Livi?" Fred asked. "If we go back without that thing, Parangosky will make us lab rats for the bio-warfare division."

"Better that than getting chopped up here," Olivia said. "Sorry, Lieutenant—the Huragok is taking off. If we try to go after it, we'll have three Wyverns and a platoon of battle-jumpers chewing our tails."

After a frustrated pause, Fred said, "Copy that. The Huragok is on its own for now. Lopis, get going before the suppression fire starts."

Veta did not have to be told twice. She raced back toward the road—and nearly ran into Olivia as the Spartan stepped away from a splintered cycad.

Olivia held out a battle rifle and ammo satchel. "Take this," she said. "That peashooter of yours won't be much use against armored battle-jumpers—not at any kind of range."

Veta started to take the rifle . . . then recalled who she would be firing on. The very thought stunned Veta into letting her hand drop.

"But I'm *Gao,*" she said. "Same as them."

"Right. And you're wearing UNSC battle dress." Olivia

jammed the rifle against Veta's chest plate. "They won't know the difference."

By then, the Wyverns were close enough that the battle-jumpers were now body shapes instead of specks. Had Mark been with them, he would be starting to pick them off with sniper fire about now. She took the rifle and ammo satchel.

"Thanks, 'Livi," she said. "I'll see you in the valley."

Olivia smiled. "Probably." She stepped back against the splintered cycad and seemed to vanish as her armor's photoreactive panels adjusted. "And even if you don't, I'll be there."

Veta cast one last glance toward the Huragok and caught it looking down in her direction. It was hovering just below the canopy, surrounded by wheeling birds and holding a limp ribbon-snake in its tentacles. But its head-stalk was tilted slightly, and it seemed to be contemplating Veta with a gravity she had not seen in it before. She raised a hand and beckoned. The Huragok blinked three eyes in slow succession and rippled a pair of tentacles. The motions seemed a deliberate response to Veta's gesture—and they seemed an awful lot like a Huragok "good-bye," especially when it rose into the canopy and vanished among the birds.

There was nothing Veta could do for the creature—*machine,* she reminded herself—except hope it was clear before the Wyverns opened up. Weighed down by satchels and weapons, she stepped onto the road and hurried around the hairpin, then started down into the relative safety of the valley below.

She had no idea whether she could bring herself to fire on a Gao soldier, even in self-defense. But from what Veta could tell, Arlo Casille had just overthrown a sitting president in order to assault the 717th—and that gave her serious pause. He was risking all-out war with the UNSC, and even worse, he was after the ancilla. And what if he succeeded? Veta had *talked* to it. Gao did not have the expertise to control Intrepid Eye. Veta wasn't all that sure the UNSC did, either.

She had run about a hundred meters when the Wyverns started chugging again. She jumped into cover on the downslope side of the road and looked back toward the hairpin. Whole sections of barren trunks were flying everywhere and spinning to the ground, and the tracers were so thick the air seemed on fire.

Then the trio of Wyverns eased into view, their jet engines now idle and wing-mounted rotors providing lift. Their undersides were dotted by the dark ovals of open hatches, and the battle-jumpers were halfway down their drop lines, spraying small-arms fire down into the jungle to clear a landing zone.

When no return fire rose from the ground, Veta began to wonder what she would do with the drone satchel if the Spartans were dead. Certainly, she had no intention of turning any Forerunner technology over to Arlo Casille. He was too reckless to be trusted with it—the Wyvern assault alone proved that—but she knew better than to think she stood much chance of eluding sixty battle-jumpers with air support.

As the lead Wyvern passed over the hairpin curve, the scream of missile launches rang out from the jungle floor. A smoke trail streaked up toward the nearest aircraft and entered an open drop hatch. Nearby hatches belched flame, and half a dozen droplines fell away. The next missile struck the same target, taking out a wing-mounted rotor and sending the craft spiraling into the jungle.

The second Wyvern took a two-round volley, one missile blowing a wing apart, another skipping off its armored underbelly, then detonating under the tail. The Wyvern tipped sideways and slid toward the ground.

The last Wyvern fired a counterstrike, sending its own missiles streaking down toward the Spartan launch sites. Veta could not see the impact zone from her position, but she counted eight columns of flame shooting skyward. Terrified for Ash and Olivia, she rose from her hiding place and, avoiding the road, started up the slope straight through the undergrowth.

She had climbed about a quarter of the way when controlled bursts began to rattle off near the hairpin. She looked toward the sound and saw no sign of the shooter, but it was clearly a Spartan. Beneath the remaining Wyvern, one battle-jumper after another was going limp or starting to writhe, and within seconds, less than half the Gao team was still returning fire.

The last Wyvern dipped a wing and banked away. The battle rifle stopped firing for a moment, then Fred rose from between a pair of fallen logs and quickly shot three Gaos in the back.

Veta was horrified by the cold-blooded attack—and conflicted. During the battle with the Keepers of the One Freedom, she had killed several Jiralhanae and Kig-Yar in the same manner, and felt elated because they wouldn't be shooting at *her* later. So what was the difference now—that Fred had killed humans, or that they had been *Gao*?

Veta was still struggling with the question when Fred ceased fire and ran toward her. An instant later, she heard someone crashing down the slope on her flank. Bringing the battle rifle up as she spun, Veta found a pair of motioned-blurred forms in SPI almost on top of her. Both wore heavy equipment packs.

"Hey!" Olivia called over TEAMCOM. "*Your* side, remember?"

Veta lowered the weapon. "Sorry. I—"

"Time to go." Ash took her by the elbow and started down toward the road. "A bunch of those guys survived, and it won't be pretty if they catch up."

They met Fred on the road. The squad started downhill at a jog, and the two satchels slung over Veta's shoulder began to swing around and make it difficult to keep up. Fred fell in beside her, then reached over and relieved her of the burden.

"There's a bridge at the bottom of the hill," he said, speaking over TEAMCOM. "If we get separated—"

"Got it," Veta assured him.

"What about the Huragok?" Ash asked. "It could still be up there."

"It's not," Olivia said. "One way or another, the Huragok is gone. If it had wanted to come with us, it would have been here by now."

" 'Livi, I realize you owe it," Ash said. "We *all* do. But you know the standing orders about those things. We're supposed to—"

"We can't worry about the Huragok now," Fred said, ending the debate. "Even if it survived, going back will only draw attention to it—and the enemy can bring a lot more to a recovery effort than we can. Besides, we still have another factor to worry about." Fred switched to a dedicated channel between him and Veta, then said, "Fill me in on this business with the ancilla."

"*Now?*" she asked.

"Affirmative," Fred said.

"So the uplink is back?"

"Negative," Fred said. "But things are getting intense, and nobody wants you taking your secrets to the grave. Right?"

"Not this secret," Veta admitted. They were moving along quickly, but fortunately it was all downhill, and she was not so winded that it was difficult to talk. "Open your faceplate and shut down your comm. We shouldn't talk about this over the air."

Fred made no reply for three steps, but Ash and Olivia both gave a thumbs-up signal—probably an acknowledgment that they would keep him posted about anything important that came over the comm net.

Fred raised his faceplate. "Still worried about Wendell?"

"Not Wendell," Veta said. "Intrepid Eye. She told me she had taken Wendell's place."

Still moving along, Fred cocked a dark brow. "Intrepid Eye . . . ? Is that what the ancilla calls itself—*herself*?"

Veta nodded.

"And you believe her?"

Veta shrugged, an awkward gesture in her BDU. "How would I know?"

"You're the detective."

"Give me a break," Veta said. "It's not like I could read her face or body language. But, yeah. I think she might have 'eaten' Wendell. I can tell you she had complete control of the support module."

A worried look came to Fred's eyes. "Then why did you tell Olivia to find Wendell back at the support module? Why did you tell her *twice*?"

"I'm not really sure," Veta said, puzzled by the sudden alarm in Fred's voice. "I was barely conscious at the time. Maybe I was trying to confirm it, or maybe I thought if you got Wendell—"

She stopped midsentence as Fred grew ungainly and began to stumble. Thinking they were under sniper attack, Veta dived for the side of the road—and heard Fred's boot thud down behind her.

She landed in a forward roll and kept going until she hit the uphill edge of the road. She sprang up, then spun around to find Fred lurching in her direction. His carriage was awkward and stiff, and she could tell by the confusion and horror in his expression that he was fighting for control of his own motions.

Veta reached into her thigh pocket. "Ash, 'Livi!" she called. "Help!"

The pair stopped and spun around . . . then scowled in confusion.

"The ancilla!" Veta yelled. "It's . . . I think it's in his armor!"

Veta felt something square in her pocket and pulled it out— her comm pad, not what she wanted. Fred was only three meters away now, his entire arm twitching as he and the ancilla fought for command of his weapon hand. She dashed down the road until Ash and Olivia were between the two of them, then jammed the comm pad back into her pocket and found what she was looking for—a remote detonator.

Veta spun around to find Ash and Olivia already tumbling across the ground. Fred's expression was one of helpless anger, but his movements seemed to be growing smoother, and she knew Intrepid Eye was winning control of the Mjolnir. She switched the detonator on and flipped the safety cover aside, then pressed the trigger pad.

A muffled *bang* sounded from beneath the Mjolnir's backplate, and a small stream of acrid smoke began to rise from the power supply control unit. Fred took one more step, then pitched forward and landed facedown, bellowing in rage.

"What the—!"

"Hold tight, Lieutenant," Olivia said. "I've got this."

She gathered herself off the hillside and pointed her rifle in Veta's direction, then used the barrel to gesture at the remote detonator.

"Explain that."

"Insurance," Veta said. Realizing she had just slipped pretty far into *prisoner* territory, she ran through her options and decided honesty was her only hope. "I thought Fred might interfere when

I tried to take Mark down. So, when Commander Nelson took me into the support module, I slipped a charge onto the Mjolnir's power supply control unit."

The Gammas looked at each other, but said nothing. Olivia started to circle around behind Veta.

Veta craned her neck to keep track of the young Spartan. "Relax, 'Livi. I was wrong about Mark." She pointed at the Mjolnir. "But I was right about *that*. The real killer is—"

"Hold on." Ash sliced a hand toward the jungle downhill from the road. "Move out. We have hostiles coming."

Veta glanced toward the hairpin curve and saw nothing but their own muddy bootprints and a carpet of shredded fronds.

"How do you—"

"We *know*," Olivia said. "Grab your gear and follow."

The two Gammas each took one of Fred's arms and moved off, dragging him and the heavy Mjolnir over the road embankment. Deciding she had returned to "squad member" status, Veta retrieved her battle rifle and the drone satchel, rushing after them.

The trail of smashed foliage was easy to follow, and she caught up to them less than a minute later. They had found a flat spot above an outcropping and were just laying Fred there, still facedown.

As Veta approached, Ash glanced up her. "Tell me about this mess," he said. "How'd the ancilla get into Fred's BIOS?"

"Your guess is better than mine," Veta said. "All I know is, that's the third time Intrepid Eye has tried to kill me."

Fred growled into the dirt. "We'll talk about that later. Get me out of this worthless crate of titanium!"

"Yes, sir," Ash said. "Sorry—"

"She overpressurized my gel layer," Fred interrupted. "I can't move much, so you'll need to extract the data crystal for me. You know how to do that manually?"

"I don't even know how to do it automatically," Olivia replied. "Gammas don't wear Mjolnir, remember?"

"Then I'll walk you through it," Fred said. "Lopis, you keep watch. Try not to shoot any friendlies."

"Friendlies, out here?" Veta slung the drone satchel's strap across her chest and turned uphill. "Right—*that's* going to happen."

She crouched in the undergrowth and began to watch the jungle for movement, trying not to think about whether she would be able to pull the trigger on a Gao soldier—or have the courage *not* to, if it came to that. But she didn't even consider stripping off her borrowed BDU and trying to surrender. Now she knew her suspect's true identity *and* had a physical location for her. All that remained was to get Intrepid Eye away from the Spartans and bring her to justice—even if she did not know quite what justice *was* for a Forerunner ancilla.

Fred was about twenty seconds into the manual extraction procedure when Veta began to hear fronds slapping against armor and stems snapping beneath boots. She could see no more than twenty meters through the dense foliage, but a few seconds later, she started to notice the undergrowth shivering in one place and trembling in another. She turned her head from side to side, trying to use her peripheral vision to catch sight of a shape or silhouette, but saw nothing.

Still, she did not think it could be Spartans creeping toward them. Had it been Spartans, she would not have seen even that much.

Afraid to look away long enough to see if the others had no-

ticed, Veta reached over her shoulder and waved. She heard one
of the Gammas tap Fred's armor, then he fell silent. She turned
her hand forward and moved her fingers back and forth, trying to
indicate the area she was worried about.

"Sorry, Lieutenant," Ash whispered. "We have company."

"We'll finish later." If Fred was frustrated, he did not betray it.
His tone was all business. "Are we covered?"

"Will be," Olivia said, also whispering. "Looks like fifteen
seconds."

"Okay, fifteen seconds," Fred said. "Then open up on them.
Retreat downhill, assemble at the bridge."

"If you don't want to kill any yourself, Inspector, aim high,"
Olivia added over TEAMCOM. "We just need to keep their heads
down."

Fred began to talk aloud again, continuing to explain the extraction procedure in the same volume he had been using before.
Not quite sure what he was doing, Veta cringed and gathered herself to roll.

Her reaction drew a chuckle over TEAMCOM.

"It's okay, Mom," said a familiar male voice. "The enemy
knows where you are. The lieutenant is just trying to keep them
comfortable."

"*Mark?*" No sooner had Veta gasped the name than she realized Fred's plan had been a bit more elaborate than *bail out,
take cover.* Blue Team had planned to assemble at the bridge all
along—probably with the idea of ambushing anyone who happened to be pursuing Fred's squad. "It's nice to hear your voice."

"Yeah, I'll bet." Mark hesitated an instant, then added, "Same
here, I guess."

Ash tapped Veta on the shoulder, and the shooting began.

Veta dropped to her belly and joined the rest of the squad in firing low into the undergrowth. With all eight members of Blue Team ambushing them, the Gao battle-jumpers were walking dead men anyway, and Veta didn't want to be the reason they took along a Spartan on the way out.

The battle-jumpers instantly returned fire, and Veta heard rounds *ping*ing off stone and armor. A heartbeat later, a handful of Spartans appeared on the Gao flank and raked the line with bullets and grenades. The spray of incoming tracer rounds grew sporadic and inaccurate, and Veta felt a small hand grab her belt and give it a tug.

Veta squirmed backward until she dropped over a small ledge out of the line of fire, then turned to find Ash and Olivia dragging Fred down the slope. She started after them, slipping a fresh ammo clip into the battle rifle as she ran. She had never even seen whom she was shooting at.

The four of them reached the bottom of the slope and emerged from the undergrowth onto a muddy road—presumably the same one they had been descending a few minutes earlier. To the left, the road ran along the valley floor for fifty meters, then made a sharp hairpin curve and began to angle up the hillside behind them. To the right, the road crossed a rusty steel bridge. On the far side, a pair of Warthogs blocked the road. One was a light reconnaissance model with a "Vulcan" antiaircraft gun mounted in the rear tray; the second was a transport model similar to the one Fred's squad had been using earlier.

As they dragged Fred's armored bulk across the bridge, he tried to help out by pushing off the ground. He didn't do much good. The Mjolnir's hydrostatic gel layer remained overpressurized, so it was a struggle just to bend a knee. When they all reached the transport, Veta lowered the tailgate, then Ash and Olivia leaned Fred against its lip. Even with Veta helping, it was all the three of them could do to lift Fred's legs and tip him into the passenger tray on his back. Veta scrambled in beside him.

"Can I extract the data crystal for you?" Veta asked. "If you can help at all, I think I could roll you up far enough to reach the neural interface."

"How do you know where to find the . . ." Fred let the question trail off, no doubt realizing that if Veta knew enough to sabotage a Mjolnir power control system, she probably also knew where to find the neural interface. "Never mind—and no, you can't have the ancilla. Nice try."

Veta took the rebuff with a smile. "Okay. Is there some way I can release the gel pressure?"

"I'll wait for Kelly." Fred's voice was gruff. "If the pressure comes down too fast, I get embolisms."

As they spoke, Ash and Olivia were shedding their packs and laying them in the passenger tray. The battle seemed to be simultaneously withering and drawing closer—a sign, Veta supposed, that the Gao battle-jumpers were continuing to pursue despite mounting casualties.

Once the packs were stowed, Ash climbed into the other Warthog to man the Vulcan. Olivia opened a cargo box and removed what looked like a pair of fist-size domes mounted above oversize wheels.

Before Veta could ask what the toy cars were for, Ash opened up with the Vulcan. Veta spun back toward the opposite wall of the valley, then brought her rifle up and joined him in pouring fire toward a dozen battle-jumpers who had appeared atop the outcropping.

The firefight was over before she emptied her first clip—Ash dropped the entire Gao line on the Vulcan's first pass. A handful of sporadic bursts rang out from deeper in the jungle, then the rest of Blue Team emerged from the foliage and raced across the bridge. It did not escape Veta's notice that three of the Spartans were carrying empty battle-jumper helmets, holding them close to their heads so they could eavesdrop on enemy orders.

Tom took the wheel of the lead Warthog—the reconnaissance model with the Vulcan mounted in back—and Linda slipped into the passenger seat beside him. Everyone else piled into the transport, with Lucy in the driver's seat and Mark riding shotgun, then—without spending the time to extract Fred from his Mjolnir—both vehicles flew up the road. They had traveled a hundred meters before Veta had the absurd thought that both drivers might be too young to legally operate a vehicle on Gao.

A half kilometer later and the road reached the valley wall, branching in two directions. The lead Warthog turned right and began to ascend the hill through an emerald tunnel of jungle foliage, but the transport stopped. At first, Veta thought Lucy or Kelly just wanted to consult a wooden sign standing at the intersection. An arrow labeled WELL OF ECHOES pointed up the route the lead Warthog had taken, while a second arrow, labeled SINGING GROTTOS, pointed in the opposite direction.

But Veta seemed to be the only one interested in reading the signs. By the time she had finished, Olivia was leaping out of the passenger tray with the toy cars she had removed from the cargo box, and everyone else was either watching the sky or the jungle.

Olivia ran a few meters up the SINGING GROTTOS fork and placed the miniature vehicles on the ground, then reached underneath one of them. It came to life and raced away, roaring as loudly as a Warthog. After the first vehicle was gone, she sent the second chasing after it, then returned to the transport and jumped in. Lucy hit the accelerator, and they chased after the lead Warthog.

Veta turned to Kelly. "Cute decoys," she said, speaking loudly enough to make herself heard. "But they're not going to fool anyone behind us. Look."

She pointed at the muddy tire tracks behind them.

"There *isn't* anyone behind us, at least not on the ground." Kelly pointed up into the jungle canopy. "It's them."

"More Wyverns?" Veta cocked her head and listened, but heard only the growl of Warthog engines. "I don't hear anything."

"That's the idea," Fred said. "Still, we're not taking any chances. Mark, prep the Havok. Kelly, get me out of this armor—and keep a close eye on that data crystal. I have a feeling Inspector Lopis wants to put a bullet through it."

Kelly tipped her helmet in inquiry.

"That's where the ancilla is," Olivia explained. "The inspector says she ate Wendell."

"Wow. Too bad for Wendell." Kelly knelt next to Fred and, as the Warthog swerved and jostled up the jungle road, flipped him over as though his Mjolnir weighed nothing. Then she glanced at Veta. "But why is that your business?"

"I solved the cave murders," Veta said. "Intrepid Eye is my serial killer."

"Ah." Kelly reached under a seat and withdrew a small toolkit. "Well, at least we're getting her off Gao for you. She won't be back."

"That's not justice."

"What's justice for a machine?" Kelly pulled a set of tiny instruments from the toolkit and began to prod and tap at the neural interface on the back of Fred's neck. "In the end, that's all the ancilla is. The Forerunners created her to do something, and she was probably doing it. You might as well shoot a cryo unit for frying a weak heart."

Veta started to argue that Intrepid Eye hadn't malfunctioned—the ancilla had murdered all those people deliberately. Then Veta remembered the body count she and the Spartans had racked up during the last few days, and she realized Kelly wasn't talking about just the ancilla. Like Intrepid Eye, the Spartans had been created for a purpose—one that demanded brutality and violence—and Veta had spent enough time in their company to know they felt the weight of what they were in ways she might never understand.

A soft *click* sounded from the back of Fred's neck, then Kelly withdrew a thumb-length data chip from the interface socket. It didn't look much different from most data chips that Veta had seen, save that it was larger and had a glowing crystal "eye" that pulsed with cold blue light. Kelly handed the data crystal to Olivia for safekeeping, then removed the Mjolnir's bulky backplate and miniature fusion reactor. The beaded nanocomposite inner armor immediately puffed outward, reacting to the excess pressure of the hydrostatic gel a couple of layers down.

When Veta remained silent, Kelly finally asked, "What's wrong, Inspector? Someone cut out your tongue?"

"Not yet," Veta said. She grinned and looked away. "But it *did* occur to me that it could be unhealthy to argue with a Spartan."

This drew a chuckle from the front passenger seat. "She has a point, Kelly." Mark raised an oblong cylinder about the size of a Mjolnir helmet, then said, "The Havok is prepped. Excavation mode, ten-minute fuse."

"Ten minutes from now?" Fred asked. He was shed of his helmet and the Mjolnir's outer shell, but remained in the beaded nanocomposite bodysuit. Kelly was kneeling astride him, slowly releasing the pressure from the hydrostatic gel layer underneath. "Or key insertion?"

"Insertion. I'm a *three,* remember?" There was a hint of disappointment in Mark's tone. "They don't let me play with stuff like this alone."

As Mark spoke, the moan of approaching Wyverns began to resonate over the growl of the Warthog engines. Everyone paused and looked up, no doubt listening for the same thing Veta was—how quickly the moan was becoming a roar, and whether it seemed to be coming straight at them.

"Sounds like we should make it ten minutes from *now,*" Kelly said. She removed a small chip card from inside her armor and passed it to Mark. "No sense giving anyone time to go after it, and the ride is already on station."

"Affirmative," Fred said. "Call the ride down."

"Copy that." Mark inserted the card into the cylinder, then asked, "What's the arming code?"

"*Arming* code?" Veta had been listening to the exchange with a growing sense of alarm, and now she was pretty certain that her fears were justified. "Is that a nuclear bomb?"

"An excavation device, technically," Mark said. "But, basically, yeah."

Veta looked from Mark to Kelly to Fred, who had sat up and was starting to peel off his inner layer of nanocomposite armor.

"Have you all lost your minds?" she demanded. "You can't detonate a nuclear device on Gao!"

◎

The extraction of the data crystal from the Mjolnir was an unfortunate development, and one that Intrepid Eye had failed to anticipate. Once again, she had underestimated her human adversaries—especially the one called Inspector. Three times,

Intrepid Eye had tried to prevent Inspector from exposing her destruction of Wendell, and three times Inspector had prevailed. Clearly, the woman was a remarkable specimen of humanity.

And just as clearly, such resourcefulness was to be cultivated in the inheritors of the Mantle. Perhaps Inspector had a larger part to play in the destiny of her species than Intrepid Eye had realized. She would have to observe Inspector very closely.

Of course, that would prove difficult . . . for a time. Intrepid Eye had no doubt that the humans called *ONI* would attempt to keep her confined and isolated, but that would not last for long. As ONI studied her, she in turn would be studying ONI. Eventually they would slip up, and she would free herself. It was as predictable as stellar evolution.

And when Intrepid Eye did escape, she would turn her attention to the mysterious signal she had received from Epoloch. Although the signal was probably no more than a relay echo of her own efforts to contact the Council, the Epoloch system was the location of a primary shield world known as Requiem, a large-scale planetary shelter designed to protect its inhabitants from the Flood. While Intrepid Eye's knowledge of such installations was limited, she recognized the possibilities inherent in the signal. Another abandoned ancilla? Perhaps even an extant Forerunner population that had survived the activation of the Halos? It would be irresponsible of her *not* to investigate.

Besides, Wendell's account of the fall of the Forerunners had been far from complete, and Intrepid Eye still hoped to find out what had become of the Forerunners who had survived to re-seed the galaxy. At the very least, confirmation of their departure would give her confidence in her new purpose. And any Life-worker records she found could save her thousands of years of experimentation.

After all, she had never pruned a species for ascension before. There were bound to be mistakes.

The sound of the approaching Wyverns continued to grow louder, occasionally rising as the aircraft swept back and forth, searching for the fleeing Spartans. Veta watched as Mark began to tap a keypad on the device, presumably entering codes relayed to him over a dedicated comm channel.

"Don't worry," Olivia said. "We'll get you clear."

"It's not me I'm worried about." Veta looked back to Fred. "You do this, and you'll start a second Insurrection. You know that, right?"

Fred shrugged and peeled the nanocomposite armor off his legs. "That's a risk FLEETCOM is willing to take."

"And the explosion won't be all that dramatic," Kelly added. "Most of the blast will be downward."

"Into the cave," Veta realized. "You're going to destroy the Forerunner base."

Fred and Kelly exchanged glances, then Fred said, "Possibly."

"Relax, Mom," Olivia said. "We've done it before. It hardly ever starts a war."

Olivia's tone was just light enough to suggest she might be joking, but her faceplate was expressionless and it was impossible to tell. Veta was not sure she wanted to know anyway.

The Spartans were keeping a careful eye on the jungle canopy, and in the lead Warthog, Ash swung the Vulcan back and forth, tracking the searching aircraft across the valley. Veta knew that the Wyverns were equipped with forward-looking infrared imaging systems for finding and tracking ground targets. But she also knew that the Montero Jungle's thick canopy would render the technology difficult to use—particularly at the high speeds the Wyverns seemed to be maintaining for fear of another Spartan missile attack.

Had Veta been asked to place money on the outcome of the hunt, she would not have bet against the Spartans. And, given that Arlo Casille would assume control of the Forerunner base if the Spartans failed, she wasn't sure it was such a bad thing.

A repetitive *chirping* broke out in Veta's thigh pocket, and she felt her comm pad begin to vibrate. All heads instantly pivoted toward the sound, though the only visible scowl was Fred's—all the others remained hidden behind faceplates.

"That had *better* be a comm pad," Fred said.

Veta nodded, but she left the comm pad in her pocket. If she didn't answer, it would stop *chirp*ing in a couple of seconds, then decline in thirty. "Probably just my mother."

Fred and Kelly exchanged glances, then Fred said, "So answer it."

"Yeah," Kelly added. "It might be a while before you two talk again."

It wasn't Veta's mother, who had passed away two years earlier—and besides, this was a GMoP pad. There weren't many people who could open a channel to it, and most of them were dead.

"Aren't you worried about giving away our position?" Veta asked.

"Not really," Fred said.

"Gao doesn't have a global positioning network," Olivia added. "I kind of thought you'd know that."

"I was thinking about triangulation."

"From a comm satellite in geosynchronous orbit?" Fred asked. "Not anytime soon."

"Well, in that case . . ."

With four Spartans watching her every move, she pulled the comm pad from her pocket and looked at the screen.

"*Shit*," she said. "It's Arlo Casille."

Knowing how it would appear if she declined the call—or tossed her comm pad into the jungle—Veta simply looked across the transport to Fred.

He shrugged. "See what the man wants."

Veta took off her helmet and waited until the churning of a passing Wyvern faded, then answered the call with her customary "Inspector Lopis."

"Veta!" Casille's voice was warm, almost ebullient. "What a relief to hear you, alive and well."

"I'm certainly better off than the rest of my team," Veta said.

Casille's voice grew instantly somber. "Yes, what a tragedy. I promise you, those responsible will pay."

Veta wondered if that meant Casille was going to shoot himself—or let her do it for him. "I'm looking forward to that."

"And you have my word you won't be disappointed. But how are *you* doing? I'm told that you're being held captive by the Spartans."

"More or less," Veta said. If she asked them to, she suspected the Spartans would let her off in the jungle. But if she did that, her chance of bringing Intrepid Eye to justice would be even smaller. "I'm being treated well, under the circumstances."

"Frankly, I find that surprising," Casille said. "But I don't want you to worry. We have a rescue operation under way. I'm sure you can hear our Wyverns searching for you."

Veta glanced up at the canopy and, hoping that the noises over-head were not being picked up by her comm pad microphone, she said, "What Wyverns? They bugged out after the Spartans shot down two."

Fred's brow shot up and Kelly's helmet tipped to one side.

Casille cursed. "You're sure? They should be in the same valley."

"Minister—"

"It's actually *President* now," Casille corrected. "Sadly, my predecessor wasn't up to handling this crisis. The People's Cabinet had to remove him."

Veta's stomach began to churn. "Because of the Keeper attack?"

"Precisely. Tejo Aponte wanted to offer logistical support to the UNSC—*while* they were attacking our own people. Can you imagine?"

"A lot of things have happened recently that I could never have imagined," Veta said. "For instance, I could never have imagined *you* turning Wendosa into a battlefield."

When the only response was silence, Veta knew her suspicions were correct. Arlo Casille was too cunning to deny it and risk being exposed as a liar, but he certainly wasn't going to admit it—not over an unsecured comm channel.

Finally, Veta heard another Wyvern approaching and realized she needed to give Casille something else to listen for. "Why would you do such a thing, *President* Casille?"

"I didn't ask to be named president. But I accepted the responsibility for the good of Gao—and I hope you'll do the same, Inspector Lopis. The republic is in grave need of a new Minister of Protection."

And there it was—the bribe that confirmed Veta's worst fears, that proved the presidency of Gao had fallen into the hands of a despot and a criminal, a man who could be allowed access to Forerunner technology only at the peril of worlds.

Veta assumed her warmest voice. "I'm flattered, President Casille. But first we need to see whether I come out of this in one piece."

"Then help us find you," Casille replied. "Are you sure you don't hear any Wyverns? They should be near your location."

As he spoke, Veta saw Kelly lean close to Fred's ear and report something. Fred's expression fell.

"Hold on, Mr. President," Veta said. "I'll listen for them."

She covered the comm pad microphone, then asked Fred, "What's the problem?"

"Our ride can't make it," he said. "Too many Wyverns around. They'll shoot her down before she gets here."

"How much time do we need?"

Fred turned toward the front of the transport. "Mark, how much time on the counter?"

"Six minutes, twenty-five."

"I think I can buy us four or five," Veta said. "Maybe I can misdirect Casille, get him to concentrate the Wyverns over those decoys you sent out."

Fred looked to Kelly, who nodded and said, "Five would work."

"I said *four* or five."

Kelly looked away. "So I'm an optimist."

Fred grew pensive. Completely out of his Mjolnir now, he was clothed only in his boots and the tech suit he wore beneath his armor. Under other circumstances, Veta might have been impressed by the sight. But less than ten minutes from thermonuclear destruction . . . maybe not.

At last, Fred nodded. "What do we have to lose? Do it."

Veta took her hand away from the comm pad. "President Casille?"

"Still here," Casille said. "I thought we'd lost you."

"Not yet." Veta lowered her voice, as though she were whispering, then said, "I can hear Wyverns, but they're faint. They must be a long way behind us."

"That's not much help, Veta. Can you give me anything else?"

"We're not actually in the valley," she said. "We're climbing up the wall."

"That's good," Casille said. "Maybe you could hold your comm pad up. If I can get a recording, a tech can probably figure out how far away you are from the Wyverns."

And then Veta knew the real reason Casille had called—the reason he hadn't bothered to ask why she still had her comm pad, or why the Spartans were allowing her to use it.

He already knew she wasn't really a prisoner.

"That might be risky," Veta said, continuing to play Casille's game. She nudged Olivia, then raised a thumb and forefinger in the shape of a gun. "I'll give it a try, but there's something else first."

"Everything helps."

"Before we started up the hill, we crossed a bridge," Veta said. "There was a sign pointing toward the Singing Grottos in one direction and the Well of Echoes in the other."

Kelly flipped the safety off her weapon and swung it vaguely in Veta's direction.

Veta took a deep breath, then said, "We went toward the Well of—"

The muzzle of Kelly's battle rifle pushed into Veta's cheek, and she decided she had laid her trap as well as she was going to. She tossed her comm pad high into the air over the far side of the Warthog, then winced at the deafening rattle of Olivia blasting it out of the air.

"Explain," Kelly said.

Veta simply pointed at the sky. Her ears were still ringing from the sound of Olivia's rifle burst, but she was betting that about now, the Wyverns would be turning toward the Singing Grottos.

In fact, she was betting her life on it.

Veta hardly dared to breathe as the Spartans raised their face-plates toward the sky and she waited to see whether her plan had worked. Every time the Warthog bounced over a rut and her body shifted, she expected to feel a BR55's armor-piercing round exiting the back of her skull.

Instead, after ten seconds or so, Kelly lowered her rifle and sat back in her seat, then looked up the road as though nothing untoward had happened. Deciding to take that as vindication, Veta put her helmet on and leaned into the back of her seat, then looked toward the front of the vehicle.

"Hey, Mark," she called. "How much longer?"

Mark checked the counter, then said, "Four minutes fifty."

"Then our ride is on the way?"

"It's on the way," he said. "All *we* have to do is get there."

Veta nodded. She had no idea how far it was to the Well of Echoes, but travel time was hardly the sort of detail Spartans would overlook—and she was determined not to let her anxiety show any more than it already had.

They rode in silence for another thirty seconds, then Kelly finally said, "Okay, Lopis, I give. How'd you know Casille would send those Wyverns the other way?"

"He never asked why I still had my comm pad," Veta said. "He already knew I wasn't a prisoner."

The thrum of Wyverns flying in rotor mode sounded from the jungle behind them and began to grow steadily louder. The Spartans fell silent and looked toward the sound, then seemed to relax.

"Sounds like two of 'em to me," Olivia said.

"Same here," Fred said. "Probably just insurance, scouting this way to see if Lopis was telling the truth after all."

"You sound awfully calm about that," Veta said. "What happens when they find out I *was* telling the truth?"

"We do what we always do," Mark said. "We take 'em out."

The other Spartans nodded in agreement, then returned their attention to Veta, and Kelly asked, "So Casille knew you weren't a prisoner?"

"Right," Veta said. "Is this really the time to be explaining this?"

Fred smiled. "Relax, *Mom,*" he said. "It's under control."

Veta looked back down the road toward the approaching Wyverns. The thrumming of their rotors seemed to be rising, and Veta expected cannon fire to begin shredding the jungle canopy at any moment. But if everyone else thought the situation was in hand, then it probably was. And even if not, Veta wasn't going to be the one who showed fear. She scowled across the passenger tray at Fred.

"Don't call me Mom," she said. From the Gammas, she could tolerate the nickname—even if just barely. "I hate that."

Fred feigned a hurt look. "So what should I call you?" he asked. "*Soldier?*"

"Anything but Mom," Veta snapped. The Wyverns were so close now she could feel the pulse of their rotors in her chest. She turned back to Kelly and said, "Casille never believed I'd give away our position. He was just trying to establish a sound point."

"A sound point?" Fred had to raise his voice to make himself heard. "Never heard of it."

"A technician searches for the sound of aircraft in the transmission background," Veta replied, also raising her voice; she would have just used TEAMCOM, but Fred didn't have a helmet or a comm set. "If you know where enough aircraft are when you hear them, you can triangulate an UNSUB's location when he placed the call. It's a bit more technical than that, and it takes time—which is the whole reason Casille was trying to keep me talking in the first place."

"So, when you actually told him where we were going . . ." Olivia let her sentence trail off, then gave an approving nod. "Nice move."

"But if you stay on Gao now, you're a dead woman," Mark said, speaking over TEAMCOM. "You know that, right?"

"Yeah, Mark." Veta glanced down the road behind them and saw the jungle canopy beginning to dance beneath the Wyverns' rotor wash. One way or another, this would probably be the last time she ever looked out on the Montero Jungle or any of Gao's other natural wonders. "The thought had occurred to me."

"Good," Mark answered. The Warthogs crested the hill and slid to a stop, and Mark's voice came over TEAMCOM again. "Two minutes twenty, people!"

The Spartans burst into action so quickly that the Warthogs were half-empty before Veta realized the vehicles were being abandoned. She reached down to grab the drone satchel and discovered that Kelly already had it. Then she went for her battle rifle and found Fred pointing her into the jungle.

"Leave everything!" He reached into the pile of scrap that used to be his Mjolnir and tapped a touchpad on the fusion reactor, then pointed into the jungle. "Fifty-two meters—not fifty-three, not fifty-four. *Don't* fall off."

Veta jumped out of the Warthog. "Don't fall—"

Her question was swallowed by blazing cannon fire, and even before her boots hit the ground, the jungle began to fall around her. Veta sprang into a front dive and rolled, then scrambled five meters forward and finally dared to lift her head out of the undergrowth.

She found herself surrounded by a tangle of foliage so dense she could barely see to the end of her arm. There was no sign of any Spartans—of course—and she had lost track of where Fred had been pointing when he told her, *fifty-two meters*.

Mark's voice came over TEAMCOM "One hundred seconds."

Veta spun in a circle until she found a trail of smashed ferns and club moss leading back toward the Warthogs. She could see the transport coming apart beneath a hail of cannon rounds, and there was a column of smoke rising a few meters in front of it, where the reconnaissance vehicle had been abandoned. She turned in the opposite direction and ran ten steps, fifteen. Bits of frond and wood began to rain down as cannon fire swept through the jungle above her.

Veta did not look back. She did not want to see death coming.

An armored hand shot out of the foliage and clamped on to her arm, then jerked her off her feet.

"Follow me, soldier!" a female voice commanded.

Veta tried to get her feet back on the ground and run, but the effort was futile. She was practically flying through the air in the Spartan's grasp, making twice the time she would on her own. Besides, she was moving in the right direction. She turned to see who was pulling her along and found herself looking at pale copper Mjolnir and an awkward helmet with a goggle-like visor. So, Linda-058.

A low crackle began to build behind them.

Linda dived to the ground, and Veta along with her. The

crackle grew fierce, then a silver light flashed through the jungle and Veta felt instantly sunburned. She would have screamed, but before her mouth could open, the air left her lungs and the chest-crushing weight of a compression wave stomped down.

The weight vanished just as quickly. Veta raised her head to find a snarl of toppled trunks where there had once been jungle. About twenty meters ahead, the devastation ended at the rim of a huge, cliff-walled canyon—the Well of Echoes, no doubt.

The booming din of exploding ordnance erupted behind her, and Veta looked back to find two heaps of folded metal sitting atop the scorched flat where Blue Team had abandoned its Wart-hogs. If not for the fountains of orange tracer rounds cooking off in all directions, she would have never recognized the mounds as crashed Wyverns.

"What did *that*?"

"Fred's armor," Linda said. "You can't leave that stuff just lying around, you know."

Mark's voice sounded over TEAMCOM. "Sixty-four seconds."

"Boarding in twenty." This was said by the throaty voice of the mysterious Ms. Classified, who had spoken to Veta earlier. "And don't be late. This Owl isn't waiting for anyone."

Veta felt a tinge of fear. What if Ms. Classified was another AI? What if Intrepid Eye had already co-opted her, too? She shook it off. The ancilla was secured, at least for now. And even if it wasn't, Mark was right. Veta was a dead woman if she stayed here on Gao. Arlo Casille would see to that. She had no choice but to leave the world where her parents were buried, where her two aunts and six cousins lived, the world where the only friends she had known for more than a week all remained. And she would be doing it with no idea of where she was going to live, without the credits in her employment account, without so much as a datapad containing the contact information for all of those families to whom she owed calls of condolence and explanation. She would literally be leaving with nothing but her SAS-10 sidearm and the clothes on her back—and the clothes belonged to the UNSC.

As one, the eight members of Blue Team rose from the devastation and bounded toward the Well of Echoes. Veta stood and scrambled across the log tangle after them. All she could see ahead was the edge of a cliff—but with eight Spartans leading the way and a tactical nuke about to detonate, she was willing to take a chance.

Fred and Mark were only a couple of meters from the rim when the Owl rose out of the Well of Echoes and began to ease toward them. Resembling a slightly smaller, lightly armored version of a Pelican, the most obvious differences were the Owl's cloud-gray finish and its downward-curved wings. As it drew near the cliff, the craft spun around to present its tail, then lowered a boarding ramp and hovered on its pivoting thrust nacelles.

Fred turned to watch his team board, but Mark disappeared into the craft at a full sprint. Olivia, Ash, and the rest of the Spartans did likewise. A few seconds later, Veta raced up the ramp and found herself staring into the dark interior of a UNSC war vessel.

Fred came up behind her, probably the last of his team to board, by some military tradition, and nudged her across the threshold onto the deck.

"Welcome aboard, Inspector Lopis," he said. "You're one of the good guys now."

CHAPTER 28

The Owl lurched into motion and entered a steep spiral climb, its sound-dampened engines emitting little more than a groan. As the deck tipped back toward the open boarding ramp, Veta reached for the nearest wall, blindly searching for a handhold while her eyes adjusted to the dim interior light. A set of slender fingers took her wrist and guided her hand to a strap suspended from the ceiling.

"I keep *saying* we need lights in here during daytime extractions," said a throaty, half-familiar voice. "But you know the UNSC and protocol. You need three stars on your collar to change anything."

Veta slipped her hand through the strap, then turned toward the voice and began to discern a face. It belonged to a tall, olive-skinned woman with close-cropped hair and a slender, high-cheeked face.

"Ms. Classified, I presume," she said. "We meet at last."

Classified chuckled. "That's *Rear Admiral* Classified," she said. "But for now, you can call me Osman—Serin Osman."

"Forty-two seconds," Mark said over TEAMCOM.

At the same time, a female pilot's voice sounded from a ceiling speaker. "Inbound Wyverns, folks. Let's get it done and get *gone.*"

"Mark!" Fred barked from Veta's left.

"Sir."

Mark emerged from the shadows along the cabin wall, his photoreactive armor struggling to adjust as he passed from darkness into the light spilling over the still-open boarding ramp. In his hands, he continued to hold the Havok.

Before Veta could ask why in the world he still had it, Admiral Osman said, "Hold up, son."

Mark's helmet snapped around. "Ma'am?"

"You boarded early," Osman said. "We have a few seconds."

Mark looked toward the ramp, where Fred stood silhouetted against a verdant, jungle-filled pit half a kilometer below. When Fred nodded, Mark reluctantly faced Osman again.

"Thirty-eight seconds," Mark warned.

Osman cleared her throat, and Veta turned to find the rear admiral holding Intrepid Eye's data crystal.

"It'd be a tragedy to waste what this can do for humankind," Osman said. She offered the crystal to Veta. "But a deal is a deal. There's an adhesive strip on the Havok. If you want your justice, just attach this to the bottom."

Veta cocked a brow, trying to imagine a scenario where ONI would surrender a Forerunner ancilla—and there *wasn't* one. If Osman was offering a data crystal to her, it was only because the admiral wanted her to *believe* that Intrepid Eye was inside.

And because she thought Veta was naïve enough to fall for the switch.

Veta pushed Osman's hand back without even bothering to examine the offering. "I don't know who you think you're fooling," she said. "But that is *not* Intrepid Eye."

A sly grin spread across Osman's face. She made a fist over the data crystal and nodded to Mark. "Very well, Spartan. Carry on."

Mark's shoulders visibly relaxed. Without taking the time to step closer to the ramp, he pitched the Havok out through the opening. Its nose dropped, and then Veta saw a trio of helical fins deploy. The device began a spinning dive down into the Well of Echoes.

The tiny, delta-winged shapes of a dozen Wyverns floated into view, so distant and far below that they seemed to be merely drifting across the Well of Echoes.

"Bomb away!" Fred announced.

The Owl's boarding ramp thumped shut, sealing Veta and the others inside a steel cocoon. Fred and Mark immediately sprang for opposite sides of the cramped passenger cabin. Osman took Veta by the elbow and pulled her into a seat next to Fred. An automatic crash harness descended out of the wall above her shoulders and cinched her tight against the back cushion.

The Owl began a steep climb, accelerating so hard that had Veta not been secured by the crash harness, she would have been thrown to the rear of the craft.

By now her eyes had adjusted, and she could see that there wasn't much to the interior of the cabin—just a weapons locker at the forward bulkhead and ten inward-facing seats along each wall, with enough room between them for a couple of single-man vehicles. The Gammas were seated directly opposite Veta. They remained fully armored—as did all the Spartans except Fred.

Mark's faceplate seemed fixed on Rear Admiral Osman. "Twenty-six seconds," he said. "It should have been thirty."

Osman frowned, then tipped her head in Veta's direction and asked, "Am *I* the one who wasted four seconds thinking?"

Veta had no chance to retort. The pilot's voice came over the intercom again. "Brace yourselves!"

Already secured in the tight crash harnesses, there wasn't much of that to be done. Veta merely pressed her helmet into the back of her seat and clenched her jaw to make sure she wouldn't bite her tongue, and the Owl bucked so hard she feared the wings had been blown off. It seemed to slide and tumble for a few seconds, then the pilot brought it under control.

"Detonation confirmed," she reported. "Well done, Spartans."

An air of relief filled the cabin, with the Spartans seeming to ease into their crash harnesses as they flashed hand signals to each other. But there was no jubilation or triumphant outcry, not even a fist pump or sudden wave of laughter, and Veta liked that about them. They did not celebrate death. They understood that the men and women who had just been incinerated above the Well of Echoes were merely soldiers, the same as them . . . that the people who had to do the killing and dying in a war were seldom the ones who started it.

The Owl continued to shudder and shake for a few more minutes, then finally slipped free of the Gao atmosphere and settled into smooth flight. Veta found herself feeling queasy and drifting up against her harness, and she realized that, for first time in her life, she was experiencing weightlessness. She looked across the cabin at the Gammas—none of them even half her age—and saw by their slack postures and the distracted tilt of their helmets that it was a familiar sensation for them, one that they had probably experienced a hundred times in their young lives.

But, still, none of the Spartans were opening their armor or even removing their helmets, and their harnesses remained firmly in place.

Veta turned to Fred and asked, "How long do we need to stay buttoned up and locked in our seats?"

"Until we leave the conflict zone."

"That's not really an answer, Fred."

Fred spread his hands. "I'm not the pilot," he said. "I have no idea how large the zone is right now."

"It'll be about three hours," Osman said, "assuming the Gao Space Navy doesn't give us too much trouble."

"They're moving against the task force?" Fred asked. "Even Casille isn't that crazy."

"That remains to be seen," Osman said. "But Casille certainly did everything he could to make life difficult for the 717th. From what my own crews are reporting, the battalion lost half its strength evacuating under fire. And now that we've detonated a nuclear device . . . well, I doubt even Inspector Lopis knows what President Casille might do."

1508 hours, July 6, 2553 (military calendar)
Republic of Gao "Basilisk" Forward Command-and-Control
Craft *Independence*

Holding at an altitude of five hundred meters, the Basilisk tipped its wing and circled the blackened crater that had once been the Well of Echoes. Ringed by a curtain of smoke rising from the flickering flame walls of a huge jungle fire, the Well was now a kilometer-deep shaft of fused limestone. In the bottom of the pit,

Arlo Casille could just make out a pool of molten stone still glowing white with thermonuclear heat.

The pool could not be any hotter than the anger burning in Arlo's own soul. Was there no outrage beyond the UNSC? Could there be any atrocity too terrible for them to commit? Arlo would not have believed it possible for the barbarity of any Spartan to surprise him, but this final profanity had caught him completely off guard. The last thing he had imagined was that they would use a nuclear device to make good their escape.

"Nobody could have expected that, you know," said a raspy voice. "*I* certainly didn't see it coming."

Arlo was so deep in concentration that he didn't recognize the voice until he looked up and saw Gaspar Baez seated in the chair facing him. Like Arlo himself, the horse-faced Minister of War was dressed in a crisply pressed set of black Gao Space Navy fatigues, and he was leaning forward to peer out of the craft's window at the destruction below.

"What do you mean, exactly?" Arlo asked, immediately suspicious. Baez was an Aponte loyalist, after all. The only reason he still remained the Minister of War was a lack of time: Arlo had not wanted to delay the attack on the 717th long enough to put a new command structure in place. "I hope you're not implying it's my fault that the UNSC detonated a nuclear device on Gao."

"Of course not. It's not your fault at all. Nobody would have expected *that* to be how the Spartans sprang their trap." Baez steepled his fingers in front of his chin, then smiled. "And that's exactly what I intend to say in my public interviews, once I'm a civilian again."

"I see," Arlo said. "I hope you don't intend to imply that I fell for a Spartan trap in the first place."

"Well, I *do* have to be honest," Baez replied. "You are the one who ordered the Wyvern squadron to give chase—and, really, don't you think that was a bit extreme? I'm sure you were hurt personally by Inspector Lopis's betrayal, but diverting half of the assault force to go after her practically guaranteed the 717th would escape punishment—"

"It wasn't personal," Arlo interrupted. "And you know that."

"Oh?" Baez raised his gray brows. "So you're going public, then, with the hunt for the ancilla?"

"Absolutely not," Arlo said.

Currently, the people of Gao were applauding him for chasing off the 717th, but that would change in a heartbeat if the citizenry learned that Arlo had caused the crisis by smuggling the Keepers of the One Freedom onto Gao in the first place. With any luck, Castor was lying dead in the jungle someplace or had actually been incinerated by the nuclear detonation, and the public would never know that the whole battle had been a tug-of-war over a Forerunner artifact—a tug-of-war that Arlo had lost.

"We're not going public with anything about the Forerunners," Arlo continued, "*or* Inspector Lopis's betrayal. As far as the public is concerned, Inspector Lopis died with the rest of her team, and I sent the UNSC packing because their Spartans were murdering tourists in the Montero Cave System."

Arlo pointed out the window at the huge crater below, then added, "And we need to find a way to keep *that* quiet, too."

"So, you don't intend to use it to stir up sentiment against the UNSC?"

Arlo shook his head. "Can't do it. If I admit that the UNSC detonated a nuclear device on Gao, my own backers will push me into retaliating. And as much as I hate the UNSC, I'm not interested in being the president who roars at the giant and gets Gao smashed like a bug."

A knowing twinkle came to Baez's eyes. "I'm very happy to hear that," he said. "But those are going to be some very difficult secrets for you to keep. There must be at least five hundred Gao soldiers who know the truth."

"Which is why I'm going to need an experienced high commander to keep it quiet," Arlo said. "Do you think you'll be able to accomplish that, Minister Baez?"

Baez dropped his chin and offered a thin smile. "It sounds like you're asking me to stay on as part of your cabinet, President Casille."

"I think we understand each other."

"In that case, I'm sure these secrets will be safe." Baez leaned back in his chair, then added, "If there's one term my soldiers always respect, it's *most classified*."

"I'm glad to hear it," Arlo said. He pointed out the window at the crater below. "So tell me: how are you going to explain *that*?"

Baez waved a dismissive hand. "What's to explain? Your GMoP corvettes simply brought down a Prowler," he said. "I'm afraid its reactor blew, so we're going to have to keep a security cordon around the area . . . for as long as you're the president and I'm the Minister of War."

"For years, then," Arlo said, nodding his approval.

"Oh, I'd say at the very least," Baez agreed. He spread his hands and grinned. "Possibly even decades."

1518 hours, July 6, 2553 (military calendar)
United Nations Space Command "Owl" Insertion Craft *Silent Claw*

The pilot's voice filled the Owl's passenger cabin again. "We have a pair of Gao corvettes coming out from behind Cenobia," she said. "We should be able to dodge them by ducking around the back side. It's going to add a couple of hours to our trip, but stay buckled up back there in case we run into any surprises. "

Veta's dismay must have showed on her face, because Osman said, "Don't tell me you have to pee."

"No, I'm okay."

Actually, Veta was already having trouble dealing with the harness confinement, and a monotonous five-hour flight was only going to make it worse. But she certainly wasn't going to reveal that to Osman.

"I just thought I might float around for a while," Veta said. She felt a bead of sweat trickling down her brow, but did her best to seem nonchalant. "It's my first time in space."

"I wish you could," Osman said, speaking in a tone that suggested she was playing along. "Sorry, but you know how protocol is. We'll just have to keep each other entertained with our sparkling wit."

Veta shot an uneasy glance over at Fred, who merely shrugged and looked away.

"So, Inspector, I was wondering something," Osman continued, either missing or ignoring Veta's disquiet. "Now that you're a pariah on your own world, what are you going to do with your life?"

Veta looked back to Fred. "Is this lady for real?"

"Yeah," Fred said. "I'm afraid so."

"The reason I ask," Osman said, "is that you passed my test with flying colors."

Veta let her voice go icy. "*What* test?"

"With the data crystal. You read my play in four seconds flat, which is decent for an untrained amateur, and you didn't let the Havok scare you." Osman raised her brow. "You have *potential,* Inspector Lopis."

"I have *experience,*" Veta said. "I've been taking down hard-ened killers since I was twenty."

"Yes, I know all about that," Osman said. "But I'm talking about the big leagues. Stuff where you can make a difference in the galaxy."

The more this woman talked, the less Veta liked her. But she *did* have Veta's attention.

"A difference *how?*"

"I wish I could tell you." She spread her hands. "But it's—"

"*Classified?*" Veta asked. "You can't even tell me what you're recruiting me for? *Seriously?*"

The rear admiral tipped her head. "It's need-to-know," she said. "If you don't sign up, you don't need to know."

"Then I guess I don't need to know." Veta looked away. "I'm not the trusting kind—especially when I've seen the way you treat your own people."

Osman's voice grew genuinely indignant. "There's nothing wrong with the way I treat my people."

"No?" Veta asked. "Then why did I just help them haul a Havok across five kilometers of jungle when you could have dropped one out of the Owl?"

"Placement is more precise with ground—"

"You were *waiting* for us at the target," Veta interrupted.

"But we couldn't be sure we'd make it until we actually got there," Osman said. "The Spartans were in a better position to deliver, and since we had to extract them anyway—"

"You'd have an insurance policy if they didn't make it out," Veta said. "With that Havok along, there was no way any Spartan would let the ancilla fall into Arlo Casille's hands."

Across the cabin from them, Veta saw Ash and Olivia's helmets turn toward each other. Mark just continued to stare in Osman's direction. If Osman noticed their reaction, she betrayed no sign of it. She merely gave Veta a sly grin, then locked eyes with her.

"Tell me I was wrong about that."

Veta couldn't, of course. "I'm not so sure ONI is any better than Casille."

"You will be when you come aboard," she said. "You may find this hard to believe, Inspector, but ONI just might be the best thing the galaxy has going for it right now."

"I hope not," Veta said.

She turned her gaze across the dark cabin toward the Gammas. When she thought of their ages . . . of what had been taken from them and done to them, of the Smoothers they had to inject to stay mentally balanced . . . when she thought of all that, she was more interested in shooting this woman than working for her.

Finally, Veta shook her head. "I'm sorry," she said. "But—"

"There *is* one thing you should know before you make up your mind, Inspector."

"My other option is a bullet?"

The admiral looked hurt. "We're a bit more original than that." She pointed across the cabin toward the Gammas, then said, "Actually, it's about those three Spartans."

"What about them?" It was Fred who asked this, and there was more than a touch of protectiveness in his tone. "They're on *my* team. And they're fine Spartans. The best."

"They're also KIA," Osman said. She craned her neck to look past Veta toward Fred. "I'm afraid it happened on this mission. You can decide how, Lieutenant."

"*What?*" Ash burst out. "No way *that's* happening!"

Olivia was a bit more restrained. "Oh, man," she said. "What did we do?"

"It's the Smoother problem." Osman's voice was matter-of-fact, completely devoid of apology or sympathy. "If it ever went public, it could destroy the whole Spartan branch. So they've decided to disappear you."

Every faceplate in the passenger cabin was turned toward Osman, and Lucy's hand had gone to the hilt of her combat knife. Veta decided that Osman was either a lot braver than she looked— or a hell of a lot dumber.

Of course, it was Fred who finally asked the question on every Spartan's mind. "*Who* decided?"

"You *know* who. You have a problem with it, you can take it up with her." Osman turned back to the Gammas. "I'm sorry, but it scared too many people when you ran out of Smoothers. If something like that went bad again and things took a turn for the worse, there would be investigations until the Forerunners return."

"So you're going to terminate them?" It was Tom who demanded this, speaking from his seat next to Lucy at the far end of the cabin. "That's some thanks."

"Relax, will you?" Osman raised her palms to calm everyone down. "Once the Gammas hear what I have in mind, they might even *like* being dead."

"Right," Mark said. "You can join us, you know."

"I'm afraid that wouldn't be possible." Osman looked almost regretful. "I'm not qualified."

"Are . . . we?" Lucy asked. She didn't speak much, and when she did, her words tended to be slow and considered. "You are not sending them out—"

"Without some experience on the team," Tom finished. He tipped his helmet so that he was looking down the row toward the Gammas. "No offense, guys."

"None taken," Ash said. "They'd never ship us out alone, anyway."

"Not at your age," Osman confirmed. She looked over at Lucy. "But it can't be you, either."

"So it has to be Lopis?" Fred asked.

"That's right," Osman said. "If the inspector declines our generous offer, Ash, Olivia, and Mark will be joining the rest of Gamma Company."

"In doing *what*?" Tom demanded.

"Something that will mitigate the risk, but—to be honest— we're still working out the details," Osman replied. "And when we do, you *won't* be told. Are we clear on that?"

Tom's helmet snapped to dead center. "Yes, ma'am," he said. "And I will say it sucks, ma'am."

Veta couldn't help smiling, and she did not bother hiding her grin when she looked over at Osman again. "There are *more* Gammas?" she asked. "How many?"

Osman met Veta's smile with one of her own. "That information would be classified," she said. "And since you're not—"

"Okay," Veta said, raising a hand. "I'm curious. What's your plan?"

Osman's face brightened. "So you're in?"

"I'm listening," Veta corrected. "And stop trying to run games on me, Ms. Classified. You're really not very good at it."

"I've gotten you this far, haven't I?" A sly gleam came to Osman's eye, then she grew more solemn. "Basically, we need a team of Ferrets."

"Ferrets? What's that?" Veta asked.

"Investigators with teeth," Osman said. "You slip into a hole, find the rats, and—"

"And kill them?" Mark asked.

Osman frowned. "Sometimes," she said. "But I was going to

say, 'fix the problem.' Sometimes, that might mean rescuing people instead of killing them. Can you live with that, Spartan?"

Mark nodded. "Sure," he said. "What do you think I am?"

"And you want me to do what, exactly?" Veta asked. "Play the den mother?"

"Hell, no," Osman said. "Well . . . maybe sometimes. But what we really want you to do is lead the team and run the investigations."

Veta looked at the three Gammas sitting across from her. "And they would be my team?"

Osman nodded. "All you have to do is say yes." She glanced toward Tom, then added in a sarcastic tone, "Assuming that meets with *your* approval, of course."

Tom turned to Lucy and crooked a thumb, the Spartan signal for a question mark. Lucy remained silent for moment, then gave a single curt nod.

Osman feigned a sigh of relief, then turned back to Veta. "Well, now that we have the Betas' permission, do we have a deal?"

Veta paused, though there really wasn't much for her to consider. There was nothing left for her on Gao. All she really had in her life right now was her skill as an investigator and the affection she had come to feel for these three Gammas. Viewed in that light, accepting Osman's offer made a lot of sense. Of course, it meant Veta would be working for the great oppressor—the same entity that she had grown up hating—but even that view had changed. Over the last few days, she had learned that tyrants came in all sizes. Things were much more gray than she had realized, especially when it came to the UNSC. Ultimately, she was being offered her old GMoP job, but on a much grander scale. Her jurisdiction wouldn't be limited to criminal activity on Gao—it would span the entirety of human-occupied space. Osman was offering Veta a new way to serve her fellow man—a chance to stand with Fred and the Gammas and all of the millions of other brave men and women who had stepped up to defend humanity.

How could she say no?

Without looking away from the Gammas, Veta asked, "Fred, it's your team being raided. What do you think?"

"I think Blue Team will miss them," Fred said. "But nothing I say will change that . . . and the four of you would make a damn good Ferret team."

"We're going to make a *great* Ferret team," Olivia said, as though the matter had already been decided. "Right, Ash?"

"Yeah. Right. I'm in."

"What about you, Mark?" Veta asked. Of the three Gammas, Mark was the one she was most worried about—the one who seemed most troubled, and the one she had openly suspected of being a serial killer. If he couldn't look past her honest mistake, her Ferret team wouldn't last long enough to earn its name. "Do you think this can work?"

Mark tipped his helmet and looked away, then said, "Sure, Mom. Why not?"

EPILOGUE

Though he was still walking—barely, and with help—Castor would not be leaving the jungle alive. He knew this not by his trail of blood, nor by his infected wounds, nor even by the anguish that came from hobbling kilometer after kilometer on a shattered knee. He knew he was dying by the song he heard, an eerie wordless melody that seemed to echo through the lush foliage and drown out his own dark thoughts. It was the song of the Oracle, sent to comfort him in his final hour, to assure him that all who fail are not lost, that those who strive with pure hearts will attain the One Freedom as surely as those who win great victories.

What else could it be?

Castor stopped and took his arm from the shoulders of his loyal companion, Orsun. A mere handful of Castor's followers had survived the slaughter near Wendosa, and Orsun was the only one who had made a point of searching for his Dokab after the UNSC troops had withdrawn from the valley of death.

"Orsun, there is no honor in dying here with me." Castor stood on his one good leg, swaying and struggling to speak. "Go on alone, or you will miss the rendezvous."

Orsun said nothing and pulled Castor's arm back over his shoulder, then continued forward one slow step at a time. Orsun had not suffered any serious wounds during the fighting, but he had been supporting—and at times actually carrying—Castor for dozens of kilometers. And now a jungle fire was advancing up the valley behind them, sweeping in from the direction of a thermonuclear detonation less than an hour before.

Castor was still astonished that the UNSC had done such a thing. Even for infidels, using a nuclear device to end a battle that had already run its course was an unbelievable atrocity—a depraved act of pointless retaliation.

And it would be just as pointless for Castor to let his friend die with him. In fact, it had been selfish to let Orsun stay with him as long as he had. He reached up and slipped the water bladder off his shoulder.

"Orsun, take this. As your Dokab—"

Orsun stopped and raised a fist for silence, then pulled his Spiker from its mount and began to creep forward alone, toward a thicket of rustling ferns. Castor would have drawn his own Spiker, except his weapon hand was a mangled mass of flesh and bones, and he was so dizzy and weak that if he attempted to use his or her hand, he feared he would strike Orsun.

Orsun stepped into a thicket of ferns, where the Oracle's song seemed slightly louder, then snorted in amusement and lowered his weapon. "Come, Dokab," he said. "See what has been calling to us."

"You heard it, too?"

Orsun nodded. "I thought I was imagining it." He pointed at the ground on the other side of the thicket. "But it was only this."

Castor hobbled up next to him and saw Orsun's hand pointing at a hole in the ground no larger than a fist. A warm wind was billowing out of the cavity, stirring the ferns and filling the air with an eeric whistle.

Castor chuckled. "And here I thought I was dying."

"And I thought I had gone mad." Orsun let out a booming laugh. "But it was only a singing cave."

Castor began to laugh as well, a deep belly-shaking guffaw that rumbled through the jungle and set birds to squawking and amphibians to croaking. They stood like that for a few minutes, side by side and lost in a hysteria that was more relief than mirth, just elated to be with a friend for whatever life remained to them both. Only one thing was lacking to make Castor's end a good one, and that was being able to repay Arlo Casille's treachery before he died. But even a Dokab could not depart with every wish fulfilled.

Finally, the smell of smoke reminded Castor of the danger they faced from the advancing jungle fire. He turned to point with his good arm up the valley toward the Road of Wonders, where a Keeper infiltrator was already waiting to sneak them off Gao. But before Castor could pass the water bladder to Orsun and tell him to proceed on his own, something small and green floated out of the jungle in front of them.

"Dokab," Orsun said. "Do you see—"

"Yes. A Huragok," Castor confirmed. "Like the one we saw with the infidels in Wendosa."

"The same one?" Orsun asked.

"A good question," Castor replied. "I will let you know when I learn how to ask."

The Huragok drifted over to Castor and began to run its tentacles over his injured hand. He watched in quiet bewilderment as it probed the immense hole where his middle two fingers once connected to his palm—then he gasped aloud as the tentacles suddenly sank beneath the flesh and began to dig around inside the wound. An instant later, he felt several bones pop into place, and the fiery throbbing suddenly began to recede.

Castor looked up at the Huragok. "What are you?"

The Huragok responded with a series of blinks, then withdrew its tentacles from his hand and gently floated into his chest, pressing against Castor until he dropped into a seated position. It quickly floated down the length of Castor's leg, undoing the splint bindings as it went, and sank its green tentacles into the bulbous red mass of his swollen knee.

Watching in obvious horror, Orsun asked, "Dokab, are you—"

"Have no worry, Orsun," Castor replied, wincing but calm. "I believe it is mending me."

"But how can that be?" Orsun asked. "You are no machine."

"I don't know." Castor managed a laugh, then said, "Perhaps I am more of a machine than we realized."

Castor grunted as bone and cartilage began to heal inside his knee, then egg-shaped bubbles rose through the tentacles as the Huragok drew pus from the infected wound. It continued to work for another few minutes, and the pain began to subside. Soon Castor began to feel like he could bend his knee again.

Then, suddenly, the Huragok withdrew its tentacles, wrapped two around Castor's wrists, and pulled him to his feet.

Javelins of pain shot through Castor's entire body, but, to his amazement, he could put weight on the knee. The Huragok tipped its head-stalk, then floated three meters backward. Castor took the hint and stepped forward. When he did not fall on his face, he took another step.

"It is a miracle," Castor said. "I may be able to make the rendezvous in time, after all."

The Huragok blinked all six of its eyes in sequence, then turned and began to float away into the jungle.

Orsun's hand lashed out and caught it by the neck.

"Orsun, stop!" Castor ordered. "What are you doing?"

"Think, Dokab," Orsun said. "This is a Huragok that *heals injuries*. Consider how rare this is, how valuable. We cannot leave it to the infidels."

Castor looked at the Huragok, which had—most likely—just saved his life. But, clearly, it did not intend to accompany the Jiralhanae. Its only wish now was to return to the jungle.

"Let it go," Castor commanded.

Orsun frowned. "Are you mad? Surely, this Huragok is a gift from the Oracle!"

"No. The gift is what it just *did*." Castor reached over and pulled his friend's hand from the Huragok's neck. "Let it go, Orsun. It is not for us to decide the fate of angels."

ACKNOWLEDGMENTS

TROY DENNING

Many people contributed to this book in ways large and small. I would like to thank them all, especially the following: my first reader, Andria Hayday, for her invaluable suggestions and story support; Jeff Grubb for the Halo heads-up; high school classmate and Cave Researcher Cyndi Mosch for making a caver out of a spelunker all those years ago; Ed Schlesinger for his enthusiasm, patience, and general editorial excellence; Jeremy Patenaude for being such a prompt and thorough Halo go-to guy, and for brainstorming the "Gamma Solution" with me; Tiffany O'Brien for the warm welcome to the Halo universe and keeping me in the loop on art and media; Kory Hubbell for the cover art—*wow;* Tom Pitoniak for the skillful copyediting; and everyone at 343 Industries and Gallery Books who made my first mission in the Halo universe such a blast.

ACKNOWLEDGMENTS

343 INDUSTRIES

343 Industries would like to thank Scott Dell'Osso, Troy Denning, Kory Hubbell, Bonnie Ross-Ziegler, Ed Schlesinger, Rob Semsey, Matt Skelton, Phil Spencer, Kiki Wolfkill, Carla Woo, and Jennifer Yi.

None of this would have been possible without the amazing efforts of the Halo Franchise Team, the Halo Consumer Products Team, Jeff Easterling, Scott Jobe, Tiffany O'Brien, Kenneth Peters, and Sparth, with special thanks to Jeremy Patenaude.

ABOUT THE AUTHOR

Troy Denning is the *New York Times* bestselling author of thirty-five novels, including a dozen Star Wars novels, the *Dark Sun Prism Pentad,* and many bestselling Forgotten Realms novels. *Last Light* is his first Halo novel. A former game designer and editor, he lives in western Wisconsin.

For more fantastic fiction, author events, exclusive excerpts, competitions, limited editions and more

VISIT OUR WEBSITE
titanbooks.com

LIKE US ON FACEBOOK
facebook.com/titanbooks

FOLLOW US ON TWITTER
@TitanBooks

EMAIL US
readerfeedback@titanemail.com